Hybrids

Books by Robert J. Sawyer

NOVELS
Golden Fleece*
End of an Era*
The Terminal Experiment
Starplex
Frameshift*
Illegal Alien
Factoring Humanity*
Flashforward*
Calculating God*

THE NEANDERTHAL PARALLAX
Hominids*
Humans*
Hybrids*

THE QUINTAGLIO ASCENSION
Far-Seer*
Fossil Hunter*
Foreigner*

SHORT-STORY COLLECTION
Iterations

ANTHOLOGIES
Tesseracts 6 (with Carolyn Clink)
Crossing the Line (with David Skene-Melvin)
Over the Edge (with Peter Sellers)

*Published by Tor Books
(Readers' group guides available at www.sfwriter.com)

Hybrids

Robert J. Sawyer

A Tom Doherty Associates Book
New York

For
Lloyd and Yvonne Penney

Wonderful Human Beings

This is a work of fiction. All of the characters and events portrayed in this book are either products of the author's imagination or are used fictitiously.

HYBRIDS

Copyright © 2003 by Robert J. Sawyer

Edited by David G. Hartwell

A Tor Book
Published by Tom Doherty Associates, LLC
175 Fifth Avenue
New York, NY 10010

www.tor.com

Tor® is a registered trademark of Tom Doherty Associates, LLC.

ISBN 0-765-34906-X
EAN 978-0765-34906-4

First edition: September 2004
First mass market edition: November 2004

Printed in the United States of America

0 9 8 7 6 5 4 3 2 1

Author's Disclaimer

The Sudbury Neutrino Observatory, Inco's Creighton Mine, Laurentian University (including its Neuroscience Research Group), and York University all really exist. However, all the characters in this novel are entirely the product of my imagination. They are not meant to bear any resemblance to the actual people who hold or have held positions with these or any other organizations.

Acknowledgments and References

For anthropological and paleontological advice, I thank Michael K. Brett-Surman, Ph.D., and Rick Potts, Ph.D., both of the National Museum of Natural History, Smithsonian Institution; Philip Lieberman, Ph.D., Brown University; Robin Ridington, Ph.D., Professor Emeritus, University of British Columbia; Gary J. Sawyer [no relation] and Ian Tattersall, Ph.D., both of the American Museum of Natural History; Milford H. Wolpoff, Ph.D., University of Michigan, and the various experts listed in the Acknowledgments to my earlier book, *Hominids*.

For advice on genetics and disease, I thank George R. Carmody, Ph.D., Department of Biology, Carleton University; Peter Halasz; Hassan Masum, a Ph.D. candidate at Carleton; Alison Sinclair, Ph.D.; and Edward Willett. For advice on the other medical matter that figures in the plot, I thank endocrinologist Christopher Kovacs, M.D., Health Sciences Centre, Memorial University of Newfoundland.

For information about and access to the Sudbury Neutrino Observatory, I thank Art McDonald, Ph.D., and J. Duncan Hepburn, Ph.D.

For drawing to my attention theories that human consciousness is an electromagnetic phenomenon, I thank Norm Nason. Two such theories, similar in most particulars, have recently and independently been developed by Johnjoe McFadden, Ph.D., School of Biomedical and Life Science,

University of Surrey, and Susan Pockett, Ph.D., Department of Physics, University of Auckland. For those interested in reading more about them, McFadden presents a general account of his version in the closing chapter of his book *Quantum Evolution: The New Science of Life* (HarperCollins UK, 2000; W. W. Norton USA, 2001), and Pockett devotes her entire book *The Nature of Consciousness: A Hypothesis* (Writers Club Press, 2000) to her version of this theory.

There was much discussion in *Humans*, the previous book in this trilogy, about paleomagnetic evidence showing that Earth's magnetic field has previously collapsed very rapidly. Since that research figures again in this book, I invite the curious to check the original study by Robert S. Coe and Michel Prévot, "Evidence suggesting extremely rapid field variation during a geomagnetic reversal," in *Earth and Planetary Science Letters*, 92:292–98 (1989), and the follow-up by Coe, Prévot, and Pierre Camps, "New evidence for extraordinarily rapid change of the geomagnetic field during a reversal" in *Nature*, 374:687–92 (1995). For other advice related to magnetic reversals, I thank Grant C. McCormick and Ariel Reich, Ph.D.

Huge thanks to my lovely wife, Carolyn Clink; my editor David G. Hartwell and his associate Moshe Feder; my agent Ralph Vicinanza and his associates Christopher Lotts and Vince Gerardis; Tom Doherty, Linda Quinton, Jennifer Marcus, Jenifer Hunt, Irene Gallo, and everyone else at Tor Books; and Harold and Sylvia Fenn, Robert Howard, Heidi Winter, Melissa Cameron, David Leonard, Steve St. Amant, and everyone else at H. B. Fenn and Company.

Many thanks, also, to the friends and colleagues who let me bounce ideas off them or otherwise provided input, including Linda Carson, Marcel Gagné, James Alan Gardner, Al Katerinsky, Herb Kauderer, and Robert Charles Wilson.

Beta testers for this novel were Ted Bleaney, Carolyn Clink, David Livingstone Clink, Richard Gotlib, Peter Halasz, Howard Miller, Ariel Reich, Alan B. Sawyer, Sally Tomasevic, Edo van Belkom, and David Widdicombe.

Interuniversal Who's Who

BARASTS (*Homo neanderthalensis*)

Ponter Boddit	quantum physicist (generation 145)
Jasmel Ket	Ponter's elder daughter (147)
Mega Bek	Ponter's younger daughter (148)
Adikor Huld	quantum physicist (145)
Lurt Fradlo	Adikor's woman-mate, a chemist (145)
Dab Lunday	Adikor's son (148)
Bandra Tolgak	geologist (144)
Harb	Bandra's man-mate (144)
Hapnar	Bandra's elder daughter (146)
Dranna	Bandra's younger daughter (147)
Vissan Lennet	geneticist (144)
Lonwis Trob	inventor (138)

GLIKSINS (*Homo sapiens*)

Mary Vaughan	geneticist, the Synergy Group
Colm O'Casey	Mary's estranged husband
Jock Krieger	director of the Synergy Group
Louise Benoît	physicist, the Synergy Group
Reuben Montego	Inco mine-site physician
Veronica Shannon	neurobiologist, Laurentian University
Qaiser Remtulla	geneticist, York University
Cornelius Ruskin	geneticist, York University

The belief in God has often been advanced as not only the greatest, but the most complete of all the distinctions between man and the lower animals.

—CHARLES DARWIN
The Descent of Man

And let me tell you, God is not so infinite as the Catholics assert. He is about six hundred meters in diameter, and even then is weak towards the edges.

—KAREL ČAPEK
The Absolute at Large

Mankind was still divided into two species: The few who had "speculation" in their souls, and the many who had none, with a belt of hybrids in the middle.

—JOHN GALSWORTHY
To Let

Chapter One

"My fellow Americans—and all other human beings on this version of Earth—it gives me great pleasure to address you this evening, my first major speech as your new president. I wish to talk about the future of our kind of hominid, of the species known as Homo sapiens: *people of wisdom..."*

"Mare," said Ponter Boddit, "it is my honor to introduce you to Lonwis Trob."

Mary was used to thinking of Neanderthals as robust—"Squat Schwarzeneggers" was the phrase the *Toronto Star* had coined, referring to their short stature and massive musculature. So it was quite a shock to behold Lonwis Trob, especially since he was now standing next to Ponter Boddit.

Ponter was a member of what the Neanderthals called "generation 145," meaning he was thirty-eight years old. He stood about five-eight, making him on the tall side for a male of his kind, and he had muscles most bodybuilders would envy.

But Lonwis Trob was one of the very few surviving members of generation 138, and that made him a staggering one hundred and eight years old. He was scrawny, although still broad-shouldered. All Neanderthals had light skin—they were a northern-adapted people—but Lonwis's was virtually transparent, as was what little body hair he had. And although his head showed all the standard Neanderthal traits—low forehead; doubly arched browridge; massive nose; square, chinless jaw—it was completely devoid of hair. Ponter, by comparison, had lots of blond hair (parted in the center, like most Neanderthals) and a full blond beard.

Still, the eyes were the most arresting features of the two Neanderthals now facing Mary Vaughan. Ponter's irises were golden; Mary had found she could stare into them endlessly. And Lonwis's irises were *segmented*, mechanical: his eyeballs were polished spheres of blue metal, with a blue-green glow emanating from behind the central lenses.

"Healthy day, Scholar Trob," said Mary. She didn't take his hand; that wasn't a Neanderthal custom. "It's an honor to meet you."

"No doubt it is," said Lonwis. Of course, he was speaking in the Neanderthal tongue—there was only one, so the language had no name—but his Companion implant was translating what he said, pumping synthesized English words out of its external speaker.

And what a Companion it was! Mary knew that Lonwis Trob had invented this technology when he was a young man, back in the year Mary's people had known as 1923. In honor of all that the Companions had done for the Neanderthals, Lonwis had been presented with one that had a solid-gold faceplate. It was installed on the inside of his left forearm; there were few Neanderthal southpaws. In contrast, Ponter's Companion, named Hak, had a plain steel faceplate; it looked positively chintzy in comparison.

"Mare is a geneticist," said Ponter. "She is the one who proved during my first visit to this version of Earth that I was genetically what they call a Neanderthal." He reached over and took Mary's small hand in his own, massive, short-fingered one. "More than that, though, she is the woman I love. We intend to bond shortly."

Lonwis's mechanical eyes fell on Mary, their expression impossible to read. Mary found herself turning to look out the window of her office, here on the second floor of the old mansion that housed Synergy Group headquarters in Rochester, New York. The gray bulk of Lake Ontario spread to the horizon. "Well," said Lonwis, or at least that was how his gold Companion translated the sharp syllable he uttered. But then his tone lightened and his gaze shifted to Ponter. "And I thought I was doing a lot for cross-cultural contact."

Lonwis was one of ten highly distinguished Neanderthals—great scientists, gifted artists—who had marched through the portal from their world to this one, preventing the Neanderthal government from severing the link between the two realities.

"I want to thank you for that," said Mary. "We all do— all of us here at Synergy. To come to an alien world—"

"Was the last thing I thought I would be doing at my age," said Lonwis. "But those short-headed fools on the High Gray Council!" He shook his ancient head in disgust.

"Scholar Trob is going to work with Lou," said Ponter, "on seeing if a quantum computer, like the one Adikor and I built, can be made using equipment that exists—how do you phrase it?—'off the shelf' here."

"Lou" was Dr. Louise Benoît, by training a particle physicist; Neanderthals couldn't pronounce the long *ee* phoneme, although their Companions supplied it as necessary when translating Neanderthal words into English.

Louise had saved Ponter's life when he'd first arrived here, months ago, accidentally transferred from his own subterranean quantum-computing chamber into the corresponding location on this version of Earth—which happened to be smack-dab in the middle of the heavy-water containment sphere at the Sudbury Neutrino Observatory, where Louise had then been working.

Because she'd been quarantined with Ponter and Mary, as well as physician Reuben Montego, when Ponter had fallen sick during his initial visit, Louise had had a chance to learn all about Neanderthal quantum computing from Ponter, making her the natural choice to head the replication effort here. And that effort was a high priority, since sufficiently large quantum computers were the key to bridging between universes.

"And when will I get to meet Scholar Benoît?" asked Lonwis.

"Right now," said an accented female voice. Mary turned. Louise Benoît—beautiful, brunette, twenty-eight, all legs and white teeth and perfect curves—was standing in the doorway. "Sorry to be late. Traffic was murder."

Lonwis tipped his ancient head, obviously listening to his Companion's translation of those last three words, but, just as obviously, completely baffled by them.

Louise came into the room, and she did extend her pale hand. "Hello, Scholar Trob!" she said. "It's a pleasure to meet you."

Ponter leaned close to Lonwis and whispered something to him. Lonwis's brow undulated—it was a weird sight when a Neanderthal who still had eyebrow hair did it; it was downright surreal, Mary thought, when this centenarian did it. But he reached out and took Louise's hand, grasping it as though he were picking up a distasteful object.

Louise smiled that radiant smile of hers, although it seemed to have no effect on Lonwis. "This is a real honor," she said. She looked at Mary. "I haven't been this excited

since I met Hawking!" Stephen Hawking had taken a tour of
the Sudbury Neutrino Observatory—quite the logistics exercise, given that the detector chamber was located two kilometers underground, and 1.2 kilometers horizontally along
a mining drift from the nearest elevator.

"My time is extremely valuable," said Lonwis. "Can we get
to work?"

"Of course," said Louise, still smiling. "Our lab is down
the hall."

Louise started walking, and Lonwis followed. Ponter
moved close to Mary and gave her face an affectionate lick,
but Lonwis spoke up without looking back. "Come along,
Boddit."

Ponter smiled ruefully at Mary, gave a what-can-you-do
shrug of his massive shoulders, and followed Louise and the
great inventor, closing the heavy, dark wooden door behind
himself.

Mary walked over to her desk and started sorting the
mess of papers on it. She used to be—what? Nervous? Jealous? She wasn't sure, but certainly it had originally made her
uneasy when Ponter spent time with Louise Benoît. After all,
as Mary had discovered, the male *Homo sapiens* here at Synergy often referred to Louise behind her back as "LL." Mary
had finally asked Frank, one of the imaging guys, what that
meant. He'd been embarrassed, but had ultimately revealed
it stood for "Luscious Louise." And Mary had to admit Louise
was just that.

But it no longer bothered Mary when Ponter was with
Louise. After all, it was Mary, not the French-Canadian, that
the Neanderthal loved, and big boobs and full lips didn't
seem to be high on the Barast list of favored traits.

A moment later there was a knock on her door. Mary
looked up. "Come in," she called.

The door swung open, revealing Jock Krieger, tall, thin, with a gray pompadour that always made Mary think of Ronald Reagan. She wasn't alone in that; Jock's secret nickname among the same people who called Louise "LL" was "the Gipper." Mary supposed they had a name for her, too, but she'd yet to overhear it.

"Hi, Mary," said Jock in his deep, rough voice. "Do you have a moment?"

Mary blew out air. "I've got *lots* of them," she said.

Jock nodded. "That's what I've been meaning to talk to you about." He came in and helped himself to a chair. "You've finished the work I hired you to do here: find an infallible method for distinguishing a Neanderthal from one of us." Indeed she had—and it had turned out to be pig-simple: *Homo sapiens* had twenty-three pairs of chromosomes, while *Homo neanderthalensis* had twenty-four.

Mary felt her pulse accelerating. She'd known this dream job, with its hefty consulting fee, was too good to last. "A victim of my own genius," she said, trying to make a joke of it. "But, you know, I can't go back to York University—not this academic year. A couple of sessional instructors"—*one of whom is an absolute bloody monster*—"have taken over my course work."

Jock raised a hand. "Oh, I don't want you to go back to York. But I *do* want you to leave here. Ponter's heading home soon, isn't he?"

Mary nodded. "He only came over to attend some meetings at the UN, and, of course, to bring Lonwis up here to Rochester."

"Well, why don't you accompany him when he goes back? The Neanderthals are being very generous about sharing what they know about genetics and   otechnology, but there's always more to learn. I'd like you to make an extended trip to the Neanderthal world—maybe a month—and learn as much as you can about their biotechnology."

Mary felt her heart pounding with excitement. "I'd *love* to do that."

"Good. I'm not sure what you'll do about living arrangements over there, but . . ."

"I've been staying with Ponter's man-mate's woman-mate."

"Ponter's man-mate's woman-mate . . ." repeated Jock.

"That's right. Ponter is bonded to a man named Adikor—you know, the guy who co-created their quantum computer with him. Adikor, meanwhile, is simultaneously bonded to a woman, a chemist named Lurt. And when Two aren't One—when the male and female Neanderthals are living separate lives—it's Lurt that I stay with."

"Ah," said Jock, shaking his head. "And I thought the *Y&R* had confusing family relationships."

"Oh, those are *easy*," said Mary with a smile. "Jack Abbott used to be married to Nikki, who was born Nikki Reed. That was after she was married to Victor Newman—for the first two times, that is, but before the third time. But now Jack is married to . . ."

Jock held up a hand. "Okay, okay!"

"Anyway, like I said, Ponter's man-mate's woman-mate is a chemist named Lurt—and the Neanderthals consider genetics to be a branch of chemistry, which, of course, it really is, if you think about it. So she'll be able to introduce me to all the right people."

"Excellent. If you're willing to head over to the other side, we could certainly use this information."

"Willing?" said Mary, trying to contain her excitement. "Is the Pope Catholic?"

"Last time I checked," said Jock with a small smile.

Chapter Two

"And, as you will see, it is only our future—the future of Homo sapiens—that I will be addressing tonight. And not just because I can only speak as the American president. No, there is more to it than that. For, in this matter, our future and that of the Neanderthals are not intertwined..."

Cornelius Ruskin was afraid the vivid nightmares would never end: that goddamned caveman coming at him, throwing him down, mutilating him. He awoke each morning soaked with sweat.

Cornelius had spent most of the day after the horrid discovery painfully lying in bed, hugging himself. The phone had rung on several occasions, at least one of which was doubtless somebody calling from York University to find out where the hell he was. But he couldn't bring himself to speak to anyone then.

Late that night, he'd called the genetics department and left a message on Qaiser Remtulla's voice mail. He'd always hated that woman, and hated her even more now that *this* had been done to him. But he managed to keep his tone calm, saying that he was ill and wouldn't be back in for several days.

Cornelius watched carefully for blood in his urine. Every morning, he felt around the wound for seepage, and took his own temperature repeatedly, to assure himself that he didn't have a fever—which he didn't, despite his frequent hot flashes.

He still had trouble believing it, was still overwhelmed by the very idea. There was pain, but it diminished day by day, and codeine tablets helped—thank God they were available over the counter here in Canada; he always had some 222s on hand, and had initially been taking five at a time, but now had himself down to the normal dose of two.

Beyond taking painkillers, though, Cornelius had no idea what to do. He certainly couldn't go see his doctor—or any doctor, for that matter. There was no way his injury could be kept secret if he did that; someone would be bound to talk. And Ponter Boddit had been right: Cornelius couldn't risk that.

Finally, when he at last managed to summon enough energy, Cornelius went to his computer. It was an old no-name 90 MHz Pentium that he'd had since his grad-student days. The machine was adequate for word processing and e-mail, but he usually saved web surfing for when he was at work: York had high-speed lines, while all he could afford for home was a dial-up account with a local ISP. But he needed answers now, and so he suffered through the maddeningly slow page-loading.

It took twenty minutes, but he finally found what he was looking for. Ponter had returned to this Earth wearing a medical belt that included among its tools a cauterizing laser scalpel. That device had been used to save the Neanderthal's life when he'd been shot outside the United Nations. Surely that was how he had—

Cornelius felt all his muscles contracting as he thought yet again of what had been done to him.

His scrotum had been slit open, presumably by the laser, and—

Cornelius closed his eyes and swallowed hard, trying to keep stomach acid from climbing his esophagus again.

Somehow—possibly even with his bare hands—Ponter had then wrenched Cornelius's testicles from his body. And then the laser must have been used again, searing his flesh shut.

Cornelius had frantically searched his entire apartment for his balls, in hopes that they could be reimplanted. But after a couple of hours, tears of anger and frustration streaming down his face, he'd had to face reality. Ponter had either flushed them down the toilet, or had disappeared into the night with them. Either way, they were gone for good.

Cornelius was furious. What he'd done had been so wonderfully appropriate: those women—Mary Vaughan and Qaiser Remtulla—had stood in his way. They'd gotten their positions, and their tenure, simply because they were female. *He* was the one with a Ph.D. from Oxford, for God's sake, but he'd been passed over for promotion as York "corrected historical gender imbalances" among its various faculties. He'd been shafted by that, so he'd shown them—the department head, that Paki bitch; and Vaughan, who had the job *he* should have had—what it was really like to get the shaft.

Damn it, thought Cornelius, feeling once more between his legs. His scrotum was badly swollen—but empty.

God damn it.

Jock Krieger went back to his office, which was on the ground floor of the Synergy Group mansion. His large window faced south toward the marina, instead of north toward Lake Ontario; the mansion was on an east–west spit of land in the Rochester community of Seabreeze.

Jock's Ph.D. was in game theory; he'd studied under John Nash at Princeton, and had spent three decades at the RAND Corporation. RAND had been the perfect place for Jock. Funded by the Air Force, it had been the principal U.S.-government think tank in the Cold War, carrying out studies of nuclear conflict. To this day, when Jock heard the initials M.D., he thought of a *megadeath*—one million civilian casualties—rather than a medical doctor.

The Pentagon had been furious about the way the initial encounter with Neanderthal Prime—the first Neanderthal to slip into *this* reality from *that* one—had gone. The story of a modern caveman appearing in a nickel mine in Northern Ontario had seemed pure tabloid stuff, akin to alien encounters, Bigfoot sightings, and so on. By the time the U.S. government—or the Canadian one, for that matter—was taking things seriously, Neanderthal Prime was out and about among the general public, making it impossible to contain and control the situation.

And so money had suddenly appeared—some from the INS, but most from the DoD—to create the Synergy Group. That had been some politician's name for it; Jock would have called it "Barast Encounter-Repetition Emergency Taskforce," or BERET. But the name—and that silly two-worlds-uniting logo—had been set before he was tapped to lead the organization.

Still, it had been no accident that a game theorist had been selected. It was clear that if contact ever did reopen, the Neanderthals and the humans—Jock still reserved that word, at least privately, for *real* people—would have different interests, and figuring out the most advantageous outcome that could be reasonably expected in such situations was what game theory was all about.

"Jock?"

Jock usually kept his door open—that was good management, wasn't it? An open-door policy? Still, he was startled to see a Neanderthal face—broad, browridged, bearded—peeking around the jamb. "Yes, Ponter?"

"Lonwis Trob brought along some communiqués from New York City." Lonwis and the nine other famous Neanderthals, plus the Neanderthal ambassador, Tukana Prat, had been spending most of their time at the United Nations. "Are you aware of the Corresponding-Points trip?"

Jock shook his head.

"Well," said Ponter, "you know there are plans to open a bigger, permanent, ground-level portal between our worlds. Apparently your United Nations has taken the decision that the portal should be between United Nations headquarters and the corresponding point on my world."

Jock frowned. Why the hell was he getting intelligence reports from a bloody Neanderthal? Then again, he hadn't yet checked his own e-mail today; maybe it was there. Of course, he'd known that the New York City option was being considered. It was a no-brainer, as far as Jock was concerned: obviously the new portal should be on U.S. soil, and putting it at United Nations Plaza—technically international territory—would appease the rest of the world.

"Lonwis says," continued Ponter, "that they are planning to take a group of United Nations officials over to the other side—*my* side. Adikor and I are going to go down to Donakat Island—our version of Manhattan—with them, to survey the site; there are considerable issues related to shielding any large-size quantum computer from solar, cosmic, and terrestrial radiation, lest decoherence occur."

"Yes? So?"

"Well, so, I thought perhaps you might like to come along? You run this institute devoted to establishing good relations with my world, but you have not yet seen it."

Jock was taken aback. He found having two Neanderthals here at Synergy just now rather creepy; they looked so much like trolls. He wasn't sure he wanted to go somewhere where he'd be surrounded by them. "When's this trip happening?"

"After the next Two becoming One."

"Ah, yes," said Jock, trying to keep up a pleasant facade. "I believe our Louise's phrase for that is, 'Par-*tay!* '"

"There is much more to it than that," said Ponter, "although you will not get to see it on this proposed trip. Anyway, will you join us?"

"I've got a lot of work to do," said Jock.

Ponter smiled that sickening foot-wide smile of his. "It is my kind that is supposed to lack the desire to see beyond the next hill, not yours. You should visit the world you are dealing with."

Ponter came up to Mary's office and closed the door behind him. He took Mary in his massive arms, and they hugged tightly. Then he licked her face, and she kissed his. But at last they let each other go, and Ponter's voice was heavy. "You know I have to return to my world soon."

Mary tried to nod solemnly, but she apparently was unable to completely suppress her grin. "Why are you smiling?" asked Ponter.

"Jock has asked me to go with you!"

"Really?" said Ponter. "That is wonderful!" He paused. "But of course . . ."

Mary nodded and raised a hand. "I know, I know. We will only see each other four days a month." Males and females lived largely separate lives on Ponter's world, with females inhabiting the city centers, and males making their homes out at the rims. "But at least we'll be in the same world— and I'll have something useful to do. Jock wants me to study Neanderthal biotechnology for a month, learn all that I can."

"Excellent," said Ponter. "The more cultural exchange, the better." He looked briefly out the window at Lake Ontario, perhaps envisioning the trip he would soon have to take. "We must head up to Sudbury, then."

"It's still ten days until Two become One, isn't it?"

Ponter didn't have to check his Companion; of course he knew the figure. His own woman-mate, Klast, had succumbed to leukemia two years ago, but it was only when Two were One that he got to see his daughters. He nodded. "And after that, I am to head down south again, but in my world— to the site that corresponds to United Nations headquarters." Ponter never said "UN"; the Neanderthals had never developed a phonetic alphabet, and so the notion of referring to something by initials was completely foreign to them. "The new portal is to be built there."

"Ah," said Mary.

Ponter raised a hand. "I won't leave for Donakat until this next Two becoming One is over, of course, and I'll be back long before Two become One once again."

Mary felt some of her enthusiasm draining from her. She'd known intellectually that even if she was in the Neanderthal world, twenty-five days would normally pass between times when she could be in Ponter's arms, but it was a hard concept to get used to. She wished there was a solution, somewhere, in some world, that would see her and Ponter always together.

"If you are going back," said Ponter, "then we can travel to the portal together. I was going to get a lift with Lou, but . . ."

"Louise? Is she going over, too?"

"No, no. But she *is* going to Sudbury the day after tomorrow to visit Reuben." Louise Benoît and Reuben Montego had become lovers while they were quarantined together, and their relationship had continued afterward. "Say," said Ponter, "if all four of us are going to be in Sudbury at the same time, perhaps we can have a meal together. I have been craving Reuben's barbecues . . ."

Mary Vaughan currently had two homes on her version of Earth: she had been renting a unit at Bristol Harbour Village here in upstate New York, and she owned a condominium apartment in Richmond Hill, just north of Toronto. It was to that latter home that she and Ponter were now heading—a three-and-a-half-hour drive from Synergy Group headquarters. Along the way, once they'd gotten off the New York State Thruway in Buffalo, they'd stopped for KFC—Kentucky Fried Chicken. Ponter thought it was the greatest food ever—a sentiment Mary didn't disagree with, much to her waistline's detriment. Spices were a product of warm climates, designed to mask the taste of meat that was off; Ponter's people, who lived in high latitudes, didn't use much in the way of seasonings, and the combination of eleven different herbs and spices was unlike anything he'd ever had before.

Mary played CDs on the long drive; it beat constantly hunting for different stations as they moved along. They'd started with Martina McBride's *Greatest Hits*, and were now listening to Shania Twain's *Come On Over*. Mary liked most of Shania's songs, but couldn't stand "The Woman In Me," which seemed to lack the signature Twain oomph. She supposed she could get ambitious someday and burn her own CD of the album, leaving that song out.

As they drove along, the music playing, the sun setting—as it did so early at this time of year—Mary's thoughts wandered. Editing CDs was easy. Editing a life was hard. Granted, there were only a few things in her past that she wished she could edit out. The rape, certainly—had it really only been three months ago? Some financial blunders, to be sure. Plus a handful of misspoken remarks.

But what about her marriage to Colm O'Casey?

She knew what Colm wanted: for her to declare, in front of her Church and God, that their marriage had never really existed. That's what an annulment was, after all: a refutation of the marriage, a denying that it had even happened.

Surely someday the Roman Catholic Church would end its ban on divorce. Until Mary had met Ponter, there'd been no particular reason to wrap up her relationship with Colm, but now she *did* want to get it over with. And her choices were either hypocrisy—seeking an annulment—or excommunication, the penalty for getting a divorce.

Ironic, that: Catholics could get off the hook for any venial sin just by confessing it. But if you'd by chance married the wrong person, there was no easy recourse. The Church wanted it to be until death do you part—unless you were willing to lie about the very fact of the marriage.

And, damn it all, her marriage to Colm didn't deserve to be wiped out, to be expunged, to be eradicated from the records.

Oh, she hadn't been 100 percent sure when she'd accepted his proposal, and she hadn't been completely confi-

dent when she'd walked down the aisle on her father's arm.
But the marriage *had* been a good one for its first few years,
and when it had gone bad it had only done so through
changing interests and goals.

There had been much talk of late about the Great Leap
Forward, when true consciousness had first emerged on this
world, 40,000 years ago. Well, Mary had had her own Great
Leap Forward, realizing that her desires and career ambi-
tions didn't have to take a back seat to those of her lawfully
wedded husband. And, from that moment on, their lives had
diverged—and now they were worlds apart.

No, she would not deny the marriage.

And that meant . . .

That meant getting a divorce, not an annulment. Yes,
there was no law that said a Gliksin—the Neanderthals' term
for a *Homo sapiens*—who was still legally married to another
Gliksin couldn't undergo the bonding ceremony with a Barast of the opposite sex, but someday, doubtless, there would
be such laws. Mary wanted to commit wholeheartedly to Ponter as his woman-mate, and doing that meant bringing a final
resolution to her relationship with Colm.

Mary passed a car, then looked over at Ponter. "Honey?"
she said.

Ponter frowned ever so slightly. It was an endearment
that Mary used naturally, but he didn't like it—because it
contained the *ee* phoneme that his mouth was incapable of
making. "Yes?" he said.

"You know we're going to spend the night at my place
in Richmond Hill, right?"

Ponter nodded.

"And, well, you also know that I'm still legally bonded to
my . . . my man-mate here, in this world."

Ponter nodded again.

"I—I would like to see him, if I can, before we head off from Richmond Hill to Sudbury. Maybe have breakfast with him, or an early lunch."

"I am curious to meet him," said Ponter. "To know what sort of Gliksin you chose . . ."

The CD changed to a new track: "Is There Life After Love?"

"No," said Mary. "I mean, I need to see him alone."

She looked over and saw Ponter's one continuous eyebrow rolling up his browridge. "Oh," he said, using the English word directly.

Mary returned her gaze to the road ahead. "It's time I settled things with him."

Chapter Three

"I said it during my campaign, and I say it again now: a president should be forward-thinking, looking not just to the next election but to decades and generations to come. It is with that longer view in mind that I speak to you tonight..."

Cornelius Ruskin lay in his sweat-soaked bed. He lived in a top-floor apartment in Toronto's seedy Driftwood district—his "penthouse in the slums," as he'd called it back when he'd been in the mood to make jokes. Sunlight was streaming in around the edges of the frayed curtains. Cornelius hadn't set an alarm—not for the last several days—and he didn't feel energetic enough to roll over and look at his clock.

But the real world would soon intrude. He couldn't remember the exact details of the sick benefits he was entitled to as a sessional instructor—but whatever they were, doubtless, after a certain number of days, the university, the union, the union's insurer, or all three of them, would require a doctor's certificate. So, if he didn't go back to teaching, he wouldn't get paid, and if he didn't get paid...

Well, he had enough to cover the rent for next month, and, of course, he'd had to pay the first and last months' rent in advance, so he could stay here until the end of the year.

Cornelius forced himself not to reach down and feel for his balls once more. They were gone; he knew they were gone. He was coming to *accept* that they were gone.

Of course, there were treatments: men lost testicles because of cancer all the time. Cornelius could go on testosterone supplements. No one—in his public life at least—would ever have to know that he was taking them.

And his private life? He didn't have one—not anymore, not since Melody had broken up with him two years ago. He'd been devastated, even suicidal for a few days. But she'd graduated from Osgoode Hall—York University's law school—finished articling, and was sliding into a $180,000-a-year associate's position at Cooper Jaeger. He could never have been the kind of power-husband she needed, and now . . .

And now.

Cornelius looked up at the ceiling, feeling numb all over.

Mary hadn't seen Colm O'Casey for many months, but he looked perhaps five years older than she remembered him. Of course, she usually thought of him as he'd been back when they were living together, when they'd been planning jointly for eventual retirement, already having set their hearts on a country house on B.C.'s Salt Spring Island . . .

Colm rose as Mary approached, and he leaned in to kiss her. She turned her head, offering only her cheek.

"Hello, Mary," he said, sitting back down. There was something surreal about a steakhouse at lunchtime: the dark wood, the imitation Tiffany lamps, and the lack of windows all made it seem like night. Colm had already ordered wine—*L'ambiance*, their favorite. He poured some in the waiting glass for Mary.

She made herself comfortable—as comfortable as she

could—and sat in the chair across the table from Colm, a candle in a glass container flickering between them. Colm, like Mary, was a bit on the pudgy side. His hairline had continued its retreat, and his temples were gray. He had a small mouth and a small nose—even by Gliksin standards.

"You've certainly been in the news a lot lately," said Colm. Mary was on the defensive already, and opened her mouth to reply curtly but before she could, Colm raised a hand, palm out, and said, "I'm happy for you."

Mary tried to remain calm. This was going to be difficult enough without her getting emotional. "Thanks."

"So what's it like?" Colm asked. "The Neanderthal world, I mean?"

Mary lifted her shoulders a bit. "Like they say on TV. Cleaner than ours. Less crowded."

"I'd like to visit it someday," said Colm. But then he frowned and added, "Although I don't suppose I'll ever get the chance. I can't quite see them inviting anyone with my academic specialty there."

That much was probably true. Colm taught English at the University of Toronto; his research was on those plays putatively by Shakespeare for which authorship was disputed. "You never know," said Mary. He'd spent six months of their marriage on sabbatical in China, and she'd never have expected the Chinese to care about Shakespeare.

Colm was almost as distinguished in his field as Mary was in hers—nobody wrote about *The Two Noble Kinsmen* without citing him. But, despite their ivory-tower lives, real-world concerns had intruded early on. Both York and U of T compensated professors on a market-value basis: law professors were paid a lot more than history professors because they had many other job opportunities. Likewise, these days—*especially* these days—a geneticist was a hot commodity, whereas there were few employment prospects outside academe for English-literature experts. Indeed, one of Mary's friends used this tag at the end of his e-mails:

> The graduate with a science degree asks, "Why does it work?" The graduate with an engineering degree asks, "How does it work?" The graduate with an accounting degree asks, "How much will it cost?" The graduate with an English degree asks, "Do you want fries with that?"

That Mary had been the real breadwinner had been only one of the sources of friction in their marriage. Still, she shuddered to think how he'd react if she told him how much the Synergy Group was paying her.

A female server came, and they ordered: steak *frites* for Colm; perch for Mary.

"How are you liking New York?" asked Colm.

For half a second, Mary thought he meant New York *City*, where Ponter had been shot in the shoulder back in September by a would-be assassin. But, no, of course he meant Rochester, New York—Mary's supposed home now that she was working for the Synergy Group. "It's nice," she said. "My office is right on Lake Ontario, and I've got a great condo on one of the Finger Lakes."

"Good," said Colm. "That's good." He took a sip of wine, and looked at her expectantly.

For her part, Mary took a deep breath. She'd been the one who'd called this meeting, after all. "Colm . . ." she began.

He set down his wineglass. They'd been married for seven years; he doubtless knew he wasn't going to like what she had to say when she used that tone.

"Colm," Mary said again, "I think it's time that we . . . that we wrapped up unfinished business."

Colm knit his brow. "Yes? I thought we'd settled all the accounts . . ."

"I mean," said Mary, "it's time for us to make our . . . the separation permanent."

The server took that inopportune moment to arrive with salads: Caesar for Colm, mixed field greens with raspberry vinaigrette for Mary. Colm shooed the server away when she offered ground pepper, and he said, in a low volume, "You mean an annulment?"

"I . . . I think I'd prefer a divorce," Mary said, her voice soft.

"Well," said Colm. He looked away, at the fireplace on the far side of the dining room, the hearth stone cold. "Well, well."

"It just seems time, that's all," said Mary.

"Does it?" said Colm. "Why now?"

Mary frowned ruefully. If there was one thing that studying Shakespeare inculcated in you, it was that there were always undercurrents and hidden agendas; nothing ever just happened. But she wasn't quite sure how to phrase it.

No—no, that wasn't true. She'd rehearsed the wording over and over in her head on the way here. It was his reaction she was unsure of.

"I've met somebody new," Mary said. "We're going to try to make a life together."

Colm lifted his glass, took another sip of wine, then picked up a small piece of bread from the basket the waitress had brought with the salads. A mock communion; it said all that needed to be said. But Colm underscored the message with words anyway: "Divorce means excommunication."

"I know," replied Mary, her heart heavy. "But an annulment seems so hypocritical."

"I don't want to leave the Church, Mary. I've lost enough stability in my life as it is."

Mary frowned at the dig; she was the one who had left him, after all. Still, maybe he was right. Maybe she owed him that much. "But I don't want to claim that our marriage never existed."

That mollified Colm and for a moment Mary thought he was going to reach across the linen tablecloth and take her hand. "Is it anyone I know—this new guy of yours?"

Mary shook her head.

"Some American, I suppose," Colm continued. "Swept you off your feet, did he?"

"He's not American," said Mary, defensively. "He's a Canadian citizen." Then, surprised by her own cruelty, she added, "But, yes, he quite literally swept me off my feet."

"What's his name?"

Mary knew why Colm was asking: not because he expected to recognize it, but because a surname could reveal much, in his view. If Colm had a failing, it was that he was his father's son, a plain-talking, thickheaded man who compartmentalized the world based on ethnic groups. Doubtless Colm was already mentally thumbing through his lexicon of responses. If Mary were to mention an Italian name, Colm would dismiss him as a gigolo. If it were a Jewish name, Colm would assume he must have lots of money, and would say something about how Mary never really was happy with a humble academic as a husband.

"You don't know him," said Mary.

"You already said that. But I'd like to know his name."

Mary closed her eyes. She'd hoped, naïvely, to avoid this

issue altogether, but of course it was bound to come out eventually. She took a forkful of salad, buying time, then, looking down at her plate, unable to meet Colm's eyes, she said, "Ponter Boddit."

She heard his fork bang against his salad plate as he put it down sharply. "Oh, Christ, Mary. The *Neanderthal?*"

Mary found herself defending Ponter, a reflex she immediately wished that she'd been able to suppress. "He's a good man, Colm. Gentle, intelligent, loving."

"So how does this work?" Colm asked, his tone not as mocking as his words. "Do you play Musical Names again? What's it going to be this time, 'Mary Boddit'? And are you going to live here, or are the two of you going to set up house in his world, and—"

Suddenly Colm fell silent, and his eyebrows shot up. "No—no, you can't do that, can you? I've read some of the newspaper articles. Males and females don't live together on his world. Jesus, Mary, what sort of bizarre midlife crisis is this?"

Responses warred in Mary's head. She was only thirty-nine, for God's sake—perhaps "midlife" mathematically, but certainly not emotionally. And it had been Colm, not her, who had first acquired a significant other after they'd stopped living together, although his relationship with Lynda had been over for more than a year. Mary settled on the refrain she'd used so often during their marriage. "You don't understand."

"You're damn right I don't understand," said Colm, clearly fighting to keep his voice down so that the few other patrons wouldn't hear. "This—this is *sick*. He's not even human."

"Yes, he is," said Mary, firmly.

"I saw the piece on CTV about your great breakthrough," said Colm. "Neanderthals don't even have the same number of chromosomes we do."

"That doesn't matter," said Mary.

"The hell it doesn't. I may only be an English professor, but I know that means they're a separate species from us. And I know that *that* means you and he couldn't have children."

Children, thought Mary, her heart jumping. Sure, when she'd been younger, she'd wanted to be a mother. But by the time grad school was finished, and she and Colm finally had some money, the marriage had begun to look rocky. Mary had done some foolish things in her life, but she at least had known better than to have a child just to shore up a faltering relationship.

And now the big four-oh was looming; Christ, she'd be menopausal before she knew it. And, besides, Ponter already had two kids of his own.

Still . . .

Still, until this moment, until Colm had spelled it out, Mary hadn't even thought about having a child with Ponter. But what Colm said was right. Romeo and Juliet were simply a Montague and a Capulet; the barriers between them were *nothing* compared with those between a Boddit and a Vaughan, a Neanderthal and a Gliksin. Star-crossed, indeed! She and he were *universe*-crossed, timeline-crossed.

"We haven't talked about having children," said Mary. "Ponter already has two daughters—in fact, year after next, he'll be a grandfather."

Mary saw Colm narrow his gray eyes, perhaps wondering how anyone could possibly predict such a thing. "A marriage is supposed to produce children," he said.

Mary closed her eyes. It had been her insistence that they

wait until she'd finished her Ph.D.—that had been the reason she'd gone on the Pill, and to hell with the Pope's injunction. Colm had never really understood that she needed to wait, that her studies would have suffered if she'd had to be mother and grad student simultaneously. But she knew him well enough even that early in their marriage to understand that the bulk of the work raising a child would have fallen to her.

"Neanderthals don't have marriages like ours," Mary said.

But that didn't appease Colm. "Of course you want to marry him. You wouldn't need a divorce from me unless you were going to do that." But then his tone softened, and for a moment Mary remembered why she'd been drawn to Colm in the first place. "You must love him very much," he said, "to contemplate excommunication just to be with him."

"I do," said Mary, and then, as if those two words had been an unfortunate echo of their own now-distant past, she rephrased the sentiment. "Yes, I love him very much."

The server came and deposited their entrées. Mary looked at her fish, quite possibly the last meal she would ever have with the man who had been her husband. And suddenly she found herself wanting to give some amount of happiness to Colm. She'd intended to hold firm on her desire for a divorce, but he'd been right—it *would* mean excommunication. "I'll agree to an annulment," said Mary, "if that's what you want."

"It is," said Colm. "Thank you." After a moment, he sliced into his steak. "I suppose there's no point in delaying matters. We might as well get the ball rolling."

"Thanks," said Mary.

"I have just one request."

Mary's heart was pounding. "What?"

"Tell him—tell Ponter—that it wasn't all my fault, our marriage breaking up. Tell him I was—I *am*—a good guy."

Mary reached over and did what she'd thought Colm was going to do earlier: she touched his hand. "Gladly," she said.

Chapter Four

"Let me begin by noting this isn't about us versus them. It isn't about who is better, Homo sapiens or Homo neanderthalensis. It isn't about who is brighter, Gliksin or Barast. Rather, it's about finding our own strengths and our own best natures, and doing those things of which we can be most proud . . ."

As soon as her lunch with Colm was over, Mary picked up Ponter from her condo in Richmond Hill. He'd been contentedly watching a classic *Star Trek* rerun on Space: The Imagination Station. They were all new to Ponter, of course, but Mary recognized the episode at once, the histrionic classic "Let That Be Your Last Battlefield," with guest stars Frank Gorshin and Lou Antonio chewing up the scenery with their faces made up to be precisely half black and half white.

They got into Mary's car, and headed out on the five-hour drive up to Reuben Montego's place—a journey that would get them there just in time for dinner.

As they motored along highway 400, Mary found herself pumping her horn and waving. Louise's black Ford Explorer with the vanity plate D2O—the formula for heavy water—had just passed them. Louise waved through her rear window and sped on ahead.

"I believe she is exceeding the limitation imposed on velocity," said Ponter.

Mary nodded. "But I bet she's really good at talking her way out of tickets."

Hours passed; kilometers rolled by. Shania Twain and Martina McBride had been replaced first by Faith Hill and then by Susan Aglukark.

"Perhaps I'm not the best spokesperson for Catholicism," said Mary in response to a comment from Ponter. "Maybe I should introduce you to Father Caldicott."

"What makes him a better spokesperson than you?" asked Ponter, taking his attention off the road—racing along highways was still very much a novel experience for him—to look at Mary.

"Well, he's ordained." Mary had developed a little hand signal—a slight lifting of her left hand—to forestall Hak, Ponter's Companion, bleeping at words she knew he wasn't familiar with. "He's had holy orders conferred upon him; he's been made a priest. That is, he's clergy."

"I am sorry," said Ponter. "I am still not getting it."

"There are two classes in a religion," said Mary. "The clergy and the laity."

Ponter smiled. "It surely is a coincidence that both of those are words I cannot pronounce."

Mary smiled back at him; she'd gotten to quite like Ponter's sense of the ironic. "Anyway," she continued, "the clergy are those who are specially trained to perform religious functions. The laity are just regular people, like me."

"But you have told me religion is a system of beliefs, ethics, and moral codes."

"Yes."

"Surely all members have equal access to those things."

Mary blinked. "Sure, but, well, see, much of the—the source material is open to interpretation."

"For instance?"

Mary frowned. "For instance, whether Mary—the biblical one, Jesus' mother—remained a virgin for her entire life. See, there are references in the Bible to Jesus' brethren— 'brethren' is an old-fashioned word for brothers."

Ponter nodded, although Mary suspected that if Hak had translated "brethren" at all, he'd already done it as "brothers," so Ponter had probably heard her say something nonsensical like, " 'Brothers' is an old-fashioned word for brothers."

"And this is an important question?"

"No, I suppose not. But there are other issues, matters of moral consequence, that are."

They were passing Parry Sound now. "Like what?" asked Ponter.

"Abortion, for instance."

"Abortion . . . the termination of a fetus?"

"Yes."

"What are the moral issues?"

"Well, is it right to do that? To kill an unborn child?"

"Why would you want to?" asked Ponter.

"Well, if the pregnancy was accidental . . ."

"How can you accidentally get pregnant?"

"You know . . ." But she trailed off. "No, I guess you *don't* know. On your world, generations are born every ten years."

Ponter nodded.

"And all your females have their menstrual cycles synchronized. So, when men and women come together for four days each month, it's usually when the women can't get pregnant."

Again a nod.

"Well, it's not like that here. Men and women live together all the time, and have sex throughout the month. Pregnancies happen that aren't wanted."

"You told me during my first visit that your people had techniques for preventing pregnancy."

"We do. Barriers, creams, oral contraceptives."

Ponter was looking past Mary now, out at Georgian Bay. "Do they not work?"

"Most of the time. But not everybody practices birth control, even if they don't want a baby."

"Why not?"

Mary shrugged. "The inconvenience. The expense. For those not using contraceptive drugs, the . . . ah, the breaking of the mood in order to deal with birth control."

"Still, to conceive a life and then to discard it . . ."

"You see!" said Mary. "Even to you, it's a moral issue."

"Of course it is. Life is precious—because it is finite." A pause. "So what does your religion say about abortion?"

"It's a sin, and a mortal one at that."

"Ah. Well, then, your religion must demand birth control, no?"

"No," said Mary. "That's a sin, too."

"That is . . . I think the word you would use is 'nuts.' "

Mary lifted her shoulders. "God told us to be fruitful and multiply."

"Is this why your world has such a vast population? Because your God ordered it?"

"I suppose that's one way of looking at it."

"But . . . but, forgive me, I do not understand. You had a man-mate for many tenmonths, no?"

"Colm, yes."

"And I know you have no children."

"Right."

"But surely you and Colm had sex. Why were there no offspring?"

"Well, um, I *do* practice birth control. I take a drug—a combination of synthetic estrogen and progesterone—so that I won't conceive."

"Is this not a sin?"

"Lots of Catholics do it. It's a conflict for many of us— we want to be obedient, but there *are* practical concerns. See, in 1968, when the whole Western world was getting very liberal about sexual matters, Pope Paul VI issued a decree. I remember hearing my parents talk about it in later years; even they had been surprised by it. It said that every instance of sex has to be open to the creation of children. Honestly, most Catholics expected a loosening, not a tightening, of restrictions." Mary sighed. "To me, birth control makes sense."

"It does seem preferable to abortion," said Ponter. "But suppose you *were* to get pregnant when you did not wish to. Suppose . . ."

Mary slowed to let another car pass. "What?"

"No. My apologies. Let us discuss something else."

But Mary got it. "You were wondering about the rape, weren't you?" Mary lifted her shoulders, acknowledging the difficulty of the subject. "You're wondering what my Church would have wanted me to do had I become pregnant because of the rape."

"I do not mean to make you dwell on unpleasant matters."

"No, no, it's all right. I'm the one who brought up the example of abortion." Mary took a deep breath, let it out, and went on. "If I'd become pregnant, the Church would argue that I should have the baby, even if it was conceived through rape."

"And would you have?"

"No," said Mary. "No, I would have had an abortion."

"Another time when you would not follow the rules of your religion?"

"I love the Catholic Church," said Mary. "And I love being a Catholic. But I refuse to relinquish control of my conscience to anyone. Still . . ."

"Yes?"

"The current Pope is old and ailing. I don't expect he will be around too much longer. His replacement may relax the rules."

"Ah," said Ponter.

They continued on. The highway had veered away from Georgian Bay. To their left and right were Canadian Shield outcroppings and stands of pine trees.

"Have you thought about the future?" asked Mary, after a time.

"I think about nothing else these days."

"I mean *our* future," said Mary.

"So do I."

"I—please don't be upset; but I think we should at least talk about this possibility: when it's time for me to return home, maybe you could come back with me. You know: move permanently to my world."

"Why?" asked Ponter.

"Well, here we could be together all the time, not just four days a month."

"That is true," said Ponter, "but . . . but I have a life in my world." He raised a large hand. "I know you have a life *here*," he said at once. "But I have Adikor."

"Maybe . . . I don't know . . . maybe Adikor could come with us."

Ponter's one continuous eyebrow rolled up his browridge. "And what about Adikor's woman-mate, Lurt Fradlo? Should she come with us, too?"

"Well, she—"

"And Dab, Adikor's son, who is to move in with him and me the year after next? And, of course, there is Lurt's woman-mate, and her woman-mate's man-mate, and their children. And my minor daughter, Megameg."

Mary blew out air. "I know. I know. It's impractical, but . . ."

"Yes?"

She took one hand off the wheel, and squeezed his thigh. "But I love you so much, Ponter. To be limited to seeing you just four days a month . . ."

"Adikor very much loves Lurt, and that is all he sees of her. I very much loved Klast, but that was all I saw of her." His face was impassive. "It is our way."

"I know. I was just thinking."

"And there are other problems. Your cities smell horribly. I doubt I could take that permanently."

"We could live out in the country. Somewhere away from the cities, away from the cars. Somewhere where the air is clean. It wouldn't matter to me where we were, so long as we are together."

"I cannot abandon my culture," said Ponter. "Or my family."

Mary sighed. "I know."

Ponter blinked several times. "I wish . . . I wish I could suggest a solution that would make you happy."

"It's not just about me," said Mary. "What would make *you* happy?"

"Me?" said Ponter. "I would be content if you were in Saldak Center each time Two became One."

"That would be enough for you? Four days a month?"

"You must understand, Mare, that I have difficulty conceiving of anything more than that. Yes, we have spent long stretches of days together here in your world, but my heart aches for Adikor while I am here."

Mary's face must have suggested that Ponter had said something insensitive. "I am sorry, Mare," he went on, "but you cannot be jealous of Adikor. People in my world have two mates, one of each sex. To be resentful of my intimacy with Adikor is inappropriate."

"Inappropriate!" snapped Mary. But then she took a deep breath, trying to calm herself. "No, you're right. I understand that—intellectually, at least. And I'm trying to come to terms with it emotionally."

"For what it is worth, Adikor is very fond of you, Mare, and he wishes you nothing but happiness." He paused. "Surely you wish him the same, no?"

Mary said nothing. The sun was low on the horizon. The car sped on.

"Mare? Surely you wish Adikor happiness, do you not?"

"What?" she replied. "Oh, of course. Of course I do."

Chapter Five

"Four decades ago, my predecessor in the Oval Office, John F. Kennedy, said, 'Now is the time to take longer strides— time for a great new American enterprise.' I was just a kid in a Montgomery ghetto then, but I remember vividly how those words made my spine tingle..."

Mary and Ponter pulled into Reuben Montego's driveway just before 7:00 P.M. Louise and Reuben both drove Ford Explorers—clear evidence, Mary thought with a grin, that they were meant for each other. Louise's was black and Reuben's was maroon. Mary parked her car, and she and Ponter headed for the front door. Mary had to pass Louise's car; she thought about feeling the hood, but had no doubt it had long since cooled off.

Reuben had a couple of acres of land in Lively, a small town outside of Sudbury. Mary quite liked his house, which was two stories tall, large, and modern. She rang the doorbell, and a moment later Reuben appeared, with Louise standing behind him.

"Mary!" exclaimed Reuben, gathering Mary into a hug. "And Ponter!" he said, once he'd released Mary, hugging him as well.

Reuben Montego was trim, thirty-five, and black, with a

shaved head. He was wearing a sweat suit with the Toronto Blue Jays logo across its chest.

"Come in, come in," said Reuben, ushering them out of the cool evening air into his home. Mary removed her shoes, but Ponter couldn't—because he wasn't wearing any. He had on Neanderthal pants, which flared out at the bottoms into built-in footwear.

"It is a quarantine reunion!" declared Ponter, appraising their little group. And indeed it was: the four of them had been locked in together for four days by the order of Health Canada when Ponter had fallen ill during his first visit.

"Indeed it is, my friend," said Reuben, acknowledging Ponter's comment. Mary looked around; she very much liked the furnishings—a smart mixture of Caribbean and Canadian, with built-in bookcases and dark wood everywhere. Reuben himself was a bit of a slob, but his ex-wife had obviously had great taste.

Mary found herself immediately relaxing in this place. Of course, it didn't hurt that this was where she'd begun to fall in love with Ponter, or that, indeed, this had become her refuge, safely locked in, with RCMP officers outside, just two days after she'd been raped by Cornelius Ruskin on the campus of Toronto's York University.

"It's a bit late in the season for it," said Reuben, "but I thought we'd try a barbecue."

"Yes, please!" said Ponter, most enthusiastically.

Reuben laughed. "All right, then. Let me get to it."

Louise Benoît was a vegetarian, but she didn't mind eating with those who were enjoying meat—which was a good thing, because Ponter *really* enjoyed meat. Reuben had put three giant slabs of beef on the grill, while Louise had busied herself making a salad. Reuben kept coming in from the backyard, working with Louise on getting everything set. Mary watched them puttering about the kitchen, working together, touching each other affectionately now and again. The early days of Mary's marriage to Colm had been like that; later, it had seemed as though they were always in each other's way.

Mary and Ponter had offered to help, but Reuben had said none was necessary, and soon enough dinner was on the table, and the four of them sat down to eat. It stunned Mary that she'd known these people—three of the most important people in her life—for only three months. When worlds collide, things change *fast*.

Mary and Reuben were eating their steaks with knives and forks. Ponter was wearing recyclable dining gloves he'd brought with him, grasping his hunk of meat and tearing chunks off with his teeth.

"It's been an amazing few months," said Reuben, perhaps thinking the same thing Mary had been. "For all of us."

Indeed it had been. Ponter Boddit had accidentally been transferred to this version of reality when a quantum-computing experiment he'd been performing went awry. Back on his version of Earth, Ponter's man-mate, Adikor Huld, had been accused of murdering him and then disposing of the body. Adikor, plus Ponter's elder daughter, Jasmel Ket, had managed to re-establish the interuniversal portal long enough to bring Ponter home—and to exonerate Adikor in the process.

Once back home, Ponter had convinced the High Gray Council to let him and Adikor try to open a permanent portal, which they quickly succeeded in doing.

Meanwhile, the magnetic field on this version of Earth had started acting up, apparently as a prelude to a pole reversal. The Neanderthal Earth had recently undergone its own reversal—and the whole thing had happened extraordinarily fast, with their field collapse beginning just twenty-five years ago and the flipping and re-establishing of the field completed just fifteen years later.

Mary, still haunted by her rape, left York University to join Jock Krieger's newly formed Synergy Group. But on a return trip to Toronto, Ponter identified Mary's rapist; Cornelius Ruskin, it turned out, had also raped Qaiser Remtulla, Mary's department head at York.

"An amazing few months indeed," said Mary. She smiled at Reuben and then at Louise; they were *such* a good-looking couple. Ponter was seated next to her; she would have taken his hand if it weren't wrapped in a bloody glove. But Reuben and Louise had no such impediment; Reuben squeezed Louise's hand, and beamed at her, the love obvious on his face.

The four of them chatted animatedly, first over their main courses, then over a dessert of fruit cocktail, and finally over coffee (for the three *Homo sapiens*) and Coca-Cola (for Ponter). Mary was enjoying every minute of it—but also feeling a little sadness, regretting that evenings like these, having dinner with Ponter and their friends, would be few and far between; Ponter's culture just didn't work that way.

"Oh, by the way," said Reuben, taking a sip of his coffee, "a friend of mine at Laurentian has been bugging me to introduce you to her." Laurentian University, in Sudbury, was where Mary had done her studies on Ponter's DNA, proving he was a Neanderthal.

Ponter lifted his one continuous eyebrow. "Oh?"

"Her name's Veronica Shannon, and she's a postdoc in the Neuroscience Research Group there."

Ponter clearly expected Reuben to say more, but when he didn't, he prodded with the Neanderthal word for yes. "*Ka?*"

"Sorry," said Reuben. "I'm just not quite sure how to phrase all this. I don't suppose you know who Michael Persinger is?"

"I do," said Louise. "I read the article about him in *Saturday Night*."

Reuben nodded. "Yeah, there was a cover story about him there. And he's also been written up in *Wired* and *The Skeptical Inquirer* and *Maclean's* and *Scientific American* and *Discover*."

"Who is he?" asked Ponter.

Reuben put down his fork. "Persinger's an American draft dodger—from the good old days when the cross-border brain drain flowed in the other direction. He's been at Laurentian for years, and invented a device there that can induce religious experiences in people, through magnetic stimulation of their brains."

"Oh, *that* guy," said Mary, rolling her eyes.

"You sound dubious," said Reuben.

"I *am* dubious," said Mary. "What a load of hooey."

"I've done it myself," said Reuben. "Not with Persinger— but with my friend Veronica, who has developed a second-generation system, based on Persinger's research."

"And did you see God?" asked Mary derisively.

"You might say that, yes. They've really got something there." He looked at Ponter. "And that's where you come in, big fella. Veronica wants to try her equipment on you."

"Why?" asked Ponter.

"Why?" repeated Reuben, as if the answer were obvious. "Because our world is abuzz over this notion that your people never developed religion. Not just that you had it and then outgrew it, but that in your whole history no one ever even conceived of the notions of God or an afterlife."

"Such notions would—how do you phrase it?—'fly in the

face' of observed reality," said Ponter. He looked over at Mary. "Forgive me, Mare. I know you believe in these things, but . . ."

Mary nodded. "But you don't."

"Well," continued Reuben, "Persinger's group believes they've found the neurological reason why *Homo sapiens* have religious beliefs. So, my friend Veronica wants to see if she can induce a religious experience in Neanderthals. If she can, then they've got some 'splainin' to do, since you guys don't have religious thoughts. But Veronica suspects that the technique that works on us won't work on you. She thinks your brains must be wired differently on some fundamental level."

"A fascinating premise," said Ponter. "Is there any danger in the procedure?"

Reuben shook his head. "None at all. In fact, I had to certify that." He smiled. "The big problem with most psychological studies is that all the guinea pigs are psych undergrads—people who have self-selected to study psychology. We know an enormous amount about the brains of such people, who may or may not be typical, but very little about the brains of the general population. I first met Veronica last year; she approached me about getting some of the miners to be test subjects—a completely different demographic than she usually gets to work with." Reuben was the mine-site physician at Inco's Creighton nickel mine, where the Sudbury Neutrino Observatory was located. "She was offering the miners a few bucks, but Inco wanted me to okay the procedure before letting them do it. I read up on Persinger's work, looked at Veronica's modifications, and underwent the procedure myself. The magnetic fields are minuscule compared to those in MRIs, and I routinely recommend *those* for my patients. It's completely safe."

"So she will pay me a few bucks?" asked Ponter.

Reuben looked shocked.

"Hey, a fellow has to eat," said Ponter. But he couldn't keep up the facade; a giant grin crossed his face. "No, no, you are right, Reuben, I do not care about compensation." He looked at Mary. "What I *do* care about is understanding this aspect of you, Mare—this thing that is so important a part of your life but that I find incomprehensible."

"If you want to learn more about my religion, come to Mass with me," said Mary.

"Gladly," said Ponter. "But I would also like to meet this friend of Reuben."

"We have to get over to your world," said Mary, sounding a bit petulant. "Two will soon be One."

Ponter nodded. "Oh, indeed—and we don't want to miss a moment of that." He looked at Reuben. "Your friend would need to make time for us tomorrow. Can she do that?"

"I'll give her a call right now," said Reuben, getting up. "I'm sure she'll move heaven and Earth to accommodate you."

Chapter Six

> *"Jack Kennedy was right: it was time then for us to take longer strides. And it's that time again. For the greatest strength we Homo sapiens have always had, since the dawn of our consciousness 40,000 years ago, is our desire to go places, to make journeys, to see what's beyond the next hill, to expand our territories, and—if I may borrow a phrase coined just four years after JFK's speech—to boldly go where no man has gone before..."*

Ponter and Mary had spent the night at Reuben's place, sleeping together on the foldout couch. Early the next morning, they headed over to the small campus of Laurentian University and found room C002B, one of the labs used by the tiny Neuroscience Research Group.

Veronica Shannon turned out to be a skinny white woman in her late twenties with red hair and a nose that until she'd met female Neanderthals, Mary would have called large. She was wearing a white lab coat. "Thank you for coming, Dr. Boddit," she said, pumping Ponter's hand. "Thank you so much for coming."

He smiled. "You may call me Ponter. And it is my pleasure. I am intrigued by your research."

"And Mary—may I call you Mary?—it is *such* a treat to meet you!" She shook Mary's hand. "I was so sorry I didn't have a chance when you were on the campus earlier, but I was back home in Halifax for the summer." She smiled, then looked away, seeming almost embarrassed to go on. "You're a bit of a hero of mine," she said.

Mary blinked. "Me?"

"There aren't that many female Canadian scientists who really make it big, but you have. Even before Ponter came along, you'd really put us on the map. The work you did with ancient DNA! First-rate! Absolutely first-rate! Who says that Canadian women can't take the world by storm?"

"Um, thank you."

"You've been quite the role model for me. You, Julie Payette, Roberta Bondar . . ."

Mary had never thought of herself in that august company—Payette and Bondar were Canadian astronauts. But, then again, she *had* gotten to another world before either of them . . .

"Thank you," said Mary again. "Umm, we really don't have that much time . . ."

Veronica blushed a bit. "Sorry; you're right. Let me explain the procedure. The work I'm doing is based on research begun here at Laurentian in the 1990s by Michael Persinger. I can't take credit for the fundamental idea—but science is all about replication, and my job is verifying his findings."

Mary looked around the lab, which had the usual university mix of shiny new equipment, battered old equipment, and beat-up wooden furniture. Veronica went on. "Now, Persinger had about an 80 percent success rate. My equipment is second-generation, a modification of what he developed, and I'm getting about 94 percent."

"It seems a bit of a coincidence that this research is going on so close to the portal between worlds," said Mary.

But Veronica shook her head. "Oh, no, Mary, not really! We're all here because of the same thing—the nickel that was deposited when that asteroid hit the Earth here two billion years ago. See, originally Persinger was interested in the UFO phenomenon: how come flying saucers are most frequently seen by guys named Clete and Bubba out in the back forty."

"Well," said Mary, "you can get beer anywhere."

Veronica laughed more than even Mary thought the joke deserved. "That's true—but Persinger decided to take the question at face value. Not that he, or I, believe in flying saucers, but there *is* a real psychological phenomenon that makes people *think* they've seen such things, and Persinger got to wondering why that phenomenon would be triggered outdoors, especially in isolated locations. Laurentian does a lot of mining studies, of course, and when Persinger started looking for possible causes for the out-in-the-countryside UFO experience, the mining engineers here suggested piezoelectric discharges."

Ponter's Companion, Hak, had bleeped a couple of times, indicating he hadn't understood some words, but neither Ponter nor Mary had interrupted Veronica, who was clearly on a roll. Apparently, though, she didn't expect Ponter to know the term "piezoelectric," and so explained it of her own accord: "Piezoelectricity is the generation of electricity in rock crystals that are being deformed or are otherwise under stress. You get piezoelectric discharges, for instance, when a pickup truck drives over rocky ground out in the country—the classic UFO-sighting scenario. Persinger managed to reliably replicate that sort of electromagnetic effect in the lab, and lo and behold, he could make just about anyone think they'd seen an alien."

"An alien?" repeated Mary. "But you'd mentioned God."

"To-may-to, to-mah-to," said Veronica, grinning a very toothy grin. "It's all the same thing."

"How?"

Veronica pulled a book off her shelf: *Why God Won't Go Away: The Biological Basis for Belief.* "Newberg and d'Aquili, the authors of this book, did brain scans of eight Tibetan Buddhists meditating and of a bunch of Franciscan nuns praying. Naturally, those people showed increased activity in the areas of the brain associated with concentration. But they also showed *decreased* activity in the parietal lobe." She tapped the side of her skull, indicating the lobe's location. "The left-hemisphere part of the parietal lobe helps define your own body image, while the right-hemisphere part helps orient you in three-dimensional space. So, collectively, those two parts are responsible for defining the boundary between where your body ends and things outside your body begin. With the parietal lobe taking a coffee break, the natural feeling is exactly what the monks report: a loss of the sense of self, and a feeling of being at one with the universe."

Mary nodded. "I saw the cover story about that in *Time.*"

Veronica politely shook her head. "It was *Newsweek,* actually. Anyway, their work combines with Persinger's and mine. They found that the limbic system lights up during religious experiences—and it's the limbic system that tags things as significant. You can show a parent a hundred babies, but they'll only react profoundly to the sight of their *own* baby. That's because the limbic system has tagged that particular visual input as important. Well, with the limbic system afire during religious experiences, the whole thing gets tagged as overwhelmingly important.

"That's why religious experiences never sound good in the telling: it's just like me telling you my boyfriend is the best-looking guy in the world, and you going, yeah, sure. So

I open my purse and show you a picture of him, and I think you'll be convinced, right? You'll go, wow, he *is* a hunk. But if I did that, you won't have that response. He's handsome beyond compare *to me* because my limbic system has tagged his appearance as having special significance for me. But there's no way I can express that to you via words or pictures. Same thing with religious experiences: no matter how much someone tells you about their own one, about how life-changing and momentous it was, you just can't get that same feeling about it."

Ponter had clearly been listening intently, alternately frowning his wide mouth and rolling his continuous blond eyebrow up his doubly arched browridge. "And you believe," he said, "that this thing your people have and mine do not—this religion—is tied to the functioning of your brains?"

"Just so!" said Veronica. "A combination of parietal-lobe and limbic-system activity. Look at what happens in Alzheimer's patients: people who've been devout their whole lives often lose interest in religion when they come down with Alzheimer's disease. Well, one of the first things Alzheimer's does is cripple the limbic system."

She paused, then continued. "It's long been known that so-called religious experiences are tied to brain chemistry, since hallucinogenic drugs can induce them—which is why such drugs form the basis of ritual in so many tribal cultures. And we've long known that the limbic system might be one of the keys: some epileptics with seizures restricted to the limbic system have incredibly profound religious experiences. For instance, Dostoevsky was an epileptic, and he wrote about 'touching God' during his seizures. Saint Paul, Joan of Arc, Saint Theresa of Avila, and Emanuel Swedenborg were all probably epileptics, too."

Ponter was leaning now against the corner of a filing

cabinet, unself-consciously shimmying left and right, scratching his back. "Those are the names of people?" he asked.

Veronica was briefly taken aback, then nodded. "Dead people. Famous religious people of the past."

Mary took pity on Ponter at this point and explained "epilepsy" for him. Ponter had never heard of anything like it, and Mary wondered—with the shiver she got whenever she contemplated it—whether epileptic genes were yet another thing the Neanderthals had dispassionately purged from their gene pool.

"But even if you're not epileptic," Veronica said, "you can get that effect. Ritual dancing, chanting, and so on have been independently developed over and over by religions around the globe. Why? Because the deliberate, repetitive, stylized body movements during such ceremonies make the limbic system tag them as being of special significance."

"This is all well and good," said Mary, "but—"

"But you're wondering what it has to do with the price of tea in China, right?"

Ponter looked completely baffled, and Mary smiled. "Just a metaphor," she said. "It means, 'With the topic at hand.' "

"And the answer," said Veronica, "is that we now understand well enough how the brain creates religious experiences to reliably reproduce them in the lab . . . at least in *Homo sapiens*. But what I'm dying to find out is whether I can induce one in Ponter."

"My own curiosity is not fatal," said Ponter, smiling, "but nonetheless I *would* like it assuaged."

Veronica looked at her watch again, then frowned. "My grad student hasn't shown up yet, unfortunately, and the equipment is quite delicate—it needs to be recalibrated daily. Mary, I don't suppose you'd be willing . . . ?"

Mary felt her spine stiffen. "Willing to *what?* "

"To take the first run; obviously, I need to know that the equipment is functioning properly before I can take any results from Ponter as significant." She held up a hand, as if to forestall an objection. "With this new equipment, it only takes five minutes to do a complete run."

Mary felt her heart pounding. This wasn't something she wanted to investigate scientifically. Like the late, lamented Stephen Jay Gould, she'd always believed science and religion were—to use his musical phrase—"nonoverlapping magesteria," each having relevance, but one having nothing to do with the other. "I'm really not sure that—"

"Oh, don't worry; it's not dangerous! The field I use for the transcranial magnetic stimulation is just one microtesla. I rotate it counterclockwise about the temporal lobes, and like I said, almost all of the people—of the *Homo sapiens*, I should say—who try this have a mystical experience."

"What . . . what's it like?" asked Mary.

Veronica said, "Excuse us" to Ponter, and she led Mary away from him—her test subject—so that the Neanderthal would not overhear. "The experience usually involves the perception that there's a sentient being standing behind them or near them," said Veronica. "Now, the *form* of that experience depends a lot on the individual's own preconceptions. You put a UFO fanatic in there, and he'll sense the presence of an alien. Put in a Baptist, and she might say she sees Christ himself. Someone who's lost somebody recently may see that dead person. Others say they've been touched by angels or God. Of course, the experience is totally controlled here, and the test subjects are fully aware that they *are* in a lab. But imagine the same effect being triggered late at night when our friends Bubba and Clete are out in the middle of nowhere. Or while you're sitting in a church or mosque or synagogue. It really would knock your socks off."

"I really don't want . . ."

"Please," said Veronica. "I don't know when I'll get another chance to check a Neanderthal—and the baseline *has* to be set first."

Mary took a deep breath. Reuben had indeed certified the process as safe, and, well, she certainly didn't want to let down this eager young woman who thought so highly of her.

"Please, Mary," said Veronica again. "If I'm right about what the results will be, this will be a huge step forward for me."

Canadian women taking the world by storm. How could she say no?

"All right," said Mary reluctantly. "Let's do it."

Chapter Seven

"Our strength is our wanderlust; our curiosity; our exploring, searching, soaring spirit . . ."

"Are you all right?" said Veronica Shannon over the speaker next to Mary's ear. "Comfortable?"

"I'm fine," said Mary, speaking into a little microphone that had been clipped to her shirt. She was seated on a padded chair inside a darkened chamber about the size of a two-piece bathroom. The walls, as she'd seen before the lights were turned out, were covered with little pyramids of gray foam rubber, presumably to deaden sound.

Veronica nodded. "Good. This won't hurt a bit—but at any time if you want me to shut the equipment off, just say so."

Mary was wearing a yellow headset that had been fashioned from a motorcycle helmet, with solenoids on the sides, directly over her temples. The helmet was attached by a bundle of wires to a rack of equipment leaning against one wall.

"Okay," said Veronica. "Here we go."

Mary had thought she would hear a buzzing, or feel a tickling between her ears, but there was nothing. Just darkness and silence and—

Suddenly Mary felt her back tense and her shoulders hunch up. Someone *was* there, in the chamber with her. She couldn't see him, but she could feel his eyes boring into the back of her skull.

This is ridiculous, thought Mary. Just the power of suggestion. If Veronica hadn't primed Mary with all her talk, she was sure that she wouldn't be experiencing anything. Christ, the things you could get research funding for sometimes amazed her. It was nothing more than a parlor trick, and—

And then she knew who it was—who was there, in the chamber with her.

And it wasn't a him.

It was a *her.*

It was Mary.

Not Mary Vaughan.

Mary.

The Virgin.

The Mother of God.

She couldn't see her, not really. It was just a bright, bright light, moving now in front of her—but a light that didn't sting the eyes at all. Still, she was sure of who it was: the purity, the serenity, the gentle wisdom. She closed her eyes, but the light did not disappear.

Mary.

Mary Vaughan was her namesake, and—

And the scientist in Mary Vaughan came to the fore. Of course she was seeing Mary. If she'd been a Mexican named Jesus—*Hay-sooz*—she'd perhaps think she was seeing the Christ. If her name were Teresa, it would doubtless be Mother Teresa she'd think she was seeing. Besides, she and Ponter had been talking about the Virgin Mary just yesterday, so—

But no.

No, that wasn't it.

It didn't matter what her brain was telling her.

Her *mind* knew that this light was something else.

Her *soul* knew it.

It *was* Mary, the Mother of Jesus.

And why not? thought Mary Vaughan. Just because she was here, at a university, in a lab, inside a test chamber, that didn't mean anything.

Part of Mary had been skeptical of modern-day miracles, but if miracles *did* happen, well, then the Virgin Mary could appear anywhere.

After all, she'd supposedly come to Fatima, Portugal.

She'd supposedly come to Lourdes, France.

And to Guadalupe, Mexico.

And La'Vang, Vietnam.

So why not to Sudbury, Ontario?

Why not to the campus of Laurentian University?

And why not to talk to her?

No. No, humility was what was called for, here in the presence of Our Lady. Humility, following her grand example.

But . . .

But still, did it make so little sense that the Virgin Mary would visit Mary Vaughan? Mary was traveling to another world, to a world that didn't know of God the Father, a world that was ignorant of Jesus the Son, a world that had never been touched by the Holy Spirit. Of course, Mary of Nazareth would take an interest in someone who was doing that!

The pure, simple presence was moving to her left now. Not walking, but moving—hovering, never touching the soil.

No. No, there was no soil. She was in the basement of a building. There was no soil.

She was in a lab!

And transcranial magnetic stimulation was affecting her mind.

Mary closed her eyes again, scrunching them tightly shut, but that did nothing. The presence was still there, still perceptible.

The wonderful, wonderful presence . . .

Mary Vaughan opened her mouth to speak to the Blessed Virgin, and—

And suddenly she was gone.

But Mary felt elated, felt like she hadn't since her first Eucharist after her confirmation, when, for the one and only time in her life, she'd really felt the spirit of Christ coming into her.

"Well?" said a female voice.

Mary ignored it, a harsh, unwelcome intrusion into her reverie. She wanted to savor the moment, to hold on to it . . . even as it dissipated, like a dream that she was struggling to transfer into conscious thought before it slipped away . . .

"Mare," said another, deeper voice, "are you okay?"

She knew that voice, a voice she'd once longed to hear again, but right now, for this moment, for as long as she could make it last, she wanted nothing but silence.

But the moment was fading fast. And after a few more seconds, the door to the chamber opened, and light—fluorescent, harsh, artificial—spilled in from outside. Veronica Shannon came in, followed by Ponter. The young woman removed the helmet from Mary's head.

Ponter loomed closer and he brought up a short, broad thumb, and wiped Mary's cheek with it. He then moved his hand away and showed her that his thumb was wet. "Are you okay?" he said again.

Mary hadn't been aware of the tears until now. "I'm fine," she said. And then, realizing that "fine" wasn't anywhere near sufficient for how she felt, she added, "I'm terrific."

"The tears . . . ?" said Ponter. "Did you . . . did you experience something?"

Mary nodded.

"What was it?" Ponter asked.

Mary took a deep breath and looked at Veronica. As much as she had taken a liking to the young woman, Mary didn't want to share what had happened with this pragmatist, this atheist, who would dismiss it as just the result of suppressed activity in her parietal lobe.

"I . . ." Mary began, and then she swallowed and tried again. "That's a remarkable device you have there, Veronica."

Veronica grinned broadly. "Isn't it, though?" She turned to Ponter. "Are you ready to try it?"

"Absolutely," he said. "If I can gain insight into what Mary feels . . ."

Veronica proffered the helmet to Ponter, and she immediately realized there was a problem. The helmet was designed to accommodate a standard *Homo sapiens* head with a high forehead, a head that was short front to back, a head with no or negligible browridges, a head, not to put too fine a point on it, that housed a smaller brain.

"It looks like it's going to be a tight fit," said Veronica.

"Let me try," said Ponter. He took the thing, turned it upside down, and looked inside, as if gauging its capacity.

"Maybe if you think humble thoughts," said Ponter's Companion, Hak, through its external speaker. Ponter scowled at his left forearm, but Mary laughed. The idea of bigheadedness apparently crossed species lines.

Finally, Ponter decided to make the attempt. He turned the helmet right-way up and pushed it down over his head, wincing as he did so. It was indeed a tight fit, but there was lining inside, and with a final massive push, Ponter got the foam to compress sufficiently to accommodate his occipital bun.

Veronica stood in front of Ponter, appraising him like one of those clerks at LensCrafters fitting new glasses, then adjusted the orientation of the helmet slightly. "That's fine," she said at last. "Now, again, as I told Mary, this won't hurt, and if you want me to stop early, just say so."

Ponter nodded, but winced again as he did so; the back of the helmet was digging into his thick neck muscles.

Veronica turned to the wall rack full of equipment. She frowned at an oscilloscope display, and adjusted a dial beneath it. "There's some sort of interference," she said.

Ponter looked puzzled for a moment, then: "Ah, my cochlear implants. They let my Companion communicate silently with me, when need be."

"Can you shut them off?"

"Yes," said Ponter. He flipped open the faceplate on his Companion and made an adjustment to the revealed control buds.

Veronica nodded. "That's the ticket; the interference is gone." She looked at Ponter and smiled encouragingly. "Okay, Ponter. Have a seat."

Mary got out of the way, and Ponter sat down on the padded chair, his broad back to her.

Veronica left the test chamber and motioned for Mary to follow. The chamber had a massive steel door on it, and Veronica had to exert herself to get it to swing shut; Mary noted that someone labeled the door "Veronica's Closet." Once it was closed, Veronica moved over to a PC and started darting her mouse pointer about, clicking buttons. Mary watched, fascinated, and after a moment she said, "Well? Is he experiencing anything?"

Veronica lifted her narrow shoulders slightly. "There's no way to tell, unless he says something." She pointed at one of the speakers hooked up to the PC. "His mike is open."

Mary looked at the chamber's closed door. Part of her hoped Ponter *would* experience exactly what she had. Even if he dismissed it as an illusion—as doubtless he would—at least he'd be able to understand what had happened to her in there, and what had happened to so many people who had felt the presence of something holy throughout *Homo sapiens* history.

Of course, maybe he'd be experiencing an extraterrestrial presence. Funny, that: she and Ponter had talked about so many things, but somehow whether or not he believed in aliens had never come up. Maybe to Ponter, to the Neanderthals, the idea of life on other worlds was as silly as the notion of a god. After all, there was a complete absence of credible evidence for extraterrestrial life, at least in Mary's version of reality. Ponter's people would say, therefore, that believing in such beings was yet another ridiculous leap of faith . . .

Mary continued to stare at the sealed door. Surely religion was more than just a neuronal trick, a microelectric self-delusion. Surely it—

"Okay," said Veronica. "I'm shutting off the current." She moved over to the steel door and managed to get it open. "You can come out now."

Ponter's first order of business was removing the tight-fitting helmet. He brought his massive hands up to each side of his head and gave what appeared to be a mighty push. The contraption came off, and he handed it to Veronica, then set about rubbing his browridge, as if trying to restore whatever circulation might normally be there.

"Well?" said Mary, when she could wait no longer.

Ponter opened Hak's faceplate and adjusted some controls, presumably reactivating his cochlear implants.

"*Well?*" repeated Mary.

Ponter shook his head, and for a heartbeat, Mary hoped it was just a further attempt to restore circulation. "Nothing," he said.

Mary was surprised by how depressed that single word made her feel.

"Nothing?" repeated Veronica, who, for her part, seemed elated by the announcement. "Are you sure?"

Ponter nodded.

"No visual phenomena?" continued Veronica. "No feeling that something was there with you? No sensation of being watched?"

"Nothing at all. Just me, alone with my thoughts."

"What were you thinking about?" asked Mary. It was possible, after all, that Ponter wouldn't recognize a religious moment.

"I was thinking about the midday meal," said Ponter, "wondering what we were going to have. And about the weather, and how soon winter will be here." He looked at Mary and must have seen the disappointment on her face. "Oh, and you!" said Ponter, quickly, apparently trying to alleviate her pain. "I thought about you, of course!"

Mary smiled wanly and looked away. Surely one test of one Neanderthal didn't prove anything. Still . . .

Still, it was provocative that she, a *Homo sapiens*, had had the deluxe, full-blown experience, and that he, a *Homo neanderthalensis*, had experienced . . .

The phrasing came unbidden to her mind, but it was the sad truth.

Ponter Boddit had experienced not a blessed thing.

Chapter Eight

"It was that questing spirit that led our ancient ancestors to spread throughout the Old World..."

Veronica Shannon was pacing back and forth in her lab. Mary was sitting on one of the office's two identical chairs; Ponter had found his chair's width between its metal arms too narrow for his bulk, and so had perched his rear on the edge of Veronica's surprisingly tidy desk.

"Do you know anything about psychology, Ponter?" asked Veronica, her hands clasped behind her narrow back.

"Some," Ponter said. "I studied it when I was learning about computer science at the Academy. It was—what would you call it?—something I had to study along with artificial intelligence."

"A co-requisite," supplied Mary.

"In every freshman psych course," said Veronica, "humans here learn about B. F. Skinner."

Mary nodded; she'd taken an introductory psychology course herself. "Behaviorism, right?"

"Right," said Veronica. "Operant conditioning; reinforcement and punishment."

"Like training dogs," said Ponter.

"Just so," said Veronica. She stopped pacing. "Now,

please, Mary, don't say a word. I want to hear Ponter's response to this without any influence from you."

Mary nodded.

"All right, Ponter," said Veronica. "Do you remember your psych studies?"

"No, not really."

The young redhead looked disappointed.

"But I do," said Hak, through its external speaker, in its synthesized male voice. "Or, more precisely, I have the equivalent of a textbook on psychology loaded into my memory. It helps me to advise Ponter when he is making an idiot of himself."

Ponter grinned sheepishly.

"Excellent," said Veronica. "Okay, here's the question: what's the best way to ingrain a behavior into a person? Not something you want to extinguish, but something you want to foster."

"Reward," said Hak.

"Reward, yes! But what kind of reward?"

"Consistent."

Veronica looked as though something incredibly significant had just transpired. "Consistent," she repeated, as if it were the key to everything. "Are you sure? Are you absolutely sure?"

"Yes," said Hak, sounding as puzzled as he ever got.

"It's not here, you know," said Veronica. "Consistent reward is *not* the best way to ingrain a behavior."

Mary frowned. She'd doubtless known the right answer at one time, but couldn't dredge it up after all these years. Fortunately, Ponter himself asked the question Veronica was waiting for. "Well, then, what *is* the best way to ingrain a behavior among your kind of humans?"

"*Intermittent* reward," said Veronica triumphantly.

Ponter frowned. "You mean sometimes rewarding the desired behavior, and sometimes not?"

"Just so!" said Veronica. "That's precisely right!"

"But that does not make sense," said Ponter.

"Of course not," agreed Veronica, grinning widely. "It's one of the strangest things about *Homo sapiens* psychology. But it's absolutely true. The classic example is gambling: if we always win at a game, the game becomes boring for us. But if we only win some of the time, it can become addictive. Or it's like kids whining to their parents: 'Buy me this toy!' 'Let me stay up late!' 'Drive me to the mall.' It's the behavior parents hate the most from their kids, but the kids can't help themselves—not because the whining *always* works, but because it *sometimes* works. The unpredictability makes it irresistible for us."

"That is crazy," said Ponter.

"Not here," said Veronica. "Not by definition: the behavior of the majority is never crazy."

"But . . . but surely it is simply irritating not to have a predictable outcome."

"You'd think," agreed Veronica amiably. "But, again, it's not—not for us."

Mary found herself fascinated. "You're obviously on to something, Veronica. What is it?"

"Everything we're doing here at the Neuroscience Research Group has been about explaining the classic religious experience. But there are lots of believers who've never had a religious experience, and yet they still believe. That's the hole in our work, the missing piece in a comprehensive explanation of why *Homo sapiens* believe in God. But this is the answer—do you see? It's this psychology of reinforcement—this bit of the way our brains are programmed—that makes us susceptible to belief in God. If there really was a God, a rational species would expect rational, predictable behavior from him. But we don't get that. Sometimes, it seems as though God protects certain people, and at other times, he'll let a nun fall down an open elevator shaft. There's no rhyme or reason to it, and so we say—"

Mary was nodding, and she finished the thought for Veronica. "We say, 'The Lord works in mysterious ways.' "

"Just so!" crowed Veronica. "Prayers aren't always answered, but people go right on praying. But Ponter's people aren't wired like that." She turned to the Neanderthal. "Are you?"

"No," said Ponter. "I do not need Hak to tell me that this is not the way we behave. If the result is not predictable—if a pattern cannot be discerned—we discard the behavior as pointless."

"But *we* don't," said Veronica, rubbing her hands together. Mary could see she had the same "Cover of *Science*, here I come!" expression Mary herself had worn years ago, when she'd succeeded in extracting DNA from the Neanderthal type specimen in Germany. Veronica beamed at Ponter, then at Mary. "Even if there is no pattern, we convince ourselves that there's some underlying logic to it all. That's why we don't just make up stories about gods; we actually *believe* them."

The religious Mary had shifted entirely to the background; this was making the scientist in her have its own peak experience. "Are you sure about this, Veronica? Because if you are—"

"Oh, I am; I am. There's a famous experiment—I'll e-mail you the citation. It had two groups of people playing a game on a grid, the rules of which hadn't been explained to the players. All they knew in advance was they'd get points for good moves and no points for bad moves. Well, for one set of players, points were given for successfully marking every other space in the lower-right corner of the grid—and, of course, after enough turns, the players easily figured that out, and could win the game every time. But the second set of players were rewarded points *randomly:* whether they got points or not had no relation to what moves they made. But those players *also* came up with rules that they said governed the game, and they were convinced that by following those rules, they were likely to do better."

"Really?" said Ponter. "I would simply lose interest in the game."

"No doubt you would," said Veronica, smiling broadly. "But we would find it fascinating."

"Or irritating," said Mary.

"Irritating, yes! Meaning it would bug us—because we just can't accept that there's no underlying design to things." Veronica looked at Ponter. "Can I try another little test? Again, Mary, if you don't mind, please don't say anything. Ponter, do you know what I mean when I talk about flipping a coin?"

Ponter didn't, so Veronica demonstrated with a loonie she fished from a pocket of her lab coat. When Ponter nodded that he understood, the skinny redhead went on. "All right, if I flip this coin twenty times, and all twenty times it happens to come up heads, what are the chances it will come up heads again on the twenty-first try?"

Ponter didn't hesitate. "One-to-one."

"Just so! Or to put it the way we would, fifty-fifty, right? An even chance."

Ponter nodded.

"Now, Mary, I'm sure you know that Ponter is absolutely right: it doesn't matter how many times heads has come up in succession before the current flip, assuming the coin isn't unbalanced. The odds that the next flip will be heads are always fifty-fifty. But when I ask first-year psych students this question, most of them think the odds must be astronomically against getting yet another heads. At some fundamental level, our brains are wired to impute motivation to random events. *That's* why even those who don't ever have the kind of experience we just manufactured for you, Mary, still see God's handiwork in what's really just randomness."

Chapter Nine

*"It was that questing spirit that moved some of us to march
thousands of miles across the Bering Land Bridge, which
linked Siberia and Alaska during the Ice Age..."*

Mary wanted to take a quick look at the Laurentian University bookstore before they headed down to the portal. She'd forgotten to bring any books from her home in Richmond Hill, and of course wouldn't be able to find reading matter for herself in the Neanderthal universe.

Also, truth be told, Mary wanted a few minutes alone to try to digest what had transpired in Veronica Shannon's lab, so she excused herself, leaving Ponter with Veronica, and was now heading down "the bowling alley"—the long, narrow, glass-walled corridor that connected Laurentian's Classroom Building and the Great Hall. Coming toward her was an attractive young black woman. Mary had never been good about remembering faces, but she saw in the expression of the other woman a brief reaction of recognition, and then, almost at once, that reaction masked.

Mary had more or less gotten used to that. She'd been in the media a lot since early August when she'd confirmed the man who had been found half-drowned in the Sudbury Neutrino Observatory was a Neanderthal. She continued walking along, then it hit her—

"Keisha!" Mary said, rotating on her heel, the black woman now having passed her.

Keisha turned around and smiled. "Hello, Mary," she said.

"I almost didn't recognize you," said Mary.

Keisha looked a bit guilty. "I *did* recognize you." She lowered her voice. "But we're not supposed to acknowledge anyone we met at the Centre, unless they acknowledge us first. That's part of ensuring privacy . . ."

Mary nodded. "The Centre" was the Laurentian University Rape Crisis Centre, where Mary had gone for counseling after what had happened at York.

"How are you doing, Mary?" asked Keisha.

Off in the distance there was a Tim Hortons coffee-and-donuts stand. "Do you have a moment?" asked Mary. "I'd love to buy you a coffee."

Keisha looked at her watch. "Sure. Or—or do you want to go upstairs, to, you know, the Centre?"

But Mary shook her head. "No. No, that's not necessary." Still, she was silent as they walked the dozens of meters to the Tim Hortons, contemplating Keisha's question. How *was* she doing?

The Tim Hortons chain was one of the few places Mary could sometimes get her favorite brew—coffee with chocolate milk—since they often had open cartons of both chocolate and white milk. She asked for it, and received it. For her part, Keisha requested an apple juice, and Mary paid for them both. They sat at one of the two small tables flush with the corridor's glass wall—mostly, people got their coffee here and ran off somewhere else.

"I want to thank you," said Mary. "You were so kind to me, back then . . ."

Keisha had a small jeweled stud in her nose. She tipped

her head down, and the jewel caught the sunlight, flashing. "That's what we're here for."

Mary nodded. "You asked how I was doing," she said. "There's a man in my life now."

Keisha smiled. "Ponter Boddit," she said. "I read all about it in *People*."

Mary felt her heart jump. "*People* did an article about us?"

The younger woman nodded. "Last week. Nice photo of you and Ponter at the UN."

Good grief, thought Mary. "Well, he's been very good to me."

"Is he going to take up that offer to pose in *Playgirl?*"

Mary smiled. She'd almost forgotten about that; the offer had come during Ponter's first visit, when they were quarantined. Part of Mary would love to show off the physique of her man to all the bimbo girls she'd endured in high school, the ones who had dated the football players, every one of whom would look scrawny in comparison to Ponter. And another part of her was tickled at the notion that there was no way Colm could resist taking a peek at a newsstand, wondering what this Neanderthal had that he didn't . . .

"I don't know," said Mary. "Ponter laughed when the invitation came, and hasn't mentioned it since."

"Well, if he ever does," said Keisha, smiling, "I want an autographed copy."

"No problem," said Mary. And she realized she meant it. She would never be over her rape—nor, she suspected, would Keisha ever be over her own—but the fact that they could joke about a man posing nude for the enjoyment of women meant that they'd both come a long way.

"You asked how I'm doing," said Mary. She paused. "Better," she said with a smile, reaching out and patting the back of Keisha's hand. "Better every day."

Once they'd finished their drinks, Mary hurried off to the bookstore, quickly bought four paperbacks, and then hustled back to room C002B to collect Ponter. They headed up to the ground floor, then out into the parking lot. It was a crisp fall day, and here, four hundred kilometers north of Toronto, the leaves had mostly turned.

"*Dran!*" exclaimed Ponter, and "Astonishment!" translated Hak, through his external speaker.

"What?" said Mary.

"What is *that?*" said the Neanderthal, pointing.

Mary looked ahead, trying to fathom what had caught Ponter's eye, then she burst out laughing. "It's a dog," she said.

"My Pabo is a dog!" declared Ponter. "And I have encountered other doglike creatures here. But this! This is like nothing I have ever seen before." The dog and its owner were coming toward them. Ponter bent down, hands on knees, to examine the small animal, at the end of a leather leash being held by an attractive young white woman. "It looks like a sausage!" declared Ponter.

"It's a dachshund," said the woman, sounding miffed. She was doing a great job, Mary thought, of being unflustered in the presence of what she must know was a Neanderthal.

"Is it—" began Ponter. "Forgive me, is it a birth defect?"

The woman sounded even more put out. "No, he's supposed to be like that."

"But his legs! His ears! His body!" Ponter rose and shook his head. "A dog is a hunter," he declared, as if the animal before him represented an affront to all propriety.

"Dachshunds *are* hunting animals," said the young woman sharply. "They were bred in Germany to hunt badgers; *Dachs* is German for 'badger.' See? Their shape lets them follow the badger down the burrow."

"Oh," said Ponter. "Ah, um, my apologies."

The woman seemed mollified. "Now, *poodles*," she said with a contemptuous sniff, "those are dumb-looking dogs."

As time passed, Cornelius Ruskin couldn't deny that he was feeling different—and a whole lot faster than he would have thought possible. Sitting in his penthouse in the slums, he pumped keywords into Google; his results improved after he stumbled on the fact that the medical term for castration was "orchiectomy," and he started specifically excluding the terms "dog," "cat," and "horse."

He quickly found a chart on the University of Plymouth's web site entitled "Effect of Castration and Testosterone Replacement on Male Sexual Behaviour," showing an immediate drop-off in such behavior in castrated guinea pigs—

But Cornelius was a man, not an animal! Surely what applied to rodents didn't—

Twirling the scroll wheel on his mouse took him farther down the same page, to a study by researchers named Heim and Hursch that showed that over 50 percent of castrated rapists "stopped exhibiting sexual behavior shortly after castration—similar to the effect in rats."

Of course, when he'd been an undergrad, the feminist rhetoric had been that rape was a crime of violence, not sex. But no. Cornelius, having more than a passing interest in the subject, had read Thornhill and Palmer's *A Natural History of Rape: Biological Bases of Sexual Coercion* when it came out in 2000. That book made the case, based on evolutionary psychology, that rape was indeed a reproductive strategy—a *sexual* strategy—for . . .

Cornelius hated to think of himself as such, but it was true; he knew it was: for males who lacked the power and status to reproduce in the normal way. It made no difference that he'd been unfairly denied that status; the fact was that he didn't have it, and couldn't get it—not in the world of academe.

He still hated the policies that had held him back. He was as much an expert on ancient DNA as Mary Vaughan was—he'd been with the Ancient Biomolecules Centre at Oxford, for Christ's sake!

It *was* unfair, totally and completely—like goddamned "slave reparations," people who never did anything wrong themselves being asked to cough up huge amounts of cash for people whose long-dead *ancestors* had been wronged. Why should Cornelius suffer for the sexist hiring policies of generations gone by?

He had spent years being *livid* over this.

But now . . .

Now . . .

Now, he was just angry: an anger that, for the first time in as long as he could remember, seemed to be under control.

There was no doubt *why* he was feeling so much less furious. Or was there? After all, it hadn't been *that* long since Ponter had cut off his balls. Was it really reasonable for Cornelius to be feeling different so quickly?

The answer, apparently, was yes. As he continued searching the web, he found an article from the *New Times* in San Louis Obispo, interviewing Bruce Clotfelter, who had spent two decades jailed for child molestation before undergoing surgical castration. " 'It was like a miracle,' Clotfelter said. 'The next morning, I realized I had gone through the night without those horrible sexual dreams for the first time in years.' "

The next morning . . .

Jesus Christ, just what was the half-life of testosterone, anyway? A few keystrokes, a couple of mouse clicks, and Cornelius had the answer: "The half-life of free testosterone in the blood is only a few minutes," said one site; another pegged the figure at ten minutes.

Some more spelunking took him to the Geocities page of a person born male who underwent castration, with no hormonal treatments before or for years after. He reported: "Four days after my castration . . . it seemed that waiting for traffic lights and other little annoyances did not bother me so much . . .

"Six days post castration I returned to work. This workday was unusually hectic . . . and yet I still felt so calm when the day was all over. I was definitely feeling the effects of castration and most certainly felt better all the time without testosterone.

"Ten days post castration I felt as a feather floating around everywhere. I just kept feeling better and better. For me the serenity was the strongest of the castration effects, followed by the decrease in libido."

Immediate change.

Overnight change.

Change in a matter of days.

Cornelius knew—*knew!*—he should be furious about what Ponter had done to him.

But he was finding it difficult to be furious about *anything . . .*

Chapter Ten

"It was that questing spirit that caused others to bravely sail boats over the horizon, finding new lands in Australia and Polynesia..."

There was a very good reason for wanting to establish a new interuniversal portal at United Nations headquarters. The existing portal was located two kilometers underground, 1.2 kilometers horizontally from the nearest elevator on the Gliksin side, and three kilometers from the nearest elevator on the Barast side.

It would take Mary and Ponter a couple of hours to get from the surface in her world to the surface in his. They began by donning hardhats and safety boots, and riding down the mining elevator at Inco's Creighton Mine. The hardhats had built-in lamps, and hearing-protection cups that could be swung over the ears if needed.

Mary had brought two suitcases, and Ponter was effortlessly carrying them for her, one in each hand.

Five miners rode most of the way down with them, getting off one level above where Mary and Ponter were to exit. That was just fine by Mary; she was always uncomfortable in this lift. It reminded her of the awkward journey she'd had in it once before with Ponter, explaining why, back then, despite his obvious attraction to her, and hers to him, she'd been unable to respond to his touch.

Once on the 6800-foot level, they began the long trudge out to the Sudbury Neutrino Observatory site. Mary was never a great one for exercise, but it was actually even worse for Ponter, since the temperature this far below the Earth's surface was a constant forty-one degrees Celsius, much too warm for him.

"I will be glad to be back home," said Ponter. "Back to air I can breathe!"

Mary knew he wasn't referring to the oppressive air here in the mine. Rather, he was looking forward to being in a world that didn't burn fossil fuels, the smell of which had assaulted his massive nose most places he went here, although Reuben's place, out in the country, had been quite tolerable, he'd said.

Mary was reminded of the theme song to one of her favorite shows when she was a kid:

> *Fresh air!*
> *Times Square!*
> *You are my wife!*
> *Goodbye, city life!*

She hoped she would fit in on Ponter's world better than Lisa Douglas had in Hooterville. But it was more than just leaving the hustle and bustle of a world of six billion souls for one of just a hundred and eighty-five million . . . million *people*; you couldn't use the word "souls" when tallying Barasts, since they didn't believe they had any.

The day before they'd left Rochester, Ponter had been interviewed on the radio; the Neanderthals were very much in demand as guests wherever they happened to be. Mary had listened with interest as Bob Smith had questioned Ponter about Neanderthal beliefs on WXXI, the local PBS station. Smith had spent a fair bit of time on the Neanderthal practice of sterilizing criminals. As they walked down the long muddy tunnel, the topic of the interview came up.

"Yes," said Mary, in response to Ponter's question, "you were fine, but . . ."

"But what?"

"Well, those things you said—about sterilizing people. I . . ."

"Yes?"

"I'm sorry, Ponter, but I really can't condone that."

Ponter looked at her. He was wearing a special orange hardhat that the nickel mine had put together for him, shaped to accommodate his Neanderthal head. "Why not?"

"It's . . . it's *inhuman*. And I guess I *am* using that word advisedly. It's just not a suitable thing for human beings to do."

Ponter was quiet for a time, looking at the drift's walls, which were covered with wire mesh to prevent rock bursts. "I know there are many on this version of Earth who do not believe in evolution," he said at last, "but those who do must understand that human evolution has—how would you say it?—ground to a halt. Since medical techniques allow almost every human to live to reproductive age, there is no longer any . . . any . . . I am not sure what your phrase is."

" 'Natural selection,' " said Mary. "Sure, I understand that; without selective survival of genes, no evolution can occur."

"Exactly," said Ponter. "And yet evolution made us what we are, turning the four basic, original lifeforms into the complex, diverse varieties exhibited today."

Mary looked over at Ponter. "The *four* original lifeforms?"

He blinked. "Yes, of course."

"What four?" said Mary, thinking perhaps she'd at last detected a hint of creationism underlying Ponter's worldview. Could it be Neander-Adam, Neander-Eve, Neander-Adam's man-mate, and Neander-Eve's woman-mate?

"The original plant, animal, fungi, and—I do not know your name—the group that includes slime molds and some algae."

"Protists or protoctists," said Mary, "depending on who you ask."

"Yes. Well, each emerged separately from the primordial prebiologic world."

"You have proof of that?" said Mary. "We generally hold that life only emerged *once* on this world, some four billion years ago."

"But the four types of life are so different . . ." said Ponter. And then he shrugged. "Well, you are the geneticist, not I. The point of this trip is to meet our experts in such matters, so you should ask one of them about this. One of you—I do not know which—has a lot to learn from the other."

Mary never ceased to be amazed at how Neanderthal science and her own brand of the stuff differed on so many fundamental matters. But she didn't want to lose track of the more important issue that—

The more important issue. Interesting, thought Mary, that she considered a moral conundrum more important than a basic scientific truth. "We were talking about the end of evolution. You're saying that your kind continues to evolve because it consciously weeds out bad genes."

" 'Weeds out'?" repeated Ponter, frowning. "Ah—an agricultural metaphor. I think I understand. Yes, you are right. We continue to improve our gene pool by getting rid of undesirable traits."

Mary stepped over a large muddy puddle. "I could *almost* buy that—but you do it not just by sterilizing criminals, but also their close relatives, too."

"Of course. Otherwise, the genes might persist."

Mary shook her head. "And I just can't abide that." Hak bleeped. "*Abide*," repeated Mary. "Tolerate. Stand."

"Why not?"

"Because . . . because it's *wrong*. Individuals have rights."

"Of course they do," said Ponter, "but so do species. We are protecting and improving the Barast species."

Mary tried not to shudder, but Ponter must have detected it regardless. "You react negatively to what I just said."

"Well," said Mary, "it's just that so often in our past, people here have made the same claim. Back in the 1940s, Adolf Hitler set out to purge our gene pool of Jews."

Ponter tipped his head slightly, perhaps listening to Hak remind him through his cochlear implants of who the Jews were. Mary imagined the little computer saying, "You know, the ones who weren't gullible enough to believe in that Jesus story."

"Why did he want to do that?" asked Ponter.

"Because he hated the Jews, pure and simple," said Mary. "Don't you see? Giving someone the power to decide who lives and who dies, or who breeds and who doesn't, is just playing God."

" 'Playing God,' " repeated Ponter, as if the phrase was appealingly oddball. "Obviously, such a notion would never occur to us."

"But the potential for corruption, for unfairness . . ."

Ponter spread his arms. "And yet you kill certain criminals."

"We don't," said Mary. "That is, Canadians don't. But Americans do, in some states."

"So I have learned," said Ponter. "And, more than that, I have learned there is a racial component to this." He looked at Mary. "Your various races intrigue me, you know. My people are northern-adapted, so we tend to stay in approximately the same latitudes, no matter where we are in terms of longitude, which I guess is why we all look pretty much alike. Am I correct in understanding that darker skin is an adaptation to more equatorial climes?"

Mary nodded.

"And the—what do you call them? On the eyes of those such as Paul Kiriyama?"

It took a moment for Mary to remember who Paul Kiriyama was—the grad student who, along with Louise Benoît, had saved Ponter from drowning in the heavy-water tank up ahead at the Sudbury Neutrino Observatory. Then it took another moment for her to remember the name for what Ponter was referring to. "You mean the skin that covers part of Asian eyes? Epicanthic folds."

"Yes. Epicanthic folds. I presume these are to help shield the eyes from glare, but my people have browridges that accomplish much the same thing, so, again, it is a trait we never developed."

Mary nodded slowly, more to herself than to Ponter. "There's been a lot of speculation, you know, on the Internet and in newspapers, about what happened to your other races. People assume that—well, that with your belief in purging the gene pool, that you wiped them out."

"There never were any other races. Although we do have some scientists in what you call Africa and Central America, they are hardly permanent residents there." He raised a hand. "And without races, we obviously have never had racial discrimination. But you do: here, racial characteristics correlate with the likelihood of execution for serious crimes, is that not correct?"

"Blacks are more frequently sentenced to death than are whites, yes." Mary decided not to add, *Especially when they kill a white.*

"Perhaps because we never had such divisions, the idea of sterilizing a segment of humanity on an arbitrary basis never occurred to us."

A couple of miners were approaching them, going the other way. They openly stared at Ponter—although the sight of a woman down here was probably almost as rare, Mary thought. Once they had passed, Mary continued. "But surely, even without visible races, there must have been a desire to favor those who are closely related to you over those who are not. That's kin selection, and it exists throughout the animal kingdom. I can't imagine that Neanderthals are exempt."

"Exempt? Perhaps not. But remember that our family relations are more . . . elaborate, shall we say, than yours, or, for that matter, than most other animals. We have a never-ending family chain of man-mates and woman-mates, and because of our system of Two becoming One only temporarily, we do not have the difficulty in determining paternity that concerns your kind so much." He paused, then smiled. "Anyway, as to the price of tea in China, my people find your notion of execution or decades of imprisonment to be more cruel than our sterilization and judicial scrutiny."

It took Mary a moment to remember what "judicial scrutiny" was: the process of viewing the transmissions made by a Companion implant, so that everything an individual said and did could be monitored as it happened. "I don't know," said Mary. "I mean, like I said in the car, I practice birth control, which is something that my religion forbids, so I can't claim that I'm morally opposed to anything that might interfere with conception. But ... but to prevent innocent people from reproducing seems wrong."

"You would accept the sterilization of the actual perpetrator, but not his or her siblings, parents, and offspring, as an alternative to execution or imprisonment?"

"Perhaps. I don't know. Under certain circumstances, maybe. If the convicted person so chose."

Ponter's golden eyes went wide. "You would let the guilty party choose its punishment?"

Mary felt her heart flutter. Was the choice of "its" Hak's attempt to render the gender-neutral personal pronoun that existed in the Barast language but not in English, or was it Ponter again dehumanizing a criminal? "Under many circumstances, I would give the criminal a choice of a range of appropriate punishments, yes," she said, thinking back to Father Caldicott giving her a choice of penances when she'd made her last confession.

"But certainly in some cases," said Ponter, "only one punishment is suitable. For instance, in ..."

Ponter stopped cold. "What?" said Mary.

"No, nothing."

Mary frowned. "You're talking about rape."

Ponter was silent for a long time, looking down at the muddy tunnel floor as he walked along. At first, Mary thought she'd offended him by suggesting he'd be so insensitive as to bring up that uncomfortable topic again, but his next words, when he finally did speak, startled her even more. "Actually," he said, "I am not just talking about rape in general." He looked at her, then back at the ground, a mishmash of boot prints illuminated by the beam from the headlight on his hardhat. "I am talking about *your* rape."

Mary could feel her heart pounding. "What do you mean?"

"I—it is our way, among our people, not to have secrets between partners, and yet . . ."

"Yes?"

He turned around and looked back down the drift, making sure they were alone. "There is something I have not told you—something I have not told anyone, except . . ."

"Except who? Adikor?"

But Ponter shook his head. "No. No, he does not know of this, either. The one person who does know is a male of my kind, a man named Jurard Selgan."

Mary frowned. "I don't remember you ever mentioning that name before."

"I have not," said Ponter. "He . . . he is a personality sculptor."

"A what?" said Mary.

"A—he works with those who wish to modify their . . . their mental state."

"You mean a psychiatrist?"

Ponter tipped his head, clearly listening to Hak speak to him through his cochlear implants. The Companion was no doubt breaking the term Mary had presented into its etymological root; ironically, "psyche" was the closest approximation to "soul" the Neanderthals had. At last Ponter nodded. "A comparable specialist, yes."

Mary's spine stiffened even as she walked along. "You've been seeing a psychiatrist? About my rape?" She'd thought he'd understood, damn it all. Yes, *Homo sapiens* males were notorious for looking at their spouses differently after they'd been raped, wondering if it had somehow been the woman's fault, if she'd somehow secretly wanted it—

But Ponter . . .

Ponter was supposed to understand!

They marched on in silence for a while, their helmet beams lighting the way.

Reflecting on it, Ponter *had* seemed desperate to know the details of Mary's rape. At the police station, Ponter had grabbed the sealed evidence bag containing specimens from Qaiser Remtulla's rape, ripped it open, and inhaled the scent within, identifying one of Mary's colleagues, Cornelius Ruskin, as the perpetrator.

Mary looked over at Ponter, a dark, hulking form against the rock wall. "It wasn't my fault," said Mary.

"What?" said Ponter. "No, I know that."

"I didn't want it. I didn't ask for it."

"Yes, yes, I do understand that."

"Then why are you seeing this—this 'personality sculptor'?"

"I am not seeing him anymore. It is just that—"

Ponter stopped, and Mary looked over. He had his head tilted, listening to Hak, and after a moment, he made the smallest of nods, a signal intended for the Companion, not for her.

"It's just *what?*" said Mary.

"Nothing," said Ponter. "I am sorry I brought the topic up."

So am I, thought Mary as they continued on through the darkness.

Chapter Eleven

"It was that questing spirit that led Vikings to come to North America a thousand years ago, that drove the Niña, the Pinta, and the Santa Maria to cross the Atlantic five hundred years ago..."

At last they reached the Sudbury Neutrino Observatory. Ponter and Mary made their way through the massive facility—all hanging pipes and massive tanks—to the control room. It was deserted now; Ponter's original arrival had destroyed the observatory's heavy-water detector tank, and the plans to repair it had been put on hold by the subsequent re-establishment of the portal.

They came to the room above the detector chamber, went through the trapdoor, and—this was the terrifying part for Mary—backed down the long ladder to the staging area, six meters off the ground. The staging area was at the end of the Derkers tube, a crush-proof tunnel that had been shoved through the portal from the other side.

Mary stood at the threshold of the Derkers tube and looked into it. The tube was twice as long on the inside as it was on the outside, and at the other end she could see the yellow walls of the quantum-computing chamber over on Ponter's version of Earth.

A Canadian Forces guard was there, and they presented

their passports to him—Ponter had received one when he'd been made a Canadian citizen.

"After you," said Ponter to Mary, a bit of gallantry he'd picked up in Mary's world. Mary took a deep breath and walked down the tube, which, when one was inside it, measured sixteen meters long and six wide. Coming to the middle, she could see the ring of ragged blue luminosity through the translucent material of the tube's wall. She could also see the shadows cast by the crisscrossing metal segments that held the tube open. Taking another deep breath, Mary stepped quickly across the discontinuity marked by the blue ring, feeling static electricity crawling over her body from front to back.

And suddenly she was *there*—in the Neanderthal world.

Mary turned around without leaving the tube and watched Ponter come toward her. She could see the blond hair on Ponter's head ruffle as he came through the discontinuity; like most Neanderthals, his natural part was exactly in the middle of his long skull.

Once he was through, Mary turned back around and continued on to the end of the tube.

And there they were, in a world that had diverged from Mary's own 40,000 years previously. They were inside the quantum-computing chamber she had glimpsed from her side, a vast room filled with a grid of register tanks. The quantum computer, designed by Adikor Huld to run software developed by Ponter Boddit, had been built to factor numbers larger than any that had ever been factored before; piercing into an alternate universe had been entirely accidental.

"Ponter!" said a deep voice.

Mary looked up. Adikor—Ponter's man-mate—came

running down the five steps from the control room onto the computing-chamber floor.

"Adikor!" said Ponter. He ran over to him, and the two men embraced, then licked each other's faces.

Mary looked away. Of course, normally—if such a word could ever be applied to her existence in this world—she would rarely see Ponter when he was with Adikor; when Two became One, Adikor would hurry off to spend time with his own woman-mate and young son.

But Two were not One, and so here, now, Ponter was supposed to be spending time with his man-mate.

Still, after a few moments, the two males disengaged, and Ponter turned to Mary.

"Adikor, you remember Mare."

"Of course," said Adikor, smiling what seemed to be a very genuine foot-wide smile. Mary tried to emulate its sincerity, if not its dimensions. "Hello, Adikor," she said.

"Mare! It is good to see you!"

"Thank you."

"But what brings you here? Two is not yet One."

There it was. A staking of claim; an establishment of turf.

"I know," said Mary. "I've come on an extended visit. I'm here to learn more about Neanderthal genetics."

"Ah," said Adikor. "Well, I'm sure Lurt will be able to assist you."

Mary tilted her head slightly—not that she had a Companion to listen to. Was Adikor just being helpful, or was he making a point of reminding Mary that she would need to seek the assistance of a female Neanderthal, who, of course, would be found in the City Center, far away from Adikor and Ponter.

"I know," said Mary. "I'm looking forward to talking with her some more."

Ponter looked at Adikor. "I will take Mary briefly to our home," he said, "and get her a few things she will need for an extended stay. Then I will arrange her transportation into the Center."

"Fine," said Adikor. He looked at Mary, then back at Ponter. "I assume it will be just the two of us for the evening meal?"

"Of course," said Ponter. "Of course."

Mary stripped naked—she was losing her self-consciousness about nudity in this world that had never had any religion to impose such taboos—and went through the tuned-laser decontamination process, coherent beams at precise wavelengths passing through her flesh to zap foreign molecules within her body. Already, similar devices were being built in Mary's world to treat many forms of infection. Sadly, though, since tumors were made of the patient's own cells, this process couldn't cure cancers, such as the leukemia that had taken Ponter's wife, Klast, two years ago.

No—not "taken." That was a Gliksin term, a euphemism that implied she'd gone somewhere, and at least by the standards of these people, she hadn't. As Ponter himself would say, she no longer existed.

And not "Ponter's wife," either. The term was *yat-dija*— "woman-mate." When in the Neanderthal world, Mary really did try to think in Neanderthal terms; it made it easier to deal with the differences.

The lasers danced over—and through—Mary's body until the square light above the door changed color, signaling that she should leave. Mary stepped out and began changing into Neanderthal clothes, while Ponter took his turn in the chamber. He'd fallen ill with equine distemper while in Mary's world the first time—members of *Homo sapiens* were immune to it, but *Homo neanderthalensis* individuals were not. This process made sure they weren't bringing the *Streptococcus equii* bacterium, or any other nasty germs or viruses, across with them; everybody who passed through the portal was subjected to it.

No one who had any choice would live where Cornelius Ruskin did. Driftwood was a rough neighborhood, full of crime and drugs. Its only appeal for Cornelius was that it was an easy walk to the York University campus.

He took the elevator down the fourteen floors to the grungy lobby of his building. Still, despite everything, he had a certain—well, affection was too strong a word, but a certain gratitude for the place. After all, living within walking distance of York saved him the cost of a car, driver's insurance, and a university parking permit—or the alternative, the monthly $93.50 for a Toronto Transit Commission Metro-Pass.

It was a beautiful day with a clear blue sky. Cornelius was wearing a brown suede jacket. He continued up the road, past the convenience shop that had bars on its windows. That seedy little store had a giant rack of porno mags and dusty tin cans of food. It was where Cornelius bought his cigarettes; fortunately he'd had half a carton of du Mauriers in his apartment.

Cornelius crossed onto the York campus, walking by one of the residence towers. Students were milling about, some still in short sleeves, others wearing sweatshirts. He suspected he might be able to get testosterone supplements at York.

Why, he could even devise a genetics project that might require them. That certainly would be an incentive to go back to his old job, but . . .

But things *had* changed in Cornelius. For one thing, the nightmares had finally ended, and he was now sleeping like a rock. Instead of lying awake for an hour or two, tossing and turning, fuming over all the things that were wrong in his life—all the slights, all his anger at having no one in his life—instead of lying awake, tortured by all that, he'd fall asleep within moments of putting his head to the pillow, sleep soundly through the night, and wake refreshed.

True, for a while, he hadn't wanted to get out of bed, but he was over that now. He felt . . . not energetic, not ready for the daily fight for survival. No, he felt something he hadn't felt for years, since the summers of his childhood, when he was away from school, away from the bullies, away from the daily beatings-up.

Cornelius Ruskin felt *calm*.

"Hello, Dr. Ruskin," said a perky male voice.

Cornelius turned. It was one of his Eukaryotic Genetics students—John, Jim . . . something like that; the guy wanted to become a genetics prof, he'd said. Cornelius wanted to tell the poor sap to drop out now; there were no decent jobs these days for white men in academe. But instead he just forced a smile and said, "Hello."

"Great to have you back!" said the student, heading off in the other direction.

Cornelius continued along the sidewalk, fields of grass on one side, a parking lot on the other. He knew where he was going, of course: the Farquahrson Life Sciences Building. But he'd never before noticed what a funny-sounding name that was: it now made him think of Charlie Farquahrson, the hick character Toronto's Don Harron had played for years on CFRB radio and the U.S. TV series *Hee Haw*. Cornelius shook his head; he'd always been too . . . too *something* . . . when approaching that building to let such a whimsical thought percolate to the surface.

Walking on autopilot, his feet trod the well-known terrain. But suddenly, with a start, he realized that he'd come to . . .

It didn't have a name, and he'd never even bestowed one upon it in his mind. But this was it: the two retaining walls that met at right angles, far from any lighting standard, shielded by large trees. This was the spot, the place where he'd thrown two different women against the wall. This was where he'd shown Qaiser Remtulla who *really* was in charge. And this was where he'd rammed it into Mary Vaughan.

Cornelius used to walk by here even in broad daylight when he needed a boost, reminding himself that at least some of the time he had been in control. Often, merely the sight of this place used to give him a raging hard-on, but this time his groin didn't stir at all.

The walls were covered with graffiti. For the same reason Cornelius chose this spot, spray-paint artists liked it, as did lovers who wanted to immortalize their youthful commitment, just as . . .

He'd long since obliterated it, but, once upon a time, eons ago, his initials and Melody's had shared a cartoon heart here.

Cornelius blinked that thought away, looked once again at this place, then turned his back on it.

It was *much* too nice a day to go to work, he thought, heading back home, the day seeming even brighter still.

Chapter Twelve

"It was that questing spirit that lifted the wings of Orville and Wilbur Wright, of Amelia Earhart, of Chuck Yeager..."

As Mary and Ponter emerged from the elevator building at the Debral nickel mine, Mary was astonished to find it was dark, given that it should only be the middle of the afternoon. She looked up and gasped.

"My God. I've never seen so many birds!" A great cloud of them was flying overhead, virtually obliterating the sun. Many were making a *kek-kek-kek* call.

"Really?" said Ponter. "They are a common type."

"Apparently so!" exclaimed Mary. She continued to look up. "Good Christ," she said, noting the pinkish bodies and the blue-gray heads. "They're passenger pigeons!"

"I doubt they could carry a passenger," said Ponter.

"No, no, no. But that's what we called them. That, or *Ectopistes migratorius*. I know them well; I'd been working on recovering DNA from them."

"I noticed the absence of these birds when I first visited your world. They are extinct there, are they not?"

"Yes."

"Through the fault of Gliksins?"

Mary nodded. "Yes." She shrugged. "We hunted them to death."

Ponter shook his head. "No wonder you had to adopt this thing you call agriculture. Our name for this bird is— Hak, do not translate the next word—*quidrat.* They are delicious, and we eat them often."

"Really?" said Mary.

Ponter nodded. "Yes. I am sure you will have some during your stay here."

As soon as Hak had regained access to the planetary information network, Ponter had had him request a travel cube. That vehicle was now barreling toward them. It was about the size of an SUV, but it worked by large fans mounted on its base and rear, plus a trio of smaller ones for steering. The cube was mostly transparent, and contained four saddle-seats, one of which was occupied by the male driver, a trim member of generation 146.

The travel cube slowed, then settled to the ground, and most of one side flipped up, providing access to the interior. Ponter clambered in, taking the far rear seat. Mary followed him, taking the other rear seat. Ponter spoke briefly to the driver, and the cube rose. Mary watched the driver operate the two main control levers, rotating the cube and setting it on its way toward Ponter's home.

Mary had strapped on a temporary Companion before leaving the elevator building; all Gliksins who visited the Neanderthal world were required to wear them, constantly monitoring their activities, and transmitting information to the alibi archives. But the damned things itched. Mary found herself sticking a ballpoint pen she'd brought with her underneath the Companion, trying to scratch with it. "Are the permanent ones this uncomfortable?" she asked, looking at Ponter.

"I am not aware of Hak's physical presence at all," said Ponter. He paused. "But, on this subject . . ."

"Yes?"

"These temporary Companions expire after twenty days or so—they are battery-powered, after all, instead of drawing power from your bodily processes. Of course, given who you are, we could certainly get you another one."

Mary smiled. She wasn't used to this notion that just being Mary Vaughan entitled her to special treatment. "No," she said. "No, I should get a permanent one, I think."

Ponter smiled broadly. "Thank you," he said. And then, presumably just to be sure, he added, "You do know that permanent means *permanent*. To remove it later will be very difficult, and might seriously damage your forearm muscles and nerves."

Mary nodded. "I understand that. But I also understand that if I don't get a permanent Companion, I'll always be an outsider here."

"Thank you," said Ponter warmly. "What kind do you want?"

Mary had been looking out at the pristine landscape—old-growth forest mixed with shield rocks. "Pardon me?"

"Well, you could get the standard sort of Companion. Or"—and here Ponter raised his left arm and faced its inner surface toward Mary—"you could opt for one like mine, with a true artificial intelligence installed."

Mary lifted her eyebrows. "I hadn't thought about that."

"Few people have intelligent Companions," said Ponter, "although I expect they will become very common in times to come. You will certainly want the processing capability that goes with an advanced unit; you will need that for real-time language translation. But it is up to you what features you get beyond that."

Mary looked at Ponter's Companion. Externally, it

seemed no different from the dozens of others she'd now seen—except, of course, the gold one Lonwis Trob had. But inside, she knew, dwelt Hak. "What's it like," asked Mary, "having an intelligent Companion?"

"Oh, it is not so bad," said Hak's voice, coming from the implant's external speaker. "I have gotten used to the big guy."

Mary laughed, half in amusement and half in surprise.

Ponter rolled his eyes, a facial expression he'd picked up from Mary. "It is a lot like that," he said.

"I'm not sure I could take it," said Mary, "having someone with me all the time." Mary frowned. "Is Hak really . . . conscious?"

"How do you mean?" asked Ponter.

"Well, I know you don't believe in souls; I know that you think your own mind is just utterly predictable software running on the hardware of your brain. But, I mean, does Hak *really* think? Is he self-aware?"

"An interesting question," said Ponter. "Hak, what do you say?"

"I am aware of my existence."

Mary lifted her shoulders. "But . . . but, I don't know, I mean, do you have wants and desires of your own?"

"I want to be of use to Ponter."

"And that's it?"

"That is it."

Wow, thought Mary. *Colm should have married one of these.* "What will happen to you—forgive me, Ponter—but what will happen to you when Ponter dies?"

"My power comes from his own biochemical and biomechanical sources. Within a few daytenths of his death, I will cease to function."

"Does that bother you?"

"I would have no further purpose without Ponter. No, it does not bother me."

"It is very useful having an intelligent Companion," said Ponter. "I doubt I would have retained my sanity during my first visit to your world without Hak's help."

"I don't know," said Mary. "It . . . well, it seems—forgive me, Hak—a bit creepy. Is it possible to upgrade later? You know, start with the basics and then add artificial intelligence at some future date?"

"Of course. My Companion originally had no intelligence."

"Maybe that's the way to go," said Mary. "But . . ."

But no. No, she was trying to fit in here, and having a Companion that could advise her and explain things to her would be very useful. "No, let's go whole hog."

"I—beg your pardon?" said Ponter.

"I mean, I'll get one that can think, just like Hak."

"You will not regret the decision," said Ponter. He looked at Mary, a proud smile on his face. "You were not the first Gliksin to visit this world," he said—and that was true. Either a woman from the Laboratory Centre for Disease Control in Ottawa or another woman from the Centers for Disease Control and Prevention in Atlanta had that distinction; Mary wasn't sure which one had actually crossed over first. "Still," said Ponter, "you will be the first Gliksin to have a permanent Companion—the first to become one of us."

Mary looked out the travel cube's transparent side, at the gorgeous autumn countryside.

And she smiled.

The driver let them off on the solar-panel array, which doubled as a landing pad, next to Ponter and Adikor's house.

Grown by arboriculture, the house's central structure was the hollow bole of a massive deciduous tree. Mary had seen Ponter's home before, but not with all the leaves having changed color. It looked magnificent.

Inside, chemical reactions produced a cool green-white light, running in ribs up the sides of the walls. Ponter's dog Pabo bounded over to greet them. Mary had gotten used to the animal's wolflike appearance, and bent down to scratch her behind the ears.

Mary looked around the circular living chamber. "It's too bad I can't stay here," she said wistfully.

Ponter took her in his arms, and Mary hugged him, resting her head on his shoulder. Still, four days a month with Ponter beat full-time with Colm.

Whenever she thought about Colm, the topic he'd raised came to mind, a topic that Mary had obviously suppressed thinking about until Colm had brought it into the open.

"Ponter," Mary said softly, feeling his chest rise and fall as he breathed.

"Yes, woman that I love?"

"Next year," said Mary, trying to keep her tone as neutral as possible, "a new generation is to be conceived."

Ponter let go of Mary and looked at her, slowly lifting his eyebrow as he did so. "*Ka.*"

"Should *we* have a child then?"

Ponter's eyes went wide. "I did not think that was an option," he said at last.

"Because we have different chromosome counts, you mean. Certainly, that would be an obstacle, but there must be some way to get around it. And, well, Jock *has* sent me here to learn about Neanderthal genetic technology. While I'm exploring that, I could look into ways in which we might be able to combine our own DNA and produce a child."

"Really?"

Mary nodded. "Of course, the fertilization would have to be done *in vitro*."

Hak bleeped.

"In glassware. Outside my body."

"Ah," said Ponter. "I am surprised that your belief system supports that process, while banning so much else related to reproduction."

Mary shrugged. "Yeah, the Roman Catholic Church is against IVF—*in vitro* fertilization. But I do want a baby. I want *your* baby. And I can't see how giving nature a little helping hand is wrong." She lowered her gaze. "But I know you already have two children. Perhaps . . . perhaps you don't want to be a father again?"

"I will *always* be a father," said Ponter, "until the day I die." Mary lifted her eyes, and was glad to see Ponter was looking right at her. "I had not thought about having another child, but . . ."

Mary felt as though she were about to burst. She hadn't realized until just this moment how very much indeed she wanted Ponter's answer to be yes. "But what?" she said.

Ponter lifted his massive shoulders, but they moved slowly, ponderously, as if he were shifting the weight of his world with them. "But we believe in zero population growth. Klast and I have two children already; they are our replacements."

"But Adikor and Lurt have only one child," said Mary.

"Dab, yes. But they may try again next year."

"Are they going to do that? Have you discussed it with Adikor?" Mary did not like the desperation that had come into her tone.

"No, I have not," said Ponter. "I suppose I could broach

the topic, but even if they are not going to try again, the Gray Council—"

"Damn it, Ponter, I'm sick of the Gray Council! I'm sick of all these rules and regulations! I'm sick of a bunch of old people controlling your life."

Ponter looked at Mary, his eyebrow lifted again in surprise. "They are elected, you know. The rules they enact are the rules my people have chosen for themselves."

Mary took a deep breath. "I know. I'm sorry. It's just— it's just that it shouldn't matter to anyone but you or me if we have a baby."

"You are correct," said Ponter. "As is, some people in my world have more than two children. Twins are not uncommon; my nearest neighbor has twin sons. And, often enough, there will be three conceptions by a woman: one when she is nineteen years old, another when she is twenty-nine, and sometimes again when she is thirty-nine."

"*I'm* thirty-nine. Why can't we try?"

"There will be those who will say such a child would be *unnatural*," replied Ponter.

Mary looked around. She moved over to one of the couches growing out of the wall, and patted the spot next to her, inviting Ponter to join her. He did.

"Where I come from," said Mary, "many people say that two men having—what did Louise call it back at Reuben's place? 'Affectionate touching of the genitals'? There are those among my species who say that *that* is unnatural, and that relations between two women are unnatural, too." Mary's face was firm. "But they're wrong. I don't know if I would have said that with such assurance before first coming to your world, but I know it now." She nodded, as much to herself as to Ponter. "The world—*any* world—is a better place when people are in love, when people care about other people, and, as long as those people are consenting adults, it's nobody's business except their own who they are. A male and a female, or two males, or two females—they're all *natural*, as long as they're in love. And a Gliksin and a Barast—*that's* natural, too, if they're in love."

"And we *are* in love," said Ponter, taking Mary's small hand in his two massive ones. "But, still, there *are* people in your world and mine who will object to our having a child."

Mary nodded sadly. "I know, yes." She let air escape from her lungs in a long, rueful sigh. "You know Reuben is black."

"More of a medium brown, I would say," replied Ponter, smiling. "A rather nice shade."

But Mary was in no mood for jokes. "And Louise Benoît is white. There are still people in my world who object to a black man and a white woman having a relationship. But they are wrong, wrong, wrong. Just as those who might object to us being together—or having a child together—are wrong, wrong, wrong."

"I agree, of course, but—"

"But what? Nothing could be a better symbol of the synergy between our worlds—and of our love for each other—than us having a baby together."

Ponter looked into Mary's eyes, his golden orbs dancing with excitement. "You are right, my love. You are absolutely right."

Chapter Thirteen

"It was that questing spirit that made brave men and women like Yuri Gagarin and Valentina Tereshkova and John Glenn ride on pillars of flame into Earth orbit..."

Every week, Jock Krieger reviewed the press coverage of the Neanderthals, both in the hundred and forty magazines Synergy subscribed to and as collected and forwarded by various print, radio, and video clipping services. The current batch of material included a preprint of an interview with Lonwis Trob coming up in *Popular Mechanics*; a five-part series from the *San Francisco Chronicle* on what Neanderthal technology was doing to the future of Silicon Valley firms; an appearance by runner Jalsk Lalplun on ABC's *Wide World of Sports*; an editorial from the *Minneapolis Star Tribune* saying Tukana Prat should win the Nobel Peace Prize for finding a way to keep contact between the two worlds open; a CNN special with Craig Ventner interviewing Borl Kadas, who headed the Neanderthal version of the Human Genome Project; an NHK documentary on Neanderthals in fact and fiction; a DVD re-release of *Quest for Fire* with an audio commentary track by a Neanderthal paleoanthropologist; a new Department of Defense study of security issues related to interdimensional portals; and more.

Louise Benoît had come down to the living room of the

old mansion that housed the Synergy Group to have a look through the materials, as well. She was reading an article in *New Scientist* that questioned why Neanderthals had ever domesticated dogs given that their own sense of smell was at least as good as that possessed by canines, meaning dogs would have added little to their ability to hunt. But she was interrupted when Jock blew out air noisily.

"What's wrong?" asked Louise, looking over the magazine at him.

"I get sick of this," Jock said, indicating the pile of magazines, newspaper clippings, audio tapes, and VHS cassettes. "I get sick to death of it. 'The Neanderthals are more peaceful than we are.' 'The Neanderthals are more environmentally conscious than we are.' 'The Neanderthals are more enlightened than we are.' Why the hell should that be?"

"You really want to know?" asked Louise, smiling. She rummaged in the pile of magazines, then plucked out the current *Maclean's*. "Did you read the guest editorial in here?"

"Not yet."

"It says that the Neanderthals are like Canadians, and the Gliksins are like Americans."

"What the hell is that supposed to mean?"

"Well, the writer says the Neanderthals believe in everything that Canada stands for: socialism, pacifism, environmentalism, humanism."

"Good grief," said Jock.

"Oh, come on," said Louise, her tone teasing. "I overheard you talking to Kevin: you agreed with Pat Buchanan when he said my country should be called 'Soviet Canuckistan.' "

"Canadians are Gliksins, too, Dr. Benoît."

"Not all of them," Louise said, still teasing. "After all, Ponter is a Canadian citizen."

"I hardly think that's the reason they keep coming off so well in the press. It's that bloody left-wing journalistic bias."

"No, I don't think so," said Louise, setting down her magazine. "The real reason the Neanderthals keep coming off better than us is that they've got bigger brains. Neanderthal cranial capacities are ten percent greater than our own. We've got just barely enough brains to think through the first stage of ideas: if we build a better spear, we can kill more animals. But, unless we make a real effort, we don't see ahead to stage two: if we kill too many animals, there won't be any left, and we'll starve. The Neanderthals, it seems, grasped the big picture from day one."

"Then why did we defeat them here, in the past of this Earth?"

"Because we had consciousness—true self-awareness—and they did not. Remember my theory: the universe split into two when consciousness first emerged. In one branch, we, and only we, had it. In the other, they, and only they, had it. Is it any wonder that, regardless of brain size or physical robustness, it was the truly conscious beings who prevailed in their respective timelines? But now we're comparing conscious beings with 1400 cc's of brain to those with over 1500." She smiled. "We've been waiting for the big-brained aliens to show up, and now they have. But they didn't come from Alpha Centauri; they came from right next door."

Jock frowned. "A big brain doesn't necessarily mean more intelligence."

"Not *necessarily*, no. Still, the average *Homo sapiens* has an IQ of 100, by definition. And it's distributed on a bell curve: for every one of us with an IQ of 130, there's another with an IQ of 70. But suppose they had an average IQ of 110 instead of 100—even before they purged their gene pool. That might make all the difference."

"You mentioned the bell curve. I read that book, and—"

"And it was full of crap. IQ simply doesn't vary between racial groups except when malnutrition has been a factor. You've met my boyfriend, Reuben Montego. Well, he's an M.D., and he's black. If *The Bell Curve* was right, he should be an incredible rarity, but of course he's not. Previous disparities were caused by economic or social barriers to higher education for blacks, not by any inherent inferiority."

"But you're saying we *are* inherently inferior to the Neanderthals?"

Louise shrugged. "There's no doubt that we are physically inferior. Why should it be so hard to accept that we also are mentally?"

Jock made a disgusted face. "I guess when you put it like that . . ." But then he shook his head. "Still, I hate it. When I was at RAND, we spent all our time trying to outfox enemies that were our match intellectually. Oh, sometimes they had a hardware advantage, and sometimes we did, but there was no notion of one side being inherently *brighter* than the other. But here—"

"We're not trying to outfox the Neanderthals," said Louise. And then, lifting her eyebrows, she added, "Are we?"

"What? No, no. Of course not. Don't be silly, young lady."

"A baby?" said Lurt Fradlo, hands on her broad hips. "You and Ponter want to have a baby?"

Mary nodded timidly. She'd left Ponter at his home, and had journeyed by travel cube to Lurt's house in Saldak Center. "That's right."

Lurt opened her arms and gave Mary a big hug. "Wonderful!" she said. "Absolutely wonderful!"

Mary felt her whole body relaxing. "I didn't know if you would approve."

"Why would I not approve?" asked Lurt. "Ponter is a wonderful person, and you are a wonderful person. You will make terrific parents." She paused. "I cannot tell with you Gliksins. How old are you, my dear?"

"Thirty-nine years," replied Mary. "About five hundred and twenty months."

Lurt lowered her voice. "For our kind, it is difficult to conceive by that age."

"Mine, too, although we have all sorts of drugs and techniques that can help. But there is one little problem . . ."

"Oh?"

"Yes. Barasts, like you and Ponter, have twenty-four pairs of chromosomes. Gliksins like me have only twenty-three."

Lurt frowned. "That will make fertilization very difficult."

Mary nodded. "Oh, yes. I doubt we could do it at all just by having sex."

"Do not give up trying, though!" said Lurt, grinning.

Mary grinned back. "Not a chance. But I was hoping to find a way that we could combine Ponter's DNA and mine. One of the chromosomes in my kind formed from the union of two of the chromosomes in the common ancestor we both share. Genetically, the actual content of the DNA sequences is very similar, but it happens to all be on one long chromosome in *Homo sapiens*, instead of two shorter ones in *Homo neanderthalensis*."

Lurt was nodding slowly. "And you hope to overcome this problem?"

"That was my thought. I think it could be done, even just with the techniques my people have available, but it would be very tricky. But your people are further along in a lot of ways. I was wondering if you knew anyone who might be an expert in this area?"

"I very much like you, Mare, but you *do* have a tendency to put your foot right in it."

"Pardon?"

"There *is* a solution to your problem—a *perfect* solution. But . . ."

"But what?"

"But it is banned."

"Banned? Why?"

"Because of the danger it posed to our way of life. There was a geneticist named Vissan Lennet. Until four months ago, she lived in Kraldak."

"Which is?"

"A town perhaps 350,000 armspans south of here. But she left."

"She left Kraldak?" said Mary.

But Lurt shook her head. "She left *everything*."

Mary felt her eyebrows shooting up. "My God—do you mean she killed herself?"

"What? No, she is still alive. At least, as far as anyone knows—not that we have any way to contact her."

Mary gestured at Lurt's forearm. "Can't you just call her up?"

"No. That is what I am trying to say. Vissan left our society. She gouged out her Companion and went to live in the wilderness."

"Why would she do that?"

"Vissan was a great geneticist, but she had developed a device the High Gray Council could not countenance. In fact, the local High Grays called me and asked my opinion of it. I did not want to see research suppressed, but the High

Grays felt they had no choice, given what Vissan had done."

"Good Christ, you make it sound as though she created some sort of genetic weapon!"

"What? No, no, of course not. She was not a lunatic. The device Vissan built was a . . . a 'codon writer,' I suppose would be the correct phrase. It could be programmed to output any sequence of deoxyribonucleic acid or ribonucleic acid imaginable, along with associated proteins. If you could think it up, Vissan's codon writer could produce it."

"Really? Wow! That sounds amazingly useful."

"It was *too* useful, at least according to the High Gray Council. You see, among many other things, it allowed the production of . . . of . . . I am not sure of your word: the half-sets of chromosomes that exist in sex cells."

"Haploid sets," said Mary. "The twenty-three—excuse me, twenty-*four* chromosomes—that are found in sperm or eggs."

"Exactly."

"But why would that be a problem?" asked Mary.

"Because of our system of justice," said Lurt. "Do you not see? When we sterilize a criminal and his or her close relatives, we are preventing them from producing haploid chromosome sets; we are preventing them from being able to reproduce. But Vissan's codon writer would have allowed the sterilized to circumvent their punishment, and still pass their genes on to the next generation, by simply programming the device to produce chromosomes for them containing their own genetic information."

"And that's why the device was banned?"

"Exactly," said Lurt. "The High Grays ordered the research halted—and Vissan was furious. She said she could not be part of a society that suppressed knowledge, and so she left."

"So . . . so Vissan is living off the land?"

Lurt nodded. "It is easy enough to do. As youths, we are all trained in the required skills."

"But . . . but it's soon going to be the dead of winter."

"Doubtless she will have built a cabin or some other shelter. In any event, Vissan's codon writer is the device you need. There was only one prototype built, before the High Gray Council banned it. Normally, of course, nothing can go missing in this world: the Companion implants see and record all. But Vissan disposed of the prototype *after* she had gouged out her Companion, and while she was alone. The prototype likely still exists, and it is clearly the ideal tool for making the hybrid child you desire."

"If I can only find it," said Mary.

"Exactly," said Lurt. "If you can only find it."

Chapter Fourteen

"And it was that questing spirit that let Eagle *and* Columbia, Intrepid *and* Yankee Clipper, Aquarius *and* Odyssey, Antares *and* Kitty Hawk, Falcon *and* Endeavour, Orion *and* Casper, *and* Challenger *and* America *fly to the moon ..."*

Mary's permanent Companion implant had to be installed by a Neanderthal surgeon. Prior to the operation, Mary had returned to the equipment room above the Debral mine where her temporary unit had originally been strapped on, since that was the only place at which its clasps would open. Then, accompanied by two burly Neanderthal enforcers, Mary had been taken to the hospital in Saldak Center.

The surgeon, a female named Korbonon, was a member of generation 145, about Mary's age. Korbonon normally worked on repairing severely damaged limbs, such as those that sometimes resulted when a hunt went horribly wrong; her knowledge of musculature and nerve tissue was second to none.

"This is going to be a bit tricky," said Korbonon. The temporary Companion was sitting on a small table, hooked up to an external power source; it was unattached to Mary, but still doing translations for her, through its external speaker. Korbonon clearly wasn't used to having her speech translated; she spoke loudly, as if Mary could understand her Neanderthal words. "Your forearm is less muscled than a Barast one, which may make anchoring the Companion difficult. But I see what they said about Gliksin proportions is true: your upper and lower arms are the same length; that should give us some extra territory to work with." Barast forearms were noticeably shorter than their upper arms; their shins were also shorter than their thighs.

"I would have thought this was a routine operation," said Mary.

Korbonon's eyebrow was a light reddish blond. It rose. "Routine? Not adding a first Companion to an adult arm. Of course, when the Companions were introduced, almost a thousand months ago, they were mostly installed in adults—but the surgeons who did that then are all long dead. No, this operation has only been occasionally performed since, mostly on those who have lost the arm that contained the implant they received in childhood."

"Ah," said Mary. She was leaning back in something that vaguely resembled a dentist's chair with stirrups—apparently an all-purpose operating platform. Her left arm was sitting on a little table that protruded from one side of the chair. The inside of her arm had been swabbed with something that wasn't alcohol—it was a pink liquid that smelled sour, but apparently served the purpose of disinfecting the skin. Still, Mary was surprised to see that Korbonon wasn't wearing a face mask. "Our surgeons usually cover their noses and mouths," said Mary, a bit concerned.

"Why?" asked Korbonon.

"To keep them from infecting the patient, and the patient from infecting them."

"I might as well operate blindfolded!" declared Korbonon.

Mary was about to question the statement, then realized what the surgeon meant: the acute Neanderthal sense of smell provided a crucial part of their perception.

"What will you do about anesthetic?" asked Mary. For the first time, she was grateful that Ponter wasn't here. Knowing his sense of humor, he would have doubtless quipped, "Anesthetic? What is that?"—to be followed, of course, after a suitable pause, with "Just kidding." She was nervous enough as it was.

"We will use a neuronal interrupter," replied Korbonon.

"Really?" said Mary, the scientist in her coming to the fore, despite her apprehension about the operation. "We use chemical agents."

The surgeon nodded. "We used to do that," she said, "but they take time to become effective, time to wear off, and are difficult to localize precisely. Also, of course, some people have allergies to chemical anesthetics."

"Yet another technology my people will doubtless want to trade for," said Mary. A second female loomed in—Mary didn't know anything about Barast medical hierarchies; she might have been a nurse or another doctor, or held some position that had no counterpart in the Gliksin world. In any event, she wrapped an elastic metalized band around Mary's left forearm just below the elbow, and then attached another one just above the wrist. Then, to Mary's astonishment, she took out what looked like a fat Magic Marker, and started drawing a complex series of lines between the two bands. Rather than ink, though, what looked like liquid metal came out. But it wasn't hot, and it quickly dried, gaining a matte finish as it did so. The color was wrong, but the effect was like that chocolate syrup for ice cream that hardens quickly into a crust. "What are you doing?" asked Mary.

The Barast with the marker made no reply. But the surgeon said, "She is tracing the appropriate nerve trunks in your forearm. The lines form electrical connections between the two destabilizers."

After a few minutes, the second female nodded, apparently to herself, and moved away, approaching a small control console. She pulled out a series of control buds, and Mary felt her forearm go numb. "Wow," she said.

"All right," said Korbonon. "Here we go." And before Mary knew what was happening, the surgeon had dived in and made a long incision parallel to Mary's radius. Mary almost threw up as her own blood welled out, spilling onto the little table, which she now noted had a raised lip all around its edge.

Mary was shocked—and was worried about going *into* shock. In her world, great efforts were taken to keep patients from being able to see themselves during surgery. But here, no thought had been given to that. Maybe having to kill your own food, even occasionally, was enough to put an end to such squeamishness. Mary swallowed hard and tried to calm herself; it really wasn't *that* much blood . . . was it?

She wondered what happened during thoracic surgery. Gliksin surgeons were presented with a patient whose face was covered, and had only a tiny, exposed surgical field. Did the Barasts do it that way, too? The main reason, after all, wasn't to keep the patient from getting covered with blood. Rather, Mary had been told by one of her doctor friends, it was a psychological aid for the surgeon—a way of keeping him or her focused on the problem in cutting and splicing, rather than thinking of themselves as carving into the home of another human soul. But the Barasts, with their complete lack of Cartesian duality and their indifference to gore, perhaps had no such need.

Korbonon slipped several blue springlike things into the wound that apparently did the same job as forceps, holding it open. Other little clips and doodads were attached to arteries, veins, and nerves. Mary could clearly see into the opening in her skin, cutting through fat and meat all the way down to the slick grayish solidity of her radius.

Moments later, the other Barast—the one who had painted the nerve-deadening lines on Mary's forearm—moved in. The Barast doctors were wearing short-sleeved yellow shirts and long blue gloves that went past their elbows; Mary thought perhaps they went that high to keep blood from getting matted into their hairy forearms.

The second Barast picked up Mary's new Companion and removed it from its sterile wrapping. Mary had gotten used to the look of the faceplates, but had never seen the other side of one. It was sculpted like a topographic model, with highs, lows, and channels, presumably to accommodate blood vessels. Mary watched in queasy fascination as her own radial artery—the suicide's favorite—was severed. It was quickly clamped at both ends, but not before a tube of blood a foot long had shot out.

Mary winced, wondering how Vissan Lennet, the creator of the codon writer, had managed to self-perform the removal of her Companion; it must have been horrendously difficult.

The surgeon next used a laser scalpel, similar to the one Mary herself had had to use when Ponter was shot outside the United Nations. The two ends of Mary's radial artery were attached to two different apertures on the underside of the Companion. She knew the Companions had no power source of their own; they were fueled by bodily processes. Well, the pumping strength of blood through the radial artery was certainly a good source of power; apparently the Companion had a hydroelectric—or would that be sangui-noelectric?—generating plant built in.

Mary kept meaning to turn away—just as she always quickly hustled past the TV series *The Operation* on The Learning Channel when surfing. But it really was interesting in an awful sort of way. She watched as the Companion installation was completed, the blood vessels cauterized, and her skin sealed by minute laser blasts. Finally a puttylike caulking was extruded all around the edges of her Companion, apparently to promote healing.

By comparison, the remaining surgery—inserting the two cochlear implants—was minor, or so it seemed, although that might have just been a consequence of Mary being unable to see that part of the operation.

At last, it was all done. Mary's arm had been wiped clean of blood, the protective film had been removed from the Companion's faceplate, and the cochlear implants had had their output balanced and tuned.

"All right," said the surgeon, reaching down to Mary's forearm and pulling out a small beadlike control bud, one of six, each a different color. "Here you go."

"Hello, Mary," said a synthesized voice. It sounded as though it were coming from the middle of her head, exactly between her ears. The voice was Neanderthaloid—deep, resonant, probably female—but it managed the *ee* phoneme in Mary's name perfectly; clearly, that problem had been addressed and solved.

"Hello," said Mary. "Um, what should I call you?"

"Whatever you wish."

Mary frowned, then: "How about Christine?" Christine was Mary's sister's name.

"That's fine," said the voice in her head. "Of course, if

you change your mind, you're free to rename me as often as you like."

"Okay," said Mary, then: "Say, did you say 'that's' and 'you're'?"

"Yes."

Mary made an impressed face. "So you can use contractions! Ponter's Companion can't."

"It wasn't a difficult programming issue," said Christine, "once the underlying concept was grasped."

Mary was startled by a tap on her shoulder. She'd blanked out the exterior world while talking with the Companion; she wondered if she had tilted her head the way Neanderthals routinely did—whether that was something that happened naturally, or was a learned behavior, a courtesy to let others know that you were momentarily preoccupied.

"So," said the surgeon, smiling down at Mary, who was still seated in the operating chair. "I take it your Companion is working?" For the first time, Mary heard a translation the way Ponter did—not through an external earpiece, but as words flowering full-blown in her head. The Companion was a good mimic; although the English words were emphasized at bizarre points—as if William Shatner were saying them—they were presented in a voice much like the surgeon's own.

"Yes, indeed," said Mary—and as soon as she'd finished, her Companion's external speaker announced what Mary recognized as the Neanderthal equivalent: "*Ka pan ka.*"

"All right, then," said the woman, still smiling. "That's it."

"Is my Companion transmitting to my alibi archive?"

"Yes," replied the surgeon, and "I am," said Christine in her own voice after translating the surgeon's "*Ka.*"

Mary got out of the chair, thanked the surgeon and her colleague, and headed on her way. When she came to the medical facility's lobby, she saw four male Neanderthals, each of which seemed to have a broken arm or leg. One was dressed in the silver of an Exhibitionist. Mary figured such a person wouldn't be offended by questions, so she walked up to him and said, "What happened?"

"To us?" asked the Exhibitionist. "Just the usual: hunting injuries."

Mary thought of Erik Trinkaus and his observation that ancient Neanderthals often had injuries similar to those of rodeo riders. "What were you hunting?"

"Moose," said the Exhibitionist.

Mary was disappointed that it wasn't something more exotic. "Is it worth it?" she asked. "The injuries I mean?"

The Exhibitionist shrugged. "Getting to eat moose is. There's only so much passenger pigeon and buffalo you can take."

"Well," said Mary, "I hope they get you all fixed up quickly."

"Oh, they will," said the Exhibitionist with a smile.

Mary said goodbye and left the hospital, going out into the late-afternoon sun; she'd probably given the Exhibitionist's audience quite a treat.

And then it hit her: she'd just entered a room that contained four males she'd never met, and rather than being terrified, as she would have been back on her world even after learning the identity of her rapist, she hadn't felt any apprehension. Indeed, she'd brazenly walked over to one of the men and struck up a conversation.

She looked down in wonder at her forearm, at her Companion, at Christine. The notion that everyone's activities were being recorded hadn't seemed real until her own permanent Companion had been made part of her. But now she understood how *liberating* it was. Here, she was safe. Oh, there might still be lots of people of ill will around her, but they would never try anything . . . because they could never get away with anything.

Mary could have had Christine call for a travel cube to take her back to Lurt's house, but it was a lovely fall day, and so she decided to walk. And, for the first time on this world, she found herself easily meeting the eyes of other Neanderthals, as though they were her small-town neighbors, as though she belonged, as though she were home.

Chapter Fifteen

"There are human footprints preserved in volcanic ash at Laetoli, made by a male and a female australopithecine, the ancestors to both Gliksins and Barasts, just wandering, walking slowly, side by side, exploring: the original small hominid steps. And there are human footprints at Tranquility Base and the Ocean of Storms and Fra Mauro and Hadley Rille and Descartes and Taurus-Littrow on the moon—truly giant leaps . . ."

Mary was exhausted from the surgery, and when she arrived at Lurt's house, she simply went to sleep, having a long nap on the recessed square filled with cushions that served as her bed. She didn't wake until Lurt got home from her lab two daytenths later.

"See!" said Mary, showing off her new Companion.

Almost all Companions looked the same, but Lurt evidently detected that Mary wanted a compliment. "It's lovely," she said.

"Isn't it, though?" said Mary. "But it's not an it; it's a she. Her name is Christine."

"Hello," said the synthesized voice from Christine's speaker.

"Christine," said Mary, "this is Scholar Lurt Fradlo. She is the woman-mate of Scholar Adikor Huld, who is the man-mate of my . . ." Mary halted, looking for the correct word, then, with a shrug, continued: ". . . of my boyfriend, Scholar—and Envoy—Ponter Boddit."

"Healthy day, Scholar Fradlo," said Christine.

"Healthy day," replied Lurt. "You may call me Lurt."

"Thank you," said the Companion.

Lurt took a deep breath, apparently inhaling scents. "Ginrald is not home yet," she said. Ginrald was Lurt's woman-mate.

"No," said Mary. "Nor is Dab or Karatal." Dab was Lurt's young son by Adikor Huld; Karatal was Ginrald's young daughter by her own man-mate.

Lurt nodded. "Good. Then perhaps we can talk. There is a circumstance we must resolve."

"Yes?"

But then Lurt remained silent, apparently reluctant to go on.

"Have I done something wrong?" asked Mary. "Have I offended you somehow?" She knew being in this world would be fraught with cultural difficulties, but she'd tried hard to follow Lurt's lead in everything.

"No, no," said Lurt. "Nothing like that." She gestured for Mary to have a seat in the circular living area. Mary moved to the couch, and Lurt straddled a nearby saddle-seat. "It's simply a question of your living arrangements."

Mary nodded. Of course. "I've overstayed my welcome," she said. "I'm sorry."

Lurt raised a large hand, palm out. "Please don't misunderstand. I enjoyed your company on your previous visit greatly. But my home is already crowded. Granted, Dab will leave us in a couple of tenmonths to go live with Ponter and Adikor, but . . ."

Mary nodded. "But that's in a couple of tenmonths."

"Exactly," said Lurt. "If you're to spend much time in this world, you must have your own home."

Mary frowned. "I have no idea how to do that. And I'll have to talk to Ponter. It's one thing to have his account debited for my incidentals, but if I'm going to buy a house—"

Lurt laughed, but it wasn't derisive. "You don't buy a house. You select one that's vacant and occupy it. Your contribution is unquestioned; you have brought much new knowledge to us. You are certainly entitled to a house."

"You mean houses aren't privately owned?"

"No. Why would they be? Ah, I think I see. Remember, we have a stable population size. There is no need for new houses, except to replace those trees that ultimately die. And trees for houses are planted and tended by the government, since, after all, it's a long time before they're big enough to be occupied. But there are always some surplus ones, to accommodate temporary visitors to Saldak. We can find you one of those. I know an excellent carpenter who can make furniture for you—I rather suspect she would enjoy the challenge of accommodating your particular needs." Lurt paused for a moment. "Of course, you would be living alone."

Mary didn't want to say that would be a relief—but, in fact, she was used to being on her own. In the years since she and Colm had split, Mary had gotten to quite enjoy her quiet evenings at home. In comparison, the hustle and bustle of Lurt's household had been nerve-wracking. And yet—

And yet, this world was so *strange*. Mary was nowhere near ready to deal with it without assistance. Even with the aid of Christine, she knew she was still in way over her head.

"Do you perhaps have a friend who could use a roommate?" asked Mary. "You know, someone who is alone, but might enjoy sharing household duties for a while with another?"

Lurt tapped her thumb against the center of her forehead, just above where the twin arches of her browridge joined. "Let me think . . . Let me think . . ." But then she tipped her head, clearly listening to a suggestion from her own Companion. "That's an excellent idea," she said, nodding. She looked at Mary. "There is a woman named Bandra Tolgak who lives not far from here. She is a geologist, and one of my favorite people. And she's absolutely fascinated by Gliksins."

"And she doesn't have a family living with her?"

"That's right. Her union with her woman-mate dissolved some time ago, and both of Bandra's children have left home now—her younger daughter just recently. She's mentioned how empty her house seems; perhaps she might be amenable to an arrangement . . ."

It was a cool fall day, with cirrus clouds finger-painted on a silvery sky. Lurt and Mary walked along. Ahead was a building about the width of a football field and, judging by the deployment of windows, four stories tall. "This is our Science Academy—the one for women," said Lurt. "Bandra Tolgak works here."

They came to one of many doors—solid, opaque, hinged. Lurt opened it, and they continued down a corridor, square in cross section, light provided by catalytic reactions inside tubes set into the walls. Many female Neanderthals of generation 147—the right age for a university education—were milling about, and a variety of spindly robots were zipping to and fro, running errands. Lurt stopped when they came to the station for a pair of elevators. Neanderthals, very sensibly, left their elevator doors open when idle, keeping the cabs from getting stuffy and making it obvious at a glance when

one was available on the current floor. Lurt led Mary into
the one that was waiting. "Bandra Tolgak's lab," Lurt said into
the air. The doors closed, and the elevator began moving
upward. After a few seconds, the doors reopened, and they
were looking out into another corridor. "Third door on your
right," said a synthesized voice.

Mary and Lurt walked to that door, opened it, and entered.

"Healthy day, Bandra," said Lurt.

A Neanderthal woman's broad back was facing them. She
turned around and smiled. "Lurt Fradlo! Healthy day!" Then
her eyes—an arresting wheat color—fell on Mary. "And you
must be Scholar Vaughan," she said. "Lurt said you were coming." She smiled again and, to Mary's astonishment, offered
her hand.

Mary took it and shook it firmly. "I—I didn't think Neanderthals shook hands."

"Oh, we don't," said Bandra, grinning. "But I have been
reading all about you Gliksins. Such a fascinating people!"
She let go of Mary's hand. "Did I do it properly?"

"Yes," said Mary. "Just fine."

Bandra was beaming. She was a 144, nine years older
than Mary—actually, eight and a half, more likely, since Mary
had been born in September, and most Neanderthals were
born in the spring. Bandra's facial and body hair was a lovely
mixture of copper and silver. "Good, good. Oh, wait! There
is another ritual!" She composed her pleasant features into
a mock-serious expression. "How *are* you?"

Mary laughed. "I'm fine, thanks. And you?"

"I am fine, too." Bandra burst out laughing. "Such wonderful people! So many little pleasantries!" She smiled at
Mary. "It really is a treat to meet you, Scholar Vaughan."

"You can call me Mary."

"No, I can't," said Bandra, laughing again. "But I would be delighted to call you 'Mare.' "

Bandra's lab was filled with mineralogical specimens—rock crystals, polished stones, beautifully prepared geodes, and more. "It's a pleasure to finally meet a Gliksin," continued Bandra. "I read everything I can find about you people."

"Um, thank you."

"So, tell me about yourself. Do you have children?"

"Not yet," said Mary.

"Ah. Well, I have two daughters and a grandson. Would you like to see pictures?"

"Um, sure."

But Bandra laughed once more. "You Gliksins and your complex manners! How wonderfully accommodating you are! I understand I could force you to look for daytenths at images I have recorded while traveling."

Mary found herself feeling very relaxed; Bandra's good humor was infectious.

"I hope you don't mind us stopping by," said Lurt, "but . . ."

"But you were in the neighborhood!" said Bandra, grinning broadly at Mary.

Mary nodded.

"Out and about," continued Bandra—saying it as "oot and aboot," the exaggerated accent that Americans ascribed to Canadians but that Mary had yet to actually hear from any of her compatriots. "Such wonderful turns of phrase you Gliksins have."

"Thank you."

"So," said Bandra, "Lurt said you had a favor to ask." She gestured at the rocks spread out around the room. "I can't imagine what help a geologist might be to you, but—and this one is one of my favorites—'I am all ears.' " Bandra beamed at Mary.

"Well, um, I . . . um, I'm looking for a place to stay, here in Saldak Center."

"Really?" said Bandra.

Mary smiled. "If I'm lying, I'm dying."

Bandra roared with laughter. "I hope you're doing neither!" She paused. "I do have a big old house, and I *am* all alone in it now."

"So Lurt said. I will only be here for a month or so, but if you'd like to have a housemate . . ."

"I *would*, but . . ." Bandra trailed off.

Mary wanted to say, "But what?" But she had no right to pry; it was hardly incumbent on Bandra to justify turning Mary down.

Still, after a moment, Bandra went on. "Only a month, you say? So, you would be here only during the next Two becoming One?"

"Yes," said Mary, "but I'll stay out of your way then, of course."

Mary could see emotions warring across Bandra's wide face—and she certainly could understand that. The Neanderthal woman was doubtless weighing the inconvenience of having a stranger move in against her scientific fascination at getting to spend time with a being from another world.

"Very well," said Bandra, at last. "What is your phrase? 'Your home is my home.' "

"I think it's the other way around," said Mary.

"Ah, yes, yes! I'm still learning!"

Mary smiled. "So am I."

Chapter Sixteen

"But it has been three decades since Eugene Cernan became the last person to walk on the moon. The last person! Who would have thought that whole generations would be born after 1972 for whom the notion of humans on other worlds would be nothing but a lesson in history class . . . ?"

Mary found Bandra's home much more comfortable than Lurt's, even though it wasn't any bigger. For one thing, the furniture was more to Mary's taste. And for another, it turned out that Bandra was both a bird-watcher and a wonderful artist: she had covered the wooden interior walls and ceilings with Audubon-quality paintings of local birds, including, of course, passenger pigeons. Mary loved birds herself: that had been why she'd been working on passenger-pigeon DNA back at York while her grad student, Daria, had had the seemingly more sexy assignment of recovering genetic material from an Egyptian mummy.

Mary found it strange to come home before Bandra did—and even stranger just to walk in the front door. But, of course, Neanderthals didn't lock their homes; they didn't have to.

Bandra had a household robot—many Barasts did. It was a spindly, insectlike being. It regarded Mary with blue mechanical eyes—not unlike those Lonwis had—but went puttering along, cleaning and dusting.

Although Mary knew she couldn't see Ponter until Two next became One, there was no reason she couldn't call him—her shiny new Companion could connect to his Companion, or any other, without difficulty.

And so Mary made herself comfortable—lying down on the couch in Bandra's living room, staring up at the beautiful mural on the ceiling—and had Christine call up Hak.

"Hi, sweetie," she said—which was even worse than "honey" as far as being an endearment that couldn't be reproduced by Ponter, but all he would have heard was the translation Christine provided.

"Mare!" Ponter's voice was full of excitement. "How good to hear from you!"

"I miss you," Mary said. She felt like she was eighteen again, talking to her boyfriend Donny from her bedroom at her parents' house.

"I miss you, too."

"Where are you?"

"I am taking Pabo for a walk. We can both use the exercise."

"Is Adikor with you?"

"No, he's at home. So, what's new?"

It was astonishing after all this time to hear Ponter using contractions—which led to Mary starting by telling him all about the installation of her permanent Companion. She went on to talk about moving into Bandra's house, and then: "Lurt said something very intriguing. She said there's a banned device that could help us have a child."

"Really?" said Ponter. "What is it?"

"She said it was the invention of someone named Vissan Lennet."

"Oh!" said Ponter. "I recall her now; I saw it on my Voyeur. She removed her Companion, and went to live in the wilderness. Some sort of conflict with the High Grays over an invention."

"Exactly!" said Mary. "She'd invented a device called a codon writer that could produce any DNA strings one might want—which is exactly what we need in order to have a baby. Lurt thinks Vissan probably still has her prototype."

"Perhaps so," said Ponter. "But if she does—excuse me. Good dog! Good dog! Here, there you go! Fetch! Fetch! Sorry, I was saying, if it does exist, it's still banned."

"That's right," said Mary. "In *this* world. But if we took it back to *my* world . . ."

"That's brilliant!" said Ponter. "But how do we get it?"

"I figure we find Vissan and simply ask her for it. What have we got to lose?"

"And how do we find her? She doesn't have a Companion."

"Well, Lurt said she used to live in a town called Kraldak. Do you know where that is?"

"Sure. It's just north of Lake *Duranlan*—Lake Erie. Kraldak is about where Detroit is in your world."

"Well, if she's living in the wilderness, she can't have gone too far from there, can she?"

"I suppose. She certainly couldn't use any form of transit without a Companion."

"And Lurt said she's probably built a cabin."

"That makes sense."

"So we could search satellite photos for a new cabin— one that isn't on maps that are more than four months old."

"You're forgetting where you are, my love," said Ponter. "Barasts have no satellites."

"Right. Damn. What about aerial reconnaissance? You know—pictures taken from airplanes?"

"No airplanes, either—although we've got helicopters."

"Well, would there be any helicopter surveys done since she left?"

"How long ago was that again?"

"Lurt said about four months."

"Well, then, yes, sure. Forest fires are a problem in summer, of course—both those caused by lightning and by human error. Aerial photographs are taken to track them."

"Can we access them?"

"Hak?"

Hak's voice came into Mary's head. "I *am* accessing them, even as we speak," the Companion said. "According to the alibi archives, Vissan Lennet's Companion went off-line on 148/101/17, and there have been three aerial surveys of Kraldak and environs since then. But although a cabin might be easily visible in winter, when the deciduous trees have lost their leaves, spotting such a thing through the summertime canopy will be difficult."

"But you'll try?" asked Mary.

"Of course."

"It's probably pointless, though," said Mary with a sigh. "Surely others have tried to track her down, if what Lurt said about Vissan's codon writer is true."

"Why?"

"Well, you know: sterilized individuals, looking to circumvent the sanction that had been imposed on them."

"Perhaps," replied Ponter, "but it's not been that long since Vissan chose to leave society, and there are not that many sterilized people. And, after all, no one on this world is looking to conceive prior to next summer, so—"

"Excuse me," said Hak. "I have found it."

"What?" said Mary.

"The cabin—or, at least, a cabin that is not on any of the older maps. It is approximately thirty-five kilometers due west of Kraldak." Hak translated the Neanderthal units for Mary, although Ponter had probably heard something like "70,000 armspans" through his cochlear implants.

"Wonderful!" exclaimed Mary. "Ponter, we *have* to go see her!"

"Certainly," he said.

"Can you go tomorrow?"

Ponter's voice was heavy. "Mare . . ."

"What? Oh, I know. I know, Two are not One but . . ."

"Yes?"

Mary sighed. "No, you're right. Well, then, can we go when Two *are* next One?"

"Of course, my love. We can do whatever you want then."

"All right," said Mary. "It's a date."

Bandra and Mary seemed very simpatico—a word Bandra relished using. They both liked to spend quiet evenings at home, and although they had an endless array of scientific things to discuss, they also touched on more personal matters.

It reminded Mary of her first days with Ponter, quarantined at Reuben Montego's house. Sharing opinions and ideas with Bandra was intellectually and emotionally stimulating, and the female Neanderthal had a wonderfully warm way about her, kind and funny.

Still, as they sat in the living room of Bandra's house, the topics sometimes got, if not heated, at least quite pointed.

"You know," said Bandra, sitting at the opposite end of a couch from Mary, "this excessive desire for privacy must be fueled by your religions. At first I thought it was just because certain appealing behaviors were forbidden, and so people required privacy to indulge in them. And, doubtless, that's part of it. But, now that you've told me about your multiplicity of belief systems, it seems that even just *wanting* to practice a minority belief required privacy. Early practitioners of your system, Christianity, hid their meetings from others, isn't that so?"

"That's true," said Mary. "In fact, our most important holy day is Christmas, commemorating the annual anniversary of Jesus' birth. We celebrate it on December 25—in winter—but Jesus was born in the spring. We know that because the Bible says it happened when the shepherds watched over their flocks by night, which only happens in the spring, when new lambs are born." Mary smiled. "Hey, you guys are like that: you like to give birth in the spring, too."

"Probably for the same reason: to give the offspring the best chance to grow before having to face winter."

But the simile had stuck in Mary's mind, and she ventured forward tentatively. "You Barasts are like sheep in other ways, too. You're so peaceful."

"Does it seem that way?" said Bandra.

"You don't have wars. And from what I've seen, you don't have much societal violence. Although . . ." She stopped herself, before she mentioned the shattering of Ponter's jaw, an unfortunate event from years ago.

"I suppose. We still hunt our own food—not all the time, of course, unless that happens to be one's particular contribution. But often enough that it provides an outlet for violent impulses. How do you say it? It gets it out of our systems."

"Catharsis," said Mary. "A purging of pent-up feeling."

"Catharsis! Oooh, another great word! Yes, indeed: smash

in a few animal skulls, or tear flesh from bone, and you feel wonderfully peaceful afterward."

Mary stopped to think if she'd ever killed an animal, for food or any other purpose. Except for swatting mosquitoes, the answer was no. "We don't do that."

"I know," said Bandra. "You consider it uncivilized. But we consider it to be part of what *makes* civilization possible."

"Still, your lack of privacy—doesn't it give rise to abuses? Couldn't someone be clandestinely—secretly—watching what you're doing, by compromising the security of the alibi archives?"

"Why would anyone want to do that?"

"Well, to prevent an overthrow of the government, say."

"Why would someone want to overthrow the government? Why not just vote it out of office?"

"Well, *today*, yes. But surely you haven't had democracy since the dawn of time?"

"What else might we have had?"

"Tribal chieftains? Warlords? God-emperors? No, scratch that last one. But, well . . ." Mary frowned. *Well, what?* Without agriculture, there were no small-scale defensible territories. Oh, primitive farmers could doubtless defend a few hundred acres, but the tens or hundreds of square miles that represented a hunting forest were beyond the abilities of small groups to protect.

And, indeed, why bother defending them? A raid on farmlands produced immediate results: plant food and fiber, stolen from the field or taken from the granary. But, as Ponter had pointed out time and again, hunting and gathering were based on knowledge: no one could just enter a new territory and profitably exploit it. They wouldn't know where the animals came to drink, where the birds laid their eggs, where the most bountiful fruit trees grew. No, such a lifestyle would engender peaceful trade, since it was far less work for a traveler to bring something of value along to swap for freshly captured game rather than to try to hunt the game himself.

Nonetheless, if push came to shove, most Neanderthals were probably robust enough to forage for themselves—just as apparently this Vissan was now doing. Besides, with a cap on population size—and the Neanderthals had had that for hundreds of years—there was plenty of unused territory for anyone who wished to strike out on their own.

"Still," said Mary, "there must have been times when people didn't like their elected officials, and wanted to get rid of them."

"Oh, yes, indeed. Yes, indeed."

"What happened then?"

"In the old days? Before the purging of our gene pool? Assassination."

"Well, there!" said Mary. "That's a reason for compromising other people's privacy: to thwart assassination attempts. If someone was plotting to assassinate you, you'd want to keep an eye on them, to prevent them from pulling it off."

"An assassination doesn't require any plotting," said Bandra, her eyebrow lifted. "You just walk up to the person you want to be rid of and smash their skull in. Believe me, that provides a wonderful incentive for elected officials to keep their constituents happy."

Mary laughed in spite of herself. "Still, surely even if the majority are happy, there will always be discontented individuals."

Bandra nodded. "Which is why we long ago saw the necessity of purging the gene pool of those who might act in an antisocial manner."

"But this purging of the gene pool . . ." Mary was trying not to be judgmental, but her tone betrayed her. "I've tried to talk to Ponter about this, but it's difficult; he's so blindly in favor of it. But even more than your lack of privacy, that notion is what creeps my people out the most."

" 'Creeps them out'! Oooh, that's a classic!"

"I'm serious, Bandra. We've attempted such things in the past, and . . . it's never gone well. I mean, we don't believe that sort of thing can be done without corruption. We've had people try to wipe out specific ethnic groups."

A bleep.

"Groups that have distinctive characteristics, based on their geographic origin."

"But diversity is of great value genetically," said Bandra. "Surely you, as a life chemist, know that."

"Yes, but—well, I mean, we have tried . . . my people, I mean . . . well, not *my* people, but bad people, bad members of my species, have tried to perform . . . we call it 'genocide,' wiping out whole other races of people, and—"

God damn it, thought Mary. Why couldn't she just chat with a Neanderthal about the weather, instead of always getting into these horrible topics? If only she could learn to keep her mouth shut.

"Genocide," repeated Bandra, but without her usual relish. She didn't have to say that her own kind, *Homo neanderthalensis*, had been the first victim of *Homo sapiens* genocide.

"But," said Mary, "I mean, how do you decide which traits to try to eliminate?"

"Isn't it obvious? Excessive violence. Excessive selfishness. A tendency to mistreat children. Mental retardation. Predisposition to genetic diseases."

Mary shook her head; she was still bothered by her aborted conversation on this topic with Ponter. "We believe everyone has the right to breed."

"Why?" said Bandra.

Mary frowned. "It's—it's a human right."

"It's a human *desire*," said Bandra. "But a right? Evolution is driven by only some members of a population reproducing."

"I guess we believe that superseding the brutality of natural selection is the hallmark of civilization."

"But surely," said Bandra, "the society as a whole is more important than any individual."

"Fundamentally, I guess my people don't share that view. We put an enormous value on individual rights and liberties."

"An enormous value? Or an enormous cost?" Bandra shook her head. "I've heard of all the security precautions you require at transportation terminals, all the enforcers you require throughout your cities. You claim not to want war, but you devote a huge proportion of your resources to preparing for it and waging it. You have terrorists, and those who exist by addicting others to chemicals, and a plague of child abuse, and—if you will forgive me—an average intelligence that is much lower than it need be."

"We've never found a way to measure intelligence that isn't culturally biased."

Bandra blinked. "How can intelligence be culturally biased?"

"Well," said Mary, "if you ask a rich child of normal intelligence what word goes with cup, he'll say 'saucer'; saucers are little plates we put underneath the cups we drink coffee—hot beverages—from. But if you ask a poor kid with normal intelligence, he might not know the answer, because his family might not be able to afford saucers."

"Intelligence is not a trivia game," said Bandra. "There are better ways to assess its strength. We look at the number of neural connections that have grown in the brain; a tally of them is a good objective indicator."

"But surely those who were denied the right to breed because of their low intelligence . . . surely they were upset by that."

"Yes. But, by definition, they were not difficult to outwit."

Mary shuddered. "Still . . ."

"Remember how our democracies are constituted: we don't let people vote until they have seen at least 600 moons—two-thirds of the traditional 900-month lifetime. That's . . . Delka?"

"Forty-eight years old," said Delka, Bandra's Companion.

Bandra continued. "That's past the age of possible reproduction for most females, and past the usual reproductive age for men. So those voting on the issue no longer had to be concerned about it themselves."

"It's not really democracy if only a minority get to vote."

Bandra frowned, as if trying to comprehend Mary's comment. "*Everybody* gets to vote—just not at every point in their lives. And unlike in your world, we have never denied anyone of sufficient age the right to vote just because of gender or dermal coloration."

"But surely," said Mary, "those who *did* vote must have been worried on behalf of their adult children, who were at reproductive age, but couldn't vote themselves."

Bandra hesitated, and Mary wondered why; she'd been on quite a roll until now. "Of course hoping for our children's happy futures is of great importance," she said finally. "But the vote was taken *before* the intelligence tests were administered. Do you see? The decision was to bar the bottom five percent of the population from reproducing for ten consecutive generations. Try to find a parent who thinks his or her own child is in the bottom five percent—it's impossible! The voters doubtless assumed none of their own children would be affected."

"But some were."

"Yes. Some were." Bandra lifted her shoulders, a small shrug. "It was for the good of society, you see."

Mary shook her head. "My people would never countenance such a thing."

"We don't have to worry much about our gene pool anymore, although there are some exceptions. Still, after ten generations of restricted breeding, we relaxed the rules. Most genetic diseases were gone for good, most violence was gone, and the average intelligence was much higher. It still falls on a bell curve, of course, but we ended up with—what do you call it? We have a concept in statistics: the square root of the mean of the squares of the deviations from the arithmetic mean of the distribution."

"A standard deviation," said Mary.

"Ah. Well, after ten generations, the average intelligence had shifted one standard deviation to the left."

Mary was about to say "to the right, you mean," but remembered that Neanderthals read from right to left, not left to right. But she did add, "Really? That much of a change?"

"Yes. Our stupid people are now as intelligent as our average people used to be."

Mary shook her head. "I just don't see any way my people would ever be comfortable with limiting who had the right to breed."

"I don't defend our way," said Bandra. "As one of your very best sayings goes, 'to each his own.'" She smiled her wide, warm smile. "But, come, Mare, enough of this seriousness. It's a beautiful evening! Let's go for a walk. Then you can tell me all about yourself."

"What would you like to know?"

"Everything. The whole ball of wax. The whole shebang. The whole nine yards. The whole enchilada. The—"

Mary laughed. "I get the idea," she said, rising to her feet.

Chapter Seventeen

"How could that have possibly happened? How could we have given up that most noble of drives that had taken us from Olduvai Gorge to the lunar craters? The answer, of course, is that we'd grown content. The century we recently left saw greater advances in human wealth and prosperity, in human health and longevity, in human technology and material comfort, than all of the forty millennia that preceded it ..."

Mary Vaughan was settling into a routine: spending days studying Neanderthal genetics with Lurt or other experts, and spending nights being very comfortable at Bandra's house.

Mary had always thought her own hips too wide, but the average Neanderthal pelvis was even wider. Indeed, she remembered Erik Trinkaus's old suggestion that Neanderthals might have had an eleven- or twelve-month gestation period, since their wider hips would have accommodated a bigger baby. But that theory had been abandoned when later work showed that the differently shaped Neanderthal pelvis was just related to their style of walking. It had been suggested they had a rolling gait, like Old West gunslingers—a fact now very much confirmed observationally.

Anyway, Mary found Neanderthal saddle-seats uncomfortable and, because most Neanderthals had shorter lower legs than upper legs, bench-type Barast chairs were a bit too low to the ground for her tastes. So she'd asked Lurt's carpenter friend to make her a new chair: a frame of knotty pine with generous cushions lashed to its back and seat.

Bandra had gotten home before Mary did that day, and was off in her bedroom. But she emerged just after Mary came in the front door. "Hi, Mare," she said. "I thought I smelled you."

Mary smiled wanly. She was getting used to it all; really she was.

"Look!" declared Bandra, pointing. "Your chair has arrived! You must try it out."

Mary did so, lowering herself onto its cushioned seat.

"Well? Well?"

"It's wonderful!" said Mary, after shifting around in it. "Really. Very comfortable."

"Just what the doctor ordered!" declared Bandra, and then she astonished Mary by making a thumbs-up sign.

Mary laughed. "Exactly."

"Right on the money! The perfect thing!"

"All of that, yes," said Mary.

"Yes!" repeated Bandra, who was enjoying herself immensely. "Bingo! Exactamundo!" Bandra beamed at Mary, and Mary smiled warmly back.

Later that evening, Mary gave her new chair a longer test, curling up in it with one of the books she'd bought at the Laurentian University bookstore.

For her part, Bandra had been working on a new bird

painting, but evidently decided it was time to take a break. She crossed the room and stood behind Mary. "What are you reading?"

Mary instinctively showed Bandra the book's cover before she realized Bandra couldn't possibly read the title—although with her delight in English, she doubted it would be long before Bandra tackled learning to read it. "It's called *The Man of Property*," said Mary, "by a writer named John Galsworthy. He won my world's top writing award, the Nobel Prize for Literature." Colm had been recommending Galsworthy for years, but Mary had only finally decided to read him after her sister Christine had raved about the new BBC adaptation of *The Forsyte Saga*, of which *The Man of Property* was the first volume.

"What's it about?" asked Bandra.

"A rich lawyer married to a beautiful woman. He hires an architect to build a country house for them, but the woman is having an affair with the architect."

Bandra said, "Ah," and Mary looked up at her and smiled. She tried again: "It's about the complexities of interpersonal relationships among Gliksins."

"Would you read some of it to me?" asked Bandra.

Mary was surprised but pleased by the request. "Sure." Bandra straddled a saddle-seat facing Mary, arms folded in her lap. Mary softly spoke the words on the page, and let Christine translate them into the Neanderthal tongue.

> Most people would consider such a marriage as that of Soames and Irene quite fairly successful; he had money, she had beauty; it was a case for compromise. There was no reason why they should not jog along, even if they hated each other. It would not matter if they went their own ways a little so long as the decencies were

observed—the sanctity of the marriage tie, of the common home, respected. Half the marriages of the upper classes were conducted on these lines: Do not offend the susceptibilities of Society; do not offend the susceptibilities of the Church. To avoid offending these is worth the sacrifice of any private feelings. The advantages of the stable home are visible, tangible, so many pieces of property; there is no risk in the status quo. To break up a home is at the best a dangerous experiment, and selfish into the bargain.

This was the case for the defence, and young Jolyon sighed.

"The core of it all," he thought, "is property, but there are many people who would not like it put that way. To them it is 'the sanctity of the marriage tie'; but the sanctity of the marriage tie is dependent on the sanctity of the family, and the sanctity of the family is dependent on the sanctity of property. And yet I imagine all these people are followers of One who never owned anything. It is curious!"

And again young Jolyon sighed . . .

"Interesting," said Bandra, when Mary eventually paused.

Mary laughed. "I'm sure you're just being polite. It must be gibberish to you."

"No," said Bandra. "No, I think I understand. This man—Soames, right?—he lives with this woman, this . . ."

"Irene," supplied Mary.

"Yes. But there is no warmth in their relationship. He wants much more intimacy than she does."

Mary nodded, impressed. "Exactly."

"I suspect such concerns are universal," said Bandra.

"I guess they are," said Mary. "I actually identify with

Irene. She married Soames not knowing what she really wanted. Just like me with Colm."

"But you know what you want now?"

"I know I want Ponter."

"But he does not come in isolation," said Bandra. "He has Adikor and his daughters."

Mary folded down her page and closed the book. "I know," she said softly.

Bandra perhaps felt she had upset Mary. "I'm sorry," she said. "I'm going to have something to drink. Would you like anything?"

Mary would have killed for some wine, but the Neanderthals didn't have such things. Still, she'd brought a kilo tin of instant coffee with her from the other side. She normally didn't drink coffee in the evening, but Neanderthal room temperature was sixteen degrees—their scale and hers were the same; the gap between the melting point and boiling point of water divided into a hundred parts. Mary preferred twenty or twenty-one degrees; a nice drinking bowl of coffee would warm her up. "Let me help," said Mary, and the two of them headed over to the food-preparation area.

Back on her version of Earth, Mary kept a liter of chocolate milk on hand to mix into her coffee. She couldn't get that here, but she'd brought along canisters of coffee whitener and hot-chocolate mix; combining them into her Maxwell House gave a reasonable enough approximation of her favorite potion.

They returned to the living room, crossing over the moss-covered floor. Bandra sat down on one of the gently curving couches that was built into the wall of the room. Mary was about to return to her own chair, but realized that she wouldn't have any place to set down her drinking bowl there. She fetched her paperback—Colm would have hated the way she'd creased the book's spine and dog-eared its pages—and took a seat at the other end of the couch, setting the drinking bowl on the pine table in front of it.

"You lived alone in your world," said Bandra. It wasn't a question; she already knew that.

"Yes," said Mary. "I have what we call a condominium apartment—a private suite of rooms in a large building that I jointly own with a couple of hundred other people."

"A couple of hundred!" said Bandra. "How big is this building?"

"It's twenty-two stories high; twenty-two levels. I'm on the seventeenth floor."

"The view must be magnificent!"

"It is indeed." But that was a reflex response, Mary knew. Her view had been of concrete and glass, of buildings and highways. It had seemed wonderful when she'd lived there, but her tastes were changing.

"What is the status of that place?" asked Bandra.

"I still own it. Once Ponter and I decide what we're doing on a permanent basis, I'll figure out what to do with it. We may want to keep it."

"And what *are* you and Ponter going to do on a permanent basis?"

"I wish I knew," said Mary. She picked up her drinking bowl and took a sip. "Like you said before, Ponter doesn't come in isolation."

"Nor should you," said Bandra, looking down, not meeting Mary's eyes.

"Pardon?" said Mary.

"Nor should you. If you are to become part of this world, you should not be alone at any time of the month."

"Um," said Mary. "On my world, most people are attracted only to individuals of the opposite sex."

Bandra looked up briefly, then dropped her gaze again. "There are no relations between women?"

"Well, sure, sometimes. But usually women involved in such relationships don't have male partners."

"That is not the way it is here," said Bandra.

Mary's voice was soft. "I know."

"I—we—you and I, we have been getting along well," said Bandra.

Mary felt her whole body tightening. "We have, yes," she said.

"Here, two women living together who like each other and are not genetically related would"—suddenly Bandra's large hand was on Mary's knee—"would be *close*."

Mary looked down at the hand. Over the years, she'd plucked the odd man's hand off her knee, but . . .

But she didn't want to give offense. After all, this woman had been kind enough to take her in. "Bandra, I . . . I'm not attracted to women."

"Perhaps . . . perhaps that is merely . . ." She sought a phrase. "Merely cultural conditioning."

. Mary frowned, considering this. Perhaps it was—but that didn't make any difference. Oh, Mary had kissed girls when she was thirteen or fourteen—but she'd just been practicing for eventually kissing boys, she and her friends being terrified that they might be no good at it.

At least, that's what they'd told each other, but—

But it *had* been fun, in its own way.

Still . . .

"I'm sorry, Bandra. I don't mean to be rude. But I'm really not interested."

"You know," said Bandra, meeting Mary's eyes, then looking away, "no one understands how to please a woman like another woman."

Mary felt her heart flutter. "I—I'm sure that's true, but . . ." She gently reached down and removed Bandra's hand. "But it's not for me."

Bandra nodded several times. "If you change your mind . . ." she said, letting the thought hang in the air, then, after a moment, she added, "It can get awfully lonely between times of Two becoming One."

That much is certainly true, Mary thought, but she said nothing.

"Well," said Bandra, at last, "I'm going to bed. Um— 'sweet dreams' is your phrase, isn't it?"

Mary managed a smile. "Yes, it is. Good night, Bandra." She watched the Neanderthal woman pass through the doorway into her sleeping chamber; Mary had her own room, the one that used to belong to Bandra's younger daughter Dranna. She thought about calling it a day herself, but decided to read some more, in hopes of clearing her head of what had just transpired.

She picked up *The Man of Property* and opened it to the turned-down page. Galsworthy employed a mocking, ironic tone; it wasn't just Neanderthals who found fault with Gliksins, after all. She read along, enjoying his splendid re-creation of upper-middle-class Victorian England. He certainly had a way with words, and—

Oh, my God . . .

Mary slammed the book shut, her heart racing.

My God.

She took a deep breath, let it out, inhaled again, exhaled. Soames had . . .

Mary's heart was pounding.

Maybe she'd misread it. After all, the language wasn't explicit. Surely it was just her own state of mind . . .

She opened the book, gingerly, carefully, the way Colm

would have, and found her place again, letting her eyes race over the cramped typesetting, and—

No, there could be no doubt. Soames Forsyte, the Man of Property, had just demonstrated that he considered his wife Irene to be nothing more than that. Despite her lack of interest in him, and in their marriage bed, he had raped her.

Mary had been enjoying the book to this point, especially the furtive, secret romance between Irene and the architect Bosinney—for it had reminded her a bit of her own strange, forbidden relationship with Ponter. But—

A rape.

A goddamned rape.

And yet she could not blame Galsworthy. It was precisely what Soames would have done.

Precisely what a *man* would have done.

Mary put down the book next to her now-cold bowl of coffee. She found herself looking at the closed door to Bandra's room, staring endlessly. After God only knew how long, Mary finally got up from the couch, and made her way into her own room, into loneliness, into darkness.

Chapter Eighteen

"Here in North America, and in India and Japan and Europe and Russia and all across this whole wide wonderful world of ours, things are mostly better than they have ever been— and they're getting even better all the time..."

Finally, it was time! Two had become One again. Mary and dozens of other females were waiting in an open field for the men to show up. Lurt was there, along with young Dab, her son by Adikor. Jasmel, Ponter's elder daughter, was there, too, but she was really waiting, Mary knew, for her own man-mate, Tryon. Mega, Ponter's younger daughter, was also there, and Mary stood next to her, holding her small hand. Mary was relieved that there was no sign of Daklar Bolbay, young Mega's guardian; that woman had made enough trouble for Mary, Ponter, and Adikor as it was.

At last the right hover-bus arrived. Ponter and Adikor came out, and Mary rushed to her man. They hugged and licked each other's faces. Ponter then hugged both his daughters, and lifted Mega up on his shoulders. Adikor, meanwhile, had already disappeared with his woman-mate and son.

Ponter had brought the trapezoidal suitcase he usually took on trips to the other Earth. Mary carried it, while he carried Mega.

They had agreed in another chat over linked Companions to go looking for Vissan on the third of the four days
of the Two-becoming-One holiday, since the forecast was for
rain in Saldak then but clear skies in Kraldak.

And so on this morning, Mary, Ponter, and Mega had a
fabulous time together. Although it was getting chilly, and
the trees had all changed color, the air was still crisp and
clean. After lunch, Mega had gone off to play with friends,
and Mary and Ponter retired to the house Mary shared with
Bandra. Neanderthals were open about sex, but Mary still
wasn't comfortable making love knowing that there was anyone else at home. Fortunately, Bandra had said she would be
away until evening with her own man-mate, Harb. And so
Ponter and Mary had the run of the place.

The sex, as always, was fabulous, with Mary climaxing
repeatedly. When they were done, they bathed together, each
lovingly cleaning the other. Then they lay on the pile of cushions, just chatting and holding each other. Mary wasn't used
to the sound of Ponter speaking with contractions, but of
course he was, since Christine was now doing the translating
instead of Hak.

Mary and Ponter spent most of the afternoon cuddling
and touching and talking and walking, just enjoying each
other's company. They took in a short comedic play—the
Neanderthals loved live theater. Electric fans at the back of
the stage blew the performers' pheromones onto the audience while clearing the audience's own out of the room.

Then they enjoyed a Neanderthal board game called *partanlar* that was something like a cross between chess and
checkers: the playing pieces were all identical, but how they
could move depended upon which squares on the hundred-
position grid they landed upon.

Later, they ate at a restaurant run by two old women

whose man-mates were no more, enjoying delicious venison, wonderful salads of pine nuts and fern leaves, fried tubers, and boiled duck's eggs. There, they sat side by side on a padded couch in the restaurant's rear, wearing Neanderthal dining gloves and taking turns feeding each other.

"I love you," said Mary, nestling against Ponter.

"And I love you," Ponter replied. "I love you so very much."

"I wish . . . I wish Two could always be One," said Mary.

"When I am with you, I wish it would never end, either," said Ponter, stroking Mary's hair.

"But it must," said Mary with a sigh. "I don't know that I'll ever fit in here."

"There are no perfect solutions," said Ponter, "but you could . . ."

Mary sat up and turned to face him. "What?"

"You could go back to your world."

Mary felt her heart sink. "Ponter, I—"

"For twenty-five days a month. And you come back here when Two become One. I promise that each time you do, I will give you the four most loving, fun-filled, passionately sexual days possible."

"I—" Mary frowned. She'd been looking for a solution that would see the two of them together constantly. But it did seem as if that wasn't possible. Still: "The commute between Toronto and Sudbury would be awkward," said Mary, "not to mention the decontamination procedures going each way, but . . ."

"You forget who you are," said Ponter.

"I . . . I beg your pardon?"

"You are Mare Vaughan."

"Yes?"

"You are *the* Mare Vaughan. Any academy—excuse me,

any *university*—would love to have you on staff."

"Well, and that's another problem. I can't possibly get four days off in a row every month."

"Again, you underestimate yourself."

"How?"

"Do I understand your academic schedules correctly? You are in session for eight months a year."

"September to April, yes. Autumn to spring."

"So four or five occurrences of Two becoming One will happen when you're not obligated to the university. Of the remaining eight, a goodly number will partially fall on those first and last days of your seven-day clusters during which you do not work."

"Still . . ."

"Still, there would be days you would have to miss being at the university."

"Exactly. And no one is going to understand that—"

"Forgive me, beloved, but *everyone* is going to understand. Even before this visit, but especially now, you know more not just about the genetics of Neanderthals than any other Gliksin, but you also know more of what Neanderthals *know of* genetics than any other Gliksin. You would be an asset to any university, and if a few accommodations have to be made to your special needs, I'm sure that could be arranged."

"I think you're underestimating the difficulties."

"Am I? The way to find out is to try."

Mary pursed her lips, thinking. He was right; it certainly couldn't hurt to ask. "Still, it takes most of a day to get from Toronto to Sudbury, especially once you add the time getting down to the portal onto the car trip. Four days could easily become six."

"If you went back to living in Toronto, yes. But why not make your contribution at Laurentian University in Sudbury?

They already know you there from the work you did during my first visit to your world."

"Laurentian," said Mary, tasting the word, tasting the idea. It was a lovely, small university, with a first-rate genetics department, and it did all that fascinating forensic work—

Forensics.

The rape. The goddamned rape.

Mary doubted she'd ever be comfortable working at Toronto's York University again. Not only would she have to face Cornelius Ruskin, but she would also have to work side by side with Qaiser Remtulla, the other woman who had been raped by Ruskin, a rape that might have been prevented if Mary had reported the attack on herself. Every time she thought of Qaiser, Mary was wracked with guilt; working with her would be devastating—and working with Cornelius would be terrifying.

There *was* a certain elegance to what Ponter was proposing.

Teaching genetics at Laurentian . . .

Living just a short drive from the Creighton Mine, the threshold to the original interuniversal portal . . .

And spending even just four days a month with Ponter would be more wonderful, more fabulous, than a 24/7 relationship with any other man she could imagine . . .

"But what . . . what about generation 149? What about our child? I couldn't bear to see my baby only once a month."

"In our culture, children live with their female parents."

"But only until they're ten, if they're male. Then, like Dab will soon, they go live with their fathers. I wouldn't be able to let my child leave me after only a decade."

Ponter nodded. "Whatever solution we find to allowing us to have a child will require manipulation of chromosomes.

Surely, in that process, it's a trivial matter to make sure our child is female. Such a child would live with her mother until she reached her two-hundred-and-twenty-fifth month—over eighteen of your years. Isn't that a typical age for children to stay with their parents, even in your world?"

Mary's head was spinning. "You are a brilliant man, Scholar Boddit," she said, at last.

"I do my best, Scholar Vaughan."

"It's not a perfect solution."

"Such things are rare," said Ponter.

Mary thought about that, then snuggled closer to Ponter and gave the left side of his face a long, slow lick. "You know," she said, pressing her face into his furry cheek, "it might just work."

Chapter Nineteen

"So: it's perfectly reasonable that we took a hiatus, that we enjoyed the first few decades of post-Cold War prosperity, that we indulged in one of the other things that makes our kind of humanity great: we stopped and smelled the roses..."

After they left the restaurant, Mary and Ponter rendezvoused with Mega, and spent a while playing with her. But soon it was her bedtime, and Mega went home to the house she shared with her *tabant*, Daklar Bolbay—which made Mary think of a brilliant idea: she and Ponter could go back to *Ponter's* house for the night, out at the Rim. After all, Adikor would not be there, and it would let Bandra and Harb have Bandra's house to themselves. Ponter was startled by the suggestion—it simply wasn't normal for a woman to come to a man's house, although, of course, Mary had been to Ponter's a couple of times now—but after Mary explained her apprehension about making love with someone else at home, Ponter quickly agreed, and they summoned a travel cube to take them out to the Rim.

After some more wonderful sex, Mary was lounging in the circular, recessed bathtub, and Ponter was sitting in a chair. He was pretending to read something on a datapad, but Mary noticed his eyes weren't tracking left to right—or right to left, for that matter. Pabo was napping quietly by her master's feet.

Ponter's posture was somewhat different from what a *Homo sapiens* male would display: although he had a long (albeit chinless) jaw, he didn't prop it up with a crooked arm. Of course, the proportions of his arms weren't quite normal. No, damn it, no; "normal" was the wrong word. Still, maybe it wasn't comfortable for him to assume the classic Rodin "Thinker" pose. Or—why hadn't Mary noticed this before? Ponter's occipital bun gave extra weight to the rear of his head, perfectly counterbalancing his heavy face. Perhaps, when brooding, he didn't prop up his head because there was no need to.

Still, brooding was unquestionably what Ponter was doing.

Mary got out of the tub and toweled off, then, still naked, made her way across the room and perched herself on the broad arm of his chair. "A penny for your thoughts," she said.

Ponter frowned. "I doubt they are worth that much."

Mary smiled and stroked his muscular upper arm. "You're upset about something."

"Upset?" said Ponter, trying on the word. "No. No, that's not it. I'm simply wondering about something."

Mary moved her arm around Ponter's broad shoulders. "Something to do with me?"

"In part, yes."

"Ponter," she said, "we decided to try to make this—this *relationship* of ours—work. But the only way we can do that is if we communicate."

Ponter looked downright apprehensive, Mary thought, and his face seemed to convey a plaintive *Don't you think I know that?*

"Well?" said Mary.

"Remember Veronica Shannon?"

"Of course. The woman at Laurentian." The woman who made Mary Vaughan see the Virgin Mary.

"There is an . . . an *implication* in her work," said Ponter. "She has identified the suite of structures in the *Homo sapiens* brain that are responsible for religious impulses."

Mary took a deep breath. She certainly hadn't been comfortable with that notion, but the scientist in her couldn't ignore what Veronica had apparently demonstrated. Still, "I suppose," is all Mary said, releasing the air she'd taken in.

"Well, if we know what *causes* religion," said Ponter, "then . . ."

"Then what?" said Mary.

"Then perhaps we could cure it."

Mary felt her heart jump, and she thought she was going to tumble backward off the chair's arm. "Cure it," she repeated, as if hearing the words in her own voice would somehow make them more palatable. "Ponter, you can't *cure* religion. It's not a disease."

Ponter said nothing, but looking down on his head from her perch on the chair's arm, Mary saw his eyebrow roll up onto his ridge as if to say, *Isn't it?*

Mary decided to speak before Ponter filled the void with more things she did not want to hear. "Ponter, it's part of who I am."

"But it's the cause of so much evil in your world."

"And of much greatness, too," Mary said.

Ponter tilted his head and turned it sideways so that he could look at her. "You asked me to speak. I was content to keep these thoughts private."

Mary frowned. If he'd been keeping them totally private,

she never would have asked him what was wrong.

Ponter went on: "It should be possible to determine what mutation caused this in Gliksins."

Mutation. Religion as a mutation. Sweet Jesus. "How do you know that it's my people who've mutated? Maybe ours is the normal state, the ancestral state, and your people are the mutants."

But Ponter simply shrugged. "Perhaps we are. If so, it wouldn't be . . ."

But Mary finished his thought for him, her tone betraying her bitterness. "It wouldn't be the only improvement since *neanderthalensis* and *sapiens* split."

"Mare . . ." said Ponter gently.

But Mary wasn't going to let it go. "See! You don't have the vocal range we do! *We're* the more advanced state."

Ponter opened his mouth to protest, but then closed it, his thought unspoken. But Mary knew what it probably was: the perfect rejoinder to her comment about vocal range, the fact that Gliksins could choke to death while drinking whereas Neanderthals could not.

"I'm sorry," said Mary. She moved over to Ponter's chair, sitting this time in his lap, draping her arms around his shoulders. "I am so sorry. Please forgive me."

"Of course," said Ponter.

"It's just a difficult notion for me. Surely you can understand that. Religion as an accidental mutation. Religion as a detriment. My beliefs as merely a biological response with no basis in any higher reality."

"I can't say I understand, for I don't. I've never believed anything in defiance of evidence to the contrary. But . . ."

"But?"

Ponter fell silent again, and Mary shifted in his lap, leaning back a bit so that she could study his broad, round, bearded face. There was such intelligence in his golden eyes, such kindness.

"Ponter, I'm sorry I reacted the way I did. The last thing I want you to do is clam up—feel intimidated about speaking openly to me. Please, tell me what you were going to say."

Ponter took a deep breath, and when he did that, it was enough to make Mary feel a breeze. "Remember I told you I had seen a personality sculptor."

Mary nodded curtly. "About my rape. Yes."

"That was the proximate cause of my visits to the sculptor, but other . . . other things, other matters . . ."

"We call them *issues*," said Mary.

"Ah. It turned out I had some other issues to resolve."

"And?"

Ponter moved in the chair, shifting both himself and Mary with ease. "The personality sculptor is named Jurard Selgan," said Ponter. An irrelevancy, buying time as he composed his thoughts. "Selgan had a hypothesis about . . ."

"Yes?"

Ponter shrugged slightly. "About my attraction to you."

Mary felt her back stiffen. It was bad enough that she was apparently the cause of Ponter's problems—but to be the subject of theories by someone she'd never met! Her voice was Pleistocene in its coldness. "And what was his hypothesis?"

"You know my woman-mate Klast died of cancer of the blood."

Mary nodded.

"And so she is no more. Completely and totally devoid of any further existence."

"Like those commemorated at the Vietnam veterans' wall," said Mary, remembering their trip to Washington, and the point Ponter had made so vigorously there.

"Exactly!" said Ponter. "Exactly!"

Mary nodded as she felt pieces fall together in her mind. "You were upset that people at the Vietnam wall were taking comfort in the notion that their loved ones might still exist in some form."

"*Ka,*" said Ponter softly; Christine didn't bother translating the Neanderthal word for "yes" if that was all a Barast said.

Mary nodded again. "You were . . . you were *jealous* of them, of the comfort they had, despite their tragic loss. The comfort that you were denied because you don't believe in heaven or an afterlife."

"*Ka,*" Ponter said again. But, after a long pause, he continued, with Christine translating: "But Selgan and I didn't speak of my visit to Washington."

"Then what?" asked Mary.

"He suggested that . . . that my attraction to you . . ."

"Yes?"

Ponter tipped his head up, looking at the ceiling with its painted mural. "I said before that I had never believed anything in defiance of evidence to the contrary. The same might be said about believing things in the *absence* of any evidence. But Selgan suggested that perhaps I *did* believe you when you said you had a soul, when you said you would continue to exist in some form, even after death."

Mary drew her eyebrows together and tilted her head to one side, absolutely baffled. "Yes?"

"He . . . he . . ." Ponter seemed unable to go on. At last, he simply lifted his left forearm and said, "Hak?"

Hak took over, speaking directly in English. "Do not feel inadequate, Mare," the Companion said. "Ponter himself could not see this, either, although it was obvious to Scholar Selgan . . . and to me, as well."

"What?" said Mary, her heart pounding.

"It is conceivable," continued the Companion, "that if you were to die, Ponter might not feel the grief as sharply as he did when Klast died—not because he loves you less, but because he might assuage his feelings with the belief that you still existed in some form."

Mary felt her whole body sag. If Ponter's arms hadn't been encircling her waist, she would have fallen off his lap. "My . . . God," she said. Her head was swimming; she had no idea what to think.

"I don't accept that Selgan is correct," said Ponter, "but . . ."

Mary nodded slightly. "But you are a scientist, and it *is* . . ." She paused, considering; a belief in an afterlife did allow such consolation. "It *is* an interesting hypothesis."

"*Ka*," said Ponter.

Ka, indeed.

Chapter Twenty

*"But now it's time to resume our journey, for it is our love
of the journey that makes us great..."*

"Guess what!" said Ponter to Mega. "Today, we're going to
take a trip! We're going to fly in a helicopter!"

Mega was all smiles. "Mare told me! Yay!"

There was much intercity travel throughout Two becoming One; a helicopter routinely flew from Saldak Center to
Kraldak Center those days, and Ponter, Mary, and Mega
headed toward where it was waiting. Ponter had brought a
leather bag with him. Mary offered to carry it for him, since
he was carrying Mega on his shoulders.

The helicopter was reddish brown, with a cylindrical hull;
it made Mary think of a giant can of Dr Pepper. The interior
cabin was surprisingly roomy, and Mary and Ponter had wide,
padded seats facing each other. Mega, meanwhile, had the
seat next to Ponter, and was having the time of her life looking out the windows as the ground dropped away.

The cabin had excellent soundproofing; Mary had only
rarely been in helicopters before, and it had always given her
a headache. "I've got a present for you," said Ponter to Mega.
He opened his leather bag and dug out a complex wooden
toy.

Mega squealed with delight. "Thank you, Daddy!"

"And I didn't forget you," he said, smiling at Mary. He reached into the bag again and pulled out a copy of *The Globe and Mail*, Canada's national newspaper.

"Where'd you get that?" asked Mary, her eyes wide.

"At the quantum-computing facility. I had one of the Gliksins pass it over from the other side."

Mary was astonished—and pleased. She had hardly thought about the world she'd been born in, but it would be good to get caught up—and she *had* been missing *Dilbert*. She unfolded the paper. According to page one, there had been a train derailment near Vancouver; India and Pakistan were hurtling threats at each other again; and the Federal Minister of Finance had handed down a new budget in Parliament.

She turned the page, the paper making a loud rustling sound as she did so, and—

"Oh, my God!" said Mary.

"What's wrong?" asked Ponter.

Mary was glad she was already sitting down. "The Pope is dead," she said softly—indeed, he obviously had been for a few days, or he'd still be on page one.

"Who?"

"The leader of my belief system. He's dead."

"I'm sorry," said Ponter. "What will happen now? Is this a crisis?"

Mary shook her head. "Well, no . . . not specifically. As I said, the current Pope was quite old and frail. It'd been known for some time that his days were numbered." Mary had gotten lazy about trying to avoid figures of speech, since Bandra knew so many of them, but she saw the puzzled expression on Ponter's face. "That he was going to die relatively soon."

"Did you ever meet him?"

"Meet the Pope?" said Mary, astonished at the notion. "No. No, it's mostly just VIPs who get to meet the Pope face-to-face." She looked at Ponter. "You would have had a much better chance of it than me."

"I . . . am not sure what I would say to a religious leader."

"He was more than just that. In Roman Catholicism, the Pope is the actual conduit for instructions to humanity from God."

Mega wanted to get out of her chair and climb into Ponter's lap just now. He helped her to do so. "You mean the Pope speaks to God?"

"Supposedly."

Ponter shook his head ever so slightly.

Mary forced a smile. "I know you don't believe that's possible."

"Then let's not rehash it. But . . . you *do* look sad. And yet you didn't personally know the Pope, and you said his death isn't a crisis for your belief system." Ponter was speaking softly, and so Mega was pretty much ignoring him. But Christine pumped her translation of Ponter's words at normal volume through Mary's cochlear implants.

"It's just a shock," said Mary. "And, well . . ."

"Yes?"

Mary blew out air. "The new Pope will make policy decisions about fundamental issues."

Ponter blinked. "Such as?"

"The Roman Catholic Church is . . . well, a lot of people say it hasn't kept pace with the times. You know it doesn't allow abortion, and it doesn't allow divorce—the dissolution of a marriage. But it also doesn't allow its clergy to have sex."

"Why not?" Mega was contentedly looking out Ponter's window.

"Well, having a sexual life is supposed to interfere with

the ability to perform spiritual duties," said Mary. "But most other religions don't require celibacy of their clergy, and many Roman Catholics think it's an idea that does more harm than good."

"Harm? We tell adolescent boys not to deny themselves, because they might fill up with sperm and explode. But that's just a joke, of course. What harm comes from this celibacy?"

Mary looked away. "Priests—members of the celibate clergy—are known to . . ." She closed her eyes, started again. "It's only a very small percentage of priests, you understand. Most of them are good, honest men. But some of them have abused children."

"Abused them how?" asked Ponter.

"Sexually."

Ponter looked down at Mega; she seemed to be paying no attention to what they were saying. "Define 'children.' "

"Little boys and girls, three, four years old, and up."

"Then it's good that these priests are celibate. The gene for this activity should become extinct."

"You'd think," said Mary. She shrugged. "Maybe you guys *do* have it right, sterilizing not just the perpetrator, but also those who share at least half his genetic material. If anything, it seems that priestly child abuse is reaching epidemic proportions." She hefted the *Globe*. "At least, that's the impression you get by reading newspapers."

"I cannot read them," said Ponter, "although I hope to learn. But I have seen your television news and heard news on the radio from time to time. I have heard the comments: 'When are we going to see the dark side of Neanderthal civilization? Surely they must have bad qualities, too.' But I tell you, Mare"—Christine could have substituted Mary's full name for Ponter's utterance, but she didn't—"we have nothing to compare with your child molesters, with your polluters, with your makers and users of bombs, with your slavery, with your terrorists. We are hiding nothing, and yet the belief persists that we must have comparably bad things. I don't know if this fallacy is related to your religious impulses, but it does seem to do similar damage: your people believe that a certain amount of evil is inevitable, unavoidable. But it's not. If any benefit comes from the contact between your world and mine, perhaps it can be that realization."

"Maybe you're right," said Mary. "But, you know, we *do* make progress over time. And that's where the new Pope comes in."

"Daddy, look!" said Mega, pointing out the window. "Another helicopter!"

Ponter craned his neck. "So there is," he said, stroking his daughter's hair. "Well, you know, lots of people have to travel to go see their loved ones when Two become One."

Mary waited until Mega had gone back to staring out the window. "A lot depends," she said, "on what the new Pope decides to do—or, to put it as my faith would, on what God tells him to do. The last Pope wasn't effective in dealing with the problem of child abuse by priests. But the new Pope could really go to town on that. And he could put an end to the celibacy requirement for priests. He could come up with a less-extreme anti-abortion policy. He could recognize homosexuals."

"Recognize them how? Do they look different?"

"No, what I mean is that my Church considers same-sex relationships to be a sin. But the new Pope might lighten up on that, and on everything else."

"What are you own beliefs in these matters?"

"Me?" said Mary. "I'm pro-choice—that is, in favor of letting a woman choose whether or not to complete a pregnancy. I've got nothing against homosexuality. I don't think that priests should be forced to be celibate. And I certainly don't think marriages should be hard to dissolve. That's the big one for me right now, of course: Colm and I agreed to get an annulment—basically, stating before the Church and God that our marriage never existed, so that it could be expunged from the records. Now, though . . ." She paused, then went on. "Now, I guess we should wait a bit to see what the new Pope is likely to do. If he allows Catholics to divorce without leaving the Church, I'd be much happier."

Another Neanderthal leaned over just then. "We're about to land in Kraldak, sir. You'll have to strap your daughter in."

Ponter summoned a travel cube to take him, Mary, and Mega out to the location Hak had identified. The male driver did not seem to want the assignment—the cabin was far beyond Kraldak Rim—but Ponter finally convinced him. The cube flew over rocky outcroppings, negotiated around stands of trees, and cut across several small lakes, until at last it arrived at the spot Hak had identified.

They got out and approached the structure. It was a sort of log cabin, but the logs were standing on their ends, rather than stacked horizontally. Ponter knocked on the door, but there was no response. He operated the starfish-shaped handle, opening the door, and—

And little Mega let out a great yelp.

Mary felt her own blood run cold. Facing her, on the opposite wall, illuminated by a shaft of light entering from a window, was the giant skull of . . .

It couldn't be, but . . .

But it certainly looked like one: a cyclops. A deformed skull, with a massive central eye socket.

Ponter had picked up his daughter, and was soothing her. "It's just a mammoth skull," he said. Mary realized he was right. The tusks had been removed, and the central hole had accommodated the trunk in life.

Ponter called out Vissan's name, but the cabin was just a single large room, with a central eating table, a single chair, hide rugs on the floor, a stone fireplace and a cluster of logs, and a pile of clothing in one corner; there was no way anyone could be hiding within. Mary turned around, looking back at the countryside, hoping to spot Vissan, but she could be *anywhere* . . .

"Scholar Boddit!" It was the driver of the travel cube.

Ponter went back to the door. "Yes?" he shouted.

"How long will we be?"

"I don't know," said Ponter. "A daytenth or more, I should think."

The driver considered this. "Well, then I'm going to go hunting," he declared. "It's been months since I've been this far out in the country."

"Have fun," said Ponter, waving at the man. Ponter then went back into the cabin, and headed over to the pile of clothing in the corner. He picked up a shirt, and brought it to his face, inhaling deeply. He did the same thing with several other pieces of clothing, then nodded to Mary. "Okay," he said, "I've got her scent."

Ponter boosted Mega up on his shoulders, and went out the front door. Mary followed, closing the door behind her. Ponter flared his nostrils, sucking in air, and walked most of the way around the house, before he stopped. "That way," he said, pointing to the east.

"Great," said Mary. "Let's go."

Little Neanderthal girls knew all about gathering but

rarely got to see a hunter at work, and Mega seemed to be loving the adventure. Even with her perched on his shoulders, Ponter managed a brisk pace over the rock outcroppings and through the forest. Mary struggled to keep up. At one point, they startled some deer, who ran away; at another, their arrival set a flock of passenger pigeons into flight.

Mary wasn't good at judging distance in the wilderness, but they must have gone six or seven kilometers before Ponter finally pointed to a figure in the distance, bent over, near a stream.

"There she is," he said softly. "She's upwind of us, so I'm sure she doesn't know we're here yet."

"All right," said Mary. "Let's get closer."

Ponter admonished Mega to be quiet, and they moved to within about forty meters of the female Neanderthal. But then Mary stepped on a stick, which cracked loudly, and the woman looked up, startled. The tableau held for a second, with Ponter, Mary, and Mega looking at the woman, and the woman looking back at them—and then the female Neanderthal took off, running away.

"Wait!" shouted Mary. "Don't go!"

Mary hadn't expected her words to do any good, but the female stopped dead in her tracks and turned around. And then it hit Mary: she'd shouted in English, and although Christine had dutifully translated a moment later, the woman had probably never heard either a voice so high-pitched or that strange alien language before. Someone who had been living on her own, without a Companion or a Voyeur, since early in the summer would have no idea that a portal had opened up to a parallel universe.

Ponter, Mega, and Mary closed some of the distance, getting within twenty meters of the woman, who had a look of absolute astonishment spread across her broad face.

"What—what are you?" she said in the Neanderthal tongue.

"I'm Mary Vaughan," called Mary. "Please, don't run off! Are you Vissan Lennet?"

The female's broad jaw dropped—and Mary realized she'd said words that contained the never-before-heard *ee* phoneme.

"Yes," said Vissan in the Neanderthal tongue. "I'm Vissan—but please don't hurt me."

Mary looked at Ponter, surprised, but then called back. "Of course we won't hurt you!" Then, to Ponter: "Why would she be afraid of us?"

Ponter spoke softly. "She has no Companion. No record is being made for her benefit of this encounter, and she has no status under our law—she could never order a review of our own recordings at the alibi archives."

"Don't be afraid!" called out Mega helpfully. "We're nice!"

Ponter, Mary, and Mega had managed to get another five meters closer to Vissan without her running off. "What are you?" said Vissan again.

"She's a Gliksin!" said Mega. "Can't you tell?"

Vissan stared at Mary. "No, really. What are you?"

"Mega's right. I am what you'd call a Gliksin."

"Astonishment!" said Vissan. "But—but you are an adult. If someone had recovered Gliksin genetic material many ten-months ago, I would surely have known."

It took a moment for Mary to figure out what Vissan meant; she thought Mary was a clone, made from ancient DNA.

"No, that's not it. I'm—"

"Let me," said Ponter. "Vissan, do you know who I am?"

Vissan narrowed her eyes, then shook her head. "No."

"That's my daddy," said Mega. "His name's Ponter Boddit. He's a 145. I'm a 148!"

"Do you know of a chemist named Lurt Fradlo?" asked Ponter, looking at Vissan.

"Fradlo? Of Saldak? I know her work."

"She's Adikor's woman-mate," said Mega. "And Adikor is my daddy's man-mate."

Ponter put a hand on Mega's shoulder. "That's right. Adikor and I are both quantum physicists. Together, he and I accessed an alternative reality in which Gliksins survived to the present day and Barasts did not."

"You're ruffling my back hair," said Vissan.

"No, he's not!" said Mega. "It's true! Daddy disappeared into another world, down in the Debral nickel mine. Nobody knew what happened to him. Daklar thought Adikor had done something bad to Daddy, but Adikor's a good guy; he'd never do anything like that! Jasmel—that's my sister—she worked with Adikor to bring Daddy back. But then they made a portal that's always open, and Mare came through from the other side."

"No," said Vissan, looking down. "She *must* be of this world. She has a Companion."

Mary looked down, as well; a bit of Christine's faceplate was protruding past her jacket's sleeve. She took off her jacket, rolled up her shirtsleeve, and held out her arm. "But my Companion has only recently been installed," said Mary. "The wound is still healing."

Vissan took her first step toward Mary, then another, then one more. "So it is," she said at last.

"What we are saying is true," said Ponter. He gestured at Mary. "You can *see* that it's true."

Vissan placed her hands on her broad hips, and studied Mary's face, with its tiny nose, high forehead, and bony projection from the lower jaw. Then, her voice full of wonder, she said, "Yes, I suppose I can."

Chapter Twenty-one

"Scientists tell us that our kind of humans moved up to the northern tip of Africa, looked north across the Strait of Gibraltar, and saw new land there—and, of course, as seems natural to us, we risked crossing that treacherous channel, moving into Europe..."

Vissan was a 144, most of a decade older than Mary. She had green eyes and hair that was predominantly gray, with only a few blond streaks betraying its original color. She was wearing fairly ragged manufactured clothing that had been patched here and there by pieces of hide, and was carrying a leather bag, presumably containing the bounty she'd gathered that morning.

The four of them were walking back toward Vissan's cabin. "All right," she said, looking at Mary, "I accept your story of who you are. But I still don't know why you have sought me out."

They had come to a small stream. Ponter picked up Mega and hopped over it first, then he offered his hand to help Mary across. Vissan forded the stream herself.

"I'm a life chemist, too," said Mary. "We're interested in your codon writer."

"It is banned," said Vissan, lifting her shoulder. "Banned by a bunch of short-headed fools."

Ponter made a silencing motion. Up ahead were some more deer. Mary looked at the beautiful creatures.

"Vissan," whispered Ponter, although Christine gave the translation a greater volume, since only Mary could hear that. "Do you have enough food? I would gladly bring down one of those deer for you."

Vissan laughed, and spoke in a normal voice. "You are kind, Ponter, but I am doing fine."

Ponter dipped his head, and they continued on, until the deer scattered of their own accord. Up ahead, Vissan's cabin was visible.

"My interest in the codon writer isn't just academic," said Mary. "Ponter and I wish to have a child."

"I'm going to have a little sister!" said Mega. "I already have a big sister. Not many people get to have a big sister *and* a little sister, so I'm special."

"That's right, darling," said Mary. "You're *very* special." She turned back to Vissan.

"What of your Barast woman-mate?" asked Vissan, looking now at Ponter.

"She is no more," said Ponter.

"Ah," said Vissan. "I'm sorry."

They had reached the cabin. Vissan opened the door and motioned for Ponter, Mary, and Mega to follow her in. Vissan took off her fur coat—

—and Mary saw the hideous scarring on the inside of her left forearm, where she'd carved out her Companion.

Ponter sat down with Mega at the table, giving her some attention. Mega had picked up a pine cone and two nice stones on the way back that she wanted her father to see.

Mary looked at Vissan. "So," she said, "does your prototype still exist?"

"Why do you need it?" asked Vissan. "Has one of you been sterilized by the government?"

"No," said Mary. "It's nothing like that."

"Then why do you need my device?"

Mary looked over at Ponter, who was listening intently to Mega, who was now telling him about things she'd been learning in school. "Barasts and Gliksins, plus chimpanzees, bonobos, gorillas, and orangutans, all have a common ancestor," said Mary. "That ancestor apparently had twenty-four pairs of chromosomes, as do all of its descendants except Gliksins. In Gliksins, two chromosomes have fused into one, meaning we only have twenty-three pairs. The overall genome is the same length, but the differing chromosome count would make a natural conception problematic."

"Fascinating!" said Vissan. "Yes, the codon writer could easily produce a matched diploid set of chromosomes that combined Ponter's DNA and your own."

"So we'd hoped," said Mary. "Which is why we're interested in whether the prototype still exists."

"Oh, it exists, all right," said Vissan. "But I can't let you have it—it's a banned device. As much as I hate that fact, it *is* the reality. You would be punished for possessing it."

"It is banned here," said Mary.

"Not just here in the vicinity of Kraldak," said Vissan. "It is banned all over the world."

"All over *this* world," said Mary. "But not in *my* world. I could take it back there; Ponter and I could conceive there."

Vissan's eyes went wide under her undulating browridge. She was quiet for a few moments, and Mary knew better than to interrupt her thinking. "I suppose you could, at that," said Vissan, at last. "Why not? Better that somebody get the benefit of it, rather than no one." She paused. "You would need medical aid still," said Vissan, "to remove an egg from your body. Your natural haploid set of chromosomes would be vacuumed out of it, and a doctor would add in a full diploid set of chromosomes created using the codon writer. The egg would then be implanted in your womb. From that point on, it will be precisely like a regular pregnancy." She smiled. "Cravings for salted tubers, morning sickness, and all."

Mary had been enthusiastic when it had all been abstract—a magical, black-box solution. But now ... "I ... I hadn't realized you would eliminate my natural DNA. I thought we'd just remap Ponter's DNA so that it was compatible with mine."

Vissan raised her eyebrow. "You said you are a life chemist, Mare. You know there's nothing special about deoxyribonucleic acid produced by your body, or by a machine. In fact, it would be impossible for you to tell a natural string and a manufactured string apart. There is no chemical difference between them."

Mary frowned. She'd chided her sister often enough for paying a premium for "natural" vitamins, which were chemically indistinguishable from those produced in labs. But ... "But one of them came from my body, and the other came from a machine."

"Yes, but ..."

"No, no, you *are* right," said Mary. "I've been telling my students for years that DNA is nothing but coded information." She smiled at Ponter and Mega. "As long as it's *our* coded information, it will still be our baby."

Ponter looked up and nodded. "Our personal genetic material will need to be sequenced, of course."

"Easily done," said Vissan. "In fact, the codon writer can do that, too."

"Wonderful!" said Mary. "Is the prototype here?"

"No. No, it's hidden. Buried. But I wrapped it in plastic and metal to protect it. It's not far away, though; I can easily retrieve it."

"It would mean a great deal to us," said Mary. Then a thought struck her. "Would you like to come back with me? To my world? I can guarantee you that we won't ban your device there, or stop you from continuing research related to it."

"What an astonishing idea!" said Vissan. "What is your world like?"

"Well, it's different. Um, we have a bigger population, for one thing."

"How big?"

"Six billion."

"Six billion! I think you hardly need a device to aid conceptions, then . . ."

Mary nodded, conceding that. "And males and females live together all the time."

"Madness! Don't they get on each other's nerves?"

"Well . . . yes, I suppose they do sometimes, but . . . As I said, it's a different place. And we have many wonderful things. We have a space station—a permanent habitat orbiting our planet. We have buildings that tower into the sky"— although, Mary thought ruefully, not as many as we used to. "And we have much more varied cuisine."

"Ponter, have you been there?"

"My daddy's been there *three* times now!" said Mega.

"Would I like it?" asked Vissan.

"That depends," said Ponter. "Do you like it here, in the wilderness?"

"Very much. I have gotten quite used to it."

"Do smells bother you?"

"Smells?"

"Yes. For power, they burn oil and coal, so there is a stench in their cities."

"That hardly sounds appealing. I think I will stay here."

"Whatever makes you happy," said Mary. "But could you teach us how to operate the codon writer, then?"

Vissan looked at Ponter. "How do you feel about this? I have willingly shed myself of the trappings of civilization, and so the Grays—High or Low—have no authority over me. But you . . ."

Ponter looked at Mary, then back at Vissan. "I have defied the High Grays before; I chose to flout their order to return to this universe so that the portal could be shut down. Indeed, I would still be in Mare's universe if an ambassador hadn't convinced others to cross over. And . . ."

"Yes?"

"And, well, sometimes people are sterilized without it being right, so . . ."

Ponter trailed off, and Mary spoke up. "He's referring to his man-mate, Adikor. When Ponter first disappeared into my world, they thought Adikor had killed him and disposed of the body. They were going to sterilize him." She turned to Ponter. "Isn't that right, Ponter?"

"What?" said Ponter, his tone odd. "Oh, yes. Yes, that was what I meant, of course . . ."

"Well, if you are comfortable with having the codon writer," said Vissan, "I am content to let you have it." She gestured toward the door. "I'll go get it. Just don't ever tell anyone—in this world, at least—that you have it."

Chapter Twenty-two

"Likewise, some of our Barast cousins, natives of Europe, came south to Gibraltar, with its famous rock, that wonderful symbol of permanence and stability. And from their vantage point, the Neanderthals could see south to the unknown lands of Africa..."

"Jock, can I have a word with you?"

Jock Krieger looked up from his desk. He was, perhaps, a bit paranoid about showing his appreciation for just how beautiful Louise was. It was a generational thing, he knew—he was thirty-six years older than Louise, after all—but he'd seen some of his colleagues at RAND get in trouble for supposedly sexist comments. "Ah, Dr. Benoît," he said, rising—that much of the manners his parents had drilled into him he couldn't suppress. "What can I do for you?"

"Remember when we were talking before about the effect a planetary magnetic-field collapse might have on consciousness?"

"How could I forget?" said Jock. "You said that human consciousness had booted up during a magnetic-field collapse."

"That's right. Forty thousand years ago, when the Great Leap Forward occurred, Earth's magnetic field was undergoing a collapse, just like it's beginning to now. In our universe, the field came up with its orientation the same as it had been before the collapse—which it will do half the time, leaving no record here. But in the other universe, the orientation came up flipped, and so it *was* recorded in their geological record. As I said, it couldn't be a coincidence that hominid consciousness booted during a field collapse, and—"

"And you said this time it might have effects on our consciousness again, possibly even causing a crash."

"Exactly. Now, when I first suggested that, it was only because of the coincidence that the Great Leap Forward occurred during a time when Earth's magnetic field had collapsed; obviously, there was a correlation between magnetic fields and consciousness. But since then, I've been digging, trying to find what research, if any, has been done about the electromagnetic nature of consciousness—and, frankly, Jock, I'm even more worried than I was before."

"Why? The Neanderthals have been through one collapse since—the one that began a quarter of a century ago in their world—and they had no problems." Jock had been astonished when he'd read the research by Coe and Prévot showing that, in fact, his Earth's geological record provided evidence that field collapses took place in a matter of weeks, not centuries. "If they came through their collapse just fine, why shouldn't we?"

"As much as I like the Barasts"—calling a Neanderthal a Neanderthal was no longer politically correct, apparently—"they *are* a different species, with differently constructed brains," said Louise. "All you have to do is look at their skulls to see that. Just because they came through all right doesn't mean we will."

"Oh, come on, Louise!"

"No, really. I've been searching the web for information

on the relationship between electromagnetic fields and consciousness, and I came across something very interesting called CEMI theory."

"Semi-theory?" repeated Jock. *Perfect name for a half-baked idea* . . .

"CEMI, with a *C*," said Louise. "It's short for Conscious Electromagnetic Information theory. A couple of researchers independently developed it, Johnjoe McFadden at the University of Surrey and Susan Pockett in New Zealand." She looked out Jock's window, apparently gathering her thoughts, then: "Look, we've identified all sorts of specific areas in the human brain: where visual images are created, where mathematical operations occur, even—I'm sure you've read about this in the press—where the seat of religious feelings is. But the one thing we've *never* located is the physical site, the actual location, of *consciousness* in the brain. Well, McFadden and Pockett think they've found it—not *in* the brain, but surrounding it and permeating it: an electromagnetic field. Such a field would allow neurons that are separated by great distances in the brain to nonetheless connect with each other, binding together all the little bits of information into an integrated whole, a coherent picture of reality."

"Wireless communication in the brain?" said Jock, intrigued despite himself.

"Exactly. Back in 1993, Karl Popper proposed that consciousness was the manifestation of a force field in the brain, but he thought it must be some *unknown* kind of force field, since he'd figured we'd have discovered it already if it consisted of energy we were familiar with. But McFadden and Pockett say the field is simply electromagnetic."

"And they've detected it?"

"Oh, there certainly *is* electromagnetic activity in and

around the brain; that's what EEGs measure, after all. But remember, our Barast friends have unified electromagnetism and the strong nuclear force—in other words, there's much more to electromagnetic fields, including both the Earth's and the ones produced by our brains, than we've ever been aware of."

"But have these researchers you mentioned proved that such fields are actually linked to consciousness?" asked Jock.

Louise brushed dark hair out of her eyes. "No, not yet. And I will admit that there's a lot of resistance from some quarters to the very notion. Good old René Descartes believed in dualism—the notion that the body and the mind are separate things—but that's been out of fashion for quite some time now, and, well, some see CEMI as an unwelcomed return to it. But CEMI theory makes *sense* from an information-processing standpoint. Essentially McFadden and Pockett are saying that awareness and information are the same phenomenon viewed from different reference frames, and—"

"Yes, so?"

"Well," said Louise, "if consciousness is an electromagnetic phenomenon, then it's perhaps no surprise that its first appearance was during a geomagnetic field collapse. Now, as I said, we know from the recent Barast experience that such a collapse *on its own* won't cause problems with consciousness—but I'm a solar physicist, remember. I may specialize in neutrinos, but I'm interested in the whole range of solar radiation—and our brains, with these delicate electromagnetic fields, will be hit by an onslaught of normally deflected solar radiation for years or decades during the collapse. The more I look into this, the more I think a consciousness crash of some sort just might occur."

"But that's crazy," said Jock. "Consciousness *can't* be electromagnetic. I had an MRI last year, and I assure you, young lady, that I was fully conscious throughout the procedure."

"That's the most common objection to this theory," said Louise, nodding. "McFadden addressed that directly in his most recent paper in the *Journal for Consciousness Studies.* He contends that fluid within the brain ventricles effectively creates a Faraday cage, insulating the brain from most external electric fields. And, as for MRIs, he points out that those are *static* electric fields—changing only the direction of moving charges, and so they don't have physiological effects. Likewise, Earth's magnetic field is static and pretty uniform—or was, at least until the collapse began. But changing—as opposed to static—external electromagnetic fields *do* induce electric currents in the brain. And these do affect brain activity; in fact, there are strict guidelines for repetitive transcranial magnetic stimulation that have to be followed to prevent inducing seizures in normal people."

"But—but if consciousness is electromagnetic, why can't we detect it?"

"Actually, we can. Susan Pockett has enumerated all sorts of research that says that the brain's electromagnetic field does change in replicable ways when experiencing specific qualia: you can measure changes in the brain's electromagnetic field when you're looking at something red as opposed to blue, or hearing a middle C instead of a high C, and so on. She's really good at shooting down objections to this theory. For instance, if the corpus callosum—the bundle of nerves that connects the left and right hemispheres—is severed, you'd expect there to be no communication at all between the two halves of the brain. And yet, except in very contrived situations, split-brain patients perform quite normally; despite there being no physical connection between their two hemispheres, their consciousness *is* integrated—

precisely, says Pockett, because consciousness is manifested in the electromagnetic field that contains the entire brain, not through neural-chemical reactions."

"So you're saying—what?—that the two halves of the brain communicate telepathically? Oh, come on!"

"They *are* communicating, even in the absence of the hard-wired link between them," said Louise. "That's a fact."

"Then why don't I pick up your thoughts when I'm standing next to you?"

"Well, first, remember the brain is essentially enclosed in a Faraday cage, shielding it. Second, Pockett believes the major oscillations associated with consciousness are in the range of one to one hundred hertz, with most of the power around forty hertz. That means they have a wavelength of about 8,000 kilometers, and the ideal antenna for picking up an electromagnetic signal is one wavelength long. Without either a truly giant receiver or *very* sensitive equipment, you'd never pick up any part of my consciousness by just being close to me. But that the field is integrated over the volume of a single brain *does* make sense. One of the big issues in consciousness is the so-called binding problem. Look at that book, there." She pointed at a volume sitting on Jock's desk, an old RAND nuclear-warfare study. "One part of the brain recognizes that it's green. Another part picks out the outline of the object from the background. A third part digs up the word 'book' to describe it. We *know* that's how the brain works—a bunch of compartmentalized functions. But how do all those bits get bound together, producing the thought that we're looking at a green thing called a book? CEMI says the electromagnetic field is what does the binding."

"This is all very speculative," said Jock.

"It's all very cutting edge, but it *is* a good, solid scientific theory that makes falsifiable predictions. I tell you, Jock, I hadn't thought a lot about exactly what constitutes consciousness until all this stuff with alternative worlds began, but it's a fascinating area of research."

"And you're worried that our consciousness might get scrambled as Earth's magnetic field collapses?"

"I don't say anything is going to happen—after all, you *are* right when you say the Neanderthals went through their own magnetic-field collapse recently and nothing happened to them. But, well, yes—I *am* worried. And I think you should be, too."

Chapter Twenty-three

"But the Neanderthals didn't cross the Strait of Gibraltar. There, at Gibraltar, we saw the difference between us and them. For, when we saw a new world, just a short distance away, we took it . . ."

"This," said Vissan, placing a pale green device on the table in her cabin, "is the prototype codon writer."

Mary looked at the machine. It was about the size and shape of three loaves of bread, placed end to end—although no Neanderthal would ever think of it that way.

"It can synthesize any string of deoxyribonucleic acid, or ribonucleic acid, if you prefer, as well as the additional proteins needed to manufacture chromosomes or other structures."

Mary shook her head in wonder. "It's a life factory." She looked at Vissan. "In my world, you would have won the Nobel Prize for this—our top honor for scientific work."

"But here," said Vissan, "it is banned." Her voice was bitter. "My intentions were so benign."

Mary frowned. "What *were* your intentions?"

Vissan was quiet for a moment. "I have a younger brother who lives in an institution." She looked at Mary. "We have eliminated most inheritable genetic disorders, but there are still things that can go wrong, things that are genetic but not inherited. My brother has—I don't know what you call it. He has an extra chromosome twenty-two."

"Chromosome twenty-one, you mean," said Mary. Then: "No, of course you don't. It *would* be number twenty-two here. We call that Down syndrome."

"Are the symptoms the same in Gliksins?" asked Vissan. "Mental and physical feebleness?"

Mary nodded. But Down also caused facial abnormalities in Gliksins, including a protruding tongue, a slack jaw, and epicanthic folds even in occidentals. Mary wondered what a Barast with Down syndrome would look like.

"My mother was a member of generation 140. She should have had her first child when she was twenty years old, but failed to conceive then—or when she was thirty. She had me when she was forty, and my brother Lanamar when she was fifty."

"Conceptions that late in life increase the likelihood of Down in my people, too," said Mary.

"Because the body's ability to produce clean sets of chromosomes has deteriorated. I wanted to overcome that—and I did. My codon writer could have eliminated all copying errors, all—"

"All what?" said Mary.

"I'm sorry," said Christine. "I don't know how to translate the word Vissan has used. It refers to when there are three chromosomes where there should only be a pair."

"Trisomy," supplied Mary.

"Had my parents had access to such technology," continued Vissan, "letting them output a perfect diploid set of chromosomes despite their age, Lanamar would be normal. And, of course, there are a host of similar conditions that also could be avoided."

Indeed there are, thought Mary. One in 500 Gliksin children were born with a sex-chromosome difficulty, such as Klinefelter syndrome (two or more X chromosomes and a Y, or often a mosaic), triple-X syndrome, Turner syndrome (a single X chromosome either completely lacking a mate or with a truncated second sex chromosome), or XYY syndrome, which could predispose males to violence—she suspected Cornelius Ruskin had an extra Y; he certainly had the body type and personality. Other combinations occurred, but they mostly resulted in miscarriages.

"But that's not all," said Vissan. "Preventing trisomy and similar disorders was only the initial impetus for my work. Once I got into my research, other wondrous possibilities occurred to me."

"Yes?" said Ponter.

"Yes, indeed! I wanted to eliminate the randomness in gene selection, leaving the choices of traits up to the parents."

"How do you mean?" asked Ponter.

Vissan looked at him. "You inherited a bunch of traits from your father and another bunch from your mother; half of your deoxyribonucleic acid came from each of them, and in total, those two halves make up your forty-eight chromosomes. But each sperm you produce has a random selection of all those traits. You—Ponter Boddit—have DNA that contains both your father's contribution to your eye color and your mother's, plus your father's contribution to your hair color and your mother's, your father's contribution to your browridge shape and your mother's, and so on. But your sperm contain only twenty-four chromosomes, with just half your deoxyribonucleic acid. Any given sperm you make will contain *either* your father's contribution to a given trait or your mother's, but not both. One sperm might contain your mother's contribution to eye color, your father's to hair color, and your mother's to browridge shape. Another might have exactly the opposite combination. A third might contain only your mother's contributions to those things. A fourth, only your father's. And so on, for all the tens of thousands of different genes you possess. No two sperm you ever produced will likely have the same combination of traits coded into it. The same sort of thing happens in the production of eggs, and, again, it's a virtual certainty that no two eggs share the same combination of the mother's mother's genetic material and the mother's father's genetic material."

"All right," said Ponter.

"In fact—Mega here is your daughter, right?"

"Yes, I am!" said Mega.

Vissan crouched down to be at Mega's face height. "Now, she has brown eyes, whereas you have golden ones," said Vissan. "Do you have any other children?"

"An older daughter, named Jasmel."

"And what color are Jasmel's eyes?"

"The same as mine."

"She's so lucky!" said Mega, pouting.

"Indeed she is," said Vissan, rising and patting the girl on her head. She looked at Ponter. "Brown is dominant; golden is recessive. The chances of a child of yours inheriting your eye color through natural processes were one in four. But if you'd let the codon writer output your genetic material for you, you could have chosen to give both your children golden eyes—or any other trait you or your woman-mate carried the genetic code for."

"Aww," said Mega. "I wish I had golden eyes!"

"Understand?" said Vissan. "What happens in a natural conception is that a set of traits selected entirely at random ends up being combined together."

Ponter nodded.

"But don't you see?" said Vissan. "That's a crazy way to do it! An absolute gamble as to what you are going to get. And it doesn't have to be related to things as inconsequential as eye color. You possess two genes related to the flexibility of the lens in your eye: one from your mother, and one from your father. Say the one you got from your mother is a good one that lets you see without corrective eyewear well into old age, but the one you got from your father is a bad one that would require you to use corrective eyewear from childhood. You will pass one, and only one, of those two on to your own offspring. Which would you choose?"

"My mother's one, of course," said Ponter.

"Exactly! But, in natural conception, there is *no* choice— no choice at all. It's pure luck of the draw which one your child will get . . . because you let inefficient nature produce your sperm. But if we sequenced your deoxyribonucleic acid, we could choose the better one of each pair of traits you yourself had inherited, and then we could manufacture a haploid set of chromosomes containing only those better traits. We could also do the same thing with Mary, here, pro- ducing a haploid set representing only the better traits from her repertoire. And then we could combine them together to produce the best child you could possibly have. The child would still absolutely be one-half its father genetically and one-half its mother, but it would have the best possible com- bination of their respective genetic material."

"Wow," said Mary, shaking her head. "It's not quite de- signer babies, but . . ."

Vissan shook her head. "No, although that's technically possible with the codon writer, too: we *could* code in alleles that are present in neither parent. But that was never my intention. Generation 149 is to be conceived shortly—and I wanted it to be the greatest generation ever, bringing forth all the positive characteristics of the people who begat it, but none of the negative ones." She shook her head again, and her tone grew even lower than normal. "It could have done as much to improve our species as the purging of the gene pool did." After a moment, though, she seemed able to push her bitterness aside, at least temporarily. "That will never be, apparently. But at least the two of you can benefit from this capability."

Mary felt as though her heart were going to burst. She was going to be a mother! It was really going to happen. "This is *fabulous*, Vissan. Thank you! Can you show us how it works?"

"Certainly," she said. "I hope its batteries are still charged . . ." She touched a control, and a moment later a square screen came to life in the center of the unit. "Of course, you can attach a bigger display. Anyway, you pour appropriate raw chemicals into this aperture here." She pointed to a hole on the right side of the unit. "And the output comes out here, suspended in pure water." She indicated a spigot at the left end. "Obviously, you'll want to hook it up to appropriate sterilized glassware."

"And how do you specify the output?" asked Mary, staring at the machine in fascination.

"One way is by voice," said Vissan. She pulled out a control bud and addressed the device. "Produce a string of deoxyribonucleic acid 100,000 nucleotides long, consisting of the codon adenine-cytosine-thymine over and over again." She looked at Mary. "That's the code for the amino acid—"

"For threonine," said Mary.

Vissan nodded. "Exactly."

Several green lights appeared on the device. "Ah, there— it's saying it needs to be fed raw materials." She pointed to the screen. "See? They're specified here. Anyway, you can also use one of several keypads to input data." She pointed at a toggle switch. "You select either deoxyribonucleic-acid or ribonucleic-acid mode here. And then you can input data at any level of resolution, right down to individual nucleotides." She indicated a square arrangement of four buttons.

Mary nodded. The toggle must have been set for DNA mode, since the buttons were displaying the Neanderthal glyphs for adenine, guanine, thymine, and cytosine. She pointed to another cluster of buttons, arranged in an eight-by-eight grid. "And these must be for specifying codons, right?" Codons were the words of the genetic language, and there were sixty-four of them, each consisting of three nucleotides. Each codon specified one of the twenty amino acids that are used to make proteins. Since there were more codons than there were amino acids, multiple codons meant the same thing—genetic synonyms.

"Yes, that's right," said Vissan. "Those buttons let you choose codons. Or, if you do not care which codon is used to specify a given amino acid, you can just select the amino acid by name here." She pointed at a cluster of twenty buttons, arrayed in four lines of five.

"Of course," continued Vissan, "these controls are normally only used for fine editing; it would be incredibly tedious to specify a lengthy deoxyribonucleic-acid sequence by hand. Normally, one interfaces this device to a computer and simply downloads the genetic design one wishes to manufacture."

"Amazing," said Mary. "You wouldn't believe the gyrations we go through to do gene splicing." She looked at Vissan. "Thank you."

"My pleasure," said Vissan. "Now, let's get down to work."

"Now?" said Mary.

"Of course. We won't produce the actual DNA, but we'll

get the process set up. First, we'll take samples of your deoxyribonucleic acid and Ponter's, and then sequence them."

"You can do that here?"

"The codon writer can. We just feed in a sample of deoxyribonucleic acid, and let it analyze it. It should take about a daytenth for each specimen."

"Only a daytenth to sequence an entire personal genome?" said Mary, astonished.

"Yes," said Vissan. "Let's get it started, and then I'll go catch us something to eat."

"I'd be glad to help in the hunt," said Ponter. He smiled and raised a hand. "Although I know you don't need it."

"I would welcome the company," said Vissan. "But first, let's collect some genetic material from each of you . . ."

Chapter Twenty-four

"If the dangers posed by the collapsing of this Earth's magnetic field teaches us anything, it is that humanity is too precious to have but a single home—that keeping all our eggs in one basket is folly..."

Ponter called the travel-cube driver and told him to head back to Kraldak; they would summon another cube later in the day to take them home.

Mary and Mega stayed back in the cabin, while Vissan and Ponter went off hunting. Mega showed Mary how her new toy worked; Mary paraphrased part of Kipling's *The Jungle Book* for Mega; and Mega taught Mary to sing a short Neanderthal song. It was a kick spending time with Mega—and Mary knew it would be even more wonderful to have a child of her own.

Finally, Vissan and Ponter returned with a pheasant they'd caught for dinner, which Vissan proceeded to cook while Ponter made a salad. It turned out there were solar panels on the roof of Vissan's cabin, and she had a vacuum box for storing food, an electric heater, some luciferin lamps, and more; friends had given her farewell gifts when she'd chosen to leave structured Neanderthal society. All in all, Mary thought it actually might not be that bad a life, as long as one had plenty to read. Vissan showed Mary her datapad, and how she could recharge it from the solar array on the cabin's roof. "I have some four billion words of text stored on this," she said. "My access to new works has been cut off, of course—but that's all right; the new stuff is all garbage, anyway. But the classics!" Vissan hugged the little device to her chest. "How I love reading the classics!"

Mary smiled. Vissan sounded just like Colm, extolling the virtues of Shakespeare and his contemporaries; she'd had to keep her Harlequin romances out of his sight, lest an argument ensue.

The dinner was delicious, Mary had to admit—or maybe, she reflected, she was just famished after all the hiking she'd done that day.

The codon writer had been moved to the floor during dinner, but once they'd finished eating, Vissan lifted it back up onto the table. Mega curled up in a corner and had a nap, while the three adults sat around the table: Vissan on the one chair, Ponter on the end of a log, and Mary, facing the cyclopean mammoth skull, perched atop the vacuum box.

"All right," said Vissan, peering at the display. "It's finished sequencing." Mary was looking at Vissan, rather than the square screen, since, with a few exceptions that she'd picked up along the way, she couldn't understand the glyphs it was showing. But Vissan was oblivious to that, and pointed at the screen. "As you can see, it's made a list of the 50,000 active genes in your deoxyribonucleic acid, Mare, and the 50,000 in Ponter's."

"Fifty thousand?" said Mary. "I thought there were only 35,000 active genes in human DNA. That's our latest count."

Vissan frowned. "Ah, well, you're missing out on . . . I'm not sure what you call it. A kind of exonic redoubling. I can show you later how that works."

"Please," said Mary, fascinated.

"In any event, the device has now made a list of 50,000 gene alleles you each possess. That means the codon writer could now just go ahead and produce what you need: a pair of gametes that have the same number of chromosomes. But . . ."

"Yes?" said Mary.

"Well, I told you the original intention of this device: to let parents pick and choose from the alleles they could offer a child."

"I think we'll be happy to just try our luck randomly." The words were out before Mary really had time to think about them; perhaps, she realized, it was some of her natural Catholic revulsion at tinkering with the stuff of life coming to the surface . . . although *any* use of this machine certainly qualified as major tinkering!

Vissan frowned. "If you were both Barasts, I would be content to accept that answer—but then again, as you yourself observed, Mare, if you were both Barast, you wouldn't need the codon writer just to randomly combine your genetic material." She shook her head. "But you are not both Barasts." She looked down at Ponter's forearm. "I never thought I'd use one of these again, but . . . Companion of Ponter!"

"Healthy day," said a male voice from the device's external speaker. "My name is Hak."

"Hak, then," said Vissan. "Surely studies have been done of the differences between Barasts and Gliksin deoxyribonucleic acid since contact was made with Mare's people?"

"Oh, yes," said Hak. "It has been quite the hot topic."

"Are those studies available through the planetary information network?"

"Of course."

"Good," said Vissan. "We will need to access them as we go along." She looked up and shifted her gaze from Mary to Ponter, then back to Mary again. "I strongly advise against just slapping your deoxyribonucleic acid together. We are talking about combining two species here. Now, yes"—she gestured at the codon writer's screen—"it's clear that the genomes for Barasts and Gliksins are almost identical, but we should really examine where they diverge, and carefully select combinations." She pointed at Mary. "Are tiny noses like that typical of your species?"

Mary nodded.

"Well, there, you see? It would be ridiculous to code for a tiny Gliksin nose and a giant Barast olfactory bulb. Traits should be chosen with care so that they enhance, or at least do not interfere with, each other."

Mary nodded. "Right. Of course." Butterflies were pirouetting in her stomach, but she tried to sound jaunty. "So, what's on the menu?"

"Hak?" said Vissan.

"The genetic divergence—"

"Wait!" said Vissan. "I haven't asked you a question yet."

Ponter smiled. "Hak is a very intelligent Companion," he said. "Do you know Kobast Ganst?"

"The artificial-intelligence researcher?" said Vissan. "I know *of* him."

"Well," said Ponter, "about ten months ago, he upgraded my Companion. You weren't the only one trying to improve the lot of Barasts, of course. Kobast wants everyone in generation 149 to have the benefit of truly intelligent Companions."

"Well, let's hope they don't shut Ganst's work down as well—although if they do, I'll be happy to have a neighbor. In any event, I was about to ask Hak to summarize what is known about how the Gliksin genome differs from the Barast one."

"And I was about to tell you," said Hak, sounding slightly miffed. "There are, as you observed, about 50,000 active genes in any Gliksin or Barast. But 98.7% of those have allele forms that exist in both populations; only 462 genes have forms that exist in Barasts but not in Gliksin, or vice versa."

"Fine," said Vissan. She looked at Mary. "You can leave the rest to chance, if you like, but I really think we should carefully look at those 462 genes, and make sensible choices for each of them."

Mary looked at Ponter, to see if he had any objection. "That's fine," she said.

"All right—although, before we start, there are two big questions we must resolve. With the codon writer, we will make a diploid set of chromosomes combining deoxyribonucleic acid from both of you. Do we make twenty-three pairs of chromosomes, or twenty-four? That is, at the level of the chromosome count, do you want your child to be a Barast or a Gliksin?"

"Wow," said Mary. "That's a good question. The work I did in my world was about defining which species a person belongs to for immigration purposes. It seems likely that chromosome count will be adopted as the legal standard."

"Your child can be a hybrid in many ways," said Vissan. "But in this, it must be one or the other."

"Um, gee . . . Ponter?"

"You are the geneticist, Mare. I rather suspect that matters of chromosome count are—how would you put it?— 'nearer and dearer to your heart' than they are to mine."

"You don't have a preference?"

"Not on an emotional level, no. I suspect, though, that

there are legal advantages to making our child genetically Gliksin."

"How so?"

"We have a unified world government—the High Gray Council. You have 191 member states in your United Nations, plus some more besides that are not members, and immigration issues will arise with each of them, no?"

Mary nodded.

"It seems easier to convince one world government that a being with twenty-three pairs of chromosomes should be able to live and work anywhere in my world than it will be to convince some 200 governments in your world that a being with twenty-four pairs of chromosomes should be accorded the same rights."

Mary looked at Vissan. "We're not actually going to manufacture the DNA for our child today, right?"

"No, no, of course not. That will be done back in your world, I presume, when you are ready to become pregnant. I am just taking you through the issues you must deal with."

"So we don't have to decide right now."

"That is correct."

"Well, then, let's table that one."

Vissan looked at the table in front of her. "Pardon?"

"I mean, let's set it aside for now. What's next?"

"Well, this has nothing to do with your special circumstances but must also be decided, since it affects how the codon writer apportions Ponter's deoxyribonucleic acid. Do you want a boy or a girl?"

"We've already discussed that," said Mary. "We're going to have a daughter."

Vissan touched a control on the codon writer. "A girl it is," she said. "Now, let's see what else we've got . . ." She looked at the display.

"The next gene sequence displayed," said Hak, "refers to hair part. Barasts have a natural part along the centerline of the scalp, right above the sagittal suture. Gliksins tend to have natural parts off to the sides. Mary seems to have alleles only for side parts; both alleles from Ponter's personal genome are, of course, for center parts. You could take one of each, and discover experimentally which is dominant, or you could take both of Ponter's and neither of Mare's, or both of Mare's and neither of Ponter's, and be reasonably sure of the outcome."

Mary looked at Ponter. The Neanderthals did indeed part their hair like bonobo chimpanzees. At first she'd found it quite startling, but she'd since gotten used to it. "I don't know."

"The side," said Ponter. "If she is going to be a girl, she should take after her mother."

"Are you sure?" asked Mary.

"Of course."

"The side then," said Mary. "Use both of my alleles."

"Done," said Vissan, touching some more controls. She indicated the square display. "You see how it's done? These touch-points on the screen select alleles?"

Mary nodded. "Quite straightforward."

"Thank you," said Vissan. "I worked hard to make it easy to use. Now, I recognize the next group of alleles, at least on Ponter's side: they are for eye color. Mare, your eyes are blue—something we never see here. Ponter's are a golden brown shade we call *delint*; it is uncommon, but prized all the more because of that."

"Blue eyes are recessive in Gliksins," said Mary.

"As are *delint* here. So we can either take both your alleles, and make your daughter blue-eyed, both of Ponter's and make her golden-eyed, or throw in one of each and be surprised by the outcome . . ."

They continued on in that vein for quite some time, interrupted only by Mary, then Ponter, having to take bathroom breaks—meaning using a wooden chamber pot.

"And now," said Vissan, "we come to an interesting neurological item. I'd be very reluctant to take one of Mare's alleles and one of Ponter's at this point, since we just don't know what effect mixing them at this site will have. I think it would be much safer for the child to go all one way or all the other, rather than try to blend the characteristics. In a Barast, this gene is well known for governing development of the part of the brain's parietal lobe that is located in the left hemisphere. You surely don't want to risk brain damage, and—"

"Did you say the parietal lobe?" said Mary, leaning forward. Her heart was pounding.

"Yes," said Vissan. "Now, if that doesn't form properly, aphasia can result, as can difficulties with motor function, so—"

Mary turned on Ponter. "Did you put her up to this?"

"I beg your pardon?" said Ponter.

"Come on, Ponter. The part of the parietal lobe in the left hemisphere!"

Ponter frowned. "Yes?"

"It's what Veronica Shannon said is responsible for religious thinking in my kind of people. The out-of-body experience; the sense of being at one with the universe. All of that is rooted there."

"Oh," said Ponter. "Right."

"You mean to say you didn't know this was going to come up?"

"Honestly, Mare, I had no idea."

Mary looked away. "You've been talking about a 'cure' for religion, for Pete's sake. And now, lo and behold, we have one."

"Mare," said Vissan, "Ponter and I did not discuss this in advance."

"No? You were alone together hunting long enough . . ."

"Really, Mare," said Vissan, "I am not aware of the research you mentioned."

Mary took a deep breath, then let it out very slowly. "I'm sorry," she said at last. "I should know better. Ponter would never blindside me."

Ponter's Companion bleeped, but he didn't ask for an explanation.

Mary reached out with her left hand. "Ponter, you *are* my man-mate, even if we haven't yet undergone the bonding ceremony. I know you would never deceive me."

Ponter said nothing.

Mary shook her head. "I didn't expect to have to face this issue. I mean, eye color and hair color, sure. But atheist or believer? Who'd have thought that that would be a genetic choice?"

Ponter squeezed Mary's hand. "This issue is far more significant to you than it is to me. I understand that much, at least. We will do whatever you wish."

Mary took another deep breath. She could talk it over with Father Caldicott, she supposed—but, geez, a Roman Catholic priest wouldn't approve of *any* part of this process. "I'm not blind, you know," said Mary. "I've seen how peaceful this world of yours is, at least most of the time. And I've seen how . . ." She trailed off, thought for a moment, then shrugged, finding no better word than the one that had first occurred to her ". . . how *spiritual* your people are. And I keep thinking about all the things you've said, Ponter—back at Reuben's place, when we watched that Roman Catholic Mass together on TV, and at the Vietnam veterans' wall, and . . ." She shrugged again. "I *have* been listening, but . . ."

"But you're not convinced," said Ponter gently. "I don't blame you. After all, I am no sociologist. My musings about the"—he, too, paused, clearly aware that this was a most delicate topic right now, but then he went on, also, apparently, unable to find a better word—"evil that religion has caused in your world are just that: musings, philosophical ramblings. I can't prove my case; I doubt anyone could."

Mary closed her eyes. She wanted to pray, to ask for guidance. But none had ever come in the past; there was no reason to think this time would be different. "Maybe," she said at last, "we should simply leave it up to fate; let the genes fall where they may."

Vissan's voice was soft. "If this involved any other part of the body, I might agree with you, Mare. But we're talking about a component of the brain that is demonstrably different between the two species of humanity. To simply throw together one allele from a Gliksin and another from a Barast, then just hope for the best hardly seems prudent."

Mary frowned, but Vissan was right. If they were going to go ahead with having a hybrid child, a decision had to be made, one way or the other.

Ponter let go of Mary's hand, but then started stroking its back. "It's not," he said, "as if we are choosing whether or not our daughter will have a soul. At most, we're choosing whether or not she will *believe* she has a soul."

"You do not have to decide this today," said Vissan. "My intent, as I said, is only to walk you through the process of using the codon writer. You won't want to produce the diploid chromosome set until it is time for it to be implanted in you, anyway, Mare." She folded her hands. "But when that time comes, you *will* have to make this choice."

Chapter Twenty-five

"So, yes, indeed, now is the time to take longer strides. But it's not just time for a great new American enterprise. Rather, it's time, if I may echo another speech, for black men and white men, Jews and Gentiles, Protestants and Catholics—and Hindus and Muslims and Buddhists, and men and women of all faiths, and men and women of none—for individuals from every one of our 191 united nations, for members of every race and religion that make up our unique, varied brand of humanity—to go forward together, in peace and harmony, with mutual respect and friendship, continuing the journey we Homo sapiens had briefly interrupted..."

"I think," said Vissan, "that the two of you have some things to discuss. Perhaps I will take Mega, and we will go look at the stars." Mega had roused from her nap. "Would you like that, Mega?"

"Sure!" said Mega.

Vissan got up from her chair, found her fur coat, wrapped Mega in a couple of oversized shirts, and they headed for the door.

Mary felt a cold wind on her face as the door swung open. She watched Vissan and Mega leave, the wooden door closing behind them.

"Mare . . ." said Ponter.

"No, no, let me think," said Mary. "Just let me think for a few minutes."

Ponter shrugged amiably, headed over to Vissan's stone fireplace, and set about making a fire.

Mary got up off the vacuum box, and took Vissan's vacated seat, resting her chin on her hand.

Her chin . . .

A *Homo sapiens* trait.

But a trivial one, completely unimportant.

Mary sighed. Except for the question of living arrangements, she didn't care if they had a boy or a girl.

And she certainly didn't care where their child parted her hair. Or what color her eyes were. Or whether she was muscled like a Neanderthal. Or what sort of sense of smell she had.

As long as she's healthy . . .

That had been the mantra of parents for millennia.

Except in Veronica's lab, Mary had never had a full-blown religious experience, but nonetheless she really did believe in God. Even now, knowing that her predisposition to such belief was hardwired into her brain, she still really did believe.

Did she want to deny their daughter the comfort that went with that belief? Did she want to prevent her from ever knowing the religious rapture that had eluded Mary outside of that lab but had apparently touched so many others?

She thought about this world she was in, and rhetoric from the newscasts of her youth welled up in her mind. Words she'd avoided until now.

Godless people.

Communists.

But, damn it all, the Neanderthal system *worked*. It worked better than the corrupt, morally bankrupt capitalism of her world—the world of Big Tobacco and Enron and WorldCom and all the others that had been exposed since, people driven by nothing but greed, taking obscene amounts for themselves while others ended up without even enough food to eat.

And it worked better than the religious institutions of her world—her own Church sheltering child abusers for decades, her religion and so many others oppressing women, religious fanatics flying planes into skyscrapers . . .

Ponter was making progress with the fire. Wisps of smoke were rising from the logs he'd placed atop the stones within the fireplace.

At last, when he'd fanned the flames to vigorous life, Mary got up from the chair and walked over to her man, still crouching by the hearth.

He looked up at her, and although the light from the fire threw his browridge and massive nose into sharp relief, he still looked loving and gentle. "I will accept whatever choice you make," he said, rising to his feet.

Mary put her arms around his shoulders. "I—I wish I could think about this for a good long time."

"There is *some* time," said Ponter. "But a finite amount. If our child is to be part of generation 149, she must be conceived on schedule."

Mary knew her voice sounded petulant. "Maybe she won't be part of 149. Maybe we'll have her the following year. Or the year after that."

Ponter's tone was soft. "I know that your people give birth every year. If our child will be principally raised in your world, then it does not matter when she is conceived. But if we wish her to be raised in whole or in part in this world, or ever really to have the option of fitting in to this society, then it really must be done on schedule."

"It," said Mary, pulling back, looking at Ponter.

Ponter's eyebrow went up.

"*It*," Mary repeated. " 'It must be done on schedule.' Hardly sounds romantic."

Ponter drew her close again. "We face a few . . . special challenges. But what could be more romantic than the child of people who are in love?"

Mary forced a smile. "You're right, of course. Sorry." She paused. "And you're right that we should do it at the correct time." Mary's own birthday was late in the year; she knew what it was like to be even six months younger than some of the other kids on the school playground. She couldn't imagine how devastating it would feel to be a year or two younger than everyone else. Yes, their daughter would be raised principally in Mary's world, but when she was all grown up, she might choose to make her home in the Neanderthal universe—and she would never fit in here if she wasn't part of a specific generation.

Ponter was quiet for a time. "Are you prepared to decide?"

Mary looked over Ponter's shoulder, into the flames.

"My brother Bill married a Protestant," she said at last. "Ho boy, was my mom upset about that! Bill and Dianne— that's his wife—had to work out which religious traditions they were going to raise their children in. I only heard bits and pieces, and of course only from Bill's point of view, but it was apparently a big battle. And now you're asking me if I'm ready to decide whether or not my child should be predisposed to believing in God?"

Ponter said nothing; he just held her, and stroked her

hair. If Ponter was dying to know what Mary's decision was going to be, he gave no sign of it—and Mary was grateful to him for that. If he'd seemed anxious, she'd have known that he had a preferred choice, and that would have made it harder for her to sort through her feelings. As to *what* his preferred choice, if any, might be, still Mary couldn't say. Her first thought was that he'd want his child to be like him, devoid of the . . .

She hated the term, but it had already percolated into the popular press, even before the bridge to the Neanderthal world had opened.

. . . devoid of the "God organ."

Then again, Ponter was bright enough to know, despite everything they'd done here today, that you couldn't order up a person the way you ordered a pizza: "Give me a number two, hold the onions." Everything blended, making the whole. Perhaps he *wanted* his new daughter to have his mother's faith? Indeed, perhaps this was the test he'd been waiting for of the personality sculptor's hypothesis? Would his feelings toward a daughter who believed in an afterlife be different than his feelings toward Jasmel and Mega?

Mary would never ask him about it, not after the decision had been made. Once the appropriate genes were coded into the chromosomes of their child, there would be no point having regrets or reopening an old debate.

There was a scene in *Star Trek V*—the one William Shatner directed, the one in which Spock's half brother Sybok went off on a search for God—that portrayed Spock's own birth, in a cave, of all places, his human mother Amanda attended by a Vulcan midwife. When the infant Spock was presented to Sarek, his Vulcan father, Sarek said only two words, each filled with infinite disappointment: "*So human . . .* "

Mary shook her head at the memory. What the hell had Sarek expected to see? Why did he set out to have a hybrid child, and then act disappointed that it had characteristics of its mother's species? Mary and Ponter were truly seeking the best of both worlds—and that meant *including* things.

"It's not a defect," said Mary, at last, not bothering to define "it." "It's not something *wrong* with the Gliksin brain. Being able to believe in God—if we want to, if we so choose—is part of who my people are." She took Ponter's hand. "I know what religion has caused—what *organized* religion has caused. And I even am starting to agree with you about the harm the mere belief in an afterlife has done in my world, too. So much of our inhumanity *does* seem related to believing that all injustices will eventually be righted in an existence yet to come. But, nonetheless, I want my daughter—*our* daughter—to at least potentially believe in those things."

"Mare . . ." began Ponter.

She pulled away from him. "No. No, let me finish. Your people sterilize criminals, and say it's just to maintain the health of the gene pool. But it's more than that, isn't it, at least when the criminals are male? You don't just sterilize them by, for instance, performing a vasectomy. No, you *castrate* them—you remove that part of their anatomy that is responsible not just for aggression, but also for sexual desire, too."

Ponter looked quite uncomfortable, Mary thought, but, then again, she supposed no man liked thinking about castration. She pressed on. "I stand here as one who has been raped, who has been a victim of the very worst that testosterone makes possible. But I also stand here as someone who has known all the joy of sex with a passionate male lover. Perhaps, maybe, in some circumstances, removing the testosterone-producing glands is appropriate. And perhaps even in some cases removing the God organ would be appropriate, too. But not at the beginning, not at the outset."

Mary again looked at Ponter. "My Church has this notion of original sin: that all people are born tainted, carrying guilt and evil because of the actions of their ancestors. But I reject that. Veronica Shannon talked to us about behaviorism, Ponter—about the idea that you can inculcate any behavior, any response, into a human being. The mechanism—intermittent reinforcement versus consistent reinforcement—may differ slightly between Gliksins and Barasts, but the underlying concept is the same. A new child, a new life, is nothing but potentials to be developed one way or another—and I want our child, our daughter, to have *all* the potentials she can and, through your love and mine as her parents, to become the best possible human being she can be."

Ponter nodded. "Whatever you want is fine by me."

"This," said Mary. "This is what I want. A child who can believe in God."

Chapter Twenty-six

"And so I stand here today to usher in the next phase. It is time, my friends, for at least some of us to move on, to leave our version of Earth and take the next giant leap..."

Mary, Ponter, and Mega spent the night at Vissan's place, sleeping on the floor. The next day, with the codon writer wrapped in furs so that no one would notice it, the three of them had a travel cube come and take them to Kraldak Center, and from there they flew by helicopter to Saldak Center ...just in time for the end of Two becoming One.

Ponter met up with Adikor, and the two of them boarded a hover-bus heading back out to male territory. Ponter, Mary knew, had another trip coming up tomorrow. That's when he would accompany the contingent from the United Nations, including Jock Krieger, down to Donakat Island.

Mary's heart was aching, and she was already counting the days until Two would become One again—not that she expected to still be living on this world at that point; she would have to return to the Synergy Group before then. But of course she'd return here for the holiday.

Mary felt extraordinarily jealous of Adikor. It was unfair, she knew, but the whole thing had left her feeling like the Other Woman, as if Ponter had snuck away for a rendezvous with an illicit lover, only to have to return to his real family.

Mary began the long, slow walk back to the house she shared with Bandra, carrying the fur-wrapped codon writer. Many other women were milling around, but none seemed sad. Those who were talking among themselves were laughing; those walking alone mostly had smiles on their broad faces—not smiles of greeting, but secret, personal smiles, smiles of remembering.

Mary felt like an idiot. What the hell was she doing here, in this world, with these people? Yes, she'd enjoyed her time with Ponter. The lovemaking had been just as fabulous as it always was, the conversation just as fascinating, and the trip with Ponter and Mega to meet Vissan had been wonderful in all sorts of ways. But it was another twenty-five days until she and Ponter could be together again!

A cloud of passenger pigeons temporarily blocked the sun. They were a migratory bird, Mary knew, shuttling between two homes, one in the north and the other in the south. Mary let out a long sigh and continued to walk. She knew why the female Neanderthals she was passing could smile. It wasn't as though they were going back to a lonely existence. Rather, they were returning to their female lovers, to their children if they had any, to their families.

Mary lifted the collar of her mammoth-hair coat; a cold breeze had come up. She hated winter in Toronto—and suspected she'd hate it here even more. Toronto was so big, with so much industry, so many people, and so many cars, that it modified the local environment. North of the city—and south of the city, in Western New York—everything got hammered by snow. But in Toronto, there were only a few snowfalls each year, and usually no major ones before Christmas. Of course, she wasn't in what corresponded to Toronto;

Saldak was 400 kilometers farther north, where Sudbury was in Mary's world, and Sudbury *did* get tons of snow. Saldak must get even more of it.

Mary shuddered, even though it wasn't *that* cold yet. As she walked along, she thought about asking her Companion to tell her about winters here, but she suspected Christine would just confirm her worst fears.

At last she came to the distended, squat tree that formed the main structure of the house she shared with Bandra. Its leaves were falling off. Mary entered the house. She was wearing Neanderthal-style pants, with built-in shoes, but she'd instinctively reached down to try to remove her footwear as soon as she'd come through the door. She sighed again, wondering if she'd ever get used to this place.

Mary went into her bedroom, put down the codon writer, and came back into the living room. She could hear the sound of running water. Bandra must already be home, her man-mate perhaps having gone back to the Rim aboard an earlier hover-bus. The sound of the water must have masked the noise made by Mary entering, and since the door to the bathroom was closed—a nod to sanitation, not privacy, Mary knew—doubtless Bandra couldn't smell Mary yet.

Mary went to the kitchen and got herself some fruit juice. She'd heard that the Neanderthals who worked in the south harvesting fruit shaved off all their head and body hair to help them better survive the warm temperatures. She tried to envision what Ponter would look like without hair. Mary had seen bodybuilders on TV, and for some reason they all had hairless chests and backs. Either they shaved them, or else the steroids they took had that effect. Anyway, she decided Ponter looked just fine the way he was.

Mary had expected Bandra to emerge from the bathroom by now, but she hadn't—and Mary really needed to pee. By sheer necessity, she'd forced herself to overcome her privacy concerns about sharing one washroom. She walked over to the closed door and pushed it open with the flat of her hand.

Bandra was standing in front of the washbasin, hunched over, leaning into the square mirror above the sink.

"Excuse me," said Mary. "I just need to—oh, my! Bandra, are you okay?"

It had taken a moment for Mary to see that there were splatters of blood on the polished granite washbasin; the red drops were difficult to make out against the pink stone.

Bandra didn't turn around. Indeed, she seemed to be making an effort to hide her face. Mary loomed in.

"Bandra, what is it?" Mary reached up and took hold of Bandra's shoulder. Had Bandra really wanted to, she could have stopped Mary from turning her around—she was certainly strong enough. But although she resisted a bit at first, she did allow Mary to turn her.

Mary felt herself sucking in air. The left side of Bandra's face was bruised horribly, a yellow rim around a black-and-blue area perhaps ten centimeters across running from just above her browridge, down her wide, angled cheek to the corner of her mouth. There had been a central scab, half the diameter of the bruise, but Bandra had picked much of it away; that's where the fresh blood was coming from.

"My God," Mary said. "What happened to you?" Mary found a cloth—square, coarse—dipped it into the water, and helped Bandra clean the wound.

Tears were running down Bandra's face now, falling from the deep wells of her eyes, detouring around her massive nose, flowing over her chinless jaw, and dropping onto the granite washbasin, diluting the blood there. "I—I never should have let you come here," said Bandra softly.

"Me?" said Mary. "What did I do?"

But Bandra seemed lost in her own thoughts. "It's not so bad," she said, looking in the mirror.

Mary set down the washcloth and put one hand on each of Bandra's broad shoulders. "Bandra, what happened?"

"I was trying to remove the scab," said Bandra softly. "I thought maybe I could cover the bruise, and you wouldn't notice, but . . ." She sniffled, and when a Neanderthal sniffled it was a loud, raucous sound.

"Who did this to you?" asked Mary.

"It doesn't matter," said Bandra.

"Of course it matters!" said Mary. "Who was it?"

Bandra rallied a little strength. "I took you into my home, Mare. You know we Barasts require very little privacy—but in this matter, I must insist upon it."

Mary felt nauseous. "Bandra, I can't stand by while you're being hurt."

Bandra picked up the washcloth and dabbed it against the side of her face a few times to see if the bleeding had stopped. It had, and she put the cloth back down. Mary led her out into the living room and got her to sit down on the couch. Mary sat next to her, took both of Bandra's large hands, and looked into her wheat-colored eyes. "Take your time," said Mary, "but you must tell me what happened."

Bandra looked away. "It had been three months since he'd done it, so I thought he wouldn't do it this time. I thought maybe . . ."

"Bandra, who hurt you?"

Bandra's voice was almost inaudible, but Christine repeated the word loud enough for Mary to hear. "Harb."

"Harb?" said Mary, startled. "Your man-mate?"

Bandra moved her head up and down a few millimeters. "My . . . God," said Mary. She took a deep breath, then nodded, as much to herself as to Bandra. "All right," she said. "This is what we're going to do: we'll go to the authorities and report him."

"*Tant*," said Bandra. *No.*

"Yes," said Mary firmly. "This sort of thing happens on my world, too. But you don't have to put up with it. We can get you help."

"*Tant!*" said Bandra, more firmly.

"I know it will be difficult," said Mary, "but we'll go to the authorities together. I'll be with you every step of the way. We'll put an end to this." She gestured at Bandra's Companion. "There has to be a recording of what he did at the alibi archives, right? He can't possibly get away with it."

"I will not make an accusation against him. Without a victim's accusation, no crime has been committed. That's the law."

"I know you think you love him, but you don't have to stand for this. No woman does."

"I don't love him," said Bandra. "*I hate him.*"

"All right, then," said Mary. "Let's do something about it. Come on, we'll get you cleaned up and into some fresh clothes, and we'll go see an adjudicator."

"*Tant!*" said Bandra, slapping the flat of her hand against the table in front of her. It made such a loud sound, Mary thought the table was going to splinter into kindling. "*Tant!*" Bandra said again. But her tone wasn't one of fear; rather, it was filled with conviction.

"But why not? Bandra, if you think it's your duty to put up with—"

"You know *nothing* of our world," said Bandra. "*Nothing.* I can't go to an adjudicator with this."

"Why not? Surely assault is a crime here, no?"

"Of course," said Bandra.

"Even between those who are bonded, no?"

Bandra nodded.

"Then why not?"

"*Because of our children!*" snapped Bandra. "Because of Hapnar and Dranna."

"What about them?" asked Mary. "Will Harb go after them, too? Was—was he an abusive father?"

"You see!" crowed Bandra. "You understand nothing."

"Then *make* me understand, Bandra. Make me understand, or I will go to the adjudicator myself."

"What is it to you?" asked Bandra.

Mary was taken aback by the question. Surely it was *every* woman's business. Surely . . .

And then it hit her, like a meteor crashing from above. She hadn't reported her own rape, and her department head, Qaiser Remtulla, had gone on to be Cornelius Ruskin's next victim. She wanted to make up for that somehow, wanted to never again feel guilty about letting a crime against a woman go unreported.

"I'm just trying to help," said Mary. "I care about you."

"If you care, you will forget you ever saw me like this."

"But—"

"You must promise! You must promise me."

"But why, Bandra? You can't let this go on."

"I *have* to let this go on!" She clenched her massive fists and closed her eyes. "I have to let this go on."

"Why? For God's sake, Bandra . . ."

"It has nothing to do with your silly God," said Bandra. "It has to do with reality."

"What reality?"

Bandra looked away again, took a deep breath, then let it out. "The reality of our laws," she said at last.

"What do you mean? Won't they punish him for something like this?"

"Oh, yes," said Bandra bitterly. "Yes, indeed."

"Well, then?"

"Do you know what the punishment will be?" asked Bandra. "You are involved with Ponter Boddit. What punishment was threatened against his man-mate Adikor when Adikor was falsely accused of murdering Ponter?"

"They would have sterilized Adikor," said Mary. "But Adikor didn't deserve that, because he didn't do anything. But Harb—"

"Do you think I care what happens to him?" said Bandra. "But they won't just sterilize Harb. Violence can't be tolerated in the gene pool. They will also sterilize everyone who shares fifty percent of his genetic material."

"Oh, Christ," said Mary softly. "Your daughters . . ."

"Exactly! Generation 149 will be conceived soon. My Hapnar will conceive her second child then, and my Dranna will conceive her first. But if I report Harb's behavior . . ."

Mary felt like she'd been hit in the stomach. If Bandra reported Harb's behavior, her daughters would be sterilized, as, she supposed, would any siblings Harb had, and his parents, if they were still alive . . . although she supposed Harb's mother might be spared, since she was presumably postmenopausal. "I didn't think Neanderthal men were like that," she said softly. "I am so sorry, Bandra."

Bandra lifted her massive shoulders a bit. "I've carried this burden for a long time. I'm used to it. And . . ."

"Yes?"

"And I thought it was over. He hadn't hit me since my woman-mate left. But . . ."

"They never stop," said Mary. "Not for good." She could

taste acid at the back of her throat. "There must be something you can do." She paused, then: "Surely you can defend yourself. Surely that is legal. You could . . ."

"What?"

Mary looked at the moss-covered floor. "A Neanderthal can kill another Neanderthal with one well-placed punch."

"Yes, indeed!" said Bandra. "Yes, indeed. So you see, he must love me—for if he did not, I would be dead."

"Hitting is no way to show love," said Mary, "but hitting back—hard—may be your only choice."

"I can't do that," said Bandra. "If the decision was taken that I hadn't needed to kill him, a violence judgment would be brought against me, and again my daughters would suffer, for they share half my genes as well."

"A goddamned catch-22," said Mary. She looked at Bandra. "Do you know that phrase?"

Bandra nodded. "A situation with no way out. But you're wrong, Mare. There *is* a way out. Eventually I, or Harb, will die. Until then . . ." She lifted her hands, unclenched her fists, and turned her palms up in a gesture of futility.

"But why don't you just divorce him, or whatever you call it here? That's supposed to be easy."

"The legalities of what you call divorce are easy, but people still gossip, they still wonder. If I were to dissolve my union with Harb, people would question me and him about it. The truth might come out, and again my daughters would be at risk of sterilization." She shook her head. "No, no, this way is better."

Mary opened her arms and took Bandra into them, holding her, stroking her silver and orange hair.

Chapter Twenty-seven

"It is time, my fellow Homo sapiens, *that we go to Mars . . ."*

This has to be absolutely galling for him, thought Ponter Boddit, who was enjoying every beat of Councilor Bedros's discomfort.

After all, it was Bedros who had ordered him and Ambassador Tukana Prat to return from Mare's version of Earth as a prelude to shutting down the interuniversal portal. But not only had Ponter refused to return, Tukana Prat had convinced ten eminent Neanderthals—including Lonwis Trob—to cross over to the other reality.

And now Bedros had to greet the Gliksin contingent from that world. Ponter had been on hand down in the quantum-computing chamber as the delegates came through; it wouldn't do if the closest thing the fractious Gliksins had to a world leader was cut in two by the portal flickering closed as he was walking down the Derkers tube.

Bedros hadn't gone down into the depths of the Debral nickel mine today. Instead, he'd waited up on the surface for the amanuensis-high-warrior and the other United Nations officials to come up.

Which was what they had just done. It had taken two trips in the circular mineshaft elevator to get them all topside, but

now they were here. Four silver-clad Exhibitionists were on
hand as well, letting the public watch what was unfolding.
The dark-skinned United Nations leader had come out of
the elevator house first, followed by Ponter, then three men
and two women with lighter skin, and then Jock Krieger, the
tallest member of the group.

"Welcome to Jantar," said Bedros. He'd obviously in-
structed his Companion not to translate the Barast name for
their planet. For their part, the seven Gliksins had no Companions, not even temporary strap-on units. Apparently,
there had been much debate about this, but that same bizarre "diplomatic immunity" Ponter had encountered before
had led to them being exempted from having everything
they said and did recorded at the alibi archives. Actually, if
Ponter understood matters correctly, Jock really wasn't entitled to this special treatment, but nonetheless he also wasn't
wearing a Companion.

"It is with great hopes for the future that we welcome
you here," continued Bedros. Ponter fought hard to suppress
a smirk; Bedros had had to be coached by Tukana Prat—the
ambassador who had flouted his authority—in what constituted an appropriate speech by Gliksin standards. He went
on for what seemed like daytenths, and the amanuensis-high-
warrior responded in kind.

Jock Krieger must have been a Barast at heart, thought
Ponter. While the other Gliksins seemed to be enjoying the
pomp, he was clearly ignoring it, looking around at the trees
and hills, at every bird that flew by, at the blue sky overhead.

Finally, the speechmaking was over. Ponter sidled up to
Jock, who was wearing a long beige coat tied at the waist by
a beige sash, leather gloves, and a brimmed cap; the Gliksin
contingent had waited down in the mine while their clothes

were decontaminated. "Well, what do you think of our world?"

Jock shook his head slowly back and forth, and his voice was full of wonder. "It's *beautiful*..."

The Voyeur in Bandra's house was attached to the living-room wall, its surface gently following the curvature of the round room. The big square was divided into four smaller squares, each showing the perspective of one of the four Exhibitionists on hand at the Debral nickel mine as the delegation from the United Nations emerged. Bandra was in no shape to be seen in public today, and Mary and she stayed home, ostensibly to watch the arrival of other Gliksins on the Voyeur.

"Oh, look!" said Bandra. "There's Ponter!"

Mary had been hoping to catch a glimpse of him—and, unfortunately, that seemed to be all she was going to get. The Exhibitionists weren't interested in a fellow Barast. Their attention was on the group of Gliksins.

"So, who is who?" asked Bandra.

"That man there"—she had the usual Canadian fear of being thought a racist that prevented her from saying "the black man" or "the man with the dark skin," even though that was the most obvious difference between Kofi Annan and the rest of the group—"is the secretary-general of the United Nations."

"Which one?"

"That one. On the left, there."

"The one with brown skin?"

"Um, yes."

"So, he's your world's leader?"

"Well, no. No, not really. But he *is* the highest official at the UN."

"Ah. And who is that tall one?"

"That's Jock Krieger. He's my boss."

"He has—he looks . . . predatory."

Mary considered this. She supposed Bandra was right. "A lean and hungry look."

"Ooooh!" said Bandra, delighted. "Is that a saying?"

"It's a line from a play."

"Well, it fits him." She nodded decisively. "I don't like his bearing. There is no joy in his expression." But then Bandra seemed to realize that she might be giving offense. "I'm sorry! I shouldn't speak that way about your friend."

"He's not my friend," said Mary. She adhered to the rule of thumb that a friend was someone to whose home you had been, or who had been to your home. "We just work together."

"And look!" said Bandra. "He's not wearing a Companion!"

Mary peered at the screen. "So he isn't." She surveyed other parts of the four images. "None of the Gliksins are."

"How can that be?"

Mary frowned. "Diplomatic immunity, I guess. Which means . . ."

"Yes?"

Mary's heart was pounding. "It usually means a diplomat can travel without having his luggage examined. If I can get the codon writer to Jock, he should be able to take it back to my world without difficulty."

"Perfect," said Bandra. "Oh, look! There's Ponter again!"

The flight from Saldak to Donakat Island took two daytenths, which, Ponter knew, was much longer than the comparable journey would have taken in Mare's world. He spent most of it thinking about Mare and about Vissan's device that would let them conceive a baby, but Jock, who was sitting next to Ponter in the wide cabin of the helicopter, interrupted his reverie at one point. "You never developed airplanes?" he said.

"No," said Ponter. "I have wondered about that myself. Certainly, many of my people have been fascinated by birds and flight, but I have seen the long—'landing strips,' do you call them?"

Jock nodded.

"I have seen the long landing strips that your airplanes require. I think only a species that was already used to clearing large tracts of land for farming would have considered it natural to do the same for runways, or even roadways."

"I never thought about it that way," said Jock.

"Well," continued Ponter, "we certainly do not have roads the way you do. Most of us are—how would you put it? stay-at-home types. We do not travel much, and we prefer to have food right outside our doors."

Jock looked around the helicopter. "Still, this is very comfortable. Lots of room between seats. We tend to cram people into planes—and trains and buses, too, for that matter."

"Comfort is not the specific goal," said Ponter. "Rather, it is to keep other people's pheromones out of one's nose. I have found it very difficult flying on your big airplanes, especially with the pressurized cabins. One of the reasons we do not fly nearly as high as you do is so that our cabins do not have to be sealed; we bring in fresh air constantly to avoid the build up of pheromones, and—" Ponter stopped talking, and tipped his head. "Ah, thank you, Hak." He looked at Jock. "I had asked Hak to let me know when we were passing over the spot that corresponds to Rochester,

New York. If you look out the window now . . ."

Jock pressed his face up against a square of glass. Ponter moved over and looked through another window. He could see the south shoreline of what he knew Jock called Lake Ontario.

"It's just forest," said Jock, astonished, turning back to Ponter.

Ponter nodded. "There are some hunting lodges, but no large-scale habitation."

"It's hard to even recognize the geography without the roads."

"We will pass over one of the Finger Lakes shortly—our name for them is the same as yours; the imagery is obvious. You should have no trouble recognizing them."

Jock looked out the window again, mesmerized.

The Exhibitionists didn't get to fly south with the contingent from the United Nations, although Bandra said there would be others on hand when they arrived at Donakat Island. In the interim, Bandra told the Voyeur to shut off, and it did so. She then turned to Mary. "We didn't speak much last night about . . . about my problem with Harb."

Mary nodded. "Is that—is that why your woman-mate left?"

Bandra got up and tipped her head back, looking at the ceiling. Hundreds of birds were painted on it, representing dozens of species; each meticulously rendered by her. "Yes. She could not take seeing what he did to me. But . . . but in a way, it's better that she's gone."

"Why?"

"It's easier to hide one's shame when no one else is around."

Mary got up and put an arm on each of Bandra's shoulders and stepped back a pace so that she could look her full in the face. "Listen to me, Bandra. You've got nothing to be ashamed of. You've done nothing wrong."

Bandra managed a small nod. "I know, but . . ."

"But *nothing*. We will find a way out of this."

"There is no way," said Bandra, and she moved a hand up to wipe her eyes.

"There *must* be," said Mary. "And we'll find it. Together."

"You don't have to do this," said Bandra softly, shaking her head.

"Yes, I do," said Mary.

"Why?"

Mary shrugged a little. "Let's just say I owe womankind one."

"And here we are, ladies and gentleman," said Councilor Bedros. "Donakat Island—what you call Manhattan."

Jock couldn't believe what he was seeing. He knew New York like the back of his hand—but this!

This was *gorgeous*.

They were flying over the South Bronx—except that it was old-growth forest, walnut, cedar, chestnut, maple, and oak, the leaves afire with autumn colors.

"Look!" shouted Kofi Annan. "Rikers Island!"

And indeed it was, *sans* penal colony, of course, and only a third the size of the artificially expanded island Jock knew. As the chopper went over it, Jock saw that there was no bridge leading south to Queens. Nor, of course, was there any airport off to the left, where LaGuardia was in his world. Instead, there was a harbor there. Jock was taken aback when he spotted what looked like an aircraft carrier—he hadn't thought the Neanderthals had such things. He hated encouraging the Neanderthal next to him to begin his endless chatting again, but he had to know. "What's that?"

"A ship," said Ponter in a tone that made it sound as though the answer were obvious.

"I know it's a ship," replied Jock, miffed. "But why does it have that wide, flat top?"

"Those are solar collectors," said Ponter, "to power its turbines."

The pilot had clearly been told to meander in, giving them the grand tour. They were flying west now, over Wards Island, which was dotted around its periphery with buildings that looked like cottages.

The helicopter continued on. It was as if Central Park had expanded right across the width of Manhattan, from East River Drive to Henry Hudson Parkway.

"Donakat Island makes up the 'Center' of the city we call Pepraldak," said Ponter. "In other words, it's female territory. In Saldak, there are many kilometers of countryside separating the Rim from the Center. Pepraldak's 'Rim' and 'Center' are simply separated by what you call the Hudson River."

"So the men live in New Jersey?"

Ponter nodded.

"How do they get across? I don't see any bridges."

"Travel cubes can fly over water," said Ponter, "so they use those in summer. In winter, the river freezes, and they simply walk over."

"The Hudson River doesn't freeze over."

Ponter shrugged. "It does in this world. Your activities modify your climate more than you think."

The chopper had now turned south, and was flying along the river. They quickly came to a slight jog in its course, meaning they must now be passing the untamed wilderness of Hoboken. Jock looked out to the left. The island was there, all right: hilly—didn't Manhattan mean "Island of Hills"?—dotted with lakes . . . and utterly devoid of skyscrapers. There were clearings containing brick buildings, but none taller than four stories. Jock turned his attention back to the right side. What would have been Liberty State Park was all forest. Ellis Island was there, as was Liberty Island, but of course there was no statue on it. That was just as well, thought Jock; he didn't really want to see a 150-foot-tall Neanderthal, although—

Jock could hear shouts going up from those around him as others spotted the same thing he just had. There were two right whales in Upper New York Bay; they must have swum up The Narrows from the Atlantic. Each was about forty feet long, with a dark gray back.

The chopper turned east, flying over water between Governors Island and Battery Park, then heading along the East River. Jock could see hundreds of arboriculture houses along the shoreline, and—"What's that?"

"An observatory," said Ponter. "I know you put your big telescopes in hemispherical enclosures, but we prefer these cubic structures." Jock shook his head. Imagine it ever being dark enough in Greenwich Village to look at the stars!

"Is there much wildlife?" asked Jock.

"Oh, yes. Beavers, bears, wolves, foxes, raccoons, deer, otters—not to mention quail, partridge, swans, geese, turkeys, and of course millions of passenger pigeons." Ponter paused. "It's too bad it's autumn; in the spring, you'd see roses and many other wildflowers."

The chopper was quite low now as it continued up the East River, the blue waters roiling in the downdraft from the blades. They came to where the river bent to the north, and the pilot continued to follow its course for another couple of miles then brought the craft in for a landing on a wide open field of tall grass, surrounded by orchards of apple and pear trees. Councilor Bedros got out first, then Ponter and Adikor, then the secretary-general. Jock followed him, and the rest of the group followed Jock. The air was sweet and clean, crisp and cool; the sky overhead was a blue Jock knew from Arizona summers, but had never seen in the Big Apple.

A contingent of local female officials and two local silver-clad Exhibitionists were on hand, and again speeches were made, including remarks by a woman introduced as the president of the local Gray Council. She was, Jock guessed, about his own age—which would make her what? Part of generation 142, he supposed. She had shaved off all her head hair except for a long silver ponytail protruding directly from her occipital bun; Jock thought she looked repellent, even for a Neanderthal.

She concluded her remarks by mentioning the meal they were going to enjoy later that day, with huge oysters and even huger lobsters. Then she called on Ponter Boddit to say some more.

"Thank you," said Ponter, moving out to stand in front of everyone. Jock was having a bit of trouble hearing him; the Neanderthals had no notion of microphone stands or loudspeakers for speeches, since voices were picked up by and relayed to Companions without any such extra equipment.

"We have worked hard," continued Ponter, "to try to find the exact spot on our version of Earth that corresponds to the location of your United Nations headquarters. As you know, we do not have satellites—and so we do not have anything as good as your global positioning system. Our surveyors are still arguing among themselves—we might be off by several tens of meters, although we are hoping to resolve that issue. Still . . ." He turned and pointed. "See those trees there? We believe that they mark the location of the main entrance to the Secretariat building." He turned. "And that swamp, over there? That is where the General Assembly is located."

Jock looked on in amazement. This was New York City—without the millions of people, without the air that made your eyes sting, without the bumper-to-bumper traffic, the thousands of taxis, the jostling crowds, the stench, the noise. This was Manhattan . . . as it had been only a few hundred years ago, as it had been back in 1626 when Peter Minuit bought it from the Indians for $24, as it had been before it had been paved over and built up and polluted.

The others in the delegation were chatting among themselves; those who were speaking English seemed to be echoing Jock's thoughts.

Ponter began walking, heading toward the shore of the East River. It was closer than it should have been—but, then again, much of modern Manhattan was recovered land. The Neanderthal knelt by the shore and dipped curved hands into the river, splashing water repeatedly against his broad face.

Jock noted that a few of the others wore bland expressions, the significance lost on them. But it wasn't lost on him.

Ponter Boddit had just washed his face with raw, untreated, unprocessed, unfiltered, *unpolluted* water from the East River.

Jock shook his head, hating what his people had done to their world, and wishing there was some way they could start over, with a fresh, clean slate.

Chapter Twenty-eight

"I believe we, the humans of this Earth, should commit our-selves, before another decade has gone by, to launching an international team of women and men to the red planet . . ."

Mary and Bandra had watched the transmissions from the Exhibitionists on Donakat Island. It was fun seeing Ponter on what amounted to Neanderthal TV, and certainly the project to establish another portal was fascinating.

Ponter had spent some time describing the difficulties with building a portal on the surface; his original quantum computer had been buried deep underground to shield it from solar radiation that might promote decoherence of the quantum registers. But even when Ponter and Adikor had made their breakthrough—literally breaking through into another universe—a second group of Barast researchers in Europe had been attempting to factor similarly large numbers. The members of that team had been female, and they apparently were *en route* to Donakat by ocean ship to provide their expertise in shielding techniques.

"It looks like you've got yourself a good man there," said Bandra.

Mary smiled. "Thanks."

"How long have you known him?"

Mary looked away from Bandra's wheat-colored eyes. "Only since August 3rd."

Bandra tipped her head, listening to her own Companion translate the date. Mary thought Bandra was going to say something scolding about how short a period of time it was; after all, Mary had never lost an opportunity to tell her sister Christine that she was moving too fast, falling head over heels for one "real find" after another. But instead Bandra said, "You are very lucky to have found him."

Mary nodded. She *was* lucky. And, besides, she knew lots of people who had had whirlwind romances before. Yes, she'd known Colm a lot longer than she'd known Ponter by the time Colm proposed and she accepted, but she'd had doubts back then.

She had no doubts now.

When something felt this right, there was no reason to delay.

"*Carpe diem,*" said Mary.

Bandra's translator bleeped.

"Sorry," said Mary. "That's Latin—another language. It means 'seize the day.' Don't spend your whole life fretting; just grab the moment, and go for it."

"A good philosophy," said Bandra. She got up from the couch. "We should attend to the evening meal."

Mary nodded, rose, and followed Bandra into the food-preparation area. Bandra had a large vacuum box that stored food without refrigeration, and a laser cooker, which employed the same sort of tunable-laser technology used in the decontamination chambers.

The top of the vacuum box had a square screen set into it, displaying an inventory of the contents so that the seal didn't have to be broken to determine what was inside. "Mammoth?" said Bandra, looking at the list.

"My goodness, yes!" said Mary. "I've been dying to try some."

Bandra smiled, opened the vacuum box—which hissed when she did so—and selected a pair of chops. She transferred them to the laser cooker and spoke some instructions to it.

"It must be hard, hunting mammoth," said Mary.

"I've never done it myself," replied Bandra. "Those whose contribution it is to do so say there's a simple technique." She shrugged a little. "But, as you would say, the putative evil one lurks in minutiae."

Mary blinked, trying to decipher Christine's translation of what Bandra had just said. " 'The devil is in the details,' you mean."

"Exactamundo!" said Bandra.

Mary laughed. "I'm going to miss you when I leave."

Bandra smiled. "I'm going to miss you, too. Whenever you need a place to stay in this world, you're welcome here."

"Thank you, but . . ."

Bandra raised one of her large hands. "Oh, I know. You only plan to come to visit when Two are One, and then you'll be spending time with Ponter. And I will . . ."

"I'm so sorry, Bandra. There must be something we can do."

"Let's not dwell on it. Let's just enjoy the time we've got before you have to leave."

"*Carpe diem?*" said Mary.

Bandra smiled. "Exactamundo."

———

The dinner was excellent; mammoth had a rich, complex flavor, and the maple-sugar salad dressing Bandra prepared was to-die-for.

Mary leaned back in the saddle-seat and sighed contentedly. "It's a pity you people don't have wine."

"Wine," repeated Bandra. "What is that?"

"A beverage. Alcohol. Fermented grapes."

"Is it delicious?"

"Well, um, that's not the point—or, at least, it's only *part* of the point. Alcohol affects the central nervous system, at least in Gliksins. It makes us feel mellow, relaxed."

"I am relaxed," said Bandra.

Mary smiled. "Actually, so am I."

The Globe and Mail Ponter had brought Mary had reported the results of a study to determine the funniest joke in the world. That didn't mean the one that made people laugh the hardest—it wasn't an attempt to replicate Monty Python's secret-weapon joke, which would cause anyone who heard it to die laughing. Rather, it was a project to find a joke that cut across cultural lines so that almost all human beings found it funny.

Mary decided to try it out on Bandra; since it happened to be a hunting joke, she thought the Neanderthal might enjoy it. She slipped a few appropriate references into their conversation, so that Bandra would have the required background, and then, around 9:00 P.M.—late in the sixth daytenth—she trotted it out:

"Okay, okay. So, there are these two guys, see, and they're out hunting, right? And one of them suddenly collapses—just falls to the ground. He doesn't seem to be breathing, and his eyes are glazed over. So the other guy, he calls 9-1-1. That's our emergency telephone number, since we don't have Companions. And the guy—he's on a cell phone, see?—he's all panicky, and he says, 'Hey, I'm out here hunting with my friend Bob, and he just keeled over. I'm afraid he's dead. What should I do? What should I do?'

"And the emergency operator says, 'Calm down, sir. Take a deep breath; let's take this one step at a time. First, let's make sure that Bob is really dead.'

"So the guy says, 'Okay,' and the operator hears him put down the phone and walk away. And then—*blam!*—there's a gunshot. And the guy comes back on the phone and says, 'Okay. Now what?' "

Bandra exploded with laughter. She'd been drinking pine tea; the way the Neanderthal throat was hooked up prevented it from spurting out her nostrils, but if she'd been a Gliksin, doubtless it would have, given how hard she was laughing. "That's *awful!*" she declared, wiping away tears.

Mary was grinning, probably wide enough to rival Ponter. "Isn't it, though?"

They spent the rest of the evening talking about their families, telling jokes, listening to recorded Neanderthal music pumped simultaneously into their cochlear implants, and just generally having a wonderful time. Mary had had several close female friends before she'd married Colm, but had drifted away from all of them during the marriage, and hadn't really acquired any new ones since the split. One of the nice things about the Neanderthal system, Mary mused, was that it would leave plenty of time for her friendships with other women.

And, despite them coming literally from different worlds, Bandra was certainly the kind of friend she would choose: warm, witty, giving, and brilliant—someone she could share a silly joke with, as well as discuss the latest breakthroughs in science.

After a bit, Bandra brought out a *partanlar* set—the same game Mary had played with Ponter. Ponter's board had been made of polished wood, with the alternating squares stained either light or dark. As befitted a geologist, Bandra's was made of polished stone, the squares black or white.

"Oh, good!" said Mary. "I know this game! Ponter taught me."

In chess and checkers, players sat opposite each other, each trying to move their armies of pieces toward the other's side of the board. But *partanlar* didn't have that directionality of play—there was no advancing or retreating. And so Bandra set the board up on a little table in front of one of the couches, and then sat on the couch, leaving plenty of room for Mary to sit beside her.

They played for about an hour—but it was the pleasant something-to-do kind of play that Mary liked, not the competitive let's-see-who's-better competition Colm favored. Neither Mary nor Bandra really seemed to care who won, and they each took delight in the other's clever moves.

"It's fun having you around," said Bandra.

"It's fun being here," said Mary.

"You know," Bandra said, "there are those of my kind who don't approve of the contact between our worlds. Councilor Bedros—remember him from the Voyeur?—is one such. But even if there are—another phrase of yours I like—even if there are a few bad apples, they do not spoil the bunch. He is wrong, Mare. He is wrong about your people. You are proof of that."

Mary smiled again. "Thank you."

Bandra hesitated for a long moment, her eyes shifting from Mary's left to her right and back again. And then she leaned in and made a long, slow lick up Mary's left cheek.

Mary felt her entire spine tighten. "Bandra . . ."

Bandra dropped her gaze to the floor. "I'm sorry . . ." she said softly. "I know it's not your way . . ."

Mary placed her hand under Bandra's long jaw, and slowly lifted her face until she was facing Mary.

"No," Mary said. "It's not." She looked into Bandra's wheat-colored eyes. Her heart was racing.

Carpe diem.

Mary leaned in closer, and, as she brought her lips into contact with Bandra's, she said, "This is."

Chapter Twenty-nine

"And although our Neanderthal cousins will be welcome to join us in this grand Mars adventure, should they so choose, it is something it seems few of them will desire..."

Cornelius Ruskin knocked on the office door. "Come in," called the familiar female voice with its slight Pakistani accent.

Cornelius took a deep breath, then opened the door. "Hi, Qaiser," he said, waking into the office.

Professor Qaiser Remtulla's metal desk was at right angles to the doorway, the long edge against one wall, the left short edge underneath her window. She was wearing a dark green jacket and black pants. "Cornelius!" she declared. "We were getting quite worried about you."

Cornelius couldn't manage a smile, but he did say, "That's very kind."

But Qaiser's round face creased into a small frown. "I wish you'd called to let me know you'd be in today, though. Dave Olsen has already come in to teach your afternoon class."

Cornelius shook his head a bit. "That's fine. In fact, that's what I want to talk to you about."

Qaiser did what just about every academic has to do when a visitor comes: she got up from her own swivel chair and took the pile of books and papers off the one other chair in the room. In her case, it was a metal-framed stacking chair with orange vinyl cushions. "Have a seat," she said.

Cornelius did just that, crossing his legs at the ankles and—

He shook his head again, wondering if he'd ever get used to the sensation. He'd spent his whole life subtly aware of the pressure on his testicles whenever he sat like this, but there was no such feeling anymore.

"What can I do for you?" prodded Qaiser.

Cornelius looked at her face: brown eyes, brown skin, brown hair, a trio of chocolate shades. She looked to be about forty-five, ten years older than he was. He'd seen her crying in anguish, seen her begging him not to hurt her. He didn't regret it; she *had* deserved it, but . . .

But.

"Qaiser," he said, "I'd like to take a leave of absence."

"There are no paid leaves for sessional instructors," she replied.

Cornelius nodded. "I know that. I—" He'd rehearsed all this, but now hesitated, wondering if it was really the right approach. "You know I've been sick. My doctor says I should take a . . . a rest leave. You know, some time off."

Qaiser's features shifted to concern. "Is it something serious? Is there anything I can do to help?"

Cornelius shook his head. "No, I'll be fine, I'm sure. But I—I just don't feel up to being in the classroom anymore."

"Well, the Christmas break is coming up in a few weeks. If you could just stick it out until then . . ."

"I'm sorry, Qaiser. I really don't think I should."

Qaiser frowned. "You know we're shorthanded as is, what with Mary Vaughan having left."

Cornelius nodded but didn't say anything.

"I have to ask," said Qaiser. "This is a genetics department, after all. There are lots of things here that potentially could have made you sick, and . . . well, I have to worry about the health of the students and the faculty. Is your problem related to any chemicals or specimens you encountered here?"

Cornelius shook his head again. "No. No, it's nothing like that." He took a deep breath. "But I can't stay here any longer."

"Why not?"

"Because . . ." A few weeks ago, he'd have been unable to discuss this topic without getting apoplectic, but now . . .

He shrugged a bit.

"Because you've won."

Qaiser's eyebrows pulled together. "Pardon?"

"You've won. The system here—it's won. It's beaten me."

"What system?"

"Oh, come on! The hiring system, the promotion system, the tenure system. There's no place for a white man."

Qaiser apparently couldn't meet his eyes. "It's been a difficult issue for the university," said Qaiser. "For *all* universities. But you know, despite the presence of me and a few others, the genetics department is still way below the university's guidelines in terms of number of tenure-stream positions held by women."

"You're supposed to have forty percent," said Cornelius.

"Right, and we're nowhere near that—not yet." Qaiser's voice took on a defensive note. "But, look, even so, it should be half, and—"

"Half," repeated Cornelius; he said it so calmly it surprised him, and apparently surprised Qaiser, too, since she immediately stopped talking. "Even when only twenty percent of the applicants are female?"

"Well, all right, then—but, anyway, the target isn't half. It's just forty percent."

"How many tenured or tenure-track positions are there in this department?"

"Fifteen."

"And how many are held by females?"

"Currently? Counting Mary?"

"Of course counting Mary."

"Three."

Cornelius nodded. He'd gotten back at two of them; the third was in a wheelchair, and Cornelius hadn't been able to bring himself to . . .

"So the next three tenure-track openings have to go to women, don't they?" he said.

"Well, yes. Assuming they're qualified."

Cornelius surprised himself; those last three words would have set him off before. But now . . .

"And if Mary's leave turns out to be permanent," he said, his tone still even, "as it probably will, you'll have to replace her with a woman, too, right?"

Qaiser nodded, but she still wasn't meeting his eyes.

"So the next *four* tenure-track appointments have to go to women." He stopped himself—rather more easily than he'd expected to be able to do so—before adding, "Preferably crippled black ones."

Qaiser nodded again.

"How often does a tenure-track position open up?" he asked, as if he himself didn't already know the answer.

"It depends on when people retire, or move on to other things."

Cornelius waited, saying nothing.

"Every couple of years or so," Qaiser finally replied.

"More like three years, on average," said Cornelius. "Trust

me; I've done the math. Meaning it'll be twelve years before you're looking for a male, and even then it'll be a disabled or minority male, isn't that right?"

"Well . . ."

"Isn't that right?"

But there was no need for Qaiser to reply; Cornelius had read the relevant part of the collective agreement between the Faculty Association and the Board of Governors so often he could recite it from memory, despite the awkward bureaucratic phrasing:

(i) In units where fewer than 40% of the tenure stream faculty/librarian positions are filled by women, when candidates' qualifications are substantially equal the candidate who is a member of a visible/racial minority, an aboriginal person or a person with a disability and female shall be recommended for appointment.

(ii) If there is no candidate recommended from (i) above then when candidates' qualifications are substantially equal a candidate who is female or who is a male and a member of a visible/racial minority, an aboriginal person, or a person with a disability shall be recommended for appointment.

If there is no candidate recommended from (i) or (ii) above then the candidate who is male shall be recommended for appointment.

"Cornelius, I'm sorry," said Qaiser, at last.

"*Everybody* is in line in front of an able-bodied white male."

"It's only because . . ."

Qaiser trailed off, and Cornelius fixed her with a steady gaze. "Yes?" he said.

She actually squirmed a bit. "It's only because able-bodied white males cut to the front of the line so often in the past."

Cornelius remembered the last time someone had said that to him—a bleeding-heart liberal white guy at a party, last spring. He'd jumped down the guy's throat, and practically tore out his lungs, saying he shouldn't be punished for the actions of his ancestors, and just . . .

He realized it now.

Just basically making an ass of himself. He'd left the party in a huff.

"Perhaps you're right," said Cornelius. "In any event, what's that old prayer? 'God, grant me the serenity to accept the things I cannot change, courage to change the things I can, and the wisdom to know the difference.' " He paused. "In this case, I do know the difference."

"I'm sorry, Cornelius," said Qaiser.

"And so, I should leave." *Take my balls and go home*, he thought—but, of course, he couldn't do that anymore.

"Most universities have similar affirmative-action programs, you know. Where would you go?"

"Private industry, maybe. I love to teach, but . . ."

Qaiser nodded. "Biotech is superhot, right now. Lots of job openings, and . . ."

"And since biotech is mostly an industry of start-ups, no historical imbalances to correct," said Cornelius, his tone even.

"Say," said Qaiser, "you know what you should do? Go to the Synergy Group!"

"What's that?"

"It's the U.S.-government think tank devoted to Neanderthal studies. They're the group that hired Mary Vaughan away."

Cornelius was about to dismiss the notion—working with Mary now would be as difficult as working with Qaiser—but Qaiser continued: "I heard they offered Mary a hundred and fifty grand U.S."

Cornelius felt his jaw dropping. That was—Christ, that was close to a quarter of a million dollars a year Canadian. It was indeed the kind of money a guy like him, with a Ph.D. from Oxford, should be pulling down!

Still . . . "I don't want to muscle in on Mary's turf," he said.

"Oh, you wouldn't be doing that," said Qaiser. "In fact, I hear she's left Synergy. Daria Klein had an e-mail from her a while ago. She's apparently gone native—moved permanently over to the Neanderthal world."

"Permanently?"

Qaiser nodded. "That's what I heard."

Cornelius frowned. "I suppose it couldn't hurt to apply there, then . . ."

"Absolutely!" said Qaiser, apparently eager to do something for Cornelius. "Look, let me write you a letter of reference. I bet they'll need another DNA expert there to replace Mary. Your graduate work was at Oxford's Ancient Biomolecules Centre, right? You'd be a perfect fit."

Cornelius considered. He'd done what he'd done in the first place because of frustration over his stalled career. It would be a nice bit of closure to have that ultimately lead to him getting the kind of job he deserved. "Thank you, Qaiser," he said, smiling at her. "Thank you very much."

Chapter Thirty

"But whether the Neanderthals come with us or not to the red planet, we should adopt their view of that world's color. Mars is not a symbol of war; it is the color of health, of life—and if it is, perhaps, barren of life now, we should not let it remain so any longer . . ."

It was time for Mary to get the codon writer to Jock, so that he could take it back to . . .

Well, to where?

Mary had laughed when she'd seen Councilor Bedros on the Voyeur referring to the Barast world as "Jantar." There was no single name for the version of Earth that Mary called home. "Earth" was just the English term; it was called different things in other languages. *Terra* was the word in Latin and many of its descendants. The French—and the French-Canadians—called it *Terre*. In Esperanto, it was *Tero*. The Greek term—*Gaea*—was popular among environmentalists. Russians called it *Zemlja*; the Swedes *Jorden*. In Hebrew it was *Eretz*; in Arabic, *Ard*; in Farsi, *Zamin*; in Mandarin, *Diqiu*; and in Japanese, *Chikyuu*. The most beautiful of the lot, thought Mary, was the Tahitian, *Vuravura*. Ponter simply called it "Mare's world," but Mary doubted that was going to catch on in general use.

In any event, Mary now had to get the codon writer to Jock so that he could take it safely back to . . . to Gliksinia.

Gliksinia? No, too harsh. How about Sapientia? Or—

The travel cube Mary had called for arrived, and she clambered into one of the two rear seats. "The Debral nickel mine," said Mary.

The driver gave her a cool look. "Going home?"

"Not me," said Mary. "But somebody else is."

Mary's heart leaped when she caught sight of Ponter, part of the group returning from Donakat Island. But she had promised herself she would behave like a proper native of this world, and not run into his arms. After all, Two were not One!

Still, when no one else was looking, she blew him a kiss, and he smiled broadly back at her.

But it wasn't him she'd really come to see. It was Jock Krieger. Mary sidled up to him, carrying her long wrapped package under her arm. "Beware of Gliksins bearing gifts!" she said.

"Mary!" exclaimed Jock.

Mary motioned for Jock to move out of earshot of the others. A silver-clad Exhibitionist tried to follow them, but Mary turned around and glared at him until he scuttled away.

"So," said Mary, "what do you think of this world?"

"It's *astonishing*," said Jock. "I knew in an intellectual sort of way that we'd screwed up our environment, but until I saw all this . . ." He gestured at the countryside. "It's like finding Eden."

Mary laughed. "Isn't it, though? Too bad it's already occupied, eh?"

"It is indeed," said Jock. "Are you going to come back home with us, or do you want to spend some more time in the garden?"

"Well, if it's all the same to you, I'd like to stay a few more days." She tried not to smile. "I've been making . . . great progress." She presented the package. "But I do have something I want you to take back."

"What is it?"

Mary looked left and right, then checked over her shoulder. She then looked down, just to make sure that Jock hadn't been forced to strap on a Companion. "It's a codon writer—a Barast DNA synthesizer."

"Why do you need me to take it back? Why don't you just bring it yourself when you come?"

Mary lowered her voice. "This is banned technology. I'm not really supposed to have it—no one is. But it's the most amazing thing. I've written up some notes for you about it; they're included in the package."

Jock lifted his eyebrows up toward his pompadour, clearly impressed. "Banned technology? I knew I was doing the right thing when I hired you . . ."

Suddenly Mary was awake. It took her a moment to orient herself in the darkness, to figure out where she was.

A large, warm form was sleeping quietly next to her. Ponter?

No, no. Not yet, not tonight. It was Bandra; Mary had been sharing Bandra's bed these last few nights.

Mary glanced at the ceiling. Neanderthal digits were gently glowing there, specifying the time. Mary was good at deciphering them when wide awake, but her vision was blurry right now, and it took her a few seconds—a few *beats*—to remember that she had to read them from right to left, and that a circle was the symbol for five, not zero. It was the middle of daytenth nine; a little after 3:00 A.M.

There was no point leaping out of bed, even though that's what she felt like doing. And it had nothing to do with the fact that she was sleeping next to another woman; indeed, she was surprised how easy it had been to get used to that. But the thought that had forced her awake was still in her head, burning brightly.

Occasionally she'd awoken in the middle of the night with brilliant thoughts before, only to fall back asleep and have them completely gone by morning. Indeed, many years ago she'd briefly fancied herself a poet—she and Colm had met at one of his poetry readings—and she'd kept a pad at her bedside, along with a small book-light, so that she could make notes without disturbing him. But she'd given that up soon enough, since the notes had turned out, when reviewed in the morning, to be mostly gibberish.

But *this* thought, this notion, this wonderful, wonderful idea, would still be there in the morning, of that Mary was certain. It was too important to let slip away.

She hugged herself, nestled back into the cushions, and soon was asleep, very much at peace.

The next morning Christine gently woke Mary at the agreed upon time—two-thirds of the way through the tenth daytenth. Bandra's Companion had been asked to wake her simultaneously, and did indeed seem to be doing so.

Mary smiled at Bandra. "Hey," she said, reaching out to touch the Barast woman's arm.

"Healthy day," said Bandra. She blinked a few times, still waking up. "Let me get to work on breakfast."

"Not yet," said Mary. "There's something I want to talk to you about."

They were facing each other on the bed, only a short distance between them. "What?"

"When Two were last One," said Mary, "Ponter and I had a talk about . . . about our future."

Bandra evidently detected something in Mary's tone. "Ah," she said.

"You know we had some . . . some matters to work out."

Bandra nodded.

"Ponter proposed a solution—or at least a partial solution."

"I have been dreading this moment," Bandra said softly.

"You knew that this situation could not last," said Mary. "I . . . I can't stay here forever."

"Why not?" said Bandra, her voice plaintive.

"Just yesterday, Jock—my boss—was asking me when I'm coming home. And I *do* have to go back; I still have to complete the annulment of my marriage to Colm. Besides, I . . ."

"Yes?"

Mary moved the shoulder that she wasn't leaning on. "I just can't take it—being here, in this world, with Ponter so close and yet being unable to see him."

Bandra closed her eyes. "So what are you going to do?"

"I'm going to return to my world," said Mary.

"And that's it? You're leaving Ponter? You're leaving me?"

"I'm not leaving Ponter," said Mary. "I will come back here every month, when Two become One."

"You will travel back and forth between worlds?"

"Yes. I will finish my contract at the Synergy Group, then try to get a job in Sudbury—that's where the portal is located in my world. There's a university there."

"I see," said Bandra, and Mary could hear the effort she

was making to keep her tone even. "Well, I suppose that makes sense."

Mary nodded.

"I will miss you, Mare. I will miss you greatly."

Mary touched Bandra's arm again. "This doesn't have to be goodbye," said Mary.

But Bandra shook her head. "I know what Two becoming One is like. Oh, for a few months, perhaps, you might make a token effort to see me briefly during each trip here, but you will really want to spend all your time with your man-mate." Bandra raised a hand. "And I understand that. You have a good man, a fine human being. If I had the same . . ."

"You don't need a man-mate," said Mary. "No woman, on either side of the portal, does."

Bandra's voice was soft. "But I *have* a man-mate, so for me there is no alternative."

Mary smiled. "A funny word, that: alternative." She closed her eyes briefly, remembering. "I know, in your language, it is *habadik*. But unlike some words that only translate approximately, that one is an exact counterpart: the choice between two, and only two, possibilities. I have some biologist friends who would argue that the concept of alternatives is ingrained in us because of our body form: on the one hand, you could do this; on the other hand, you could do that. An articulate octopus might have no word for the condition of having only two choices."

Bandra was staring at Mary. "What are you talking about?" she said at last, clearly exasperated.

"I'm talking about the fact that there are other possibilities for you."

"I will do nothing to jeopardize my daughters' ability to reproduce."

"I know that," said Mary. "Believe me, that's the last thing I would want."

"Then what?"

Mary pushed herself forward on the cushions, closing the distance between her and Bandra, and she kissed Bandra full on the lips. "Come with me," said Mary, when she was done.

"*What?*"

"Come with me, to the other side. To my world. To Sudbury."

"How would that solve my problem?"

"You would stay in my world when Two become One. You would never have to see Harb again."

"But my daughters . . ."

"Are just that: *daughters*. They will always live in the City Center. They will be safe from him."

"But I would die if I could never see them again."

"So come back when Two are separate. Come back when there is no chance of you seeing Harb. Come back and visit your daughters—and their children—as often as you wish."

Bandra was clearly trying to take it all in. "You mean you and I would both *commute* between the two worlds, but we would each come back here at different times?"

"Exactly. I'd only come for visits when Two *are* One—and you'd only come for visits when they aren't. Work schedules in Canada are five days on, two days off—we call the days off 'weekends.' You could come back for each weekend that didn't happen to fall during Two becoming One."

"Harb would be furious."

"Who cares?"

"I would have to travel to the Rim in order to use the portal."

"So just don't ever do it alone. Make sure there's no way he could approach you there."

Bandra sounded dubious. "I . . . I suppose it might work."

"It *will*," said Mary firmly. "If he objected, or tried to see you at the wrong times of the month, the truth about him would come out. He may not care about what happens to you or to his daughters, but he doubtless doesn't wish to be castrated himself."

"You would do this for me?" said Bandra. "You would make a home with me in your world?"

Mary nodded and hugged her close.

"What would I do there?" asked Bandra.

"Teach, at Laurentian, with me. There's not a university in my world that would turn down a chance to add a Neanderthal geologist to its faculty."

"Really?"

"Oh, yes, indeed."

"So we could live and work together in your world?"

"Yes."

"But . . . but you told me that it was not the way of your people. Two women together . . ."

"It is not the way of *most* of my people," said Mary. "But it is of some. And Ontario, where we'll live, is one of the most understanding places in all my world about such things."

"But . . . but would this make you happy?"

Mary smiled. "There are no perfect solutions. But this one comes close."

Bandra was crying, but they were clearly tears of joy. "Thank you, Mary."

"No," said Mary. "Thank you. To you, and to Ponter."

"Ponter I can understand, but me? Why?"

Mary hugged her again. "You both showed me new ways of being human. And for that, I'll always be grateful."

Chapter Thirty-one

"Of course, once we're there, once we have planted flowers in the rusty sand of the fourth planet from our sun, once we've nurtured them with water taken from Mars' polar caps, we Homo sapiens might again briefly pause to smell those roses..."

"Asshole!"

Jock knew the other driver couldn't hear him—it was too cold a day for anyone to have their windows down—but he hated it when morons cut him off.

The traffic seemed intolerable today. Of course, Jock reflected, it was probably no worse than any other day driving here in Rochester, but everything seemed unbearable in comparison to the clean, idyllic beauty he'd seen on the other side.

"The other side." Christ, his mother used to talk about heaven that way. "Things'll be better on the other side."

Jock didn't believe in heaven—or hell, for that matter—but he couldn't deny the reality of the Neanderthal world. Of course, it was pure dumb luck that they hadn't made a mess of things. If real humans had noses like that, we probably wouldn't have been willing to wallow in our own garbage, either.

Jock stopped at a traffic light. A front page from *USA*

Today was blowing across the street. Kids were smoking at the bus stop. There was a McDonald's a block ahead. Sirens were wailing in the distance, and car horns were honking. A truck next to him belched smoke out of a vertical exhaust pipe. Jock looked left and right, eventually spotting a single tree growing out of a concrete planter half a block away.

The radio newsreader started with a disgruntled man having shot and killed four coworkers at an electronics plant in Illinois. He then gave ten seconds to a suicide bombing in Cairo, a dozen more to what looked like impending war between Pakistan and India, and rounded out his minute with an oil spill in Puget Sound, a train derailment near Dallas, and a bank robbery here in Rochester.

What a mess, Jock thought, tapping his fingers against the steering wheel, waiting for the signal to go. *What a goddamned mess.*

Jock came in the front door of the Synergy Group mansion. Louise Benoît happened to be in the corridor. "Hey, Jock," she said. "So is it as beautiful as they say over on the other side?"

Jock nodded.

"I don't know about that," said Louise. "You missed the most amazing aurora while you were gone."

"Here?" said Jock. "This far south?"

Louise nodded. "It was incredible; like nothing I'd ever seen before—and I'm a solar physicist. Earth's magnetic field is really beginning to act up."

"You seem to still be conscious," Jock said wryly.

Louise smiled, and indicated the package he was holding. "I'm going to let that remark pass, since you brought me flowers."

Jock looked down at the long box Mary Vaughan had given him. "Actually, it's something Mary wanted me to bring back for her."

"What is it?"

"That's what I'm going to find out."

Jock headed down the corridor to the desk where Mrs. Wallace, who served as receptionist and Jock's administrative assistant, sat.

"Welcome back, sir!" she said.

Jock nodded. "Any appointments today?"

"Just one. I set it up while you were away; I hope you don't mind. A geneticist looking for a job. He came very highly recommended."

Jock grunted.

"He'll be here at 11:30," said Mrs. Wallace.

Jock checked his e-mail and voice mail, got himself some black coffee, and then unwrapped the package Mary had given him. It was obvious at a glance that it was alien technology: the textures, the color scheme, the overall appearance—everything was different from what a human would have made. The Neanderthal fondness for squares was very much in evidence: a square cross section, square display, and control buds arranged in squares.

Various controls were labeled—some, to his surprise, in what looked like Neanderthal handwriting. It clearly wasn't a mass-produced device; maybe it was a prototype of some sort . . .

Jock picked up his telephone, and dialed an internal number. "Lonwis? It's Jock. Can you come down to my office, please . . ."

———

Jock's door opened—no knock first—and in came Lonwis Trob. "What is it, Jock?" said the ancient Neanderthal.

"I've got this device here"—he indicated the long contraption sitting on his desktop—"and I was wondering how to turn it on."

Lonwis moved across the room; Jock could almost hear the Neanderthal's joints creaking as he did so. He bent over —this time the creak was definitely audible—bringing his blue mechanical eyes closer to the unit. "Here," he said, pointing to an isolated control bud. He grabbed it between two gnarled fingers, and plucked it out. The unit began to hum softly. "What is it?"

"Mary said it's a DNA synthesizer."

Lonwis peered some more at it. "The housing is a standard unit, but I have never seen anything quite like this. Can you pick it up for me?"

"What?" said Jock. "Oh, sure." He lifted the device off the desktop, and Lonwis stooped to look at its underside. "You will want to hook it up to an external power source, and—yes, good: it has a standard interface port. Dr. Benoît and I have built some units that allow Neanderthal technology to be hooked up to your personal computers. Would you like one of those?"

"Um, sure. Yes."

"I will have Dr. Benoît attend to it." Lonwis headed for the door. "Have fun with your new toy."

Jock spent hours examining the codon writer, and reading over the notes Mary had prepared on it.

The thing could make DNA, that much was clear.

And RNA, too, which Jock knew was another nucleic acid.

It also seemed to be able to produce associated proteins, such as those used to bind deoxyribonucleic acid into chromosomes.

Jock had a cursory understanding of genetics; many of the studies he'd been involved with at RAND concerned biowarfare. If this device could produce nucleic-acid strings and proteins, then . . .

Jock steepled his fingers. What the boys at Fort Detrick would give for this!

Nucleic acids. Proteins.

Those were the building blocks of viruses, which were, after all, just scraps of DNA or RNA contained in protein coats.

Jock stared at the machine, thinking.

The phone on Jock's desk made its distinctive internal-call ring. Jock picked up the handset. "Your 11:30 appointment is here," said Mrs. Wallace's voice.

"Right, okay."

A moment later a thin, blue-eyed man in his mid-thirties came through the door. "Dr. Krieger," he said, extending his hand. "It's a pleasure to meet you."

"Have a seat."

The man did so, but first handed Jock a copy of a lengthy *curriculum vitae*. "As you can see, I have a Ph.D. in genetics from Oxford. I was associated with the Ancient Biomolecules Centre there."

"Did you do any Neanderthal work?"

"No, not specifically. But lots of other late-Cenozoic stuff."

"How did you hear about us?"

"I was with York University, where Mary Vaughan used to be, and—"

"We generally do our own recruiting, you know."

"Oh, I understand that, sir. But I thought, with Mary having gone to the other universe, you might have need of a geneticist."

Jock glanced at the object on his desktop. "As a matter of fact, Dr. Ruskin, I do."

Chapter Thirty-two

"But smelling Martian roses will be only a pause, only a
brief catching of breath, a moment of reflection, before we
will again take up the journey, driving ever outward, farther
and farther, learning, discovering, growing, expanding not
only our borders but our minds..."

It had been almost three weeks since the United Nations
contingent, including Jock, had returned home. Ponter and
Adikor were working down in their quantum-computing facility, a thousand armspans below the surface, when the message came through: a courier envelope, passed along the
Derkers tube by a Canadian Forces officer.

Ponter himself happened to open the package. The interior envelope bore the bisected-globe logo of the Synergy
Group, and so Ponter at first assumed it was for Mare. But it
wasn't. To his astonishment, the inner envelope was addressed to him, in both English letters and Neanderthal
glyphs.

Ponter opened the envelope, with his beloved Adikor
looking over his shoulder. Inside was a memory bead. Ponter
popped it into the player on his control console, and a three-
dimensional image of Lonwis Trob appeared, his mechanical
blue eyes shining from within. The image was about a third

of life-size, and it floated a handspan above the console.

"Healthy day, Scholar Boddit," said Lonwis. "I need you to return to the Synergy Group headquarters, here on the south side of Lake Jorlant—what the Gliksins still insist on calling Lake Ontario, despite me having corrected them repeatedly. As you know, I am working here with Dr. Benoît on quantum-computing issues, and I have a new idea about preventing decoherence even in surface-level systems, but I require your expertise in quantum computing. Bring your research partner, Scholar Adikor Huld; his expertise would be of considerable utility, too. Be here within three days."

The image froze, meaning the playback had come to an end. Ponter looked at Adikor. "Would you like to come along?"

"Are you kidding?" asked Adikor. "A chance to meet Lonwis Trob! I'd love to come."

Ponter smiled. Gliksins said that Barasts lacked the desire to explore new places. Maybe they were right: until now, despite it being his hardware that had made the portal possible, Adikor hadn't shown any interest in seeing the Gliksin world. But now he was going to go over—so he could meet one of his Barast heroes.

"Three days gives us plenty of time to pack," said Ponter. "It's not far from here—the here that is there, I mean—to the Synergy Group headquarters."

"I wonder what Lonwis has behind his ridge?" asked Adikor.

"Who knows? But I'm sure it's brilliant."

The control room was empty except for Ponter and Adikor, although a Neanderthal technician was working on the computing floor, and a Neanderthal enforcer was seated by the mouth of the portal, just in case.

"I must invite Mare to join us," said Ponter.

Adikor's eyes narrowed. "It's not yet time for Two to become One."

Ponter nodded. "I know. But that rule doesn't apply in her world, and she would never forgive me if I went over there and didn't bring her."

"Scholar Trob did not ask for her," said Adikor.

Ponter reached out and touched Adikor's arm. "I know this has been difficult for you. I've spent far too much time with Mare, and far too little with you. You know how much I love you."

Adikor nodded slowly. "I'm sorry. I'm trying—I really am—not to be petty about Mare and you. I mean, I *want* you to have a woman-mate; you know that. But I never thought you'd find a woman-mate who would intrude on our time together."

"It has been . . . complex," said Ponter. "I apologize for that. But shortly your son Dab will come to live with us—and then *you* will have less time for me."

As soon as he'd said those words, Ponter regretted them. The hurt was obvious on Adikor's face. "We will raise Dab together," Adikor said. "That is the way; you know that."

"I do know. I'm sorry. It's just that . . ."

"That this is so rotted *awkward*," said Adikor.

"We will resolve it all soon," said Ponter. "I promise."

"How?"

"Mare will move to the other side of the portal and live there, in her world, except when Two become One. Things will go back to being normal between you and me, Adikor."

"When?"

"Soon. I promise."

"But you want her to come on *this* trip—come with us to the Synergy Group, come with us to see Lonwis."

"Well, her current contribution *is* as a researcher at the Synergy Group. Surely it makes sense for her to return there from time to time."

Adikor's broad mouth was frowning. Ponter used the back of his hand to gently rub Adikor's cheek, feeling his whiskers. "I do love you, Adikor. Nothing will ever come between us."

Adikor nodded slowly, and then, taking the initiative himself, he spoke into his Companion. "Please connect me to Mare Vaughan."

After a moment, Christine's imitation of Mare's voice emerged from Adikor's Companion's external speaker, a translation of what Mare had said in her language: "Healthy day."

"Healthy day, Mare. This is Adikor. How would you like to take a trip with Ponter and me?"

"This is astonishing!" said Adikor as they drove through Sudbury, Ontario. "Buildings everywhere! And all these people! Men and women together!"

"And this is just a *small* city," said Ponter. "Wait till you see Toronto or Manhattan."

"Incredible," said Adikor. Ponter had taken the back seat so that Adikor could ride up front. "Incredible!"

Before heading out on the long trip to Rochester, they stopped first at Laurentian University to inquire about employment opportunities for Mary and Bandra. Ponter had been absolutely right: the meeting started with the head of the genetics and geology departments, but soon the university's president and its chancellor had shown up as well. Laurentian very much wanted to hire them both, and was more than happy to work out a schedule that would accommodate four consecutive days' leave per month for Mary.

Since they were at Laurentian, they went down to the basement lair of Veronica Shannon. Adikor went into "Veronica's Closet," wearing a newly built test helmet that easily accommodated Neanderthal skulls.

Mary had hoped that Adikor might experience something when the left-hemisphere part of his parietal lobe was stimulated, but he didn't. On the off-chance that Neanderthal brains were mirror images of Gliksin ones (unlikely, given the prevalence of right-handedness in Neanderthals), Veronica tried a second run, stimulating the right-hemisphere part of Adikor's parietal lobe, but that also produced no response.

Mary, Ponter, and Adikor then drove down to Mary's condo in Richmond Hill, Adikor looking out at the highway and all the other cars in absolute amazement.

When they reached Mary's home, she picked up her huge stack of accumulated mail from the concierge's desk in the lobby, and then they went up the elevator to her unit.

There, Adikor went out on the balcony, amazed by the view. He seemed content to just keep looking, so Mary ordered up a dinner she knew Ponter would like: Kentucky Fried Chicken, coleslaw, french fries, and twelve cans of Coke.

While they waited for it to arrive, Mary turned on her TV, hoping to catch up on the news, and before long, she found herself glued to her set.

"*Habemus papam!*" said the news anchor, a white woman with auburn hair and wire-rimmed glasses. "That was the word today from Vatican City in Rome: we have a Pope."

The image changed to show the plume of white smoke emerging from the chimney on the Sistine Chapel, indicating the burning of ballots after a candidate had received the required majority of two-thirds plus one. Mary felt her heart pounding.

Then a still image appeared: a white man of perhaps fifty-five, with salt-and-pepper hair and a narrow, pinched face. "The new Pontiff is Franco, Cardinal DiChario, of Florence, and we are told that he is taking the name of Mark II."

A two-shot now, of the anchor and a black woman of about forty, wearing a smart business suit. "Joining us here at the CBC Broadcasting Centre is Susan Doncaster, professor of religious studies at the University of Toronto. Thank you for coming in, Professor."

"My pleasure, Samantha."

"What can you tell us about the man born Franco Di-Chario? What sort of changes can we expect him to make in the Roman Catholic Church?"

Doncaster spread her arms a bit. "Many of us were hoping for a breath of fresh air with the appointment of a new Pope, perhaps a relaxation of some of the Church's more conservative stances. But already wags are noting that his chosen name sounds like he's just the latest iteration of what's already been established: the Pope, Mark II. You'll note we're back to having an Italian on St. Peter's Throne, and as a cardinal, Franco DiChario was very much a conservative."

"So we won't see a lightening up of policies on, for instance, birth control?"

"Almost certainly not," said Doncaster, shaking her head. "DiChario is on record calling Pope Paul's *Humanae Vitae* the most important encyclical of the second millennium, and one whose tenants he believes should guide the Church throughout the third millennium."

"What about the celibacy of the clergy?" asked Samantha.

"Again, Franco DiChario spoke frequently about how important the standard vows—poverty, chastity, and obedience—

were to the taking of Orders. I can't see any possibility of Mark II reversing Rome's stance on that."

"I get the impression," said the anchor, smiling slightly, "that there's no point in asking about the ordination of women, then."

"Not on Franco DiChario's watch, that's for sure," said Doncaster. "This is a Church under siege, and it is fortifying its traditional barricades, not tearing them down."

"So no likelihood of a softening of rules about divorce, then, either?"

Mary held her breath, even though she knew what the answer must be.

"Not a chance," said Doncaster.

Mary had put her TV remote control away in a drawer back at the beginning of the summer; she was trying to lose weight, and that had seemed a simple enough way to force herself to move around more. She got up off the couch, crossed over to the fourteen-inch RCA set, and touched the button that turned it off.

When she turned back around, she saw that Ponter was looking at her. "You're not pleased by the choice of new Pope," he said.

"No, I'm not. And a lot of other people won't be, either." She lifted her shoulders slightly, a philosophical shrug. "But, then again, I suppose there's rejoicing going on in many places, too." She sighed.

"What will you do?" said Ponter.

"I—I don't know. I mean, it's not like I'm about to be excommunicated; I did promise Colm that I'd agree to an annulment rather than a divorce, but . . ."

"But what?"

"Don't get me wrong," said Mary. "I *am* glad that our child will have the God organ. But I am getting tired of all these ridiculous restrictions. It's the twenty-first century, for Christ's sake!"

"This new Pope may surprise you," said Ponter. "As I understand it, he has made no announcements of his own since being named to the office. All we have heard is speculation."

Mary sat back down on the couch. "I know that. But if the cardinals had wanted a real change, they would have elected somebody different." She laughed. "Listen to me! That's the secular view, of course. The choice of Pope is supposed to be divinely inspired. So what I should be saying is if *God* had wanted a real change, *he* would have selected somebody different."

"Regardless, as that woman said, you have a Pope—and he looks young enough to serve for many tenmonths to come."

Mary nodded. "I *will* get an annulment. I owe that to Colm. I'm the one who left the marriage, and he doesn't want to be excommunicated. But even if an annulment means I *could* stay in the Catholic Church, I'm not going to. There are lots of other Christian denominations, after all— it hardly means giving up my faith."

"This sounds like a big decision," said Ponter.

Mary smiled. "I've been making a lot of those lately. And I can't stay Catholic." She was surprised at how easily the words came. "I can't."

Chapter Thirty-three

> "We—the kind of humanity called Homo sapiens, the kind
> our Neanderthal cousins call Gliksins—have a drive unique
> among all primates, a drive singular in the realm of con-
> scious beings . . ."

"Hello, Jock," said Mary Vaughan as she came into his office
at the Synergy Group.

"Mary!" Jock exclaimed. "Welcome back!" He got up out
of his Aeron chair, crossed in front of his desk, and shook
her hand. "Welcome back."

"It's good to see you." She motioned outside the door,
and her two traveling companions stepped into view. "Jock,
you remember Envoy Ponter Boddit. And this is Scholar Adikor Huld."

Jock's bushy gray eyebrows shot up toward his pompadour. "My goodness!" he said. "This *is* a surprise."

"You didn't know we were coming?"

Jock shook his head. "I've been wrapped up with . . .
other matters. I get reports on all Neanderthal comings and
goings, but I'm behind in looking at them."

Mary thought briefly of an old joke: the bad news is that
the CIA reads all your e-mail; the good news is that the CIA
reads *all* your e-mail.

"Anyway," said Jock, moving in and shaking Ponter's hand, "welcome back." He then shook Adikor's hand. "Welcome, Dr. Huld, to the United States of America."

"Thank you," said Adikor. "It is . . . overwhelming."

Jock managed a thin smile. "That it is."

Mary indicated the two Barasts. "Lonwis Trob asked for Ponter to return, and this time to bring Adikor with him."

Ponter smiled. "I'm sure that I'm too much of a theoretician for Lonwis's tastes. But Adikor actually knows how to build things."

"Speaking of Neanderthal ingenuity," said Mary, pointing at a worktable that had been set up in a corner of Jock's office, "I see you've been examining the codon writer."

"Yes, indeed," said Jock. "It's an astonishing piece of equipment."

"That it is," said Mary. She looked at Jock, wondering whether to tell him. Then, too excited not to, she said, "It's going to allow Ponter and me to have a baby, despite our differing chromosome counts."

Jock sat up straight in his Aeron chair. "Really? My . . . goodness. I didn't . . . I didn't think that would be possible."

"Well, it is!" said Mary, beaming.

"Um, well, ah, congratulations," said Jock. "And to you, too, of course, Ponter. Congratulations!"

"Thank you," said Ponter.

Suddenly Jock frowned, as if something important had occurred to him. "A hybrid between *Homo sapiens* and *Homo neanderthalensis*," he said. "Will it have twenty-three pairs of chromosomes or twenty-four?"

"You mean, will it be Gliksin or Barast, according to the test I worked out?" asked Mary.

Jock nodded. "Just—you know—an idle curiosity."

"We talked about that a lot. We finally decided to give it twenty-three pairs of chromosomes. It'll appear as a Gliksin—a *Homo sapiens*—at that level."

"I see," said Jock. He seemed slightly displeased at the notion.

"Given that the embryo is going to be placed in my womb"—she patted her belly—"we're trying to avoid triggering any immunological responses there."

Jock glanced down. "You're not pregnant now, are you?"

"No, no. Not yet. Generation 149 won't be conceived until next year."

Jock blinked. "So the child is going to live in the Neanderthal world? Does that mean you're going to move there permanently?"

Mary looked over at Ponter and Adikor. She hadn't expected to get into this just yet. "Actually," she said slowly, "I'm going to mostly stay in this world . . ."

"It sounds like there's a 'but' coming," said Jock.

Mary nodded. "There is. You know I finished the task you hired me for here at Synergy much faster than we'd originally anticipated. I'm thinking it's time I moved on. I've been offered a full-time tenured position in the genetics department at Laurentian."

"Laurentian?" said Jock. "Where's that?"

"It's in Sudbury—you know, where the portal is. Laurentian is a small university, but it's got a great genetics department—and it does DNA forensic work for the RCMP." She paused. "I find myself interested in that area these days."

Jock smiled. "Who'd have thought 'location, location, location' would ever apply to Sudbury?"

"Hello, Mary."

Mary dropped the mug she was holding. It shattered, and

coffee laced with chocolate milk splattered across the floor of her office. "I'll scream," said Mary. "I'll call for Ponter."

Cornelius Ruskin closed the door behind him. "There's no need for that."

Mary's heart was pounding. She looked around for anything she could use as a weapon. "What the hell are you doing here?"

Cornelius managed a small smile. "I work here. I'm your replacement."

"We'll see about that," said Mary. She scooped up the handset of her desk phone.

Cornelius moved closer.

"Don't you touch me!" said Mary. "Don't you dare!"

"Mary—"

"Get out! Get out! Get out!"

"Just give me two minutes, Mary—that's all I ask."

"I'll call the police!"

"You can't do that. You know you can't, not after what Ponter did to me, and—"

Suddenly Cornelius stopped talking. Mary's heart was pounding furiously, and her face must have betrayed something that Cornelius detected.

"You don't know!" he said, his blue eyes wide. "You don't know, do you? He never told you!"

"Told me what?" said Mary.

Cornelius's lean form went limp, as if his limbs were only loosely connected to his body. "It never occurred to me that you weren't involved in planning it, that you didn't know . . ."

"Know what?" demanded Mary.

Cornelius backed away. "I won't hurt you, Mary. I *can't* hurt you."

"What are you talking about?"

"Do you know that Ponter came to see me, at my apartment?"

"What? You're lying."

"No, I'm not."

"When?"

"Back in September. Late at night . . ."

"You *are* lying. He never—"

"Oh, yes he did."

"He would have told me," said Mary.

"So I would have thought," agreed Cornelius with a philosophical shrug. "But apparently he didn't."

"Look," said Mary. "I don't care about any of that. Just get the hell out of here. I came down here to get away from you! I'm going to call the police."

"You don't want to do that," said Cornelius.

"Just watch me—and if you come one step closer, I'll scream."

"Mary—"

"Don't come any closer."

"Mary, Ponter *castrated* me."

Mary felt her jaw drop. "You're lying," she said. "You're making that up."

"I'll show you, if you like . . ."

"No!" Mary almost vomited, the notion of seeing his naked flesh again too much to bear.

"It's true. He came to my apartment, maybe two in the morning, and he—"

"Ponter would never do that. Not without telling me."

Cornelius moved a hand to his zipper. "Like I said, I can prove it."

"No!" Mary was gasping for air now.

"Qaiser Remtulla told me you'd gone native—moving permanently to the other side. I never would have come down here otherwise, but . . ." He shrugged again. "I need this job, Mary," said Cornelius. "York was a dead end for me—for any white male of my generation. You know that."

Mary was close to hyperventilating. "I can't work with you. I can't even be in the same room as you."

"I'll stay out of your way. I promise." His voice softened. "Damn it, Mary, do you think I like seeing you? It reminds me of"—he paused, and his voice cracked, just a little—"of what I used to be."

"I hate you," hissed Mary.

"I know you do." He shrugged a little. "I—I can't say that I blame you, either. But if you spill the beans about me to Krieger, or anyone else, it will be game over for Ponter Boddit. He'll go to jail for what he did to me."

"God damn you," said Mary.

Cornelius just nodded. "No doubt he will."

"Ponter!" said Mary, storming into the room at Synergy where he was working with Adikor Huld and Lonwis Trob. "Come with me!"

"Hello, Mare," said Ponter. "What's wrong?"

"Now!" snapped Mary. "Right now!"

Ponter turned to the other two Neanderthals, but Christine continued to translate. "If you'll excuse me for a moment . . ."

Lonwis nodded, and made a crack to Adikor that it must be Last Five. Mary marched out of the room, and Ponter followed.

"*Outside!*" snapped Mary, and without looking back, she headed down the mansion's carpeted main-floor corridor, took her coat from the rack, and went out the front door.

Ponter followed, taking no coat. Mary marched across

the brown lawn and crossed the road, until they were at the boardwalk of the deserted marina. She wheeled on Ponter. "Cornelius Ruskin is here," she said.

"No," said Ponter. "I would have smelled him if—"

"Maybe slicing off his balls has changed his scent," snapped Mary.

"Ah," said Ponter, and then: "Oh."

"That's it?" demanded Mary. "That's all you've got to say?"

"I—um, well . . ."

"Why the hell didn't you tell me?"

"You wouldn't have approved," said Ponter, looking down at the sidewalk, which was half-blanketed with dead leaves.

"You're damn right I wouldn't have! Ponter, how could you *do* something like that? For Christ's sake . . ."

"Christ," Ponter repeated softly. "Christ taught that forgiveness was the greatest of virtues. But . . ."

"Yes?" snapped Mary.

"But I am not Christ," he said, his voice sounding very sad indeed. "I could not forgive."

"You told me you wouldn't hurt him," said Mary. A seagull wheeled overhead.

"I told you I would not *kill* him," said Ponter. "And I did not, but . . ." He shrugged his massive shoulders. "My honest intention had been simply to warn him that I had identified him as the rapist, so that he would never commit that crime again. But when I saw him, when I smelled him, smelled the stench of him, the stench he'd left on his latest victim's clothing, I could not help myself . . ."

"Jesus, Ponter. You know what this means: he's got the upper hand. Anytime he wants, he could blow the whistle on you. The issue of whether he was guilty of rape wouldn't even figure in your trial, I suspect."

"But he is guilty! And I couldn't stand the thought of him getting away with his crime." And then, perhaps to defend himself even more, he repeated the last word in the plural—"Crimes," reminding Mary that she had not been Cornelius Ruskin's only victim, and that the second rape had happened because Mary had failed to report her own.

"His relatives," said Mary, the moment the thought came to her. "His brothers, sisters. Parents. My God, you didn't do anything to them, did you?"

Ponter hung his head, and Mary thought he was going to admit further attacks. But that wasn't the cause of his shame. "No," he said. "No, I have done nothing about any other copies of the genes that made him what he was. I wanted to punish *him*—to hurt *him*, for hurting you."

"But now he can hurt *you*," said Mary.

"Don't worry," said Ponter. "He won't ever reveal what I did."

"How can you be sure of that?"

"To accuse me would mean that his own crimes would come to light. Perhaps not at my own trial—but in separate proceedings, no? Surely the enforcers here wouldn't let the matter drop."

"I suppose," said Mary, still furious. "But a judge might rule that he'd already been punished enough by you. After all, Canadian law considers castration too great a penalty even for rape. So, if he'd already been punished to that level, a judge might deem it pointless to impose the lesser, legal penalty of imprisonment. If that's the case, he would have nothing to lose by seeing to it that you were jailed for what you did to him."

"Regardless, it would become public knowledge that he had been a rapist. Surely there would be social consequences of that which he would not risk."

"You should have talked to me first!"

"As I said, I had not intended to exact this . . . this . . ."

"Revenge," said Mary, but the word came out in a plain tone, as if she were merely providing another bit of vocabulary. She shook her head slowly back and forth. "You should not have done this."

"I know."

"And to do it, but then not tell me! Damn it, Ponter—we're not supposed to have secrets! Why the hell didn't you tell me?"

Ponter looked out at the marina, at the cold gray water. "I'm sure I am safe from repercussions in *this* world," he said, "for, as I said, Ruskin will never reveal what I did to him. But in my world . . ."

"What about it?" snapped Mary.

"Don't you see? If it were to become known in my world what I'd done, I'd be judged excessively violent."

"You trust bloody Ruskin to keep a secret, but not me!"

"It's not that. It's not that at all. But everything is recorded. There would be a record in my alibi archive of me telling you, and there would be a record in yours of the same thing. Even if neither of us ever let the matter slip out, there would always be a chance that the courts might order access to your archives or mine, and then . . ."

"What? What?"

"And then not only I would be punished, but so would Mega and Jasmel."

Oh, Christ, thought Mary. *It comes full circle.*

"I am sorry," said Ponter. "I really am—about what I did to Ruskin, and about not letting you know." He sought out her eyes. "Believe me, it has not been an easy burden to bear."

Suddenly Mary got it. "The personality sculptor!"

"Yes, this is why I saw Jurard Selgan."

"Not because of my rape . . ." said Mary slowly.

"No, not directly."

". . . but because of what you'd *done* about my rape."

"Exactly."

Mary let out a long sigh, anger—and much else—exiting her body. He hadn't thought less of her because she'd been raped . . . "Ponter," she said softly. "Ponter, Ponter . . ."

"I do love you, Mare."

She shook her head slowly back and forth, wondering what to do next.

Chapter Thirty-four

"And that drive will compel us onward and outward..."

Bristol Harbour Village was the dream of a developer named Fred Sarkis: five luxury condominium-apartment buildings perched atop a shale cliff on the shore of Canandaigua Lake. One of upstate New York's Finger Lakes, Canandaigua was a long, deep gouge in the landscape formed by Ice Age glaciers.

BHV had been built in the early 1970s, before the economies of Rochester, and so many other upstate cities, had gone into the toilet. It was a bizarre artifact of its time, like Habitat from Expo '67. When Mary first saw it, at Louise Benoît's recommendation, she'd thought they should film the next Spider-Man movie there: there were all sorts of bridges linking its multilevel outdoor parking garages with the actual apartment buildings that would have been perfect for the web-slinger.

Apparently, though, the development had never quite worked out the way it had been planned, and despite such luxuries as a Robert Trent Jones golf course just up the street and nearby Bristol Mountain for skiing in winter, there were always a large number of units for sale or rent. The real-estate agent Mary had spoken to went on about how Patty Duke and John Astin, back when they were married, had stayed there one summer. Mary rather suspected that once she learned that two Neanderthals were now here, that fact would become a new part of her sales pitch.

The apartment Mary had rented was a two-bedroom, 1000-square-foot unit split over two levels. It still had what must have been the original god-awful orange shag carpet; Mary hadn't seen anything like it in decades. Still, the view was beautiful—looking directly across the width of the lake. The upper balcony, off the master bedroom, had an unobstructed panorama; the lower balcony looked out into the top of the tenacious trees that had grown up out of the crumbling cliff face. From either of them, one could see the cement walkway jutting out to the outdoor elevator shaft that dropped the hundreds of feet to the marina and man-made beach below.

"Now, *this* is an interesting place!" said Ponter as he stood on the lower balcony, clutching the railing with both hands. "Modern conveniences amid nature. I almost think I am back on my world."

Mary was using an electric grill on the balcony to cook steaks she'd bought at Wegman's. Ponter continued to look out at the lake, while Adikor seemed more interested in a large spider that was working its way along the railing.

When the steaks were done—just a shade past raw for the boys, medium well for her—Mary served them, and Ponter and Adikor tore into theirs with gloved hands, while Mary carved hers with a knife. Of course, dinner was the easy part, thought Mary. At some point, though, someone was bound to bring up the question of—

"So," said Adikor, "where shall we sleep?"

Mary took a deep breath, then: "I thought Ponter and I would—"

"No, no, no," said Adikor. "Two are not One. It's I who should be sleeping with Ponter now."

"Yes, but this is *my* home," said Mary. "My world."

"That's irrelevant. Ponter is *my* man-mate. You two have not even bonded yet."

"Please!" said Ponter. "Let's not fight." He smiled at Mary, then at Adikor, but said nothing for a few moments. Then, in a tentative voice, he offered, "You know, we could all sleep together . . ."

"No!" said Adikor, and "No!" said Mary simultaneously. *Good grief!* thought Mary. A hominid *ménage à trois!*

"I really think," continued Mary, "that it makes sense for Ponter and me—"

"That's gristle," said Adikor. "It is obvious that—"

"My beloved," said Ponter, but perhaps since *mare* was the Neanderthal word for "beloved," he started again, using a different approach. "My two loves," he said. "You know how deeply I care about each of you. But Adikor is right—under normal circumstances, I would be with him at this time of month." He reached out and touched Adikor affectionately. "Mare, you must get used to this. It's going to be a reality for the rest of my life."

Mary looked out at the lake. This side was in shade, but sun was still falling on the far shore, a mile and a half off. There were four air-conditioning/heating units in the apartment, Mary knew—one at each end of each floor. She'd been turning on the fan on the one in the master bedroom before going to bed each night, so that the white noise would drown out the cacophony of birds that hailed the dawn. She supposed if she put it on high, it might keep her from hearing any noise coming from the other bedroom . . .

And Ponter *was* right. She *did* have to get used to this.

"All right," she said, at last, closing her eyes. "But you guys have to make breakfast, then."

Adikor took Ponter's hand, and smiled at Mary. "Deal," he said.

There was already a large safe in Jock's office, built into the far wall; it had been the first renovation Jock had ordered when the Synergy Group had bought this old mansion. The safe, embedded in concrete, met Department of Defense guidelines for being both secure and fireproof. Jock kept the codon writer in it, only bringing it out for supervised study.

Jock sat at his desk. On one corner of it was the conversion box Lonwis had put together that would allow designs created on Jock's PC to be downloaded into the codon writer. Jock was looking at one such design. His monitor—a seventeen-inch LCD, with a black bezel—was showing the notes and formulas Cornelius Ruskin had prepared. Of course, Jock had told Cornelius that his interest was purely defensive—wanting to see what a worst-case scenario would be if a device like the codon writer fell into the wrong hands.

Jock knew he should have turned this device over to the Pentagon—but those bastards would want to use it against *humans*. No, this was his opportunity—his one chance—and he had to seize it. Right now, early on in the contact between the two worlds, it would look like an accident: a nasty bug that had slipped through to the other side. Regrettable, but it would leave Eden uninhabited, and there'd only be one *Homo sapiens* casualty—Cornelius Ruskin, after he was no longer of any use.

Ruskin, of course, only knew what was necessary. For instance, as far as he, and most of the genetics community, knew, the natural reservoir for the Ebola virus—the place it lurked when not infecting humans—was unknown. But Jock was privy to things Ruskin was not: the U.S. government had isolated the reservoir back in 1998: *Balaeniceps rex*, the shoebill, a tall wading bird found in swamps in eastern tropical Africa. The information had been classified, lest an unfriendly power make use of it.

Ebola was an RNA virus whose genome had been completely sequenced, although, again, Ruskin wouldn't know that; that information had also been classified, for the same reason. So, presumably as far as Ruskin was aware, the sequence Jock had asked him to manipulate was just a random viral string, not the actual genetic code of Ebola.

Ebola came in several strains, named for the locations at which they had been first identified. Ebola-Zaire was by far the most deadly, but it was only transmitted through bodily fluids. In contrast, Ebola-Reston, which doesn't affect humans, is transmitted through the air. But Ruskin had had no trouble—purely as part of an exercise, of course—in programming the codon writer to swap a few genes, thereby producing a hybrid version that should have Ebola-Zaire's virulence combined with Ebola-Reston's ability for airborne transmission.

A few more tweaks cut the modified virus's incubation time to one-tenth of what it had been in nature, and boosted the kill rate from ninety to better than ninety-nine percent. And one final tweak had changed the genetic markers that specified the virus's natural reservoir . . .

The second part of the project had been harder, but Cornelius had taken to it like a dog to a bone; it's amazing how much a $200,000 consulting fee can motivate someone.

The concept was simple enough on paper: keep the virus from being activated unless the host cell had certain characteristics. Fortunately, when Ambassador Tukana Prat brought ten of the most famous Neanderthals of all with her to the United Nations, they had freely shared much knowledge. One of them, Borl Kadas, had provided all the information that had been gleaned from the sequencing of the Neanderthal genome, which had been completed back in the year Jock knew as 1953. That database had provided the information needed to make sure the virus would kill only those it was supposed to kill.

Now only one problem remained: getting the virus over to the other side. At first, Jock had thought the simplest solution would be to infect himself with it—after all, it would have no effect on a hominid with twenty-three pairs of chromosomes. But the tuned-laser technology used for decontaminating people crossing between worlds would have easily zapped it from his body. Even diplomatic pouches were decontaminated, so simply storing a supply of the virus in one of them wouldn't work, either.

No, he needed to get an aerosol bomb over in some sort of container that was opaque to the laser pulses used by the Neanderthals' decontamination equipment. Jock himself had no idea what would do the trick, but his optics team—originally assembled to study the imaging technology in Companion implants, and handpicked from the best Bausch & Lomb, Kodak, and Xerox had to offer—would certainly be able to work it out, especially since the tuned-laser technology was also one of those the Neanderthals had freely shared with *Homo sapiens*.

Jock picked up the phone on his desk, and dialed an internal extension. "Hello, Kevin," he said. "It's Jock. Would you, Frank, and Lilly please come down to my office? I've got a little job for you . . ."

Mary found a simple short-term solution to the problem of working in the same building as Cornelius Ruskin. She would come in late in the day and work on into the evening; Cornelius would leave shortly after she arrived—or, if she was lucky, even before she got in.

Ponter and Adikor came in from Bristol Harbour Village with Mary; they had no way to get around except for having her drive them. But they spent most of their time working on the quantum-computing project with Lonwis Trob, and often with Louise Benoît—although she kept more normal hours, and had already gone home today.

Mary was writing a report for Jock, detailing everything she'd learned from Lurt, Vissan, and others about Neanderthal genetics. The work simultaneously elated and depressed Mary: elated her because she'd learned so much, and depressed her because the Neanderthals were decades beyond her people in this area, meaning so much of the work she'd done in the past was hopelessly obsolete, and—

Massive footfalls—someone running down the corridor.

"Mare! Mare!"

Adikor had appeared in Mary's doorway, his broad, round face terrified. "What is it?" Mary asked.

"Lonwis Trob—he's collapsed! We need medical aid, and—"

And, except for Bandra, who knew the joke about the hunters calling 9-1-1, the Neanderthals had no idea how to summon such a thing; nor could their Companions call anyone on this side of the portal. Mary rose and ran down the corridor to the quantum-computing lab.

Lonwis was flat on his back, his eyelids fluttering. When they opened, they showed only smooth blue-metal spheres; the parts with the mechanical irises had apparently rolled up into his head.

Ponter was kneeling beside Lonwis. He was using the back of one hand, effortlessly it seemed, to compress Lonwis's chest over and over again—a Neanderthal version of CPR. Meanwhile, Lonwis's golden Companion was speaking aloud in the Neanderthal language, describing Lonwis's vital signs.

Mary picked up the phone on one of the desks, dialed 9 for an outside line, then 9-1-1.

"Fire, police, or ambulance?" said the operator.

"Ambulance."

"What's wrong?"

"A man having a heart attack," said Mary. "Hurry!"

The operator, a woman, must have had the address on a screen in front of her, based on the incoming phone number. "I'm dispatching an ambulance now. Do you know how to perform CPR?"

"Yes," said Mary. "But someone else is already doing that, and—look, I should tell you up front. The man having the heart attack is a Neanderthal."

"Ma'am, it's a serious crime to—"

"*I'm not joking!*" snapped Mary. "I'm calling from the Synergy Group. We're a U.S.-government think tank, and we've got Neanderthals here."

Ponter was continuing to compress Lonwis's chest. Adikor, meanwhile, had opened up Lonwis's medical belt and was using a compressed-gas injector to pump something into Lonwis's neck.

"Can I have your name?" said the operator.

"Is the ambulance coming? Have you sent it yet?"

"Yes, ma'am. It's on its way. Can I have your name?"

"It's Mary N. Vaughan. That's V-A-U-G-H-A-N. I'm a geneticist."

"How old is the patient, Ms. Vaughan?"

"A hundred and eight—and no, I am *not* joking. It's Lonwis Trob, one of the Neanderthals who visited the United Nations last month."

Stan Rasmussen—a geopolitical expert who worked down the hall—had appeared in the doorway. Mary covered the handset and spoke quickly to him. "Lonwis is having a heart attack. Get Jock!" Rasmussen nodded and hurried away.

"I'm going to transfer you to the paramedics," said the 9-1-1 operator.

A moment later a different female voice came on. "We're five minutes away," she said. "Can you describe the patient's condition?"

"No," said Mary, "but I'll put his Companion on." She picked up the desk set and carried it across the room, setting it down near Lonwis. She then spoke to Lonwis's implant: "Switch to English, and answer all the questions you hear. Help is on its way . . ."

Chapter Thirty-five

"And yet, some of us will stay permanently on Mars. Now, in the pages of science and science fiction there have long been notions of terraforming Mars—making it more Earth-like, by enhancing its atmosphere and liberating its frozen water, thus creating a world better suited for human habitation..."

Jock, Ponter, and Adikor had rushed off to Strong Memorial Hospital, along with the still-unconscious Lonwis Trob. There was nothing Mary could do to help, and, at Jock's urging, she had stayed back at the Synergy Group.

It took Mary a good hour to calm down enough to get back to her work, but finally she did so . . . only to have it blow up in her face.

One of Mary's friends back at York had been a Linux evangelist, trying to convince everyone in the genetics department that they should abandon Windows and switch instead to the open-source operating system. Mary tended to stay out of computer wars—she'd remained neutral years before in the Mac-versus-PC skirmishes—but every time her Windows-based PC displayed that blue screen of death, she felt like throwing her support in with the Linux crowd.

And now it had happened again, for the second time today. Mary did the three-fingered salute, but after sitting through the interminable wait for the system to reboot, she found that it stubbornly refused to reacquire its network connection.

Mary sighed. It was 7:00 P.M., but she could hardly call it a day; Ponter and Adikor would need her to give them a lift back to Bristol Harbour Village whenever they returned from the hospital.

Of course, there were lots of other computers here in the old mansion that housed the Synergy Group, but, well . . .

Jock had one of those nifty Aeron chairs Mary had read about in the Sharper Image catalog. It was supposed to be super-comfortable, an ergonomic heaven. Granted, he had probably adjusted all its heights and tilts for his rangy body, but, still, she could get a feel for it if she worked in his office.

Mary got up, and headed down the staircase, which was carpeted in a wine red. Jock's office door was wide open, and Mary walked in. Jock had a big bay window, looking south over the marina. Mary shivered at the view, despite it still being warm inside.

She walked over to Jock's super-chair, all black metal and plastic, with a fine-meshed black back that was supposed to allow one's skin to breathe while seated. Feeling like a mischievous kid, she lowered herself into the chair and leaned back.

My God, she thought. *A product for which the hype was actually true!* It was wonderfully comfortable. She used her feet to rotate the chair left and right. Mary knew Aerons cost an arm and a leg, but she *had* to get herself one of these . . .

After relaxing in the chair for a few more moments, she settled back to work. Jock, who had left this room in a hurry when Lonwis Trob had his heart attack, was still logged onto the network. Mary suspected her own password would work from here, but wasn't positive, and so she decided to leave well enough alone, and continued working as if she were Jock. She opened up the "Neanderthal genetics" folder on the server, and—

Mary's eyebrows shot up. She spent most of her time in this folder, but there were two icons displayed that she'd never seen before. She felt nervous: although Mary was pretty good at backing up, she was afraid the crash she'd had upstairs had corrupted the directory tree.

She decided to check by double-clicking on one of the icons she didn't recognize—it showed a red-and-black double helix. Mary knew most of the genetics apps on the market, and their accompanying document icons, but this one was unfamiliar.

After a moment a window opened. It said "USAMRIID Geneplex—Surfaris" in the title bar, and a screenful of text and formulas appeared below it. USAMRIID was an acronym that appeared often enough in the genetics literature: United States Army Medical Research Institute of Infectious Diseases. And Geneplex was obviously the program's name. But "Surfaris" didn't mean a thing to Mary.

Still, she looked at the window's contents, and was absolutely astonished. Some of her own earlier work here at Synergy had involved trying to use the quorum-counting facility of bacteria to determine an actual tally of how many chromosome pairs were present—twenty-three or twenty-four. But that hadn't worked. First, the quorum mechanism seemed to lack the ability to distinguish quantities that precisely. And, second, chromosomes only resolved themselves out of the chromatin during mitosis, which, of course, was hardly the usual state of affairs within a cell.

But Jock had apparently had someone else also working on this problem, and that geneticist had come up with a much simpler technique. In a Gliksin, what had been ances-

tral chromosomes two and three had fused, producing a
much longer chromosome. The genes that had been at the
end of chromosome two now abutted the genes at the beginning of chromosome three, somewhere in the middle of the
new, combined chromosome.

The same genes existed in a Neanderthal, but they did
not abut. Rather, the last gene on chromosome two was followed by a telomere—the junk-DNA cap that did nothing
but protect the tip of the chromosome, like the little plastic-
wrapped bit at the end of a shoelace. Likewise, the first gene
in chromosome three was preceded by another telomere, the
end cap on the leading edge of that chromosome. So, in a
Neanderthal, you'd find these sequences:

> *At the end of chromosome 2:*
>   ... [other genes][gene ALPHA][telomere]

> *At the beginning of chromosome 3:*
>   [telomere][gene BETA][other genes] ...

Those sequences wouldn't exist anywhere in Gliksin
DNA. Conversely, in Gliksin DNA, millions of base pairs away
from any telomere, you'd find this sequence, a combination
completely absent from Neanderthal DNA:

... [other genes][gene ALPHA][gene BETA][other genes] ...

A logical extension of Mary's original work—and a perfect, infallible way of distinguishing between the two kinds
of humans, even when a cell wasn't undergoing mitosis. It
was precisely what Jock said he'd wanted: a simple, reliable
method to distinguish a Gliksin from a Barast.

Mary was pleased to see that all the tests were invoked.

In theory, one could test for only one of the three conditions. Finding either of the first two sequences—either gene AL-PHA or gene BETA next to a telomere—clearly denoted *Homo neanderthalensis*. And finding the third sequence—genes ALPHA and BETA adjacent to each other—denoted *Homo sapiens*. But things could always go wrong, and so the test to identify a Neanderthal used a little logic tree, explained, presumably for Jock's benefit, in plain English:

> *Step 1: Are Genes ALPHA and BETA found side by side?*
> If **yes**, abort (this isn't a Neanderthal)
> If **no**, this is probably a Neanderthal: go to Step 2
>
> *Step 2: Is Gene ALPHA found next to a telomere?*
> If **yes**, this is still likely a Neanderthal: go to Step 3
> If **no**, abort (this should never happen in a Neanderthal)
>
> *Step 3: Is Gene BETA found next to a telomere?*
> If **yes**, this is definitely a Neanderthal: go to Step 4
> If **no**, abort (this should never happen in a Neanderthal)

The abort conditions in steps two and three were fail-safes. They occurred if the genes ALPHA and BETA were not side by side (as determined in step one) *and* neither ALPHA nor BETA were next to a telomere—combinations that should never be found in either kind of hominid DNA.

It was a pig-simple program for a computer to execute, but it was a bit more complex to code into a cascade of biochemical reactions, although apparently that was what Jock's geneticist had done. Mary had no trouble following the formulas for enzymes produced at each stage of the reaction, and could see that the results would indeed follow the intended logic. At the end of it all, she expected to just see an enzyme or other marker produced whose presence could be easily tested for: an unambiguous flag saying, yup, this is a Neanderthal, or nope, it's not.

But she wasn't anywhere near the end of the process, as she saw when she scrolled down to the next screen full of formulas and text. Mary's jaw dropped as she continued to read, discovering what step 4 was. Jock and many members of his team had come from RAND; Mary had gotten used to them speaking in cold-war clichés, but the next term stopped her heart for a second: "Payload delivery."

If, and only if, the test subject was found to be a Neanderthal, a new cascade sequence was invoked that ultimately resulted in . . .

Mary could hardly believe her eyes. Her specialty was ancient DNA—that's what had gotten her involved in all this to begin with, after all—but that didn't mean she was ignorant of more recently identified sequences, especially those that had made front-page news around the world.

If the specimen was a Neanderthal, a payload was indeed delivered: a payload based on a filovirus that would result very rapidly in the development of a hemorrhagic fever.

A fatal hemorrhagic fever . . .

Mary leaned back in Jock's chair. She could taste bile climbing her throat.

Why on Earth would someone want to wipe out the Neanderthals?

But, of course, the question really should be, Why, with *two Earths*, would someone want to wipe out the Neanderthals?

Hemorrhagic fevers were contagious. Gliksins couldn't cure them, and she very much doubted Barasts could, either, for two reasons. First, by virtue of never having developed agriculture and animal husbandry, the Neanderthals had also never had to develop techniques for dealing with plagues. And, second, all known hemorrhagic fevers were tropical diseases—something the northern-living Neanderthals would have had very little experience with.

Mary swallowed hard, trying to force down the biting, sour taste.

But why? Why would someone want to kill the Neanderthals? It didn't make . . .

Suddenly Mary remembered her little exchange with Jock back at the Debral nickel mine:

"*It's* astonishing," Jock had said. "*I knew in an intellectual sort of way that we'd screwed up our environment, but until I saw all this* . . . " He'd indicated the pristine countryside. "*It's like finding Eden.*"

And Mary had laughed. "*Isn't it, though?*" she'd said. "*Too bad it's already occupied, eh?*"

A little joke—that's all it was. But Jock hadn't laughed. All you had to do was get rid of those pesky Neanderthals, and an Eden awaited . . .

It was horrific—but Jock had spent his life dealing with scenarios of mass destruction. What was horrific to Mary was just another day at the office for him.

Mary's first thought was to erase the computer files—but, of course, that would accomplish nothing. There would doubtless be backups.

Her second thought was to pick up the phone and call— well, as a good Canadian, she naturally thought of the CBC, which could then spread the news to the four corners of this world. There was no way people would stand for this sort of genocide.

But she didn't know how far along Jock was. If he was ready to go, Mary certainly didn't want him to feel cornered, since he might release his disease vector as soon as he heard that the public had gotten wind of his plan.

Mary needed help, ideas, support—not just from Ponter or Adikor, but from another Gliksin, someone who understood how this world worked.

There were people she trusted back in Toronto, but was there anyone she could rely on here in the United States? Her sister Christine—the real Christine—of course, but she was in Sacramento, clear across the continent, thousands of—of *miles*—away.

And then it hit her.

The obvious answer, as much as her youth and beauty rankled Mary.

The woman who had saved Ponter Boddit's life when he'd first arrived in this reality.

The quantum-physics postdoc that Jock had scooped up to try to replicate the Neanderthal computing technology.

Louise Benoît.

Not that Louise would be much help in medical matters, but—

But her boyfriend! Granted, Reuben Montego was no specialist, but he'd be a lot more help dealing with a disease vector than would a physicist.

Mary knew that she might never again get access to these computer files. She looked around Jock's office and found a spindle of blank CDs (Kodak brand, of course, this being Rochester). She took one, put it in the computer's CD drive, and clicked on the CD-burning application. Just to be on the safe side, she selected all the files in the folder. The whole thing topped out at 610 meg—small enough to fit on a single CD. She clicked the "copy files" button, and leaned back in the Aeron chair—which, just now, didn't seem comfortable at all—wishing she knew some way to calm her racing heart.

Chapter Thirty-six

"But there have been objections to terraforming Mars from those who feel that, even if it has no indigenous life, we should leave its stark natural beauty pristine and unspoiled— that if we visit it, we should treat it as we do our Earthly parks, taking nothing but memories and leaving behind nothing but footprints . . ."

Ponter and Adikor had ended up spending the whole night at the hospital with Lonwis and Jock. Mary had eventually gone home alone to Bristol Harbour Village, without having had a chance to tell Ponter what she'd discovered.

Exhausted, she didn't get in to Seabreeze until 11:00 A.M., but Ponter, Adikor, and Jock still hadn't come in yet. After getting an update from Mrs. Wallace on Lonwis's condition—stable—she climbed the stairs to Louise Benoît's lab. "How about some lunch?" Mary asked.

Louise looked pleasantly surprised. "Sure," she said. "When?"

"How about right now?" said Mary.

Louise looked at her watch and was clearly surprised by how early it was. But something in Mary's voice had obviously got her attention. "*Bon,*" she said.

"Great," said Mary. Their coats were on a rack by the mansion's front door. They put them on and headed outside, into the crisp November day, a few snowflakes blowing around.

There were several restaurants on either side of Culver Road. Many were seasonal—Seabreeze was a summer resort, after all—but some were open year-round. Mary started walking purposefully to the west, and Louise fell in beside her.

"So," said Louise, "what do you feel like?"

"I was in Jock's office last night," said Mary, without preamble, "while he was off at the hospital with Lonwis. He's had a virus designed to kill Neanderthals."

Louise's accented voice was filled with disbelief. "What?"

"I think he's going to wipe them out—all of them."

"Why?"

Mary looked over her shoulder, just to be sure they weren't being followed. "Because the grass *is* greener on the other side of the fence. Because he wants to claim their version of Earth for our kind of humans." She kicked some litter out of her way. "Maybe so we can start over without all this."

Up ahead, on the left side of the road, an amusement park was visible, closed for the winter, its roller coaster a lump of rusty intestines. "What—what should we do?" said Louise. "How do we stop him?"

"I don't know," said Mary. "I only stumbled onto the virus design by accident. My network connection went down, and so I went to his office to use his workstation, since he was gone for the day. But he'd left in such a hurry when Lonwis had his heart attack that he hadn't logged off his account. I copied the virus designs onto a CD, but I think what I'd really like to do is get back into his account again, and modify the master file so that it won't produce anything deadly. I presume he's planning to feed those instructions into the codon writer, and then release the virus into the Neanderthal world."

"What if he's already made the actual virus?" said Louise.

"I don't know. If he has, we may be sunk."

They were walking along a narrow sidewalk. A car drove by them.

"Have you thought about just going to the media with the CD—you know, blowing the whistle?"

Mary nodded. "But I want to . . . to *defuse* his virus before I do that. And I'll need help finding a way back into Jock's computer."

"The Synergy Group network uses RSA encryption," said Louise.

"Is there any way to crack that?"

Louise smiled. "Before we met our Neanderthal friends I would have said no, there was no practical way. After all, most encryption systems, including RSA, are based on keys that are the products of two large prime numbers. You have to be able to figure out the prime factors of the key number to crack the code, and with 512-bit encryption, like our system here uses, it would take conventional computers millennia to try all the possible factors. But quantum computers—"

Mary got it in a flash. "Quantum computers try all possible factors simultaneously." But then she frowned. "So, what are you proposing? That we have the portal shut down so that Ponter's quantum computer can crack Jock's encryption for us?"

Louise shook her head. "Setting aside the fact that Ponter's is hardly the only quantum computer that exists in the Neanderthal world—it's just the biggest one, that's all—we don't need to go there to get this problem solved." She smiled. "You may have spent the last couple of months gallivanting over two universes, but I've been hard at work right here, and my job was to build our own quantum computer, based on what I'd learned from Ponter during our quarantine. We've got a perfectly fine little quantum computer in my lab here at Synergy. It's got nowhere near enough registers to do what Ponter's big unit did—open a stable portal to another universe—but it certainly can crack 512-bit encryption codes."

"You're wonderful, Louise."

Louise smiled. "Nice of you to finally notice."

As soon as Ponter and Adikor returned from the hospital, Mary said they should go for lunch—hoping that Mrs. Wallace wouldn't remark to Jock that this was the *second* time she'd supposedly gone out to lunch today. Once they were outdoors, Mary led them out to the back of the mansion, and they walked along the sandy beach, a cold wind coming across the gray choppiness of Lake Ontario.

"Something is clearly upsetting you," said Ponter. "What is it?"

"Jock has created a biological weapon," Mary said. "It's a virus that determines if the host cell belongs to a Neanderthal. If it does, it invokes a hemorrhagic fever."

She heard Ponter's and Adikor's Companions bleep; not surprisingly, the subject of tropical diseases had not come up so far. "Hemorrhagic fevers are fatal," said Mary. "Ebola is the classic example from my world; it causes blood to leak out of the eyes and other orifices. Such fevers are highly contagious and we don't have a cure for them."

"Why would anyone make such a thing?" asked Ponter, his voice full of revulsion.

"To wipe your world free of indigenous humans, so that my kind could claim your version of Earth—as a second home, maybe."

Ponter apparently could find no word in his own language to convey the sentiment he wanted to express. "*Christ,*" said his untranslated voice.

"I agree," said Mary. "But I'm not sure how to stop Jock. I mean, he might be acting alone, or his government—and possibly mine, too—might be behind this."

"Have you told anyone besides us?" asked Ponter.

"Louise. And I've asked her to tip off Reuben Montego, too."

Adikor said, "Are you sure they can be trusted?"

But before Mary could answer, Ponter spoke. "I would trust those Gliksins with my life."

Mary nodded. "We can count on them. But we can't be sure about anyone else."

"Well," said Ponter, "not anyone else in *this* world. But *everyone* in my world stands to lose if Jock releases his virus. We should go there, and . . ."

"And what?" said Mary.

Ponter lifted his shoulders. "And shut down the portal. Sever the link. Protect our home."

"There are more than a dozen Barasts here, on this side of the portal," said Mary.

"We must get them home first, then," said Ponter.

"The reason they're here is to *keep* the High Gray Council from closing the portal," said Adikor. "It won't be easy to convince them to return—and, regardless, who knows when we'll be able to move Lonwis?"

Ponter frowned. "Still, it's too dangerous to let Jock have a way of transmitting his virus to our world."

"Maybe we've got it wrong," said Adikor. "Maybe Jock just hates the fact that there are Barasts *here*, on this Earth. Maybe he intends to release his virus here."

"In which case," said Ponter, "the first step is still to get all Barasts back to our side. But you heard what he said: 'I get reports on all Neanderthal comings and goings.' It would be easier for him to simply track down the handful of Barasts already here and kill us by more conventional means."

Adikor took a deep breath. "I guess you're right." He looked at Mary, then back at Ponter. "When you returned from your first visit to this world, I asked you whether the Gliksins were good people, whether we should try to re-establish contact with them."

Ponter nodded. "I know. This is my fault. It's—"

"*No*," said Mary emphatically. If there was one thing all the brochures Keisha had given her had taught her, it was that you can't blame the victim. "No, it is not your fault, Ponter."

"You are kind," said Ponter. "So, how should we proceed?"

"I'm going to get back into Jock's computer tonight, after he leaves," said Mary, "and modify the viral design, so that it isn't dangerous. Let's just pray he hasn't already output the actual virus."

"Mare . . ." said Ponter gently.

"I know, I know. You don't pray. But maybe you should start."

Chapter Thirty-seven

"Who would have thought that both destinies for Mars could be fulfilled? But, of course, now they can. We will travel to the Mars of this universe, the one that graces the night skies of the Americas, Africa, Europe, Asia, and Oceania, and, as has ever been our way, we will conquer this new frontier, making an additional home for Homo sapiens there..."

When they returned to the mansion, Jock was waiting for them. Mary thought her heart was going to explode. "Adikor, Ponter," said Jock. "I'm afraid you're going to have to leave us."

"Why?" said Adikor.

"The hospital called. Lonwis's condition is deteriorating, and they don't know what to do. He's going to be rushed back to the Neanderthal world, so that he can be treated there. I've arranged for a U.S. Air Force plane to take him up to Sudbury, but he wants the two of you to accompany him. He says—I'm sorry, gentlemen, but he says he may not last much longer, and he needs to go over his quantum-computing ideas with the two of you."

Ponter looked at Mary. Mary lifted her eyebrows, wishing there were some alternative. "I'll drive you to the airport," she said.

"Say, guys," said Jock, "before you go, one question."

"Yes?" asked Ponter.

"When does—what do you call it?—'Two becoming One'? When does that happen next?"

"Three days from now," said Adikor. "Why?"

"Oh, no special reason," said Jock. "Just curious."

The codon writer remained in Jock's safe, dammitall. Mary really wanted to take it with her when she and Louise fled to Canada, but that wasn't going to be possible. Still, although the safe was apparently impregnable, Jock's computer files were not. Louise had had no trouble compromising Jock's password file—his password turned out to be "minimax," a term Mary vaguely recognized as having something to do with game theory—and after everyone else had left for the evening, Mary slipped back into Jock's office, while Louise returned to her own lab.

Mary entered "minimax" at the password prompt, gaining access to the hidden files on the Synergy server. She then clicked on the Surfaris icon, and the USAMRIID Geneplex program opened, displaying the virus's design. Mary set about modifying it.

It was a heady experience. Despite her scientific training, despite everything Vissan had said, down deep, some part of Mary still thought there was something mystical about life; that, at its core, it was more than just chemistry. But of course it wasn't; the geneticist in her knew that. Program the right sequence of nucleotides, and you'll ultimately produce a series of proteins that will do precisely what you wish. Still, Mary could scarcely believe what she was doing. It was like back when she was married to Colm. He'd written poetry in his spare time, selling—in the poet's sense of the word, meaning giving away in exchange for copies of the publication—dozens of poems to places like *The Malahat Review*, *White Wall Review*, and *HazMat*. Mary had always been astonished that he could sit down at his keyboard, pounding away in WordStar—would he ever give that program up?—and produce something beautiful, meaningful, and unique out of absolutely nothing.

And now Mary was doing the same thing: specifying sequences that would eventually be output as an actual lifeform—or, at least, as a virus—that had never existed before. Of course, she was really only modifying the existing Surfaris template that some other geneticist had created, but, still, the resulting virus would indeed be novel.

And yet, the virus she was creating wouldn't actually do anything. Whereas the original design would have aborted only if it was hosted in the cell of a Gliksin, rather than a Barast, Mary's version would abort *regardless* of the input it received: it would do nothing no matter what sort of cell it was within. It was only the branching logic Mary was changing. She left the code that would produce the hemorrhagic fever intact not out of any desire to see it ever invoked, but rather to make sure that, at a cursory glance at least, her sequence would look like the one Jock had intended the codon writer to produce.

Mary wanted a name to mentally distinguish her version from Jock's. She frowned, trying to think of something appropriate. Jock's original had been named "Surfaris"—a word that even the on-line Oxford English Dictionary didn't have in its database. But then it occurred to Mary that it might be a plural form, and so she tried what she guessed would be the singular, although that looked like it could be a plural in its own right: "surfari."

And there it was: a blending of "surfing" and "safari,"

referring to the search surfers make for decent waves. Mary couldn't see the relevance, so she typed the term, in the plural form Jock had used, into Google.

Of course.

The Surfaris. A rock group who in 1963 recorded what went on to be a standard on golden-oldie stations, "Wipeout."

Sweet Jesus, thought Mary. *Wipeout.*

She shook her head in disgust.

Well, what's the opposite of "wipeout?"

At thirty-nine, Mary was young enough—barely—to remember the heyday of vinyl 45-rpm records. Doubtless "Wipeout" had been released in that format. But what had been on—she still remembered the term—the flip side? Google to the rescue: "Surfer Joe," written by Ron Wilson. Mary honestly couldn't remember ever hearing that song, but then again, that was often the fate of B-sides.

Regardless, it was as good a code name as any: she'd think of Jock's original as the Wipeout virus, and her modified, do-nothing version as Surfer Joe. Of course, she saved Surfer Joe with the same filename Jock's geneticist had used for the Wipeout version, but at least she could keep them straight in her mind now.

Mary leaned back in her chair.

It *did* feel like playing God.

And, she had to admit, it felt good.

She allowed herself a little chuckle, wondering what Neanderthals called megalomaniac thoughts. Surely not playing God. Maybe "pulling a Lonwis" . . .

"Mary!"

Mary's heart jumped. She'd thought she was alone here. She looked up and—

God, no.

Cornelius Ruskin was standing in the doorway.

"What are you doing here?" Mary said, her voice trembling. She grabbed a heavy malachite paperweight off the worktable.

Cornelius held up a hand; in it was a brown leather wallet. "I forgot my wallet at my desk. I just came in to pick it up."

Suddenly it hit Mary. The other geneticist. The one Jock had been using to code this . . . this *evil*. It was Cornelius. It had to be.

"What are you doing in Jock's office?" asked Cornelius.

Cornelius couldn't see Jock's LCD screen from the doorway. "Nothing. Just looking for a book."

"Well," said Cornelius. "Mary, I—"

"You've got your wallet. Get out."

"Mary, if you'd just—"

Mary's stomach was roiling. "Louise is upstairs, you know. I'll scream."

Cornelius stood in the doorway, his expression weary. "I just want to say I'm sorry—"

"Get out! Get the hell out of here!"

Cornelius hesitated for a moment, then turned. Mary listened to his footfalls go down the corridor, and the sound of the heavy door to the mansion opening and closing.

Her vision was blurry, and she felt nauseous. She took a deep breath, then another one, trying to calm herself. Her hands were slick with sweat, and there was a sour taste at the back of her throat. *Damn him, damn him, damn him . . .*

The rape exploded in Mary's mind again, with a vividness that she hadn't felt for weeks. Cornelius Ruskin's cold blue eyes visible behind the black ski mask, the stench of cigarettes on his breath, his arm pushing her back against that retaining wall.

God damn Cornelius Ruskin.

God damn Jock Krieger.

Damn them both to hell.

Damn *men* to hell.

Only men would create something like the Wipeout virus. Only men would do something so heinous, so abominable.

Mary snorted. There weren't even proper words left for such evil. "Heinous" had been robbed of its power by Keanu Reeves using it in *Bill & Ted's Excellent Adventure*, and "abominable" was almost always followed by "snowman," as if such evil could only exist in the realm of myth.

She'd always associate such evil with this world, the world of Genghis Khan and Adolf Hitler and Pol Pot and Paul Bernardo and Osama bin Laden.

And Jock Krieger.

And Cornelius Ruskin.

A world of *men*.

No, not just of men. A very specific *kind* of man. Male *Homo sapiens*.

Mary took a deep breath, calming herself. Not all men were evil. She knew that. She really did. There was her dad, and her brothers, and Reuben Montego, and Fathers Caldicott and Belfontaine.

And Phil Donahue and Pierre Trudeau and Ralph Nader and Bill Cosby.

And the Dalai Lama and Mahatma Gandhi and Martin Luther King, Jr.

Compassionate men, admirable men. Yes, there were *some*.

Mary had no idea how to distinguish genetically between great men and evil ones, between visionaries and psychopaths. But there was one glaring genetic marker for male violence: the Y chromosome. Granted, not everyone who had a Y chromosome was an evil man; indeed, the vast majority weren't. But every evil man, by definition, had to have a Y chromosome, the shortest of all *Homo sapiens* chromosomes and yet the one that had the biggest impact on psychology.

And history.

And the safety of women and children.

Cornelius Ruskin had a Y.

Jock Krieger likewise.

Y.

Why?

No. No, it was too much. It really was too redolent of playing God.

But she *could* do it. Oh, she'd never dream of unleashing such a thing here, in this world. She was no murderer—that much of her own personal code of ethics Mary was certain of, for the man she hated most, the man she most wanted to see punished, was Cornelius Ruskin, and when Ponter had proposed killing him, Mary had insisted he not do it.

And, despite Adikor's suggestion, Mary was sure Jock Krieger never meant for his Wipeout virus to be introduced to *this* version of Earth. It was doubtless intended for the other version, the Neanderthal world, a serpent for the un-spoiled Eden.

Of course, if everything went as planned, if she managed to stop Jock, no virus would be released in the Neanderthal world.

But if one was to be, well, hopefully it would be Mary's Surfer Joe, either in the version she'd just produced, which did nothing, or . . .

Or . . .

She could make a more radical revision, producing a ver-sion that modified the original logic to act only if—

It was simple, so simple.

A version that would act only if the host cell the virus had invaded *did not* belong to a Neanderthal, and *did* contain a Y chromosome.

If, and only if . . .

Mary frowned. A revised Surfer Joe.

A Mark II—just like the new Pope, taking it all one step further.

She shook her head. It was madness. Sinful.

Or was it? She'd be protecting an entire world from male *Homo sapiens*. After all, if she and the paleoanthropologists who shared her view were right, it had been male *Homo sapiens*—the hunters in the clan, not the gatherers, not the women—who had slaughtered their browridged cousins here until not a single one was left.

And now, using the tools of the twenty-first century and technology borrowed from the Barasts themselves, male *Homo sapiens* were preparing to do again what male *H. sap* had done once before.

Mary looked at Jock's computer screen.

It would be so simple. So very simple. The logic tree was already in place. She only needed to change the sequences being tested for, and which way the logic branched.

Testing for a Y chromosome was easy enough: just pick a gene from the Human Genome Project database that appeared only on that chromosome. Mary rummaged on Jock's desk for pen and paper, then wrote out the logic in longhand on a yellow ruled pad:

> Step 1: Is a Y chromosome present?
> If **yes**, this is a male: go to Step 2
> If **no**, abort (this isn't a male)

Step 2: Is Gene ALPHA found next to a telomere?
If **yes**, abort (this is a Neanderthal)
If **no**, this is probably a Gliksin: go to Step 3

Step 3: Is Gene BETA found next to a telomere?
If **yes**, abort (this should never happen in a Gliksin)
If **no**, this is definitely a Gliksin: go to Step 4

Mary looked at what she'd written over and over again, but couldn't find a flaw. There was no point at which the logic could get caught in an infinite loop, and there were not one but two checks to make sure she was really dealing with a *Homo sapiens* male and not a *Homo neanderthalensis* one.

Of course, it was all moot—surely Jock *would* be stopped before he could release his virus. Modifying it now was just a safeguard, in case somehow it made it over to the other side.

Mary shook her head and looked at her watch. It was well after midnight—the start of a new day.

She should just go home now. Jock's Wipeout virus had been defused; it would do nothing at all, assuming, as Mary fervently hoped, that he hadn't yet used the codon writer to output the actual viral molecules. Surfer Joe would harm no one. That's all she'd set out to accomplish, after all.

That's all that needed to be done.

And yet . . .

And yet.

No one would have to get hurt. She'd find a way to disseminate the information, to make sure that everyone on this Earth knew that it was unsafe for male Gliksins to travel to the Neanderthal world. The Barast tuned-laser decontamination technology would make sure the Surfer Joe virus never got back across the portal to this world. Male Gliksins—the majority that were decent, and the horrible minority that did so very much harm—would be safe, just as long as they left Ponter's world the hell alone.

Mary took a deep breath, then let it out slowly.

She folded her hands in her lap, the left still showing the pale indentation on the third finger where her wedding ring had once been.

And Mary Vaughan thought and thought and thought.

And at last she unfolded her hands.

And then, of course, she did the only thing she could do.

Chapter Thirty-eight

"And although someday we may also travel to Dargal—for that is what the Neanderthals named the red planet of their universe, the crimson beacon that beams down upon the continents of Durkanu, Podlar, Ranilass, Evsoy, Galasoy, and Nalkanu—we will leave that version of Mars as we find it. Truly, like so much in this new era we are now entering, we will have our cake and eat it, too . . ."

Mary Vaughan sat bolt upright in her bed at Bristol Harbour Village, suddenly awake.

When does—what do you call it?—'Two becoming One'? When does that happen next? That's what Jock had asked yesterday. Mary had been too upset about Lonwis's deteriorating condition and Ponter's impending departure to really think about it then, but it hit her now, forcing her awake: why Jock should care.

While Two were One would be the perfect time to release his virus. It would be far easier to infect at least the local population in Saldak when everyone of both sexes was together in the Center—and, of course, there was more intercity traffic during Two being One than at any other time of the month; the virus would be spread rapidly.

The four-day holiday would begin the day after tomorrow. That meant Jock wouldn't act until then—meaning Mary had to act *before* then.

She looked up at the ceiling to see what time it was—but she was *here*, not *there*, and there was nothing on her ceiling. She turned to the digital clock on the night table, the red digits glowing: 5:04 A.M. Mary fumbled to turn on the table lamp, then picked up her phone and called Louise Benoît's home number in Rochester.

"*Allô?*" said a sleepy voice after six rings.

"Louise, it's Mary. Look—Two become One the day after tomorrow. I'm sure that's when Jock is going to release his virus."

Louise was clearly struggling to consciousness. "Two becoming . . ."

"Yes, yes! Two becoming One. It's the only time on the Neanderthal world when there's high population density in their cities, and a lot of intercity traffic. We have to do something."

"*D'accord,*" said Louise, her voice raw. "*Mais quoi?*"

"What you said we should do: go to the media, blow the whistle. But, look, it'll be safer for both of us if we're back in Canada before we do that. I'll be out of here in half an hour, meaning I can pick you up by 6:30 A.M. We'll drive up to Toronto."

"*Bon,*" said Louise. "I'll be ready."

Mary clicked off and headed for the bathroom, starting the shower running. Now, if she only knew *how* to blow the whistle. Of course, she'd been interviewed on TV and radio plenty of times now, and—

She thought of a nice female producer she'd met at CBC Newsworld in 1996, back when the only Neanderthals known were fossils, back when Mary had isolated a DNA sample from the Neanderthal type specimen at the Rheinisches Landesmuseum. CBC on-air personalities probably didn't have listed phone numbers, but there was no particular reason why a producer wouldn't. Mary headed back into the bedroom, scooped up the telephone handset, dialed 1-416-555-1212, Toronto directory assistance, and got the number she needed.

A minute later she had another groggy woman on the phone. "H-hello?"

"Kerry?" said Mary. "Kerry Johnston?"

She could almost hear the woman rubbing her eyes. "Yes. Who's this?"

"This is Mary Vaughan. Remember me? The geneticist from York—the expert on Neanderthal DNA?"

A small part of Mary was disappointed that neither Louise nor Kerry had offered up the cliché, "Do you have any idea what time it is?" Instead, Kerry seemed now to be instantly awake. "Yes, I remember you," she said.

"I've got a huge story for you."

"I'm listening."

"No, it's nothing I can tell you about by phone. I'm down in Rochester, New York, right now, but I'll be in Toronto in about five hours. I need you to put me live on Newsworld when I get there . . ."

Mary and Louise were driving along the Queenston-Lewiston bridge over the Niagara River. Exactly in the middle of the bridge three flags snapped salutes in the breeze, marking the border: first the Stars and Stripes, then the robin's-egg-blue UN flag, and finally the Maple Leaf. "Nice to be back home," said Louise as they passed them.

As she always did, Mary felt herself relax a bit now that they had returned to her home and native land. Indeed, an old joke came to mind: Canada could have had British culture, French cuisine, and American know-how . . . but instead ended up with American culture, British cuisine, and French know-how.

Still, it *was* nice to be back.

Once off the bridge, they were confronted by a row of customs booths. Three of the four that were open had small lineups of cars in front of them; the fourth had a longer queue of trucks. Mary joined the middle car line and waited for the vehicles ahead of them to be dealt with, tapping the steering wheel impatiently with the flat of her left hand.

At last, it was their turn. Mary pulled up to the booth and rolled down her window. She expected to hear a Canadian customs official's usual greeting: "Citizenship?" But instead, to her astonishment, the female officer said, "Ms. Vaughan, right?"

Mary's heart jumped. She nodded.

"Pull over up ahead, please."

"Is there—is there something wrong?" asked Mary.

"Just do as I say," she said to Mary, then picked up a telephone handset.

Mary felt her palms go moist on the steering wheel as she drove slowly ahead.

"How'd they know it was you?" asked Louise.

Mary shook her head. "License plate?"

"Should we make a run for it?" asked Louise.

"My name's Mary, not Thelma. But, Christ, if—"

A balding customs agent, paunch flopping over his belt, was coming out of the long, low inspection building. He waved for Mary to pull into one of the angled parking spots in front of it. She'd only ever stopped here before to use the public washroom—and then only when desperate; it was rather squalid.

"Ms. Vaughan? Ms. Mary Vaughan?" said the agent.

"Yes?"

"We've been waiting for you. My assistant is putting a call through right now."

Mary blinked. "For me?"

"Yes—and it's an emergency. Come along!"

Mary got out of the car, and so did Louise. They went into the customs building, and the fat man brought them around behind the counter. He picked up a phone, hit a line key. "I have Ms. Vaughan," he said into the handset, then he passed it to Mary.

"This is Mary Vaughan," she said.

"Mary!" exclaimed a Jamaican-accented voice.

"Reuben!" She looked over and saw Louise smile broadly. "What's up?"

"God, woman, you need to get a cell phone," said Reuben. "Look, I know you and Louise are heading to Toronto, but I think you'd better get up here to Sudbury—and fast."

"Why?"

"Your Jock Krieger has gone through the portal."

Mary's heart jumped. "What? But how'd he get up there so quickly?"

"He must have flown, and that's what you should do, too. It'd take six hours to drive up here from where you are. But I've got *The Nickel Pickle* waiting for you in St. Catherines." *The Nickel Pickle* was Inco's corporate Learjet, painted dark green on its sides. "I only found out he'd gone over by accident," continued Reuben. "Saw his name on the mine-site visitors' log when I was signing somebody else in."

"Why didn't anybody stop him?" asked Mary.

"Why *should* they have? I checked with the Canadian Forces guys down at the neutrino observatory; they said he had a U.S. diplomatic passport, so they ushered him right through to the other side. Anyway, look, I've faxed a map to the customs station, showing how to get to the airfield . . ."

Chapter Thirty-nine

"And it is a new era we are entering. The Cenozoic—the era of recent life—is indeed all but over. The Novozoic—the era of new life—is about to begin ..."

"Medical emergency!" snapped Reuben Montego. His shaved black head glistened in the harsh lights of the giant building. "We're going straight down to the 6800-foot level."

The elevator technician nodded. "Right you are, Doc."

Mary knew that the cage had been waiting here on the surface in response to a call Reuben had made from his office. The three of them hurried inside, and the technician, who would stay up top, pulled down the heavy cage door. He then gave five blasts on the buzzer—express descent with no stops. The elevator began its drop down a shaft five times as deep as each of the World Trade Center towers had been tall—until, of course, some male *Homo sapiens* had destroyed them ...

On the way in, Mary, Louise, and Reuben had grabbed hardhats and mining coats from the racks in the changing area. They struggled to get them on as the elevator made its noisy descent.

"What sort of police force do they have on the other side?" asked Reuben in his deep, Jamaican-accented voice.

"Hardly any," said Mary, half shouting to be heard above

the racket. *And it should stay that way*, she thought: a world free of crime and violence.

"So it's up to us?" said Reuben.

"I'm afraid so," said Mary.

"What about taking some of the Canadian Forces guys with us?" asked Louise.

"We still don't know who's behind this," said Mary. "It could be Jock acting alone—or it could go all the way to the DND and the Pentagon."

Louise looked at Reuben, and Mary saw him draw her close. If they were half as scared as Mary felt, she couldn't blame them for wanting to hold each other. Mary moved over to the far side of the mud-covered lift and made a show of watching the levels go by, so that Reuben and Louise could have a few minutes to themselves.

"My English vocabulary is clearly still wanting," said Christine's voice through Mary's cochlear implants. "What does juh-tahm mean?"

Mary hadn't made out a thing; evidently the Companion's microphones were more discerning. She whispered so that the others wouldn't be able to hear her. "That's not English, it's French: *'Je t'aime.'* It means 'I love you.' Louise told me Reuben always switches to French to say that."

"Ah," said Christine. They continued down, until the lift finally shuddered to a halt. Reuben hoisted the door, revealing the mining drift, heading off into the distance.

"What time did he go through?" demanded Mary, once they'd finally reached the staging area to the portal, built on a platform in the barrel-shaped six-story-tall Sudbury Neutrino Observatory chamber.

A Canadian Forces man looked up, eyebrows lifted. "Who?"

"Jock Krieger," said Mary. "From the Synergy Group."

The man—blond, light-skinned—consulted a clipboard. "We had a John Kevin Krieger go through about three hours ago."

"That's him," said Mary. "Did he have anything with him?"

"Forgive me, Dr. Vaughan," began the officer, "but I really don't think I'm supposed to divulge—"

Reuben moved forward and showed him an ID card. "I'm Dr. Montego, the mine-site physician here, and this is a medical emergency. Krieger may be highly infectious."

"I should call my superior," said the soldier.

"Do that," snapped Reuben. "But first tell us what he was carrying."

The man frowned, thinking. "One of those overnight bags that rolls on wheels."

"Anything else?"

"Yes, a metal box, about the size of a shoebox."

Reuben looked at Mary. "Damn," she said.

"Was the box put through decontamination?" asked Louise.

"Of course," said the soldier, his tone defensive. "Nothing goes through without being decontaminated."

"Good," said Mary. "Let us through."

"Can I see your identification?"

Mary and Louise slapped their passports down. "All right?" said Mary. "Now, let us through."

"What about him?" said the soldier, pointing at Reuben.

"Damn it, man, I just showed you my Inco card," said Reuben. "I don't have my passport with me."

"I'm not supposed to—"

"For Pete's sake!" said Mary. "This is an emergency!"

The soldier nodded. "All right," he said at last. "All right, go ahead."

Mary ran on, leading the way to the Derkers tube. As soon as she got to its mouth, she continued on through, and—

Blue fire.

Static electricity.

Another world.

Mary could hear two sets of footfalls behind her, so she didn't look back to see if Louise and Reuben were following as she hurried out of the tube. A burly male Neanderthal technician looked up, astonished. Probably no one had ever come running out of the portal before.

The Neanderthal was one Mary knew on sight. He clearly recognized her, too, but, to Mary's astonishment, he was making a beeline to tackle Reuben, who was just behind Mary.

Mary suddenly realized what was going on: the Neanderthal thought Louise and Reuben were chasing Mary, not following her. "No!" shouted Mary. "No, they're with me! Let them pass!"

Her own shouting meant that Christine had to wait until she'd finished her exclamation before translating the words, lest her external speaker—capable of a healthy volume, but nowhere near as loud as a shouting human—be drowned out. Mary listened to the Neanderthal words that came from her forearm: "*Rak! Ta sooparb nolant, rak! Derpant helk!*"

By about halfway through the translation, the Neanderthal technician tried to abort his run, but he slipped on the polished granite computing-chamber floor and went sliding into Reuben, sending the M.D. flying. Louise tumbled over the Neanderthal, somersaulting onto her back.

Mary reached down and helped Louise up. Reuben was getting to his feet, too.

"*Lupal!*" called the Neanderthal. *Sorry!*

Mary headed up the half flight of stairs into the control room, passing another startled Neanderthal, then continued on toward the drift that connected the quantum-computing facility to the rest of the nickel mine.

"Wait!" shouted the second Neanderthal. "You have to go through decontamination!"

"There's no time," Mary shouted back. "This is an emergency, and—"

But Reuben interrupted her. "No, Mary, he's right. Remember how sick Ponter got when he first came to our side? We're trying to prevent a plague, not start one."

Mary swore. "All right," she said. She looked at Reuben and Louise, the black Jamaican-Canadian with the shaved head and the pale Québecois with the long brunette hair. They'd doubtless seen each other naked many times, but neither had seen Mary that way. "Strip down," she said decisively. "Everything off, including watches and jewelry."

Louise and Reuben were used to decontamination procedures from working at the Sudbury Neutrino Observatory, which had been kept in clean-room conditions until Ponter's original arrival destroyed the detector. Still, they each hesitated for a moment. Mary started undoing her blouse. "Come on," she said. "There's no time to waste."

Reuben and Louise began removing their clothing.

"Just leave your clothes here," said Mary as she tossed her panties into a round hamper. "We can pick up Neanderthal clothing in the next room."

Mary, now totally nude, entered the cylindrical decontamination chamber. It had been designed to comfortably hold one adult Neanderthal, but at Mary's insistence, all three of them piled into it, in order to save time. Mary was too nervous to be embarrassed as Louise's backside pressed against her own, or as Reuben, who had ended up facing toward Mary, was pressed face first against her breasts.

Mary pulled out a control bud. The floor started slowly rotating, and lasers began firing. Mary was used to the procedure by now, but she could hear Louise gasp as the formidable-looking beam emitters hummed to life.

"It's okay," said Mary, trying to ignore the part of her brain that was calculating exactly what portions of Reuben were pressed up against her. "It's perfectly safe. The lasers know which proteins should be in a human body—including those in intestinal bacteria, and so on—and they pass right through them. But they break down foreign proteins, killing any pathogens."

Mary could feel Louise squirm slightly, but she sounded fascinated. "What kind of lasers can do that?"

"Quantum-cascade lasers," said Mary, parroting something she'd heard Ponter say. "In the trillion-cycles-per-beat range."

"Tunable terahertz lasers!" exclaimed Louise. "Yes, of course. Something like that *could* selectively interact with large molecules. How long does the process take?"

"About three minutes," said Mary.

"Say, Mary," said Reuben. "You should have someone look at that mole on your left shoulder . . ."

"What?" said Mary. "Jesus, Reuben, this isn't the time—" But she cut herself off, realizing he was doing exactly what Louise had just been doing: retreating into a technical mindset, trying to keep professional. After all, Reuben was buck naked with two women, one of whom was his lover and the other his lover's friend. The last thing he—or Mary—needed right now was for him to be composing a letter to *Penthouse* in his head. "I'll see a dermatologist," she said, softening her tone. She shrugged as much as the tight confines would allow. "Damned ozone layer . . ."

Mary rotated her head slightly. "Louise, there should be a square light above the door in front of you. Do you see it?"

"Yes. Oh, it's green! Good." She shifted slightly, as if making to exit.

"Freeze!" snapped Mary. "Green is the Neanderthal color for 'halt'—green meat is rotten meat. When it turns red, that means it's okay to proceed. Let us know as soon as it does."

Louise nodded; Mary could feel the back of the younger woman's head going up and down. Maybe it had been a mistake to bring along two people who had had no preparation for the Neanderthal world. After all, it could be—

"Red!" exclaimed Louise. "The light is red!"

"All right," said Mary. "Push the door open. The handle looks like a starfish—see it? It slides up to unlatch the door."

Mary could feel Louise squirming some more, and then suddenly the pressure was off Mary's back as Louise stepped out of the chamber. Mary took a backward step, turned around, and hurried out of the chamber as well. "This way!" she shouted.

They entered a room whose walls were covered with cubic cubbyholes, each containing a set of Neanderthal clothes. "Those should fit you, Reuben," said Mary, pointing at one set. "And those should do for you," she said, indicating another.

Mary was an old hand now at getting into Barast garments, but Louise and Reuben were clearly baffled. Mary shouted instructions at Reuben, and bent down next to Louise, who was having trouble with the footwear built into the Neanderthal pants. Mary did up her instep and ankle ties for her.

They then hurried out into the drift. Mary had hoped there would be a vehicle of some sort waiting there, but, of course, if there had been one, Jock himself would have taken it.

A three-kilometer-long run, thought Mary. Sweet Jesus, she hadn't done anything like that since her undergrad days, and even then she'd been terrible. But adrenaline was pumping through her like there was no tomorrow—which, she knew, might very well be the case for the Barasts. She ran off down the tunnel, its floor covered with flat wooden boards.

There was much less illumination in this tunnel than in the corresponding one on the Gliksin side. The Neanderthals used robots for mining that didn't need much light. For that matter, neither did Neanderthals, whose sense of smell gave them an excellent mental picture of what was going on around them.

"How . . . far . . . is . . . it?" called Louise from behind.

Despite the urgency of the situation, Mary was pleased to hear the young woman sounding winded already. "Three thousand meters," Mary shouted back.

Something suddenly cut across the path in front of Mary. If her heart hadn't already been pounding, it probably would have started then. But it was just a mining robot. She called out that fact so that Reuben and Louise wouldn't be startled, then she found herself shouting to the robot, "Wait! Come back here!"

Christine obliged with a translation, and a moment later the robot reappeared. Mary got a good look at it now: a low, flat, six-legged contraption, like a two-meter-long crab, with conical bores and hemispherical scoops projecting forward on articulated arms. The thing was built for hauling rock, for Christ's sake. It *had* to be strong enough. "Can you carry us?" asked Mary.

Her Companion translated the words, and a red light winked on the robot's shell. "This model is incapable of speech," added Christine, "but the answer is yes."

Mary clambered up onto the machine's silver carapace, severely banging her right shin as she did so. She turned back to Reuben and Louise, who had come to a stop behind her. "All aboard!"

Louise and Reuben exchanged astonished looks but they soon hauled themselves onto the robot's back, as well. Mary slapped the thing's side. "Giddyup!"

Her Companion probably didn't know that word, but surely understood Mary's intention and conveyed it to the robot. Its six legs flexed once, as if to gauge how much weight it was now carrying, and then it set off in the direction they'd been heading, moving fast enough that Mary felt hot wind on her face. There were puddles of muddy water at various points, and every time one of the robot's splayed feet came down into one, Mary and the others got splashed with dirty liquid.

"Hold on!" Mary called out repeatedly, although she doubted Reuben and Louise really needed any urging to do just that. Still, Mary herself felt as though she was going to be bounced right off the carapace a few times, and her bladder was objecting strenuously to the abuse.

They passed another mining robot—a spindly, upright model that reminded Mary a bit of a praying mantis—and then, about 600 meters farther along, they passed a pair of male Neanderthals going in the other direction, who leaped out of the way of the charging robot just in time.

Finally, they made it to the elevator station. Thank God

those two Neanderthals had just come down: the lift was still at the bottom. Mary scrambled off the robotic crab and dashed over to the elevator. Louise and Reuben followed, and as soon as they were all in the cylindrical car, Mary stomped on the floor-mounted switch that started the up-ward journey.

Mary took a moment to see how the others were doing; everything had a slightly greenish cast under the luciferin lights. For once, Louise looked nothing like a fashion model: sweat was running down her face, her hair was matted with mud, and her Neanderthal clothing was absolutely filthy with mud and what, after a second, Mary realized was grease, or something akin to it, from the robot.

Reuben was in even worse shape. The robot had bounded along, and at some point Reuben's bald head must have hit the mine's roof. He had a nasty gash running along his pate, and was gingerly probing it with his fingers, wincing while he did so.

"All right," said Mary. "We've got a few minutes until the elevator reaches the surface. There will be an attendant or two there, and they won't let you pass without having temporary Companions strapped on. You might as well allow that—it'll take less time than to convince those guys that it's an emergency. And, besides, Companions let us communicate with each other, and with any other Neanderthals we need to speak to. All the ones stored here at the mine have the translation database."

Mary knew the elevator cab was gently corkscrewing through 180 degrees as it rose up the shaft, but she doubted Louise and Reuben could tell. She lifted her forearm and spoke to it. "Have you reacquired the planetary information network yet, Christine?"

"No," said the voice coming from Mary's cochlear implants. "I probably won't be able to reconnect until we are only a short distance beneath the surface, but I will keep— wait, wait. Yes, I've got it. I am on the network."

"Great!" said Mary. "Get me Ponter."

"Calling," said the implant. "No answer yet."

"Come on, Ponter," urged Mary. "Come on . . ."

"Mare!" came Ponter's voice, as translated and imitated by Christine. "What are you doing back on this side? "Two don't become One until the day after tomorrow, and—"

"Ponter, *shush!*" said Mary. "Jock Krieger has made it over here. We have to find him and stop him."

"He will be wearing a strap-on Companion," said Ponter. "I saw the arguments in the High Gray Council on my Voyeur after Gliksins were let through before without them. Trust me: that is never going to happen again."

Mary shook her head. "He's no idiot. It's certainly worth getting an order to triangulate on his Companion, but I bet he's removed it somehow."

"He can't have," said Ponter. "That would have set off numerous alarms. And he certainly can't be just wandering around on his own. He's probably with Bedros or some other official. No, we should be able to locate him. Where are you?"

The elevator cab shuddered to a halt, and Mary gestured for Reuben and Louise to hurry out. "We've just exited into the equipment room above the Debral nickel mine. Louise and Reuben are with me."

"I'm at home," said Ponter. "Hak, call for travel cubes for Mare and for me, and contact an adjudicator." Mary heard Hak acknowledge the command, then Ponter continued: "Any idea where Krieger might be?"

"At the moment, no," said Mary, "although my guess is that he plans to release the virus in the Center when Two are One."

"That makes sense," said Ponter. "It's the time of maximum population density, and there's lots of intercity travel when its over, so—"

Hak's voice came on, interrupting, untranslated, speaking to Ponter.

"Mare," said Ponter, a moment later. "Hak has reached an adjudicator for me. When your travel cube arrives, head to the alibi-archive pavilion in the Center. I'll meet you there."

A male Neanderthal attendant was now clamping a temporary Companion onto Reuben's left forearm. A moment later he came over to Louise and attached one to her, as well. Mary held up her own arm to show the attendant that she had a permanent unit. "Okay," she said to Louise and Reuben. "Grab some coats and let's go!"

It had snowed since Mary was last here; the glare from the white ground was fierce. "The adjudicator is getting hold of two more adjudicators," Ponter said, coming back on-line, "so that they can order judicial scrutiny of Jock's Companion's transmissions. Once that's done, they can triangulate on him."

"Christ," said Mary, holding a hand over her eyes and scanning the horizon for the travel cube. "How long will that take?"

"Not long, hopefully," said Ponter.

"All right," said Mary. "I'll call you back. Christine, get me Bandra."

"Healthy day," said Bandra's voice.

"Bandra, honey, this is Mary."

"Mare, my darling! I didn't expect you to be back until the day after tomorrow. I'm so nervous about Two becoming One. If Harb—"

"Bandra, get out of the Center. Don't ask me why, just do it."

"Is Harb—"

"It's got nothing to do with Harb. Just get a travel cube, and get going, anywhere far away from the Center."

"I don't understand. It's—"

"Just do it!" said Mary. "Trust me."

"Of course I—"

"And Bandra?" said Mary. She looked at Louise and Reuben, then thought to hell with it. "Bandra, I should have said this before now. I do love you."

Bandra's voice was full of joy. "I love you, too, Mare. I can't wait until we can be together again."

"I've got to go," said Mary. "Hurry, now. Get out of the Center!"

Mary looked defiantly at Louise, who had a "what was *that* all about?" expression on her face. But then Louise pointed past Mary. Mary turned. The travel cube was approaching, flying over an open area covered with a blanket of snow. They ran toward it, and as soon as it had settled to the ground, Mary straddled the saddle-seat beside the driver, a redheaded male 144. She watched as Reuben and Louise climbed into the back and awkwardly mounted the two seats there. "Saldak Center, as fast as possible," Mary said to the driver. Agonizing seconds were lost as her Companion translated her words, and the driver's response.

"Yes, I know Two are separate!" snapped Mary. "And I know he's a male," she said, tossing her head in Reuben's direction. "This is a medical emergency. Go!"

Christine was a clever little device. Mary recognized the Neanderthal imperative "*Tik!*" as the first word she uttered, meaning she had moved "Go!" up to the beginning of her translation. As the driver got the car into motion, the Companion added the rest of what Mary had said.

"Christine, get me Ponter."

"Done."

"Ponter, why the hell does it take *three* adjudicators to order that Jock be tracked?"

Ponter's translated reply started to come into Mary's cochlear implants again. She pulled out a bud on her Companion's silver faceplate, and the rest of his reply was shunted to the external speaker, so that Louise and Reuben could hear: "Hey, you're the one who was saying we didn't have enough safeguards for privacy in our alibi-archive system. In fact, it takes unanimous consent of three adjudicators to order judicial scrutiny of a Companion when no criminal accusation has been made."

Mary glanced at the landscape speeding by—at least it was by Neanderthal standards; the cube was probably only doing sixty kilometers an hour. "Well, can't you accuse him of a crime?" asked Mary. "Then you'll only need one adjudicator, right?"

"This way will be faster," said Ponter. "An accusation requires a complicated procedure, and—ah, here's my travel cube." Mary could hear the sound of a vehicle descending and a few clangings and bangings as Ponter boarded. He snapped the Neanderthal words for "alibi archives," which Mary recognized, then turned his attention back to Mary.

"All right," he said. "Now let's—oh, wait a beat . . ." The connection went dead for a few seconds, then Ponter's voice came back on. "The adjudicators have ordered the judicial scrutiny. A technician at the alibi-archive pavilion is getting a fix on Jock's location now."

Reuben leaned forward so that he could talk into Mary's Companion. "Ponter, this is Reuben Montego. As soon as they've located Krieger, get them to clear the area. I'm safe, and so are Louise and Mary, but any Neanderthals exposed to Jock's virus are as good as dead."

"I will do so," said Ponter. "We can broadcast an emergency message to every Companion. I'll be at the alibi pavilion shortly; I'll make sure it happens."

Ahead, the buildings of Saldak Center loomed. Dozens of women were out putting up decorations for Two becoming One.

"We've located him," said Ponter's voice. "Hak, cease translating; transmit directly." Ponter began to shout in the Neanderthal language, clearly addressing the driver of Mary's travel cube.

The driver replied with several words, one of which was "*Ka.*" The car started veering off.

"He's in Konbor Square," said Ponter, his words once more being translated. "I've told your driver to take you there. I'll meet you there."

"No," said Louise, leaning forward. "No, Ponter, it's too risky for you—for any Neanderthal. Leave it to us."

"He is not alone. The adjudicators are looking at his Companion transmissions right now; he's with Dekant Dorst."

"Who is that?" asked Mary.

"One of Saldak Center's elected officials," said Ponter. "She's a female of generation 141."

"Damn," said Mary. Normally, she'd trust any female Barast to restrain just about any male Gliksin, but 141s were seventy-eight years old. "We don't want this devolving into a hostage-taking. We have to get her out of there."

"Indeed," said Ponter.

"Dekant Dorst must have cochlear implants, right?" said Mary.

"Of course," said Ponter.

"Christine, get me Dekant Dorst."

"Done."

Mary spoke immediately, before the Barast woman could respond to the chirp her Companion would have just made between her ears. "Dekant Dorst, don't say a word, and don't give any sign to Jock Krieger that you are communicating with anyone. Just cough once if you understand."

A cough emanated from Christine's external speaker.

"All right, good. My name is Mary Vaughan, and I'm a Gliksin. Jock is currently under judicial scrutiny. We believe he is smuggling a dangerous substance into Saldak Center. You have to get away from him at the first opportunity. We're on our way to your location now. All right?"

Another cough.

Mary felt awful; the old woman must be terrified. "Any suggestions?" Mary said to Reuben and Louise.

"She could tell Jock that she has to go to the washroom," said Louise.

"Brilliant! Ponter, where are Jock and this woman right now? Indoors or out?"

"Let me ask the adjudicator . . . They are outdoors, heading on foot to the central plaza."

"Jock's Wipeout virus is designed for airborne transmission," said Mary. "He must have some sort of aerosol bomb in that metal box he's carrying. He probably intends to plant it in the central plaza, with it set to go off during the Two becoming One festivities."

"If so," said Ponter, "he'll likely time it to go off right at the end of the holiday, so that all the males will go back home before anyone shows signs of illness. Not only will that get it out to Saldak Rim, but there are many males who come in from further locations."

"Right," said Mary. "Dekant, when the chance presents itself, tell Jock you've got to go into a public building to use the washroom, but that he'll have to stay outside because he's male. Okay? We'll be there soon."

Another cough, and then, for the first time, Mary heard Dekant's voice, sounding quite nervous. "Scholar Krieger," she said, "you must forgive me, but this old body of mine . . . I'm afraid I have to urinate. There's a facility in there that I can use."

Jock's voice, muffled, distant: "Fine. I'll just . . ."

"No, you must wait outside. Two aren't yet One, you know—not yet!"

Jock said something that Mary couldn't quite make out. About twenty seconds later, Dekant spoke. "All right, Scholar Vaughan. I'm safely indoors now."

"Good," said Mary. "Now, if—"

But she was interrupted by a female Neanderthal voice emerging from all four Companions in the travel cube—and, presumably, from every other Companion linked to Saldak's alibi archives. "This is Adjudicator Mykalro," said the voice. "We have an emergency. Immediately evacuate Saldak Center. Do it on foot, by hover-bus, or by travel cube, but get out right now. Do not delay. There may soon be a contagious fatal disease in the air. If you see a male Gliksin with silver hair, avoid him! He is under judicial scrutiny, and is currently located in Konbor Square. I repeat . . ."

Suddenly the driver dropped the travel cube to the ground. "This is as close as I'm going," he said. "You heard the adjudicator. If you want to go further in, you'll have to do it on foot."

"Damn you," said Mary, but Christine didn't translate that. Then: "How far are we?"

The driver pointed. "That's Konbor Square over there."

Off in the distance, Mary could see a series of low buildings, a short stack of travel cubes, and an open area.

Mary was furious, but she pushed up the starfish control that opened her side of the cube and got out. Louise and Reuben followed. As soon as they were clear, the travel cube rose again and began flying back the way they'd come.

Mary started running in the direction the driver had indicated. Jock was in an open area that was covered with well-trod snow. Mary could see other travel cubes moving away from the Center, heading out toward the Rim. She'd hoped the adjudicator had had the good sense not to broadcast her warning to Jock's strap-on Companion. Mary, Reuben, and Louise rapidly closed the distance, getting within twenty meters of him. After catching her breath, Mary called out, "It's over, Jock."

Jock had on a typical mammoth-fur coat and was carrying the metal box the Canadian Forces officer had described— presumably his aerosol bomb. He turned around, looking surprised. "Mary? Louise? And—my goodness! Dr. Montego, isn't it? What are you doing here?"

"We know about the Surfaris virus," said Mary. "You can't get away."

To Mary's astonishment, Jock grinned. "Well, well, well. Three brave Canadians, come to save the Neanderthals." He shook his head. "You people have always made me laugh, with your silly socialism and misguided bleeding hearts. But you know what strikes me as the funniest thing about Canadians?" He reached into his jacket and pulled out a semiautomatic pistol. "You don't carry guns." He aimed the weapon squarely at Mary. "Now, my dear, how was it again that you were going to stop me?"

Chapter Forty

"The dawn of the Cenozoic, the famed Cretaceous-Tertiary boundary when the dinosaurs died out, was marked by a layer of clay, found on both versions of Earth. The beginning of the Novozoic in this universe, our universe, the universe of Homo sapiens, will be marked by the footsteps of the first colonist on Mars, the first member of our species to leave the cradle that is this Earth, never to return ..."

Ponter and the three adjudicators were in the largest viewing room at the alibi-archive pavilion, watching everything unfold from multiple points of view. Not only had the adjudicators switched Jock Krieger's Companion over to judicial scrutiny, they had also done the same for Mary Vaughan's, Louise Benoît's, and Reuben Montego's. Four meter-wide holographic bubbles floated in the room, each one showing the surroundings of one of the four Companions on the scene.

Ponter and the three adjudicators were at risk, too, of course. Although the archive pavilion was located on the periphery of the Center, it was still far too close to where the standoff was occurring. "The female Gliksin with the dark hair was right," said Adjudicator Mykalro, a chunky 142. "You must leave, Scholar Boddit. We all must."

"The three of you go," said Ponter, folding his arms in front of his chest. "I'm staying."

And then Ponter saw Jock pull his gun. His whole spine stiffened; Ponter hadn't seen a gun since he'd been shot by that would-be assassin outside United Nations headquarters. He relived the moment of the bullet tearing into him, hot and piercing and—

And he couldn't let that happen to Mare.

"What sort of weapons are stored here?" demanded Ponter.

Mykalro's white eyebrow went up. "Here? At the archive pavilion?"

"Or next door," said Ponter, "at the Council chamber."

The Neanderthal woman shook her head. "None."

"What about the tranquilizer guns enforcers use?"

"They're kept in the enforcement station, in Dobronyal Square."

"Don't enforcers carry them?"

"Not normally," said another one of the adjudicators. "There's no need. Saldak's Gray Council only authorized the acquisition of six such units; I suspect they're all in storage right now."

"Is there any way to stop him?" asked Ponter, pointing at one of the floating images of Jock.

"Not that any of those puny Gliksins could manage," said Adjudicator Mykalro.

Ponter nodded, understanding. "I'm going to help them. How far away are they?"

The second adjudicator squinted at a status display. "About 7200 armspans."

He could easily run that. "Hak, have you got the exact location noted?"

"Yes, sir," said the Companion.

"All right, Adjudicators," said Ponter, "get to safety. And wish me luck."

"You can't just shoot us," said Mary, trying to keep her voice from quavering, unable to take her eyes off the gun. "There will be a record at the alibi archives."

"Oh, yes, indeed," Jock said. "A fascinating system they've got here, I must say: remote black boxes for every man, woman, and child. Of course, it'll be easy enough to find the archive blocks for the four of us, and once all the Neanderthals are dead, there will be no one to stop me from waltzing into the pavilion and destroying those blocks."

Out of the corner of her eye, Mary saw that Reuben was inching away from her. There was a tree a few meters beyond him; he might be able to get behind it, meaning Jock wouldn't be able to shoot him without changing position. Mary could hardly blame Reuben for trying to protect himself. Louise, meanwhile, was somewhere behind her and presumably off to her right.

"You can't expect your virus to have a worldwide effect from one deployment," said Mary. "The Neanderthals don't have the population density to support a plague. It'll never get past Saldak Center."

"Oh, don't worry about that," said Jock, hefting the metal box. "In fact, I have you to thank, Dr. Vaughan: it was your earlier research that made this possible. We've changed the natural reservoir for this version of Ebola from African shoebills to passenger pigeons. Those birds will carry the virus all over this continent."

"The Neanderthals are peaceful—" said Louise's voice.

"Yes," said Jock. As his eyes shifted to Louise so did his gun. "And that will be their downfall—here, now, just as it was 27,000 years ago, the last time we defeated them."

Mary was thinking about making a run for it, and—

And Reuben did just that, bursting into motion. Jock swung toward him and squeezed off a round. The report startled a flock of birds—passenger pigeons, Mary saw—into flight, but Jock missed, and Reuben was now behind the tree, safe at least for the moment.

When Reuben had made his break to Mary's left, Louise had seized the moment and torn off to the right. Like most of Northern Ontario in either universe, the ground here was strewn with erratics: boulders deposited by glaciers that had receded at the end of the Ice Age. Louise ran, then dove, making it behind a lichen-covered boulder barely big enough to conceal her body.

Mary was still caught in the center, both the tree on her left and the boulder on her right too far to reach without being picked off by Jock Krieger.

"Ah, well," said Jock, shrugging to convey that he felt Louise's and Reuben's temporary shelters were nothing but a minor inconvenience. He aimed the pistol back at Mary. "Say your prayers, Dr. Vaughan."

Ponter ran faster than he ever had before, legs pounding up and down. Although there was a lot of snow on the ground, there were many walking paths that had been cleared, and he was making good progress. He took care to breathe solely through his nose, letting his vast nasal cavities humidify and warm the crisp air before it was drawn into his lungs.

"How far away am I?" Ponter asked.

Hak replied into his cochlear implants. "Assuming they haven't moved, they're just over the next rise." A beat. "You should take pains to be silent," continued the Companion.

"You don't want to alert Jock to your presence."

Ponter frowned. *You don't have to tell an old hunter how to sneak up on his prey.*

Mary's Companion spoke into her cochlear implants. "Ponter is only fifty meters away now. If you can keep Jock talking a little longer . . ."

Mary nodded just enough for Christine to detect the movement. "Wait!" said Mary. "Wait! There's something you don't know!"

Jock's aim didn't waver. "What?"

Mary thought as fast as she could. "The—the Neanderthals . . . they're . . . they're psychic!"

"Oh, come on!" said Jock.

"No, no—it's true!" Suddenly Ponter appeared from over a ridge, behind Jock, silhouetted against the lowering sun. Mary fought to keep her expression neutral. "That's why we have religious feelings, and they don't. Our brains are trying to contact other minds, but can't; something's wrong with the neural wiring—it makes us think there's some higher presence that we can't quite connect with. But in them, the mechanism works properly. They don't have religious experiences"—Christ, she wasn't buying this herself; how could she expect him to?—"they don't have religious experiences because they are *always* in contact with other minds!"

Ponter was moving his splayed legs in an exaggerated fashion, carefully stepping across the snow, making barely any sound. Jock was downwind of Ponter; if he'd been a Neanderthal, he'd doubtless have detected him by now, but he wasn't a Neanderthal, thank God . . .

"Think of the value of telepathy in covert operations!" said Mary, raising her voice without making it obvious that she was trying to cover what little sound Ponter was making. "And I'm on the trail of the genetic cause of it! You kill me and the Barasts, and the secret is gone for good!"

"Why, Dr. Vaughan!" exclaimed Jock. "An exercise in disinformation. I'm most impressed." Ponter was now as close as he could get to Jock without his own long shadow—damn the low winter sun!—falling into Jock's field of view. Ponter interlocked his fists, ready to smash them down on Jock's head, and—

Jock must have heard something. He began to wheel around a fraction of a second before Ponter's hands came crashing down. Instead of staving in Jock's skull, the fists connected with Jock's left shoulder. Mary heard the sound of cracking bone, and Jock let out a yowl of pain and dropped the bomb box. But he still had the gun in his right hand and he squeezed off a shot. Jock didn't have a Neanderthal's shielding browridge, and when he'd turned toward the sun, the glare had blinded him for an instant; the shot went wide.

There was no way Mary could reach Ponter safely, so she did the next best thing: she ran to her left, joining Reuben behind the tree. Ponter let out a great bellowing roar and swung again, a roundhouse that sent Jock sprawling facedown in a snowbank. The Neanderthal moved quickly, yanking Jock's right arm back, pulling it in a direction it was not meant to go, splitting the air with another hideous *craaack!* Jock screamed, and, in a blur of motion, Ponter had the gun. He tossed it away with such force that it made a whizzing sound as it sliced through the cold, dry air. Ponter then swung Jock around so that he was facing him, and Ponter hauled back his own right arm, its massive fist balled.

Jock rolled to the right, and using his one good arm, he clutched at the silver box, drawing it closer to him. He did something to it, and white gas started pouring out of the box. Ponter was only intermittently visible through the cloud, but Mary saw him grab Jock by the throat and haul back with his other arm, aiming his fist for the center of Jock's face.

"Ponter, no!" shouted Louise, running out from behind the boulder. "We need to know—"

Ponter was already committed to his punch, but must have backed off slightly in response to Louise's words. Still, he connected with an impact that made a sound like a hundred pounds of leather dropping to the floor. Jock's head snapped back, and he slumped to the snow-covered ground, eyes closed.

The cloud continued to expand. Mary ran forward, going straight for the box. Gas continued to pour from it, obscuring her vision. She searched with her hands for some sort of cutoff valve, but found nothing.

Reuben had also run forward, but he'd headed for Jock. He was now crouching down, taking the man's pulse. "He's unconscious, but alive," he said, looking up at Ponter.

Mary took off her coat, trying to wrap up the bomb. She seemed to be managing to contain the box, but then it exploded, the coat shredding, Mary's skin being sliced in a dozen places, and the cloud expanding more and more. It was like being in a super-dense London fog; Mary could only see a meter or two ahead.

Louise was now bending over Jock. "How long will he be out?"

Reuben looked up and shrugged a little. "You heard the sound of Ponter's fist connecting. Jock's got a concussion at least, and probably a skull fracture. It'll be hours, anyway."

"But we need to know!" said Mary.

"Know what?" asked Reuben.

Mary's heart was pounding erratically, her stomach was roiling, acid was clawing up her gullet. "Which version of the virus he used!"

Reuben was completely lost. "What?" he said, getting up.

"Mary modified the virus design last night," said Louise. "If Jock made his stock of it this morning, then . . ."

Mary wasn't listening. Her head was swimming, pounding. She wanted to scream. If Jock had used the codon writer to run off the virus that morning, then he had produced Mary's modified Surfer Joe. But if he'd made it earlier, then the cloud they were standing in was the original Wipeout version, meaning—

Mary's eyes were stinging, and she was having trouble keeping her balance.

—meaning that goddamned Gliksin bastard lying there in the snow had just killed the man she loved.

Chapter Forty-one

"It has been suggested by some scientists that since there was, apparently, only one universe until 40,000 years ago when consciousness arose on Earth, then there is no other consciousness anywhere in this vast universe of ours—or, at least, none older than our own. If that is true, then exploring the rest of space isn't just our destiny, it is our obligation, for there is no one but we Homo sapiens with the desire and means to do it . . ."

At the moment, Ponter looked fine; no virus worked *that* fast. He ripped strips of mammoth hide off Reuben's coat, and Louise and Reuben used them to tie up the unconscious Jock's arms and legs. As soon as he was trussed up, Reuben and Ponter carried Jock into the nearest building—probably the one Dekant Dorst had gone into, although hopefully she had long since left. The sun had set, and it was getting bitterly cold, but, despite everything, they wouldn't leave him out at the mercy of the elements.

Reuben closed the building's door, then he and Ponter returned to where Mary and Louise were. "Come on, big fella," Reuben said. "Let's get you to the mine—we can try the decontaminating lasers there."

Ponter looked up, his blond-brown eyebrow climbing his browridge; like Mary, he clearly hadn't thought of that.

"Do you think there's a chance?" said Mary, looking now at Reuben, her eyes bloodshot, her face so desperate for a miracle.

"I don't see why not," said Reuben. "I mean, if those lasers work the way you said they do, they should zap the virus molecules, no? It will be a solution for Ponter, at least—although perhaps there's a better decontamination facility here in the Center." He looked at Ponter. "Isn't that where your hospitals are?"

Ponter shook his head. "Yes, but the most sophisticated decontamination unit ever built is the one at the portal."

"Then let's get you there," said Reuben.

"We must clear everyone out of the mine and the quantum-computing chamber first," said Ponter. "We can't risk me infecting anyone else."

"Let me call a travel cube," said Mary, and she began speaking into her Companion.

But Reuben touched her arm. "Who would fly it here? We can't risk exposing other Neanderthals."

"Then—then we'll carry him there!" said Mary.

"*Ce n'est pas possible,*" said Louise. "It's kilometers away."

"I can still walk there," said Ponter.

But Reuben shook his head. "I want to get you processed as fast as possible. We don't have the hours it would take."

"God damn it!" said Mary, her fists clenched. "This is ridiculous! There *has* to be a way to get him there in time!" And then, suddenly, she hit upon it. "Hak, you're the most experienced Companion here. Surely you can talk Ponter through driving a travel cube?"

"I can access the procedures and explain them, yes," said the voice from Ponter's forearm.

"Well, hell!" said Mary. "We passed a stack of them on our way here. Let's go!"

———

They quickly reached the stack of stored travel cubes. There was a cylindrical control unit next to the stack, and Ponter did something to it that made a forkliftlike affair lift up the top cube and place it on the ground. The cube's transparent sides swung upward.

Ponter straddled the right-front saddle-seat, and Mary took the one beside him; Reuben and Louise scrambled into the back. "All right," said Ponter, "Hak, tell me how to drive this contraption."

"To activate system power, pull out the amber control bud," said Hak through his external speaker.

Mary looked at the control cluster in front of Ponter. It was actually much less cluttered than the dashboard of her own car; the travel cubes had far fewer convenience features. "There!" she said. Ponter reached forward and pulled out the bud.

"The right-hand lever controls vertical movement," continued Hak. "The left-hand lever controls horizontal movement."

"But they're both up-and-down levers," said Reuben, confused.

"Exactly," said Hak. "It is much easier on the driver's shoulder joint. Now, to operate the ground-effect motors, you use the cluster of controls between the levers—see them there?"

Ponter nodded.

"The big control sets the rotational velocity for the main fan. Now . . ."

"Hak!" snapped Reuben from the back. "We don't have much time. Just tell him what buttons to push!"

"All right, Ponter," said Hak. "Clear your mind, and try not to think. Just do precisely what I say. Pull out the green control bud. Now the blue. Grasp the two levers. Yes, good. When I say 'go,' pull the right-hand lever fifteen percent of a circle toward you and simultaneously move the left-hand lever five percent. All right?"

Ponter nodded.

"Ready?" said Hak.

Ponter nodded again.

"Go!"

The travel cube lurched violently, but it did rise from the ground.

"Now, push in the green bud," said Hak. "Yes. Move the right-hand lever back as far as it will go."

The cube sped forward, although it was listing badly to one side. "We're not level," said Mary.

"Do not worry about it," said Hak. "Ponter, pull the right lever back one-eighth of a turn. Yes, now . . ."

It only took a few minutes to get out of Saldak Center, but it was still a long way to the mine—and it was bloody complicated operating a vehicle that could fly. Mary had never believed it on TV shows when ground controllers were able to talk passengers into landing planes after the pilots had passed out, and—

"No, Ponter!" said Hak, his volume high. "The other way!"

Ponter pulled the horizontal control toward him, but it was too late. The right side of the travel cube slammed into a tree. Ponter and Mary pitched forward. The control sticks collapsed into the dashboard, like telescopes being put away, apparently a safety feature to prevent them from impaling the driver. The cube tumbled over onto its side.

"Anybody hurt?" shouted Mary.

"No," said Reuben. And, "No," agreed Louise.

"Ponter?"

There was no reply. Mary turned to face him. "*Ponter?*"

Ponter was looking down at the Companion implant on his left forearm. It had obviously smashed into something. He opened Hak's faceplate, which clearly took some force to do; it had been deformed by the crash.

Ponter looked up, his deep-set golden eyes moist. "Hak is badly hurt," he said—Christine providing the translation.

"We've got to get going," said Mary gently.

Ponter looked for a few more seconds at his damaged Companion, then nodded. He twisted, then pushed the starfish-shaped door control, and the side of the travel cube popped open. Reuben hauled himself up and out, then dropped to the ground. Louise climbed out next. Ponter easily lifted himself out of the front compartment, then he gave Mary a hand exiting. Then Ponter turned his attention to the exposed underbelly of the travel cube. Mary followed his gaze and could see that the twin fan assemblies were horribly mangled. "It's not going to fly again, is it?" she asked.

Ponter shook his head and made a rueful "look at it" gesture with his right arm.

"How far are we from the Debral mine?" asked Mary.

"Twenty-one kilometers," said Christine.

"And where is the nearest working travel cube?"

"A moment," said Christine. "Seven kilometers to the west."

"*Merde,*" said Louise.

"All right," said Mary. "Let's start walking."

It was getting quite dark—and they were out in the middle of the countryside. Mary had seen enough big animals here during the day; she was terrified to think of what creatures might come out at night. They trudged through the snow for perhaps ten kilometers—five hours of walking in these difficult conditions. Louise's long legs tending to put her out in front.

Overhead, the stars were out—the circumpolar constellations that the Barasts called the Cracked Ice, and the Head of the Mammoth. They continued on, farther and farther, Mary's ears feeling numb from the cold, until—

"Gristle!" said Ponter. Mary turned. He was leaning against Reuben. Ponter held up his hands, and—

Mary felt her heart flutter, and she heard Louise let out a horrified sound. There was blood on Ponter's hands, looking black in the moonlight. It was too late; the hemorrhagic fever, with its artificially accelerated incubation time, had taken hold. Mary looked at Ponter's face, wincing in expectation of what she'd see, but, except for a startled expression, he looked fine.

Mary moved quickly over to Ponter, and braced his other arm, helping to hold him up. And that's when she realized that it wasn't Reuben who was helping Ponter stand; it was Ponter who was helping Reuben.

In the dim light, and against his dark skin, Mary had missed it at first: blood on Reuben's face. She hurried over to him, and almost threw up. Blood was seeping out from around Reuben's eyeballs and ears and running from his nostrils and the corners of his mouth.

Louise was over to her boyfriend in two long strides, and started wiping the blood away, first with her coat's sleeve, then with her bare hands, but it was now coming in such profusion that she couldn't keep up with it. Ponter helped Reuben down onto the snow, and the blood splashed loudly against the whiteness, seeping deeply into it.

"God," said Mary softly.

"Reuben, *mon cher . . .*" said Louise, crouching in the

snow next to him. She placed a hand gently on the back of his head, no doubt feeling the stubble that had grown today.

"Lou . . . eese," he said softly. "Darling, I—" He coughed, and blood welled out of his mouth. And then, as Mary knew he always did when he said the magic words, Reuben switched to French: "*Je t'aime.*"

Tears began dripping from Louise's eyes as the weight of Reuben's head fell backward against her hand. Mary was searching for a pulse on Reuben's right arm; Ponter was doing the same with his left. They exchanged shakes of their heads.

Louise's face contorted, and she cried and cried. Mary moved over to her, kneeling in the snow, an arm around the younger woman, pulling her close. "I'm sorry," Mary said, over and over again, stroking Louise's hair. "I'm sorry, I'm sorry, I'm sorry . . ."

After a few moments, Ponter touched Louise's shoulder gently, and she looked up. "We can't stay here," he said, again with Christine translating.

Mary said, "Ponter's right, Louise. It's getting way too cold. We've got to start walking."

But Louise was still crying, her fists balled tightly. "That bastard," she said, her whole body shaking. "That bloody monster!"

"Louise," said Mary gently, "I—"

"Don't you see?" said Louise, looking up at Mary. "Don't you see what Krieger did? He wasn't content to kill Neanderthals! He made his virus kill black people, too!" She shook her head. "But . . . but I didn't know a virus could work that fast."

Mary shrugged. "Most viral infections are caused by just a few individual virus particles, introduced at a single point on the body. Much of the incubation period is spent just amplifying those initial few particles into a large enough population of viruses to do their dirty work. But we were all literally soaked in a fog of virus, inhaling and absorbing billions of virus particles." She looked at the darkening sky, then back at Louise. "We have to find shelter."

"What about Reuben?" asked Louise. "We can't leave him here."

Mary looked at Ponter, pleading with her eyes for him to stay silent. The last thing Louise needed to hear just now was, *Reuben is no more.*

"We'll come back for him tomorrow," said Mary, "but we've got to get indoors."

Louise hesitated for several seconds, and Mary had the good sense not to prod her further. Finally, the younger woman nodded, and Mary helped her to her feet.

A bitter wind was blowing, causing the snow to drift. Still, they could see the tracks they'd made coming out this way. "Christine," said Mary, "is there any shelter around here?"

"Let me check," said Christine, then, a moment later: "According to the central map database, there is a hunting lodge not far from where our travel cube crashed. It'll be easier to reach than the City Center."

"You two head there," said Ponter. "I'm going to try to make it out to the decontamination facility. Forgive me, but the two of you would just hold me back."

Mary's heart jumped. There were so many things she wanted to say to him, but—

"I will be fine," said Ponter. "Don't worry."

Mary took a deep breath, nodded, and let Ponter draw her into a farewell hug, her body shaking. He released her, then headed off into the cold night. Mary fell in next to Louise, and they trudged ahead, taking directions from Christine.

After a time, though, Louise stumbled, falling face first into the snow. "Are you okay?" Mary asked, helping her up.

"*Oui*," said Louise. "I—my mind keeps wandering. He was such a wonderful man . . ."

It took most of an hour to get to the hunting lodge, Mary shivering all the way, but finally they came to it. The lodge looked much like Vissan's cabin, but larger. They went inside, and activated the lighting ribs, filling the interior with a cold green glow. There was a small heating unit, which they eventually figured out how to turn on. Mary looked at her watch and shook her head. Even Ponter couldn't have made it to the mine's decontamination facility yet.

They were both exhausted—physically and emotionally. Louise lay on the one couch, hugging herself, crying softly. Mary lay down on a cushioned part of the floor, and found herself crying as well, heartsick, despondent, overwhelmed by grief and guilt, haunted by the image of a good man weeping blood.

Chapter Forty-two

> "And if that notion isn't correct—if this and other universes are, as some scientists and philosophers believe, teeming with intelligent life—then we have another duty when we take our next small steps, and that is to put our best foot forward: to show all the other forms of life the greatness that is Homo sapiens, in all our wonderful and myriad diversity. . . ."

Mary prayed repeatedly throughout the night, whispering softly, trying not to disturb Louise. "God in heaven, God of grace, save him . . ."

And later: "God, please, don't let Ponter die."

And later still: "Damn you, God, you owe me one . . ."

Finally, after tossing and turning all night, tormented by dreams of drowning in a sea of blood, Mary became aware of sunlight streaming in through the lodge's small window, and the *kek-kek-kek* call of passenger pigeons heralding the dawn.

Louise was also awake, lying on the couch, staring up at the wooden ceiling.

There was a vacuum box and a laser cooker in the hunting lodge, presumably powered by solar panels on the roof.

Mary opened the vacuum box and found some chops—of what kind of animal, she had no idea—and some roots. She cooked them up, making a simple breakfast for her and Louise.

The lodge had a small square table with saddle-seats on all four sides. Mary straddled one, and Louise sat opposite her.

"How are you doing?" asked Mary gently, after they'd finished eating. She'd never seen Louise like this: bedraggled, with dark circles under her eyes.

"I'm okay," she said softly, in her accented voice, but she sounded anything but.

Mary wasn't sure what to say. She didn't know whether it was best to bring up the topic of Reuben, or to let it be, in hopes that Louise had somehow put it out of her own mind, at least for a few moments. But then Mary thought of the rape, and her utter inability to stop thinking about it early on. There was no way Louise could be thinking about anything other than her dead boyfriend.

Mary reached a hand across the table, taking one of Louise's. "He was a good man," she said, her own voice breaking as she did so.

Louise nodded, her brown eyes dry but bloodshot. "We'd talked about moving in together." Louise shook her head. "He was divorced, and, you know, nobody my age bothers getting married in Québec—the law treats you the same whether you have the piece of paper or not, so why bother? But we'd talked about making things permanent." She looked away. "It was almost a joke between us. He'd say things like, 'Well, when we move in together, we'll have to get a place with big closets,' because he thought I had too many clothes." She looked at Mary; her eyes were moist now. "Just joking stuff like that, but . . ." She shook her head. "But, you know, I thought it was really going to happen. After I finished my work at Synergy, I'd move back up to Sudbury. Or we'd go to Montréal, and Reuben would set himself up in private practice. Or . . ." She shrugged, apparently realizing it was pointless to go on enumerating options that now could never be.

Mary squeezed Louise's hand, and just sat with her for a time. Finally, though, she said, "I want to go find Ponter." She shook her head. "Damn, I got so used to these Companions letting us keep in touch, but with Hak broken . . ."

"Ponter must be okay," said Louise, realizing, apparently, that it was now her turn to provide comfort. "He wasn't showing the slightest sign of fever."

Mary tried to nod in agreement, but her head didn't seem to want to move. She was so upset, so nervous, so . . .

Suddenly there was a scratching sound at the door. Mary's heart jumped. She knew she almost certainly had nothing to fear from Neanderthals, but this was prime hunting territory—or else the lodge wouldn't have been built here. Who knew what sorts of beasts were prowling outside?

"We can't go looking for Ponter," said Louise. "Think about it: the lasers may have zapped the virus that was in him, but that hardly confers immunity, and we're infected, too, no? It may not do anything to white Gliksins, but we're carriers. He can't see us until you and I have been decontaminated, as well."

"So, what should we do then?" asked Mary.

"Get Jock Krieger," said Louise.

"What? Why? He can't hurt anyone where we left him."

"No, but if there is an antidote for the virus, or a way to neutralize it on a large scale, he's the one who would know, right?"

"What makes you think he'll tell us?" said Mary.

Louise's tone was firm for the first time since Reuben had died. "If he doesn't, I'll kill him," she said simply.

They waited until it had been many minutes since they'd heard any animal sounds from outside. Then, cautiously, they opened the lodge's door, snow swirling in.

It took most of the morning to reach the building near Konbor Square where'd they'd deposited the trussed-up Jock Krieger.

"I half expect him to be gone," said Louise as they approached the closed door. "That bastard seems to have no end of tricks up his sleeve . . ."

She pushed up the five-pronged control that unlatched the door.

Jock was not gone.

He was lying on his side. Pools of dark blood were on the floor around him. His skin was white, waxy.

Mary turned him over. There was coagulated blood all over Jock's cheeks and chin, and extending down like wine-colored sideburns from his ears. She glanced down briefly and saw that his pants were also soaked with blood, which had presumably poured out of his lower orifices.

Mary fought to keep down the tubers and meat she'd eaten for breakfast. She looked over at Louise, who was biting her lower lip. Mary turned away and tried to make sense of it all.

Two dead Gliksins.

Two dead *male* Gliksins . . .

It was almost as if . . .

Surfer Joe, Mark II.

But no. No, that was impossible. *Impossible!* Yes, Mary had doodled a design for a virus that would only kill male Gliksins, but she'd shredded those sheets of paper, and she'd certainly never coded it into Jock's program. He'd obviously made his virus *before* Mary had rendered it harmless, then, but . . .

But it *was* behaving like the one Mary had thought of, the one that would kill *Homo sapiens* who had Y chromosomes.

Mary hadn't made that virus. She had *not* . . .

Unless . . .

No, no. That was crazy.

But she'd traveled between universes, and so had Jock. And if, in one version of her reality, she had not made Surfer Joe deadly to male *Homo sapiens*, then . . .

Then, perhaps, in another version of reality she *had* gone ahead with her fantasy, had mapped out such a virus . . .

And this Jock Krieger, the one who had exsanguinated through every natural opening in his body, might have come from *that* version of reality . . .

Mary shook her head. It was all too bizarre. Besides, hadn't Ponter and Louise said often enough that the universe Mary called home and the one Ponter called home were entangled? That they were the two original branches that had split apart when consciousness first arose on Earth 40,000 years ago?

If that was the case . . .

If that was the case, then someone other than Mary had modified the virus.

But who? Why?

Chapter Forty-three

"And we are just that: a great and wonderful people. Yes, we have made missteps—but we made them because we are always walking forward, always marching toward our destiny..."

Cornelius Ruskin tried to control it as he watched the news report, but he couldn't: his whole body was shaking.

He'd intended his modification of Jock Krieger's Surfaris virus as a *defensive* weapon, not an offensive one—a way of protecting the Neanderthal world from the depredations of...

... well, of people like him. Like he used to be...

And now, two men were dead.

Of course, if all went as he'd expected from now on, no more would die. Male *Homo sapiens* would stay in their own world, denied nothing except the right to take their evil through the portal.

Cornelius had found a nice rental house in Rochester, on a tree-lined *Leave It to Beaver* street; such a wonderful contrast to his old penthouse in the slums. But it didn't feel comfortable; it felt like hell. He was gripping the arms of his new easy chair, trying to steady himself, as CNN showed the interview with Mary Vaughan, one of the women he'd raped.

Not that she was discussing that; rather, she was explaining why male Gliksins had to stay here, in this world, never traveling to the Neanderthal one. Accompanying her, looking hale and hearty, was Ponter Boddit.

The interview had been done by CBC Newsworld, and picked up by CNN; Mary had apparently stood Newsworld up a few days ago, when she'd raced off to try to stop Jock Krieger, but now she was back here, in this reality.

The reality that Cornelius Ruskin had to live with.

"So you're saying it's not safe for any male *Homo sapiens* to travel to the Neanderthal world?" asked the male Asian interviewer.

"That's right," said Mary. "The viral strain Jock Krieger released is—"

"That's the strain the U.S. Centers for Disease Control and Prevention has dubbed 'Ebola-Saldak,' correct?" asked the interviewer.

"That's right," said Mary. "We assume Krieger's intention had been to make a strain that was only fatal to Neanderthals, but instead he ended up with something that selectively kills male *Homo sapiens*. We don't know how widely dispersed that strain is now in the Neanderthal world, but we do know that it's fatal to male humans of our species within hours of exposure."

"What about this Neanderthal decontamination technology? Dr. Boddit, what can you tell us about that?"

"It uses tuned lasers to destroy foreign biomolecules in the body," said Ponter. "Both Dr. Vaughan and myself were processed by it before crossing back to this version of Earth. It's completely effective, but, as Dr. Vaughan said, any male Gliksin infected with Ebola-Saldak will die unless treated by this same process very quickly, and there are very few such decontamination stations on my world."

"And other than this laser technology, there's no cure or vaccine?"

"Not yet," said Mary. "Of course, we will try to find one. But, remember, we've been working on cures for other Ebola strains for years, so far without success."

Cornelius shook his head. When he'd realized that Jock wasn't just doing simulations but really planned to produce his virus, Cornelius had modified the code he'd written, had let Jock produce liters of the virus in sealed glassware, and then, when that was done, he'd reinstated the original code, so that if Jock checked it again, he'd never know it had been changed.

It was supposed to compensate a bit, be a step toward evening out Cornelius's karmic account—not that he could ever make up for what he'd done in Toronto. But the rapist had been the *old* him, the *angry* him. He really was a new man now—still wronged, but able to control his anger at being wronged. No, he no longer felt the way he had, back when he'd attacked Mary Vaughan, back when he'd savaged Qaiser Remtulla, back when testosterone had coursed through his veins. But *they* must still feel it, must still wake up in cold sweats, terrifying images of . . .

Well, not of *him*, he imagined, but of a man in a black ski mask. At least, that was how Qaiser must see him, for she didn't know the identity of her attacker.

But Mary Vaughan knew who he was.

It was a double-edged sword. Cornelius understood that. Mary couldn't identify Cornelius without Ponter being exposed to charges for the . . . the *cure* . . . he'd administered to him.

But, still, the images that haunted Mary surely had a face, white-skinned, blue-eyed, features twisted into anger and hatred.

And now, Cornelius realized, it mattered little that no one would likely ever be able to identify his role in Reuben and Jock's deaths. Mary had already told the world that Jock Krieger had made some mistake in designing his virus, that he'd been hoisted on his own petard, the victim of his own creation.

And, truth be told, Cornelius didn't feel too bad about the death of Krieger, who, after all, had been planning genocide for the Neanderthals.

But an innocent man was dead, too, this doctor—this *real* doctor, this healer, this saver of lives, this Reuben Montego.

Cornelius let go of his chair's arms and lifted his hands to see if they were still shaking. They were. He grabbed hold of the armrests again.

"An innocent man," he said aloud, although there was no one but him around to hear it. He shook his head.

As if there could be any such thing . . .

But, then again, maybe there was.

The obituaries and appreciations of Reuben Montego that had already appeared online spoke glowingly of him. And his girlfriend, Louise Benoît, whom Cornelius had met at the Synergy Group, was absolutely devastated by his death, saying over and over again what a kind and gentle man he'd been.

Yet again, Cornelius had caused great sadness to a woman.

He knew he'd have to do something soon about his castration. Other changes, after all, would shortly begin to occur: his metabolism would slow, fat would begin to pile up on his body. He'd already noticed that his beard came in more slowly, and he was feeling listless much of the time— listless, or depressed. The obvious solution was to start testosterone treatments. Testosterone was a steroid, he knew, produced mainly in the testicles' Leydig cells. But he also knew it could be synthesized from more readily obtainable steroids, such as diosgenin; doubtless there was a black market in it. Cornelius had tried to ignore the drug dealing going on near his old apartment in Driftwood, but surely if he'd wanted to find a dealer for testosterone, he could locate one there, or somewhere here in Rochester.

But no. No, he did not want to do that. He did not want to go back to being his old self, to feeling that way.

There was no going back for him.

And . . .

And no going forward, either.

He lifted his hands. They weren't shaking anymore; they weren't shaking at all.

He wondered what people would say about *him* after he was gone.

He'd followed all the recent debate about religious worldviews in the press. If people like Mary Vaughan were right, he'd know—even in death, he'd know. And maybe, just maybe, his having saved the Neanderthal world from the likes of himself would count for something.

Of course, if the Neanderthals were right, death would be oblivion, a simple cessation of being.

Cornelius hoped the Neanderthals were right.

He didn't want to leave any evidence of the mutilation he'd suffered. He couldn't care less what happened to Ponter Boddit, but he didn't want his own family to ever know what he'd done in Toronto.

Cornelius Ruskin headed out to the garage, and began siphoning gasoline from his car's tank.

———

"Well, Bandra, what do you think?" asked Mary.

Bandra was wearing Gliksin clothes—taupe Nikes, stone-washed blue jeans, and a loose green shirt, all bought at the same Mark's Work Wearhouse that had provided Ponter's new clothes during his first visit to Mary's world. She placed her hands on her wide hips and looked around in astonishment. "It . . . it is unlike any dwelling I have ever seen."

Mary looked around the large living room as well. "This is the kind of house most people live in—at least, here in North America. Well, actually, this is an exceptionally *nice* house, and most people live in big cities, not out in the country." She paused. "Do you like it?"

"It will take some getting used to," said Bandra. "But, yes, I *do* like it very much. It's so big!"

"Two stories," said Mary. "Thirty-five hundred square feet, plus basement." She gave Bandra's Companion a second to do the conversion, then smiled. "And there are *three* bathrooms."

Bandra's wheat-colored eyes went wide. "The lap of luxury!"

Mary smiled, recalling the slogan of the hair dye she used. "We're worth it."

"And you say the surrounding land is ours, as well?"

"Yup. All 2.3 acres."

"But . . . but can we afford it? I know here everything has a cost."

"We certainly couldn't afford this much land anywhere near Toronto. But here, outside Lively? Sure. After all, Laurentian University will be paying us both well, as academic salaries go."

Bandra sat down on the living-room couch and gestured toward the dark wood curio cabinets, filled with little carvings. "The furnishings and decorations are beautiful," she said.

"It's an unusual mix," said Mary. "Canadian and Caribbean. Of course, Reuben's family will want some of the things, and I'm sure Louise will want a few, as well, but we'll get to keep most of them. I bought the house furnished."

Bandra looked down. "I wish I had met your friend Reuben."

"You'd have liked him," said Mary, sitting next to Bandra on the couch. "He was a terrific person."

"Won't it make you sad, though?" asked Bandra. "Living here?"

Mary shook her head. "Not really. See, this is where Ponter, Louise, Reuben, and I were all quarantined together during Ponter's first visit to my world. It's where I got to know Ponter, where I started to fall in love with him." She pointed across the room, at some heavy built-in bookcases, filled with mystery novels. "I can picture him, right there, using the edge of that far bookcase as a scratching post, shimmying left and right. And we had so many wonderful conversations on this very couch. I know I'll only be with him four days a month from now on, and mostly in his world, not mine, but it's like, in a way, that this is *his* home, too."

Bandra smiled. "I understand."

Mary patted her knee. "And that's why I love you. Because you *do* understand."

"But," said Bandra, grinning now, "it won't be just the two of us much longer. It's been a long time since I've lived in a house with a baby in it."

"I hope you'll help me," said Mary.

"Of course. I know what ninth-daytenth feedings are like!"

"Oh, I don't mean that . . . although I certainly would be grateful! No, what I mean is I hope you'll help me in bringing up Ponter and my daughter. I want her to know and appreciate both cultures, Gliksin and Barast."

"True synergy," said Bandra, smiling widely. "Two really becoming One."

Mary smiled back at her. "Exactamundo."

The call came two days later, about six in the evening. Mary and Bandra had finished their first full day at Laurentian, and were relaxing in their house, the house that had been Reuben's. Mary was stretched out on the couch, finally finishing the Scott Turow novel she'd started ages ago, back before the first opening of the interuniversal portal. Bandra was reclining in the La-Z-Boy that had come with the place, the very one Mary had slept in during the quarantine. She was reading a book of her own on a Neanderthal datapad.

When the two-piece phone on the little table next to the couch rang, Mary folded down the paperback's page, sat up, and lifted the handset. "Hello?"

"Hello, Mary," said a female voice with a Pakistani accent. "It's Qaiser Remtulla from York calling."

"My goodness, hello! How are you?"

"I'm fine, but—but I'm calling with sad news. You remember Cornelius Ruskin?"

Mary felt her stomach clench. "Of course."

"Well, I'm sorry to be the one to have to tell you, but I'm afraid he's passed away."

Mary's eyebrows went up. "Really? But he was so young . . ."

"Thirty-five, I'm told," said Qaiser.

"What happened?"

"There was a fire, and . . ." She paused, and Mary could hear her swallowing hard. "And there wasn't much left, apparently."

Mary struggled to find a response. At last an "Oh" escaped her lips.

"Did you—do you want to come to the memorial service? It's going to be on Friday, here in Toronto."

Mary didn't have to think about that. "No. No, I really didn't know him," she said. *I really didn't know him at all.*

"Well, okay, I understand," said Qaiser. "I just thought we should inform you."

Mary wanted to tell Qaiser that she should sleep peacefully, now that the man who had raped her—who had raped both of them—was dead, but . . .

But Mary wasn't supposed to be aware of Qaiser's rape. Her mind was reeling; she'd find some way to eventually let Qaiser know. "I do appreciate the call. Sorry I can't make it."

They said their goodbyes, and Mary placed the handset in its cradle. Bandra had returned the La-Z-Boy to its upright position. "Who was that?"

Mary walked over to Bandra and extended her arms, helping Bandra to her feet. She then pulled Bandra close to her.

"Are you all right?" asked Bandra.

Mary hugged her tight. "I'm fine," she said.

Bandra said, "You're crying." She couldn't see Mary's face, which was nestled into her shoulder; perhaps she smelled the salt in the tears.

"Don't worry," said Mary softly. "Just hold me."

And Bandra did precisely that.

Chapter Forty-four

"My fellow human beings, my fellow Homo sapiens, we will continue our great journey, continue our wondrous quest, continue ever outward. That is our history, and it is our future. And we will not stop, not falter, not give up until we have reached the farthest stars."

Ponter and Adikor had been spending a lot of time at the United Nations, advising a committee that was trying to decide whether to continue construction of the new, permanent portal between UN headquarters and the corresponding site on Donakat Island. After all, if *men* couldn't use it, some were arguing, then all work should be abandoned. Louise Benoît had been appointed to the same committee.

Laurentian University, of course, took a Christmas break—meaning that Mary and Bandra were free for the holidays. And so they'd decided to fly down to New York to spend New Year's Eve with Louise, Ponter, and Adikor in Times Square.

"It's incredible!" said Bandra, shouting to be heard above the crowd. "How many people are here?"

"They usually get half a million," said Mary.

Bandra looked around. "Half a million! I don't think there have *ever* been half a million Barasts together in one place."

"So," said Ponter, "why do you celebrate the new year on this date? It's not a solstice or an equinox."

"Um," said Louise, "I honestly don't know. Mary?"

Mary shook her head. "I haven't a clue." She sought Louise's eyes, tried to imitate her accent above the din. "But any day's a good day to par-tay!" But a smile was too much to hope for; it was still much too soon.

"So what's going to happen tonight?" asked Adikor.

Everything was bathed in a neon glow. "See that building over there?" said Mary, pointing.

Adikor and Ponter nodded.

"That used to be the headquarters of the *New York Times* newspaper—that's why this is called Times Square. Anyway, see the flagpole on top? It's seventy-seven feet tall. A giant ball, weighing a thousand pounds, will be lowered down that pole starting precisely at 11:59 P.M., and it will take exactly sixty seconds to reach the bottom. When it does, that's the beginning of the new year, and a big fireworks display will begin." Mary held up a bag; they'd each received one, compliments of the Times Square Business Improvement District. "Now, when the ball hits the bottom—well, you're supposed to kiss your loved ones first, and shout 'Happy New Year.' But you're also supposed to toss the contents of your bag into the air. It's full of little bits of paper called confetti."

Adikor shook his head. "It's a complex ritual."

"It sounds delightful!" said Bandra. "I think we—astonishment! Astonishment!"

"What?" said Mary.

Bandra pointed. "It's us!"

Mary turned. One of the giant video screens was showing Bandra and Mary. As Mary watched—it was quite a thrill!—the image panned left, catching Ponter and Adikor. After a moment, though, the picture switched to New York's mayor, waving at the crowd. Mary turned back to the others.

"Our presence has not gone unnoticed," she said, smiling.

Ponter laughed. "Oh, we are used to that!"

"You come here every year?" asked Adikor.

A light snow was falling, and Mary's breath was visible as she spoke. "Me? I've never been here before—but I watch it on TV each year, along with about 300 million other people worldwide. It's quite the tradition."

"What time is it now?" asked Ponter.

Mary looked at her watch; there was plenty of neon light to see the display by. "Just past 11:30," she said.

"Oooh!" said Bandra, pointing again. "Now it's Lou's turn!"

The giant screen had a tight close-up on Louise's beautiful face, and she smiled enchantingly at seeing herself on the big screen. There were howls of appreciation from tens of thousands of males. Well, Pamela Anderson Lee had gotten her start on a Jumbotron, too . . .

The monitor changed to show Dick Clark, in a black silk jacket, standing on a wide stage, surrounded by hundreds of pink and clear balloons. "Hello, world!" he shouted, and then, amending himself with a giant, perfect grin: "Hello, *worlds!*"

The crowd cheered. Mary clapped her mittened hands together.

"Welcome back to *Dick Clark's New Year's Rockin' Eve!*"

More cheering. All around them, people were waving little American flags that had been given out along with the confetti bags.

"It's been an *amazing* year," said Clark. "A year that saw us meet up with our long-lost cousins, the Neanderthals."

The screen changed to show a close-up of Ponter, who took a second to spot the camera, then waved gamely, Hak's nice new faceplate sparkling in the neon rainbow.

A chant went up from the crowd. "Pon-*ter!* " "Pon-*ter!* " "Pon-*ter!* "

Mary felt as though her heart were going to burst with pride. Dick Clark kept things moving along, though. "Tonight, in addition to the biggest bands from this world, Krik Donalt is going to perform his number-one hit 'Two Becoming One' live in our Hollywood studio. But, right now, we'll— sir, sir, I'm sorry, but you'll have to leave."

Mary looked at the giant screen, baffled. Clark was alone on the stage.

"I'm sorry, sir, but we're on the air here," said Clark to empty space. He turned and shouted, "Matt, can we get this clown out of here?"

There was a murmur through the crowd. Whatever bit Clark was trying clearly wasn't working. Indeed, Bandra leaned in to Mary and said, "He's bombing . . ."

Suddenly, a man whose back had been to them turned— a tricky feat, given that the crowd was packed like cordwood—and looking right at Ponter, he said, "My God, it's you! It's you!"

Ponter smiled politely. "Yes, I—"

But the man, eyes wide, pushed Ponter aside, and said again, "It's you! It's you!" He seemed intent on making his way through the crowd, and, for the most part, it was parting to allow him to do so.

"Jesus!" shouted a woman beside Bandra, but Mary couldn't see what had upset her so. She turned back to look at the man who had pushed past Ponter and, to her astonishment, she saw him go to his knees.

Dick Clark's voice emanated from the speakers again, sounding panicky. "I can't do this with him here!"

Mary felt her throat go dry. She reached out with her left hand, hoping to steady herself. Bandra grabbed her arm. "Mare, are you okay?"

Mary forced a small nod.

"Jesus!" shouted the woman again.

But Mary shook her head.

"No," she said, ever so softly.

No, it wasn't Jesus.

It was Mary.

It was the blessed Virgin Mary!

"Ponter," said Mary, her voice shaking. "Ponter, do you see her? Do you see her?"

"Who?" said Ponter.

"She's right there," said Mary, pointing—and then, almost at once, she drew her hand back and used it to cross herself. "She's right there!"

"Mare, there are half a million people here . . ."

"But she's *glowing*," said Mary softly.

Ponter turned to Louise, and Mary forced herself to look in that direction for a second. Louise's brown eyes were wide and she was whispering over and over again, too softly for Mary to hear, but she could read Louise's lips: "*Mon Dieu, mon Dieu, mon Dieu . . .*"

"See!" said Mary. "Louise sees her, too!" But even as she said that, Mary had her doubts; the Virgin was indeed holy, but one did not greet her with "My God, my God, my God . . ."

Mary found her gaze drawn back to the perfect illuminated form in front of her, flanked by towering buildings.

Bandra was still holding on to Mary's arm. The woman on the other side of Bandra had dropped to her knees. "Mary!" she exclaimed. "The Blessed Virgin Mary!" But she was facing in completely the wrong direction . . .

"Look," shouted a voice—just one of tens of thousands of shouts going up now, but one that Mary happened to pick out from the background. "The mothership!"

Mary tilted her head up. Searchlights were crisscrossing the black, empty sky.

"Mare!" It was Ponter's voice. "Mare, are you okay? What's happening?"

A man in front of Mary had turned around and was reaching into his coat. For half a second Mary thought he was going for a gun, but what he brought out was a fat wallet, filled with cash. He opened it. "Here," he said, shoving some bills at Mary. "Here, take it! Take it!" He turned to Ponter and shoved some money at him, too. "Take it! Take it! I've got too much . . ."

From behind Mary came a loud cry of "*Allah-o-akbar! Allah-o-akbar!*"

And from in front: "*The Messiah! At last!*"

And off to her left: "*Yes, yes! Take me, Lord!*"

And to her right, someone singing: "*Hallelujah!*"

Mary wished she had her rosary. The Virgin was here—right here!—beckoning her to come forward.

"Mare!" shouted Ponter. "Mare!"

Behind Mary, someone was weeping. In front of her, someone else was laughing uncontrollably. Others were burying their faces in their hands, or clapping their hands together, or raising their hands to heaven.

A man was shouting, "Who's that? Who's there?"

And a woman was shouting, "Go away! Go away!"

And yet another person was shouting, "Welcome to Planet Earth!"

A few feet away, Mary saw a man faint, but the crowd was too closely packed for him to fall over.

"It's judgment day!" shouted a voice.

"It's first contact!" shouted another.

"*Mahdi! Mahdi!*" shouted a third.

Nearby, a woman was intoning, "Our Father, who art in heaven, hallowed be thy Name . . ."

And next to her a man was saying, "I'm sorry, I'm sorry, I'm so very sorry . . ."

And somebody else was shouting emphatically, "This cannot be happening! This cannot be real!"

"Mare!" said Ponter, taking her by the shoulders and swinging her around, away from the Blessed Virgin. "Mare!"

"No," Mary managed to say. "No, let me go. She's here . . ."

"Mare, the crowd is going wild. We have to get out of here!"

Mary twisted away, finding strength she never knew she had. She'd do anything to be with the Virgin . . .

"Adikor, Bandra, hurry!" Ponter's voice, translated, bursting into her brain, drowning out the words of Our Lady. Mary reached up her hands, bending her fingers into claws, trying to tear out the cochlear implants. Ponter continued: "We've got to get Mare and Lou out of here!"

The white light—the perfect white light—was shimmering now, prismatic scintillations along its edges. Mary felt her heart expanding, her soul soaring, her—

Gunshots!

Mary looked off to her right. A white man of about forty had a pistol out and was firing it at some unseen demon, his face contorted in terror. In front of him, people were dying, but Times Square was too crowded for them to fall. Mary saw the faces of first one person, then another, as bullets tore into them.

Screams went up, rivaling the shouts of rapture.

"Bandra," yelled Ponter. "Clear the way! I'll get Mare. Adikor, get Lou!"

Mary felt sweat pouring down her face, despite the cold. Ponter was going to try to take her away from—

No, thought the rational part of Mary, fighting its way to the front of her consciousness. *The Virgin is not here.*

Yes! screamed another part of her. *Yes, she is!*

No—no. There is no Virgin! There is no—

But there was—there must be!—for suddenly, Mary felt herself rising up off the ground, flying up . . .

Because Ponter was lifting her, high, higher still, swinging her up on his broad shoulders. Bandra, in front of them, was pushing people aside as though they were bowling pins, parting the sea, forcing an opening in the crowd. Ponter barreled forward, occupying the space Bandra was clearing before it was filled again by the crushing humanity. There were still a few areas of lower density—what was left of the lanes that had originally been set aside for emergency vehicles—and Bandra was heading for one of them.

Mary looked left and right, trying to spot the light of the Virgin again—and saw that Louise was now high up on Adikor's shoulders, and that the two of them were right behind, following Mary and Ponter.

A man came toward them, a crazed look on his face. He swung at Ponter, who easily deflected the blow. But then another man came at Ponter, shouting, "Begone, demon!"

Ponter tried to deflect his blows, as well, but it was no use. The attacker was like—*exactly* like, Mary realized—a man possessed. He smashed a fist into Ponter's broad jaw, and Ponter finally struck back, lashing out with the flat of his hand, connecting in the middle of the man's chest. Even over the cacophony, Mary heard the sound of ribs cracking, and the man went down. The crowd surged in to fill the space cleared by Bandra, and it looked as though the attacker was being trampled, but within seconds Ponter had pushed far enough ahead that Mary could no longer see what was happening to the fallen man.

Mary's perspective was bouncing wildly as Ponter surged ahead, but suddenly she caught sight of the giant lighted ball starting its descent down the flagpole—a geodesic sphere, six feet wide, covered with Waterford crystal, lit from within and without. Mary couldn't imagine that anyone had had the presence of mind to send it on its way down; there must have been a computer controlling it.

Strobe lights. Searchlights. Lasers crisscrossing through dry-ice clouds.

More screams. More gunshots. Shattering glass. Alarms wailing. An NYPD officer being bucked by his horse.

"Mary!" shouted Mary. "Save us!"

"Ponter!" Adikor's voice, from behind them. "Look out!"

Mary could feel Ponter swinging his head. Another crazed person was pushing toward him, this one brandishing a crowbar. Ponter moved to his right, knocking people over as he did so, to avoid being brained.

Bandra turned around and seized the man's wrist, closing her hand. Again, Mary heard the ricochet crack of breaking bone, and the crowbar crashed to the pavement.

Mary swung her head, searching for the Virgin. The giant ball was almost all the way down—and they were almost out of Times Square, making their way east on 42nd Street.

Suddenly the sky exploded—

Mary looked up. The heavenly host! The—

But no. No, just as the dropping of the ball must have been computer-controlled, so, too, apparently, was the fireworks display. A great peacock's tail of light was opening up behind them, followed by red, white, and blue skyrockets rising toward the heavens.

Ponter's legs were pounding up and down, muscular pistons. The crowd was thinning, and he was making good progress now. Bandra remained out in front; Adikor, with Louise still on his shoulders, fell in beside them, and they continued on, running into the night, into the new year. "Mary," called Mary Vaughan. "Blessed Mary, come back!"

United Nations headquarters was just over a mile east of Times Square. It took ninety minutes to get there on foot, fighting traffic and crowds all the way, but at last they made it, and got safely inside—a Gliksin security guard recognized Ponter, and let them in.

The visions had ended shortly after midnight, stopping as abruptly as they had begun. Mary had a splitting headache, and felt empty and cold inside. "What did you see?" she asked Louise.

Louise shook her head slowly back and forth, clearly recalling the wonder of it all. "God," she said. "God the Father, just like on the roof of the Sistine Chapel. It was . . ." She sought a word. "It was *perfect*."

They spent the rest of the night on the twentieth floor of the Secretariat Building, sleeping in a conference room, listening to the wild sounds and sirens far below—the visions were over, but the chaos had only just begun.

In the morning, they watched the sporadic news coverage—
some stations weren't operating at all—trying to piece together what had happened.

Earth's magnetic field had been collapsing for over four
months now—for the first time since consciousness had
emerged on this world. The field's strength had been fluc-
tuating, lines of force converging and diverging wildly.

"Well," said Louise, hands on hips, staring at the TV set,
"it wasn't exactly a *crash*, but . . ."

"But what?" said Mary. They were both exhausted, filthy,
and badly bruised.

"I'd told Jock the biggest problem related to the
magnetic-field collapse wouldn't be ultraviolet radiation getting through, or anything like that. Rather, I said it would be
the effects on human consciousness."

"It was like what I'd experienced in Veronica Shannon's
test chamber," said Mary, "only much more intense."

Ponter nodded. "But, as in Veronica's chamber, neither
I nor, I'm sure, any other Barast experienced anything."

"But everyone else," said Mary, and she gestured at the
television set, "across the whole damn planet it seems, had a
religious experience."

"Or a UFO abduction experience," said Louise. "Or, at
least, some sort of encounter with something that wasn't really there."

Mary nodded. It would be days—months!—before they
had accurate death tolls and damage estimates, but it seemed
clear that hundreds of thousands, if not millions, had per-
ished on New Year's Eve—or New Year's Day, in time zones
east of New York.

And, of course, the debates would continue for years

about what the experience—at least one commentator was already calling it "Last Day"—had meant.

Pope Mark II was to address the faithful later today.

But what could he possibly say? Would he validate the sightings of Jesus and the Holy Virgin while dismissing the reported encounters with deities and prophets and messiahs sacred to Muslims and Mormons, to Hindus and Jews, to Scientologists, Wiccans, and Maori, to Cherokees and Mi'kmaqs and Algonquins and Pueblo Indians, to Inuit and Buddhists?

And what about the UFO sightings, the gray aliens, the bug-eyed monsters?

The Pope had some 'splainin' to do.

All religious leaders did.

Adikor, Bandra, and Louise were absorbed by a report from the BBC, covering events that transpired yesterday in the Middle East. Mary tapped Ponter on the shoulder, and when he looked at her, she motioned for him to come to the far side of the conference room.

"Yes, Mare?" he said softly.

"It's all a crock, isn't it?" she said.

Hak bleeped, but Mary ignored it.

"Look, I've changed my mind. About our child . . ."

She saw Ponter's broad face fall.

"No, no!" said Mary, reaching out, touching his short, muscular forearm. "No, I still want to have a child with you. But forget what I said in Vissan's cabin. Our daughter should not have the God organ."

Ponter's golden eyes searched for something in her own. "Are you sure?"

She nodded. "Yes, finally, for once in my life, I'm really sure of something." She let her hand slide down his arm, and intertwined her fingers with his.

Epilogue

It had been six months since New Year's Eve, and there had been no repetition of the visions. The magnetic field enclosing that version of Earth continued to fluctuate wildly, though, so there was no guarantee that it wouldn't stimulate the minds of *Homo sapiens* in the same way again. Maybe, in fourteen or fifteen years, when the field reversal was complete, the people of Mare's world—still no consensus on a better name for it—wouldn't have to worry about a reoccurrence.

In the interim, though, Veronica Shannon, and others doing similar research, had become media celebrities as the world rebuilt, explaining what had happened . . . at least to those who would listen. In North America, church attendance had hit an all-time high—and then an all-time low. A cease-fire was holding in Israel. Muslim extremists were being ousted throughout the Arab world.

But here, on Jantar, the Barast world, whose field collapse had been over for a decade now, things continued as they always had, devoid of thoughts of gods and demons and alien beings.

Mary Vaughan had always wanted a summer wedding— her first one, to Colm, had been in February. But since Neanderthal bonding ceremonies were held outdoors, it was even more important to her this time that the festivities happen during the warm months.

The bonding ceremony would take place here, in the wilderness between Saldak Center and Saldak Rim. Mary had attended one previous bonding, that of Ponter's daughter Jasmel Ket to Tryon Rugal. It had been most awkward: Daklar Bolbay, who was Jasmel's former guardian, Adikor's accuser, and, for a brief time, Mary's rival for Ponter's affection, had shown up unexpectedly. Even with her there, though, it had been a small ceremony, as was the Barast norm.

But Mary had also always wanted a big wedding. When she and Colm had tied the knot, they'd only invited their parents and siblings—simple and, more importantly, inexpensive, an event suited to their grad students' budget.

But this time out, there were a lot of people on hand, at least by Neanderthal standards. Adikor was there, along with his woman-mate Lurt and son Dab. Also present were Ponter's parents, two of the nicest 142s you'd ever want to meet. And Ponter's daughters Jasmel and Mega were on hand, plus Jasmel's man-mate Tryon. There, too, were Hapnar and Dranna and their man-mates. Because Mary wanted a maid of honor, even though Barasts had no such thing, Louise Benoît was on hand, as well. And, because he'd asked to attend—and nothing could be denied him during the celebrations of the thousandth month since he'd liberated the Barasts by introducing Companion technology—also on hand was Lonwis Trob, now a whopping 109, and only slightly worse for wear after having a mechanical heart installed.

None of the women present were showing yet, but they would be soon: generation 149 was on its way, and Mary was expecting, as were Lurt, Jasmel, Hapnar, and Dranna.

Ponter hadn't yet arrived. It was traditional for the man who was about to be bonded to go hunting, procuring a food offering to bring to his intended. For her part, Mary had gathered a large quantity of pine nuts, roots, vegetables, edible fungi, and more as her offering.

"Here comes Daddy!" shouted little Mega, pointing. Mary looked up. Off to the west, Ponter had appeared on the horizon. He was carrying things in each of his hands, although Mary couldn't yet make out what they were.

"And here comes Mother!" said Hapnar, pointing to the east. Sure enough, Bandra was approaching from that direction.

Ponter had said that double ceremonies were rare, but Mary had thought it so very appropriate: to be bonded to her man-mate Ponter *and* her woman-mate Bandra simultaneously. The sky overhead was cloudless, and the air was warm and dry. Mary felt wonderful—in love, loved, loving life.

Ponter and Bandra had equal distances to go, but the terrain was rougher to the west, and Bandra arrived at the clearing first. She hugged her daughters, then greeted Ponter's parents—her own lived far away, but, Mary knew, were watching transmissions being sent by Bandra's Companion. She came over to Mary and kissed and licked her face.

Bandra looked so happy, it made Mary's heart want to burst. It had been ages since Bandra had seen Harb; her man-mate knew Bandra had moved to the other world, but Bandra had taken no steps to dissolve her bond to him— because, she said, if she did, he'd just seek another woman-mate. Perhaps, at some point, he'd dissolve their union himself—but enough about Harb, Mary thought. Today was a day for making, not breaking, bonds.

Bandra was wearing a backpack, which she lowered to the ground. It contained her offering of food for Mary. Mary had brought twice as much, but only half was for Bandra; the rest was for Ponter.

Soon—finally!—Ponter arrived. Mary was surprised. When she'd attended Jasmel and Tryon's bonding, Tryon had shown up with a freshly killed deer slung over his shoulders; the blood streaming from its many spear wounds had turned Mary's stomach. But Ponter was holding two large cubical containers—Mary recognized them as thermal storage units. She looked at him questioningly, but he just set them down out of the way. Then he hugged Mary, holding her for a wonderfully long time.

No officials were needed for the ceremony, of course; the whole thing, after all, was being recorded from multiple Companion viewpoints at the alibi archives. And so the three of them simply began, with Ponter standing on one side of Mary and Bandra on the other.

Mary turned to Ponter and spoke—in the Neanderthal tongue, which she'd spent the last half year learning, patiently taught by Bandra. "I promise, dear Ponter, to hold you in my heart twenty-nine days a month, and to hold you in my arms whenever Two become One."

Ponter took one of Mary's hands. She continued: "I promise that your health and your happiness will be as important to me as my own. If, at any time, you tire of me, I promise to release you without acrimony, and with the best interests of our children as my highest priority."

Ponter's golden eyes were beaming. Mary turned to Bandra. "I promise, dear Bandra, to hold you in my heart twenty-nine days a month, and to hold you in my arms whenever Two are not One. I promise that your health and your happiness will be as important to me as my own, and if, at any time, you tire of me, I promise to release you without acrimony."

Bandra, who for her part, had been becoming fluent in English—at least those words that she could pronounce—

said softly in that language, "Grow tired of you? Never in a million years."

Mary smiled, then turned back to Ponter. It was his turn to speak now, and he did so: "I promise," he said in his wonderfully deep, resonant voice, "to hold you in my heart twenty-nine days a month, and to hold you in my arms whenever Two become One. I promise that your happiness and well-being will be as important to me as my own. If you ever tire of me, I promise to release you without pain, and with the best interests of our child—our very special hybrid child—as my highest priority."

Mary squeezed Ponter's hand, and turned back to Bandra, who repeated the same vows Mary had made to her, then added, again in English, "I love you."

Mary kissed Bandra again. "I love you, too," she said. And then she turned and kissed Ponter, long and hard. "And you know I love you, big fella."

"They're bonded!" said little Mega, clapping her hands together.

Adikor moved in and hugged Ponter. "Congratulations!"

And Louise hugged Mary. *"Félicitations, mon amie!"*

"And now," exclaimed Ponter, "it's time for the feast!" He went over to the cubical containers he'd brought with him and opened them up. The lids were lined with reflective foil. Ponter pulled out large paper bags from one, and then the other, and Mary saw on them the familiar drawing of a white-haired Gliksin with glasses and a goatee.

"Astonishment!" exclaimed Mary, in good Barast fashion. "Kentucky Fried Chicken!"

Ponter was grinning his foot-wide grin. "Only the very best for you."

Mary smiled back at him. "Oh, yes, indeed, my love," she said. "The very best—of both worlds."

About the Author

Robert J. Sawyer lives in Mississauga, Ontario, Canada, and is Writer in Residence at the Toronto Public Library's Merril Collection of Science Fiction, Speculation and Fantasy.

Rob has a bachelor's degree in Radio and Television Arts from Toronto's Ryerson University—so it's no surprise that he keeps turning up on both those media. He's got 200 television appearances under his belt (including *Rivera Live* with Geraldo Rivera) and almost as many radio interviews (including National Public Radio's *Talk of the Nation*). In addition, he's hosted programs for CBC Radio and Discovery Channel Canada, and is a frequent commentator about science fiction on Space, Canada's national SF cable network, and about science fact on Newsworld, Canada's cable news network. In 2002, on the twentieth anniversary of his graduation, Ryerson presented him with its Alumni Achievement Award, making him one of only thirty out of 100,000 alumni so honored to date.

Rob's other honors include a Nebula Award from the Science Fiction and Fantasy Writers of America for Best Novel of the Year (for *The Terminal Experiment*); six best-novel Hugo Award nominations (for *The Terminal Experiment, Starplex, Frameshift, Factoring Humanity, Calculating God,* and *Hominids*); SF awards in France, Japan, and Spain; seven Aurora Awards (Canada's top honor in speculative fiction); the *Science Fiction Chronicle* Reader Award for Best Short Story of the Year; and an Arthur Ellis Award from the Crime Writers of Canada.

Since graduating in 1982, Rob has had all of two jobs: four months working at Bakka, Toronto's SF specialty store, immediately followed by eight months back at Ryerson, demonstrating TV studio-production techniques.

Ever since, he's been a full-time freelance writer, although he spent most of the 1980s doing over 200 articles for magazines and newspapers (usually about computers or personal finance), and writing brochures, newsletters, and other materials for corporations and government offices.

Rob's first novel, *Golden Fleece,* came out in 1990, and by 1992 he had given up nonfiction work to concentrate exclusively on SF. In 1997, his wife, Carolyn Clink, left her job in the printing industry to come work full-time as Rob's assistant, and in 2002 they started their own corporation, SFWRITER.COM Inc., named in honor of Rob's massive, award-winning Web site at **www.sfwriter.com**.

"The Neanderthal Parallax is tremendous storytelling, with a convincing scientific basis, but at its core, it is science fiction as social commentary. *Humans* is worth reading for the quality of Sawyer's vision and insight, the near-possibility of his scientific departures, and the depth of his social criticism."

—*Quill & Quire*

"Would it be worth it? That's the question Sawyer asks. Peace, harmony, social justice—would we *humans* give up our privacy, and our right to reproduce the way we want, to have these things? It's a thought-provoking question in the tradition of great social science fiction."   —Scifi.com

"Robert Sawyer . . . combines entertaining science-fiction with advanced scientific concepts as skillfully as any author alive."

—*The Rocky Mountain News*

"*Hominids* shuttles smoothly between its two main plots, building toward a suspenseful climax. . . . A meticulously conceived piece of anthropological science fiction."

—*San Francisco Chronicle*

"[A] polished anthropological SF yarn . . . The author's usual high intelligence and occasionally daunting erudition are on prominent display . . . in a novel that appeals to both the intellect and the heart."   —*Publishers Weekly*

"There is science aplenty, but Sawyer broadens his story to focus on what really goes on inside people and how they interact . . . Never is Sawyer afraid to reveal the emotions inherent in every connection. And that's when you soar above the equations to produce genuine artistry."   —Sfsite.com

"Rob Sawyer has carried the banner of Asimovian science-fiction into the 21st century. *Hominids* is based in cutting-edge contemporary science—paleoanthropology, quantum computing, neutrino astronomy, among others—and furnished at the same time with touching human (and parahuman) stories. Precise, detailed, and accomplished. The next volume is eagerly anticipated."   —Robert Charles Wilson